Was It Something I Said?

Was It Something I Said?

☢

Valerie Block

SOHO

Published by

Soho Press, Inc.

853 Broadway

New York, New York 10003

Library of Congress Cataloging-in-Publication Data
Block, Valerie,
    Was it something I said? / Valerie Block.
      p. cm.
    ISBN 1-56947-109-6 (alk. paper)
    I. Title.
PS3552.L6345W37   1998
813'.54—dc21   97-16735
                                         CIP

Book Design by Pauline Neuwirth, Neuwirth & Associates, Inc.

10 9 8 7 6 5 4 3

This book is dedicated to my parents.

Acknowledgments

For the vote of confidence, and all their serious efforts on my behalf, I am indebted to Melanie Fleishman, Laura Hruska and Juris Jurjevics of Soho Press, and to Gail Hochman and Marianne Merola of Brandt & Brandt.

For enthusiasm and critical assistance, I would like to thank Peter Cameron, Pamela Christman, Aimee Garn, Sally Higginson, Abby Knopp, Stephen Koch, and Richard Locke.

For technical expertise, I would like to thank Elaine Brasch, David Christman, Pam Gannon, Valerie Hartman Levy, Sharon Lesser, Robert Lobell, Ed Lord, Andrew J. Nussbaum, David Roethgen, Suzanne Sloane, and Michael Uchitel.

Chapter 1

He couldn't get himself arrested

At 7:30 A.M., Barry Cantor flew up the Saw Mill River Parkway blasting *Abbey Road*. It was five days before Christmas. He hadn't had a second date in eight months, and he hadn't had sex in over a year. It was astounding.

Barry worked, read the *Times*, watched TV; he played first base for the Condiments and Retail Sauces team. At 32, he'd won a Brammy for Best Consumer Promotion. At 33 he'd renovated the twisty seven-room apartment he'd grown up in. Three months ago, he'd hired a chef to cook for him twice a week. If he behaved himself, he'd be Group Product Supervisor in a year. In all probability, he would never learn Italian; when he was honest with himself, he admitted that he didn't really speak French.

He took the second Tarrytown exit. All of Barry's old friends were married, and most of them were fathers; he saw them on the weekends, among their families, carrying things. Possibly there was something wrong with him. He'd been losing hair steadily since his junior year at Dartmouth. On the other hand, he was taller than most men he knew. Plus, there was something seriously wrong with every single woman he'd met lately. Jack Kennedy didn't get married until he was 36.

He turned into the ice-encrusted parking lot, sick of thinking about himself. It was as if Cynthia had never existed, as if he'd never had someone sleeping next to him. And why would it ever end? Nobody wanted anything anymore.

Not true: Vince Anspacher was seeing three women simultaneously. Barry had been fascinated by Vince's situation until he'd met Vince's lineup—neurotic, abrasive, and self-involved, every single one of them, and Kiki was the kind of girl who needed a map in an elevator. Though all three of them were quite passable, visually.

Barry had met Vince at a wedding in July. Vince had seemed on his wavelength, if a little out of his league; his father was a self-made magnate whose empire was written up in the newspaper every day. In September, when Vince had asked to stay till he found a sublet, Barry instantly agreed, thinking being roommates with Vince would lead to membership to clubs he'd never heard of, and also that it might be nice to bump into someone in the hall.

Of course, all that had come of it was repeated reminders of what Barry was missing, and why. Last night, on his way to bed, he saw that Vince's door was open. Renée was probably naked on the bed. If Vince wanted a woman over—and why shouldn't he?—fine. But with the door open? The good news was that Vince traveled constantly.

Barry pulled into his parking space and paused as "Come Together" came on again. What was John Lennon singing about, and did it matter? Long before the murder, he'd felt deficient for not liking John more. John was too contrary; Barry always had the feeling that he was missing something, and he wasn't cool enough to know what it was. Paul, on the other hand, let Linda play in the band—

conciliatory to the point of ridiculous. Well, a gentleman. Any kind of critical discussion was of course impossible now.

Barry shut off the car and walked across the frigid Plaza to start the day. Christmas had come to the Maplewood Acres national headquarters in Tarrytown. It had started in November with the reindeer on the lawn. It would end in January with green tuna fish on red rolls in the cafeteria. The offices were trembling under the weight of all the garlands, lights, and desktop nativity scenes. Every year, it started earlier. Every year, it made Barry sick.

Maggie Fahey, an astonishingly beautiful Assistant Product Manager, came out of the deli and walked past him without a single word.

"Top o' the marnin to ya, lass," he called after her.

She raised her coffee without turning around by way of greeting. Very nice. He couldn't get himself arrested.

Barry kibitzed a little with the coffee guy, who always had his large/light/three sugars bagged before he'd reached the counter. He loved the coffee guy. He took the holly-decked elevator to 5, strode down the hall, and nearly collided with some people who were sucking up to John Rheinecker, Senior VP for marketing and the man behind the Susie Strudel relaunch, which was widely regarded as nothing short of brilliant. Barry hated watching people grovel for Rheinecker and he hated Rheinecker for enjoying it.

"Morning, Cantor," Rheinecker said in a dry, disdainful fashion without eye contact. His face had the color and sheen of pink grapefruit skin.

"Your Grace," Barry said, and pivoted into his office.

So he had a problem with authority. So what? On his desk were the shivering remains of Friday's trauma: the Council had decided to sell Peggy's Pickles, a beautiful little brand with a loyal following in New England. No reflection on Barry's management, but still, it grated on him.

Emily King, his putative assistant, wasn't around. He flicked the lid off his coffee. The Maplewood Acres Morale Survey was still on his desk, blank. The anonymity clause at the top was bullshit—they had everything coded. Everybody else had returned it immediately, lying robotically (the required seminar on e-mail etiquette was very important, the dental plan was very generous). If you'd told Barry ten years ago that he'd be thinking twice about voicing honest criticism, he'd have laughed out loud.

And yet: Henry Ford didn't form the Detroit Automobile Company until he was 36, didn't form the Ford Motor Company until he was 40, didn't release the Model T until he was 45. Of course, George Gershwin was dead at 39. On the other hand, he never married. Still: Gershwin had women flocking around him constantly.

Barry combed through the latest Nielsen numbers for Parson's Creek Salad Dressings. Dijon Garlic had taken a nose dive nationwide in August. Caesar With Bacon was doing a respectable business in the Rochester test market. His phone rang.

"Don't lend your father money," his mother rasped.

"But he's my father," Barry said, feeling the floor dropping away. Two years ago he'd given Ira $7,000 to tide him over till the insurance paid when his boat was shredded in Hurricane Carl. In his heart of hearts, Barry knew Ira didn't have insurance, even though he'd been kvetching about the bureaucracy, the volumes of paperwork, the mental hygiene of the inspectors.

"Fine. Go ahead," Rose said. "You'll never see it again."

His parents had been divorced for twenty-one years. Rose continued to run her coat-lining business in a dingy factory on 36th Street. His father lived on the boat in Queens with Katerina, the Albanian woman who used to clean his menswear store before his second bankruptcy. "He's got some nerve asking you," he said.

"He asked your sister. She just called me." Barry made a mental note to chew out Karen for telling Rose. "Look, I'll see you tonight," she shouted over the din. "I'm short two shipments of thread. I gotta clear it up before I get on the plane."

Barry strolled across the floor to his immediate supervisor, William Plast.

"Good weekend?" he asked at the threshold.

"Cleaned out the garage," Plast said, with morose satisfaction, motioning him inside. "Took the kids to the church auction. You?"

Barry sat in Plast's guest chair, causing a Wise Man to topple off the credenza.

"Watched the golf," Barry said, picking the figurine up and replacing him in the manger.

"Ah, the good old days," Plast said, with his harassed father look, "when you could just sit and watch the golf."

They began chatting about the year in salad dressings. Barry had also attended his college roommate's second wedding alone, and was snubbed by a stout, frosted blonde who couldn't have been under 40. This was the longest period of celibacy recorded outside Franciscan cloisters. Maybe when he got home that night, he should just walk across the hall to the Divorcée's apartment and present himself. Barry Cantor: Convenience. Amusement. Discretion. But he couldn't fuck around anymore. He'd had plenty of intrigue in his life, but other than Cynthia, nothing had ever really gotten beyond preliminary hostilities.

Pointing to the Dijon Garlic visuals, Plast said, "Is there a way of enhancing the drama of the drop?"

"Why would I want to do that?"

"To draw attention to it."

"Why would I want to do that?"

Plast looked as if he'd caught Barry cheating on a math test. He was 43 and five foot four; he was shaped like a pudgy football, and had all the spontaneity and liveliness of cold oatmeal. The idea that Plast was getting laid regularly made Barry furious.

"Look, we're not gonna get more promotion money next year by dropping our pants and asking Rheinecker for a whack."

Stu Eberhart passed by and Plast knocked over his wastebasket jumping to attention. Barry was always surprised at how small the CEO was. Tiny little guy, maybe five one or two. Since becoming CEO, he'd survived a triple bypass, and Rheinecker's maneuverings for his job. Three years ago, Eberhart had traded in his wife of 28 years for a newer model of the same kind of tootsed-up, suburban ash blonde. Last year, the second Mrs. Eberhart had sprung a serious new chest.

Plast turned his attention to Barry's coupon design. "I don't like the burst behind 'Save 50 cents,'" he said sadly. He had a fat simpering wife who agreed with his every proclamation.

"Well, I'm not personally attached to it," Barry sighed. He missed John Hearne. Hearne was the best boss he'd ever had. No: the only good one. Operating as a team, without formalities, they'd pumped up Maplewood Jam by 13 percent in two years. When Barry was promoted to Product Manager, Hearne was picked to start a low-cholesterol frozen entrées division. Since Eberhart's bypass, Hearne had a virtual green light on every line extension.

"I like a circle, not a burst," Plast said finally. "And let's do it horizontal, the way we usually do it. It works."

When Barry strolled back across the floor, Emily King was batting around in her cubicle. About a month ago, a tension had blossomed when he asked her to have a drink, which she'd misinterpreted. Like he was interested in this whiny, horse-faced incompetent? The thing had blossomed when she told him her sister was training to become a midwife, and he'd said that was the most ridiculous thing he'd ever heard. It turned out that she, Emily, was also training to become a midwife. Did she even *have* a sister? Emily: preposterous.

"Please check these numbers," Barry said, and gave her the Nielsens when she walked into his office. "I'll need them by lunch."

She glared at him in impudence, submission, and self-loathing. "How the hell am I supposed to do that by lunch?"

"Come in by 9 like everybody else?"

She suppressed whatever she was going to say, took the discs and flounced—yes, *flounced* was the word—off to her cubicle. She still had her coat on: he shouldn't see her dingy, stringy body. Lord, was she a pain in the ass.

He trotted down to John Hearne's office.

"My assistant has PMS four weeks a month," Barry began, and put his feet up on Hearne's desk, causing a flock of greeting cards to flutter to the floor. He bent down to pick up the cards. "My boss spent his weekend fiddling around with my coupon. My roommate has female guests and leaves his door open. They're selling my pickles," he added, replacing the cards one by one in a line on the desk. "Should I be taking any of this personal?"

"No," Hearne said reasonably, with a look of frank amusement. "But show a little fear with the generals, Barry. They'll love you for it," he added, like a salesman.

"Uch," Barry said, and walked.

Ever since they'd met, Hearne had been Barry's advance man in life. Hearne was one of the few people at the company who gave Barry hope. But the morale survey had been Hearne's idea, and Hearne was too deluded to see they were using it for intelligence gathering and mind control. And last week, Barry had heard the man speaking to his wife in a tone he wouldn't have used on a naughty dog. It pained him to think he'd been wrong about Hearne.

When he came back upstairs, Emily was deeply immersed in a tête-à-tête with the luscious Maggie Fahey in the tinsel-decked pantry.

"I put a big piece of quartz on my heart," Emily said, in a self-pitying tone. She was wearing a red felt Santa pin on her flat chest.

"I sing to my crystals," Maggie said proudly.

"It felt good, weighing down, because my heart was already heavy," Emily said, tragically. "And pink is a healing color."

"I hate to interrupt this beautiful moment—" Barry began, but they took no notice of him.

"I have some that I wear," Maggie continued, "and some others that I keep by the window, so they get air."

"—but I really need those numbers pronto if I'm going to make my plane." If he left for the airport by two, he'd miss Quality Control singing the product list to "Deck the Halls."

Emily looked up at him as if he'd torn skin off her heart, and stalked out like an insulted starlet on a nighttime soap.

"Talk about bad energy," Maggie said, in disgust.

Some days, Barry was reminded of Jeff Keeley, a PM on Raisin Bread who'd been dismissed after being observed relieving himself in the white-paper recycling bucket. And then there was the legendary Gary Tobias: fired after he exploded at a Beverage Review, calling Rheinecker an asshole for nixing his coffee soda idea. For Barry, there were your Keeley days and your Tobias days. Really, Emily had to go.

LaGuardia was swarming with harassed December travelers. Barry hated the holidays. The crowds, the forced sentiment, the retail pressure, the buildup, the letdown, the crap all over the buildings. Every year, he went to Miami Beach for the antidote, a dose of hot air and cranky Jews, and that made him sick too. In a few hours, he'd be seeing his mother's doughy legs—spectrally pale, crisscrossed with lines of gnarled blue knots—by the pool. He wasn't looking forward to it. The idea that he might meet someone there rather than here was laughable, but he kept his mind open just the same. Every year.

There was an exquisite woman on line in front of Barry. She had dense, sculpted black eyebrows and short straight black hair with bangs. She was in a neat black coat. She had matching, clean-looking luggage. He was falling in love with the back of her head, where her hair was shorn into an emphatic point that held his attention. Her left hand was in her pocket.

He stared at the curving point. What do you say to such a woman—I'm Barry: Fly me? While he was debating this, inwardly cursing himself as a coward, she glided up to the counter.

She wanted to upgrade to first class with frequent flier miles and she stood with her body pressed into the chest-high partition. She was gracious yet unyielding, brisk and beautiful. Her hand was still in her pocket. She was going to Phoenix at 3:45. She turned around and gazed at him. She was vivid, she was dark. "We were married in a previous life," the look said. "Don't you feel it?"

She got what she wanted. She hoisted her bags and gave him a look that said, "I wasn't looking at you before; moreover, I'm from Park Avenue, so don't fuck with me."

She disappeared beyond a pack of misbehaving kids, but he caught sight of her again as she rose through the ceiling on an escalator. Was it too much to hope that this woman, whom he loved, yes, *loved*, would give him a backward glance? The airport was throbbing. His heart was simultaneously knocking in his throat and his stomach. She was looking down at him.

It was his turn on line. "I want to change this to the 3:45 Phoenix flight," he said, out of breath and sweating.

"This is a nonrefundable ticket."

"It's a free country, I'll buy a new one," he snapped—the flight left in sixteen minutes and his wife from a previous life was escalating away.

The clerk looked up. "Coach or first class."

"First class." Barry leaned in confidentially. "I want to sit next to that woman just now with the frequent flier miles."

The pasty clerk looked up sharply with his eyes.

"I know, but I'm a nice guy," Barry pleaded. "I've never done this before." The clerk was clacking away on his keyboard—what did that mean? Would he have to explain his love to this man's superior? "Across the aisle, then." He dared not look around. "Please! I'm giving you twice the business here."

"She's in 3A. You're in 3B. You're perfect together," the WorldWide clerk said automatically. "Next?"

Barry Cantor took off for the gate with serious energy. There was nothing he couldn't do.

. . .

When he arrived at his seat, she was arranging belongings.

"Hi," he said briefly, as if to be polite. 3A looked at him in wild disbelief, and then busied herself among her bags, taking out volumes of reading material. He took out his own volumes, as a sign that he wouldn't bother her.

When they were both settled, he chanced a direct look. She gave him a polite, closed-mouth grimace of a smile, and gazed out the window.

That was okay. It was a long way to Phoenix; she'd have to use the bathroom sometime. In the meantime, the excitement had ebbed. It was nice just sitting next to her. She was somewhere between 28 and 38. Perfect. She smelled like hyacinths, tangerines, pencil shavings—strong, strange.

"Ow moy Gawd," a man behind him said, and rocked Barry's seat as he searched for something.

Maybe she'd be a horror show when she opened her mouth. It would serve him right. An ugly stewardess arrived to ask what they wanted to drink before takeoff.

"Tomato juice, please," she said, "no ice." Unplaceable accent, lovely voice.

"Ginger ale for me!" he said, with growing confidence.

He pretended to read *Progressive Grocer*. He would invite this woman to dinner at his home with his personal chef. This would impress her.

Last night, for example, when Barry got home, Pippa wasn't around, but the place smelled fabulous. There was homemade minestrone on the stove and a moldy-looking cheese laid out on a board. He tried it. It tasted like the dusty concrete floor in a dank French basement. He was in heaven.

"I saw the most amazing film," Pippa had said when she walked in with his dry cleaning. "Did you ever see it? *The Deer Hunter?*"

"Oh, I think I may have seen that one—was that a talkie?"

Her skin was bad, her eye makeup was runny, and her hair was a nightmare. There was a frazzled, undiscriminating energy about Pippa, and five weeks earlier, when she'd come to audition with a meal, he'd looked at the leather jacket and the Day-Glo orange hair, and wondered if she was on drugs. But her eyes were a lively vaporous blue, and she smiled when she talked. She didn't stop talking. She was a junior at Columbia, torn between law and architecture. She'd been Type A, but now she wasn't sure.

"Wow, what a crowd," she'd cracked, nodding at two plates in an otherwise empty cabinet. Barry was mad at himself for thinking drugs; he was getting middle-aged, for Christ's sake. She was a pretty person going through an awkward period. The food was fantastic—he couldn't have been more surprised. He'd hired her on the spot, canceling appointments with two other hopefuls who'd answered the ad he'd placed in the *Times*.

This woman in 3A looked like she liked to eat. He would invite her to dinner and ask Pippa to make something spectacular. She'd made napoleons from scratch one night her second week. He'd watched her rolling the dough out with a rolling pin. He didn't even know he owned a rolling pin.

"So, you're Jewish," his chef said, with an overcasual air, tossing flour across the dough.

The eternal issue. "Yes ma'am, I am."

She was pretending to read her cookbook. "And Vince?"

"Vince is half Jewish. The worst kind: he thinks he's better than everybody." He watched her digesting the information. "And you?"

"I'm nothing. So Vince's dad is like a big important—"

"But Christian nothing, right?" he interrupted.

"My father was Catholic and my mother was Presbyterian," she said, picking up the square of dough and slapping it down to roll it in a different direction. "They became Quakers in college and against anything organized afterwards."

Vince was wandering around in a bathrobe with a glass of Scotch. He looked like a duke's son dissipating himself at Oxford in a PBS miniseries. Pippa scooted around him shyly. She had a crush on Vince. It was irritating.

"So," Barry asked him. "How's tricks?"

Vince's eyes half closed.

"Have you thought about clearing the decks? Being alone for a while, to figure out what you want?"

"Alone," Vince said, as if it were a foreign word. "I don't think I've been alone for more than"—he paused in thought—"a week since I was 17."

What an extraordinary statement. "Well then, clearly you need to try it."

"Has it worked for you," Vince asked, bored.

"Now, now, it's not nice to make fun of the afflicted," Barry said, annoyed. Pippa was blushing at the sink as she brushed melted butter onto the pastry dough. So what, Vince was connected and rich and good-looking. He was a prick. "Do these women know about each other?"

"Not specifically," Vince yawned, and sat at the table. "They know I date other women. They're all seeing other guys."

"Laura's number one, right?" Barry asked. Vince shrugged. "Doesn't it bother you that she's seeing other guys? Let me be clear: when we say seeing, we do mean screwing—yes?"

Vince turned his palms up on the table. "Yes."

"And that doesn't bother you?"

"Well, I don't want to watch her do it, but no, not really."

Astonishing. There are only two kinds of situations a man can handle: very serious or purely sexual. Anything in between and you're in trouble. Vince was in trouble. Although: he envied Vince's ability to just coast with a girl while she was around. He, Barry, couldn't bear to spend even an evening with someone who didn't have end-game potential.

When the pre-takeoff drinks arrived, Barry turned to 3A and said, "L'Chaim." She gave him another disbelieving glance. What was with the disbelieving glances? Get over it, Girl: I am sitting next to you and we are going to Phoenix! What he would do when he got there, he had no idea. He went back to *Progressive Grocer*.

Everyone said that it happened when you least expected it. Barry was 34 years old and he hadn't even kissed a woman in ten months. So how could he not expect it? He was the only man at Maplewood Acres over 27 who wasn't married, with the exception of Bob Stenglis, head of Beverages, who was queerer than a $3 bill. Even Cynthia had gotten married. The woman next to him was making notes in the margins of a document in tiny, neat handwriting. What did that portend?

He tried to calm himself. He tried to contain his expectations. But he missed the multiformat evening where there was food, entertainment, and then going home and getting naked. Barry missed talking. Was this really too much to ask?

Both he and his intended ignored the stewardess's safety routine. What if she lived in Phoenix?

The plane skittered off to a bad start; Barry felt his stomach drop. The woman leaned back with eyes closed.

She was wearing earplugs.

What the hell was he doing?

He'd signed for the ticket without even looking at it.

How much had this date cost?

The plane was tilting and shuddering as it ascended. Long distance was not an attractive option at this stage of his life, even if she was terrific in bed.

Everything dropped suddenly; there was an audible, cabin-wide gasp as the plane pitched and a grinding rattle started. 3A sat forward, took out the earplugs, and held them tightly in her hand. Land and water veered up at dangerous angles in the windows next to her. Everyone was alert, looking around.

"Captain Don Baker has informed me," the stewardess came over the speaker, "that we are experiencing some turbulence. Please sit back with your seat belt fastened and we wish to remind you again that there is no smoking anywhere on this flight, and there are smoke detectors in the lavatories, and tampering with a smoke detector is a federal crime subject to penalty and fine."

The lurching and the terrible grinding rattle continued. Was he going to die on this plane? Not possible. There were often bad moments, but the plane always came through. Always. Barry slipped his airsick bag out just to have it handy. Throwing up on his dream girl could not be his last act before dying.

The speaker thundered, "SIT DOWN! 29D, SIT DOWN!"

Barry and the woman exchanged wordless, petrified eye contact. A smell like garlic wafted through the cabin; the plane seemed to be slowing down.

"I have a very bad feeling about this," she said, in a low voice. Her teeth were curvy and unnaturally white.

"Me too," Barry said, and without really thinking about it, he put his hand out on the drink rest between them. She put her frozen hand in his. They laced fingers. She had the loveliest brown eyes. He couldn't possibly die yet. The pilot announced in an explosion of static that they would be returning to LaGuardia.

"Fly!" he heard himself barking. "Don't talk, fly!"

The plane pressed up again, turning sharply to the right. When the about-face was completed, the grinding stopped.

There was an absolute, terrible, plane-wide silence.

The plane began to fall. Barry found himself stepping on the gas. The woman, ashen, let go his hand and grabbed at the seat in front of her. He handed her his airsick bag and she heaved, neatly, behind the sharp pleats of white plastic. He held his hand between her shoulder blades, wondering if he would live long enough to touch the point on the back of her neck.

He touched it, and she made a terrible face and heaved again into the bag. The plane plummeted and there was fear in his mouth. The stewardess began barking over the speaker, demanding calm, sounding terrified herself. The man behind them chanted, "OW MOY GAWD, OW MOY *GAWD*, OW MOY *GAWD!*"

Barry smelled smoke and burning hair. The plane was on fire? The woman handed him the airsick bag and he threw up on top of whatever she had thrown up; the idea of it made him retch again. He sat back, sweating. She handed him a Wash'n Dri. He was too weak to take it. Land was appearing and disappearing in the windows. His heart was pelting his ribs. She opened the Wash'n Dri for him. He wiped his mouth and sweating forehead.

The lights went out.

He was going to die now. And all because he couldn't get laid.

The woman was looking at him with luminous eyes. He grabbed her and they braced their arms around each other tightly. The pilot said that he was attempting an emergency landing.

"Just fly the fucking plane, Jack," Barry shouted, and at this the woman laughed, and turned her face to him and kissed him flush on the mouth. Her lips were soft, and she tasted of vomit acid; he supposed he did too. Noxious fluids were part of life too. There was another lurch, and Barry almost threw up again, almost threw up in this beautiful woman's mouth. He tried to stabilize, but he had no idea what was happening.

"Justine Schiff," she said, and squeezed his right hand so fiercely he gasped. The stewardess demanded a tuck position. They bent over their knees; the pressure from his seat belt was intolerable. The plane was fighting up again; he felt it like a creepy vibration in his lower back. Why was this taking so long?

"Land! Crash even!" He sat up indignantly and looked around: An empty plane.

This was terrifying. He quickly got down. She was looking at him from a few inches away, red-faced in her tuck position. She had the most unusual little thumbs—shallow and wide, with tiny rectangular nails way up at the very top. The variety of human life was just endless.

"I was going to a wedding," she said in a normal voice.

"Right before Christmas?"

"I know! She has some nerve."

"I think I wet my pants!" he realized. She handed him some Kleenex from her bag. "Hey, nice meeting you," he said, and she laughed.

He stared at the tiny little horizontal window of her thumbnail as if he could see his future there. He repeated her name over and over as they went down.

None of that, now

When things got very bad, and luggage went caroming through the cabin, Justine was too terrified to speak. Just because you're ruthlessly organized and thinking ahead constantly doesn't mean you're covered against every eventuality, and acts of God. However, it felt very familiar with Barry Cantor. She didn't even know his name until after she'd kissed him. She had never kissed a man first. What did it say about her life that she was comfortable kissing a stranger in a crashing plane.

There was deafening violence. If she made it through this alive, she would have to reassess her entire way of living. She was hit by things flying by in the massive crunch when the plane smashed across the ground. There was a scramble, people climbing over her to get out, pushing frantically at the door. On automatic, she slid down the yellow chute into freezing brown water, thigh-high.

She was alive. She waded through the filthy, icy swamp to the edge of the tarmac. People in orange jumpsuits and ambulances were speeding around. They were hosing down black smoke in the center of the plane. There was a big, wide wall of shrieking noise. She stepped up onto broken concrete in sopping panty hose. She was looking for Barry Cantor.

But there were so many people, so much twisted garbage. The smell of burning plastic made her gag. A huge bus came to ferry them to the terminal. She must have turned her ankle in the crush to get out of the plane. There was pushing and raised voices in the bottleneck at the door. Inside, everyone was milling around dazed, wet and flushed, wearing silver thermal sheets around their shoulders, panting white steam in the cold, gagging. She didn't see him anywhere.

Someone gave her a silver thermal sheet. Suddenly, she had never been this cold; her clothes were swampy, her thighs were chafing. Her coat was on the plane. Her shoes were gone. The ankle was throbbing.

"Passengers from WorldWide Flight 358!" a tough Brooklyn voice spat from the system. "Please proceed into the processing area." The noise was painful. She had never been this cold. There was craziness all around. She almost cried. The tough voice continued to shout at a blistering volume: "If you or a member of your party is unable to walk, please stay where you are and bring it to the attention of a member of the ground crew."

Justine realized with shame that she hadn't thought about her mother. She'd thought about her father, briefly, just after she threw up. She had wondered what kind of impact, if any, her death would have on his life. But she hadn't thought about her mother.

There was chaos in the terminal. The noise was intolerable. Justine pulled herself along a carpeted wall. She wanted a shower, dry clothes, sweaters, quiet. She spotted Barry from behind—he was the tallest man in the next lounge. He looked like somebody's husband.

She hopped up behind him and put her hand on his arm. He squeezed her in an excruciating hug. Chaos continued all around. She closed her eyes and forced herself to breathe.

Someone lurched into her and she fell forward; Barry helped her to a seat. He was exactly the sort of guy who never spoke to her. He smiled as if he wanted to cry. He really did look like somebody's husband. But did he look like her husband.

All at once, he began talking. "Can you believe this? Nothing like this has ever happened to me! I've always wondered how I would handle it—did you?"

"Not really," she said, smiling at his enthusiasm.

"I thought you handled it great! I was so impressed with you!" he said, squeezing her waist with both hands. She cringed and crossed her legs, forgetting her ankle. The whole of her leg throbbed. "I knew it was the end when the stewardess got scared."

She wanted to lie down and be still.

A woman sitting nearby began talking at them: "Did you see that elderly man going down the slide?" Blades of gray hair were plastered to her forehead. She was trying to bend her glasses back into shape. "Oh, my Lord!"

Barry took the glasses from her and tried to fix them. "Did you go out the back or the front?"

"The back," the woman said.

"We went out the front." He returned the glasses and asked a squat, lumpish man across from them, "Back or front?"

It was over. Justine wanted to go home and take a shower. She wanted to take a shower with Barry Cantor. Why was he talking to these fat old people he didn't know? A whole new group had gathered; they were exchanging stories, displaying their burns and bruises.

"This man in front of us had a seizure," a woman younger than Justine said to Barry. "Do you think he died?" she asked, screwing up her face like a little lost lamb.

"Barry," Justine said. "I have to go."

"Really?" He turned back to his new friends. "Well, adios, it's been surreal."

"I want to give you my card," the glasses woman said. They waited while she dug around. "I don't have it," she wept, making a face Justine didn't want to look at. "I don't have anything."

Barry put his arm around this woman's shoulders. "You have what God gave you," he said. "That's all anybody ever has."

Oy, she thought. She didn't want to stand around for this.

The fat guy said, "Cry, it's all right, let it all out."

Justine was disgusted. She needed to pee. "Barry? I have to go. I'll be back."

There was a cutout symbol of a woman, and she followed the arrows, limping down the fluorescent boulevard. Violently bright lights suddenly turned on behind her. The Eyewitness News Team had arrived.

In front of her, a fleet of airline personnel was coming at her, fast. She would soon be up against a wall of these uniforms. She had to go. She limped, head down. A brisk blonde in a navy blue suit planted herself firmly in front of Justine. The rest of the fleet marched on.

"Ma'am, you're gonna have to stay in the designated area for safety reasons. We'll have a doctor with you momentarily."

"Bathroom." People were rushing by with medical equipment.

The woman pointed with her whole arm towards the chaos. "Turn right at Gate 17A, there's a restroom down that concourse."

The door with the circle and the triangle was ten feet away.

"That's off limits, sorry." The woman was squeezing her inner elbow and pulling her back towards the heat and anarchy.

"It's right there," Justine shouted.

"We have regulations during an emergency situation."

"You have regulations about that bathroom? Get your fucking hands off me," Justine snarled, freeing her arm. The woman stepped back. "I'll sue your ass off." She began to limp to the door. "You personally, not WorldWide. I'm suing them separately."

Justine slammed into the empty bathroom, and sat directly on a toilet seat, in spite of a lifetime of training. She urinated with her shoulderbag resting on her thighs. Something terrible was going to happen. She sat with her arms braced over her knees, shaking. Several files were on the plane—days of research, lost.

She hung over the sink, running her wrists under cool water as if she were drunk. The tough voice sputtered, "Passengers from Flight 358! Please be patient! Everyone will be given complete and comprehensive medical attention free of charge!"

"Stop yelling at me!" Her feet were raw and numb, like frozen meat. This was terrible. She limped out smack into the airline blonde who was now with a white-hatted nurse. The nurse didn't touch her, but looked at her directly. "Are you feeling all right?"

Justine burst into tears. "I, my ankle."

"Let's have a look at it. Can you walk to those seats?"

"We are not responsible for accidents that occur in unauthorized areas," the officious bitch hovered directly behind.

"You're making me nervous," Justine snapped. "Go away."

The uniform left. Justine rolled her panty hose off, barely worrying that anyone would see. The nurse asked what her name was, where the flight had been going, what day was it, what year was it. "What is this," she asked, suddenly petrified.

"We always check for head injuries. Now blood pressure."

"Hey!" Barry sat down next to her and she felt a strange rush of relief. "How'd you get your own private nurse?"

When the nurse finished with her and turned to Barry, Justine paid close attention. He was big, and had meat on his bones without being fat. That happened sometimes with men. He squeezed her hand in time to the nurse's pumping as she took his blood pressure.

"What day is it?" the nurse asked.

"The first day of the rest of my life," he offered freely. "Did anyone die?"

"No," the nurse rose. "Okay, I'm just triage, I don't treat you. Both of you get on line three, and you stay off that foot."

A whole crew of navy blue WorldWide personnel set up shop in their lounge. She and Barry were given the numbers 67 and 68 on the third medical line. People clamored to be interviewed on television. She lay down over three seats and put her head in Barry's lap. All she wanted was quiet. He continued to talk compulsively: the turbulence, the noise, the landing, the injuries, the engine. She wrapped her legs in the silver sheet.

The night before, she'd been at the end of her third 18-hour day in a row when Chris Farlowe had called her in to ask her to work on a tender offer. She'd declined. She never declined.

Farlowe was tall, stout, unpolished, unrepentant, and often enraged. He had routinely asked her to be acting partner on choice assignments. He whipped off his glasses and said irascibly, "Trouble at home?"

"Excuse me?"

"Do you have a personal problem. Things of that nature. Don't go into it," he added quickly, a hand up in warning. "I don't want to know."

"No, but I have a wedding this weekend," she said, and his weedy gray eyebrows shot up. "Not my own," she reassured him.

"Thank God," he said offhandedly, as if the idea were so preposterous it barely qualified as a bad joke.

So of course she had to burst into tears on his desk.

"What?" he shouted angrily.

Nothing like this had ever happened before. Farlowe jumped up to slam his door. He had no tolerance for apathy, never mind hysterics. He waited—clapping his hands—for her to compose herself.

But she couldn't stop. This was beyond unprofessional. This was corporate suicide. He sat on the Management Committee, the Partnership Committee, and co-chaired the Corporate Department.

Farlowe shook his big, lolling gray head. "Come on, Schiff," he kept warning impatiently, drumming his fingers on the desk. "None of that, now."

Women were one thing at Packer Breebis Nishman Grabt. Married women were something else. A single woman trying to get married was the lowest form of life. From this moment on, no matter how many 18-hour days Justine billed, Farlowe and partners would treat her like a coed resting between shopping sprees at Saks.

Barry Cantor would not stop talking.

"It's going to be at least three hours on this line," a man with a bandaged hand told them on his way to his exit interview, and Justine almost burst into tears again.

She rose and limped to a patch of empty carpet and lay down with the silver sheet. People were rushing, screaming, crying. She'd lost her shoes, her coat, her files.

Barry squatted down by her side. "What's up?" he said very loud.

"Tired. All of a sudden."

"That's it? No problems under your clothes I can check?"

His teeth overlapped in the front. He was very charming. It was a shame he was talking so loud.

"Passengers from Flight 358! After you have seen Airline and Medical Representatives, you are free to depart the recovery area!" A small cheer erupted; Barry participated in it. "There will be vouchers for the 7 P.M. WorldWide flight to Phoenix!" There was an eruption of derisive laughter. "And there is no smoking in the terminal, subject to fine and/or imprisonment!"

Justine sat up. Why were they sitting around waiting. If she wasn't going to Phoenix, she should go in and work on that tender offer.

She rose. "I have to get out of here."

"Don't you want your luggage?"

She wondered if Barry Cantor was the kind of guy she might have slept with in college, but didn't have much use for now. On the other hand, hadn't she decided to rethink her life?

No: some things were core concerns. He was sitting there like all the other sheep, waiting for somebody else to make arrangements for him. This infuriated her.

"I'm going." She held her hand out, disappointed.

"Oh, I see, a polite handshake at ground level." He pulled her into him and squeezed. He pressed his lips to her forehead. He was tall, he was solid. There would be no question who weighed more. She was near tears again.

"Look. All I want is a shower," she said. "I want a steak."

"You need some help with that?"

I thought you'd never ask, she thought. "Yes," she said.

There was massive traffic on the Grand Central Parkway: everyone on both sides of the highway was watching the column of dirty gray smoke and the dousing of the plane. Justine tried to slow her heart down with the biofeedback exercises she'd learned at an ABA seminar in Duluth last year. She'd obtained a fast-track release by cornering a uniform and saying, "I am an attorney with Packer Breebis Nishman Grabt. If you think I'm waiting on line you've got another thing coming." After they'd signed medical waivers and release forms, a WorldWide man escorted them to the head of the taxi line and gave them booklets about postcrash trauma, psychiatric referrals, socks, toiletry kits, and packets of smoked almonds.

In the cab, Barry held her bad foot delicately. It was rapidly losing outside skin sensations, and the internal pressure was mounting. "We met in a crashing plane!" he told the driver.

She wanted to shoo him away. She wanted to kiss him again. As an experiment, she leaned her head on his chest. It was comfortable. She closed her eyes.

The car yanked forward and back.

"Hey!" Barry shouted through the partition. "We've brushed with death already once today. Don't stop and start like that."

"Well said," she said. They got comfortable again.

"Wait a minute," Barry shouted. "I don't have my wallet!"

The cab stopped short; horns honked. The driver glared at them in the rearview.

"I have it! I have it!" Justine shouted, waving her wallet.

Barry looked at her as if she'd produced a live animal from her sleeve. They sat up and separated. She wondered if she'd make it to the TriBoro without wanting to disinvite him. All well and good at 20,000 feet hurtling to the ground. Inching through Queens in a foul-smelling cab was something else. She didn't have to decide until they got to her building. She didn't owe him anything. She didn't want to talk.

"Well, we had a bonding, near-death experience, and now we're realizing that we're strangers," he said seriously. "That's normal. I'd say let's bond further in the shower, but you're not the type."

"How would you know?"

"You're the type who hands a man a moist towelette in a crashing plane. Something tells me you want your own shower." He smiled broadly: "Hey! I have two showers."

"No," she said. "Home."

He looked disappointed, but he didn't push it. A cemetery loomed up on the left side. "Mr. Khalil Abdul!" he shouted to the driver. "We almost died! And now we know what life is!" The driver turned on the radio, loud. Awful noise saturated the air.

She hadn't given this driver a passing thought since getting into the cab. Normally, she'd have been acutely aware of whether he'd try to chat her up, shortchange her, take her out of her way, or drive like a maniac. Surprising herself again, she kissed Barry on the mouth. She could tell they would be compatible this way, but she didn't want to get into it now. She was too tired. He laughed, as if amazed.

As they turned on 76th Street, she handed him money, told him to demand a receipt, and kissed his cheek, which was salty.

"Dinner?" he asked.

"Yes."

He took her card, but he didn't look at it. "Tonight?"

"No."

"I'll call you then," he said, and looked at the card. "Wait! No! I want the *home* number." She began to tell him how rarely she was at home, but he interrupted, "I need a pen. Khalil!" The driver handed back a pen. Barry Cantor wrote the number on the card, and gave her such a sweet, impressed, lovely look that she almost got back into the cab. He pulled her in and kissed her nose.

"Nice meeting you," he called, loud and sarcastic.

She stepped carefully over ice in the WorldWide socks, limping bare-legged into her lobby. Everything felt completely different.

Chapter 2

Boeuf

Pippa's roommates were in awe of her. They lounged in the living room, drinking Kahlúa and milk. They smoked Virginia Slims Menthol Luxury Lights 120s. They played Tori Amos on the stereo, and discussed Pippa's new situation late into the night.

"I say they're gay," said Benita, unwrapping a Ring-Ding. Benita was overweight and she didn't care. "Why would that guy have three women if he wasn't trying to prove something." She sunk her teeth into a puck of chocolate. Pippa shivered.

"WEREN'T trying to prove," said Daria. She was sternly beautiful, with green shadows under her eyes and bones like the young Gregory Peck. She embodied the exotic yet lived-in look that Pippa was trying to cultivate. Her parents lived in Rome.

"They're not gay," Pippa said, on the exhale. "Barry is desperate to get married." She dropped ashes into a dish Daria had stolen from The Royalton.

"Gimme a Vagina Slime," Daria said, stretching her leg out in an arabesque and tipping the Kahlúa bottle over her glass. Pippa tossed her the pack. Daria lit a cigarette and exhaled in a plume, looking disdainful and majestic. "I'm using their pad in my next film."

This made Pippa nervous. "Don't tell anyone about my job."

They looked at her for a moment, and then began a new topic: the disparity between the men they knew and the men they wanted to know.

Pippa was cooking three nights a week now. She'd never met people like this before. Vince spoke fluent Japanese and German, and Barry was certified to do scuba. She had never been in such an enormous, beautiful apartment. Ever since her first night, when she'd auditioned with a pot roast she'd never tried before and got the job, she'd had the sense that her luck was changing.

The recipe had called for ten onions, and she was sure that sounded wrong, but she did it anyway, and tossed in some extra garlic. She tasted the sauce, and it seemed fine—terrific, even—she was just lucky. They were standing there, among the mess. Amidst. Well, if they didn't want to see the mess, then why put the kitchen in the living room? Barry was tall and attractive in an older man kind of way—balding in a point, but beefy and dark. Vince was gorgeous, with long, sandy bangs and sleepy, slanty brown eyes. She tried not to look at him. The silence was unbearable.

"This recipe comes from my Uncle Hosea," she said.

Barry said, "Uncle Hosea, from the old country?"

"You could say that."

"Where is the old country?" Vince asked, undressing while he spoke, removing his tie in a noose, unbuttoning his shirt.

"Vermont." Vince hung his shirt and tie on the back of a chair, flipped open his belt, peeled off his socks, and sat down in his undershirt with his pants unzipped.

She tried not to stare. "Is dinner here always so formal?"

"Get dressed," Barry told Vince, who strolled out. Barry turned to her, his thick arms folded across his big blue-shirted chest. "You know, we have several applicants." He was at least a foot taller than she was.

"You want to shop around. That's fine."

"How much would you charge?"

"Twenty dollars an hour," she said fast, her scalp sweating. She'd been over this in the shower, on the subway, with her roommates, alone.

"The worst that could happen is you don't get the job," Daria had said. "But what if they say yes?"

They said yes. A miracle.

One night, her second week cooking, while she was chopping walnuts for a carrot cake, Barry took a cutting knife, pulled the garbage can over to the table, sat down, cracked his knuckles grandly, tilted his head from side to side, and breathed deeply. He swung a bulging shopping bag on top of the table.

"I do this a couple times a year," he said, and began slicing open envelopes. They worked separately for a while.

"So, help me out here," Barry said, and she looked up. "I have this theory, see, that women who wear velvet chokers are into bondage."

Already she was beginning to tire of Barry. "All women," she said, "not just four out of five."

"Just the ones in chokers. I notice you're wearing one: what do you think?" He looked at her directly and cocked an eyebrow.

Daria would surely have something to zing back at him—Pippa couldn't think of what. Her internship only paid $6 an hour. She needed this job. "I really don't know how to respond to that."

He smiled at her with big boxy teeth. Better to eat me with, she thought. She folded in the walnuts. She heard the knife tearing through the paper.

"Do you have a boyfriend, Pippa?"

This was the second week, but it was still the first impression.

"Does it matter?"

He turned his palms up and out. "Just making conversation."

She looked at him closely. The phone rang; he answered it and handed it to her. It was Krissel Design. Could she come in at 8 A.M. to redraft gas pipes.

Barry didn't seem angry that she'd gotten a call. In fact, he looked completely disarmed then, friendly and balding and talkative in his shirtsleeves and socks. He raised an eyebrow at her. He was just a guy doing his bills. Doing them late.

"Well, I think I'm kind of seeing someone."

"Too soon to tell?"

"Yeah." Zack, the guy from the party, had finally called two weeks later, but he called at 10:30 and asked her out for a beer right then. She said yes, but felt weird about it, but he'd already left when she called him back, so she had to go. When she got to The West End, he was in a booth with three friends and he talked to her but barely looked at her, which she considered a good sign. But he hadn't called since. She emptied her batter into the pan.

"What does he do?"

"Philosophy major. He's a senior."

"An older man. But what kind of car does he drive? Very important, Pippa. You don't want some loser in a Honda."

"He doesn't have a car."

"Not even a Honda?"

"Barry, this is New York. Nobody has a car."

"Anyone who is anyone has a car." He whisked all the bills into the shopping bag and announced he was taking a shower. He was probably like Hosea, who just said outrageous things to make sure you were awake.

Vince arrived late with Renée, who sauntered in wearing a banana minidress with perfectly matched banana stockings and banana suede shoes. She tossed her big frizzy auburn hair around and sat down at the table. She had a hairy zebra-skin belt.

"Oh, it's not meat, is it," Renée sniffed, shocked. She was a British TV producer.

"Boeuf Bourguignon," Pippa said.

"Oh," Renée whispered. "I don't eat meat."

"It slipped my mind," Vince said, waving his hand vaguely.

"Do we have any extra vegetables for Renée?" Barry asked.

"Don't bother. I'm not hungry."

Everyone sat down at the table, and Pippa served salad. Renée pushed silverware around for a while and then picked up her fork suddenly. She speared a leaf of lettuce and held it up, looking at Pippa. "What did you put in the dressing?"

"A secret," Pippa whispered.

"No, honey, I need to know."

Pippa began to tell her, but Renée interrupted and said, "It's sesame oil, isn't it."

"Is oil a problem for you?" Pippa asked.

"Sesame." She pushed her plate into the center of the table. Pippa looked at Barry; he raised a shoulder and a hand.

Suddenly, Vince focused directly on Renée and said, "Where do you come from, you wood nymph, you?" and kissed the curve of her neck. Renée moaned theatrically and rolled her head around.

This stopped conversation for a while.

When Pippa presented Vince with a plate of stew and noodles, he turned to Renée and said, "Pippa is one of my favorite people."

Now, what did that mean?

Pippa served Barry, poured wine, and waited for conversation. There was none.

"I'm thinking that drafting gas pipes isn't giving me a real taste of what it is to be an architect," she said, to break it up.

Vince chewed, in a trance. His streaky hair was standing on end.

"I know several brilliant designers who are collecting unemployment at present," Renée said. "Nobody's building."

Look at Renée at the end of the day: high heels, earrings, bracelet, scarf, perfect makeup. Pippa couldn't walk around the block in sweat pants without spilling, tearing, or losing something. "So you think I shouldn't try to be an architect?"

"Pippa," Vince said suddenly, "you'd better learn whatever it is you want to know now, because it's a fact: after 24 or 25, your memory goes, and so does all desire to learn anything new."

"That's such bullshit," Barry said heatedly.

Vince shrugged. "This is your era, Pippa, so work hard."

She looked at him closely. Was he patronizing her? She had no idea. She cleared the plates. "I'm thinking of getting a razor cut again," she told Barry. "What do you think?"

"I think that would be a mistake," he offered.

"But I need a change," she said.

"Renée, what can we do with this hair?" Barry turned to ask.

Renée took a sip of wine. "Wash it, maybe?"

"Meow!" Barry said.

"You're a fine one to talk about hair," Renée said in a malevolent, self-satisfied way. Barry smiled, but didn't bother responding.

Immediately after the main course, Renée strolled out in her heels and Vince followed her to his bedroom. This was offensive.

Barry turned on the TV and sat on the couch. Pippa cleared the dishes, glancing at the crooked jetty of hair that struggled down to Barry's forehead, and disliked Vince in a serious way. She brought Barry decaf and a piece of the cake and sat down next to him, warming her hands on her cup.

"Are you polygamous too?"

"When I'm unbelievably lucky, I get to be monogamous."

"I really don't like the way he operates," she said, increasingly on Barry's side. "At all."

This was when Barry offered her a semester's tuition if she introduced him to his future wife. She finished her coffee standing up in the kitchen, watching him watch highlights of a basketball game with the sound off. She resolved not to tell Daria about the finder's fee or the choker comment.

She took the leftovers home in a plastic tub; while listening to the flap and sweep noises of a nightly ritual from the apartment above that sounded like people bowling with live birds, she and her roommates polished off the carrot cake, discussing their parents' limitations as role models late into the night.

Little yellow sticky things

On his way out in the morning, Vince found another little yellow sticky thing on the front door. It said: "Vince: Please call super about heat. Barry."

When Vince was in Los Angeles, life was so easy, he was scarcely aware of living it. He spent sixty percent of his time traveling— Tokyo, London, wherever his deals were. But back in New York, there was so much inherent friction, it was impossible not to be constantly aware of his life. Mingus Resnick had closed the LA bureau, five people on the CMO desk had been laid off, and partners were sharing clerical staff. His stomach was corroded. His mother was always calling with family obligations. He sensed she might be disappointed. He needed to make decisions, or something.

He knew he should get his own apartment. Buy furniture. But why commit to a lease when all he really needed was closet space? He'd hoped that living with Barry would be like turning a corner, but now he wished Barry would just leave. It was a lovely apartment, and he'd never lived on the Upper West Side before.

He had to straighten out his female situation. But how could you say, "We can't go on like this," when "this" was once a month? Sometimes, in the middle of things, he forgot where he was. Who was she? Did she like it slow or fast? He missed LA.

Vince stuck a note for Pippa on the refrigerator: "Dear Pippa, Would you be an angel and call the super about the heat before the plants freeze? Thanks! Vince." He pocketed Barry's note and left for the day. Barry required too much energy.

As he crossed West End, Vince saw the horrifying man again. This man wore a suit and went around with a briefcase as if nothing was wrong, but he must have been in a terrible accident. His skin was red and mottled, most of one ear was sliced off, and there were long red scars on his neck. How could this guy wake up and look at himself? What did he do in his suit? Would you trust your business to someone who looked like The Swamp Thing?

"It's all right if you give me money!" an unwashed woman sitting on the ground near a stand of Christmas trees called to him. "I won't tell where I got it." It wasn't right to pretend she wasn't there, so he nodded sideways while looking straight ahead; he didn't want to offend anyone. He hailed a cab.

Mingus Resnick had moved the New York bureau into an old-fashioned building down among the luggage shops and technical schools in the East 30's. There were sooty venetian blinds and black-and-white linoleum floors. It was a far cry from the granite slabs at the World Financial Center. He checked LIBOR and the Prime, and followed Claudia, his secretary, into the kitchen. He sang: "Good morning, Merry Sunshine, what made you wake so soon?"

"What?" she asked, as if outraged.

Claudia had a crush on him. She took messages from his girl-friends—it made no sense.

He tried to be pleasant: "Didn't your mother sing that song to you?" he asked, and she lurched past him. What did she want from him?

His father's face was on the front page of the *Wall Street Journal*. Vince stared at the tiny gray dots. He tried to look at each one separately. He spent his morning analyzing the cash flow from the sale/lease-back he was doing in Mexico City. Laura called to tell him to pick her up at LaGuardia on Friday.

He had to restructure two deals by Monday—he didn't have time for another bad weekend with Laura. He had to do something. Stop seeing someone. Something.

Billy Friedman came in talking. "In 1986 I sold a Dutch pension fund on a 700-unit condo in Newport Beach. Guess what?"

"It's in one of your pools of nonperforming loans?"

"Yes! It was 1986! These things were idiot-proof!"

"No one has suffered more than the Dutch," Vince said.

Billy liked Vince's tie; what did Vince think of Billy's tie? Billy picked up a little black box that Vince had borrowed from an actress he'd been seeing years ago. When you put a penny in the slot, a little gnarled green hand came out and snatched it away. Billy had done this a hundred times. He put a penny in the slot, and howled at the hand. If the box ever disappeared, Vince would know where to find it.

Billy had bought a rowing machine, and wanted to discuss his training. Vince excused himself and took Inside Mortgage News to the men's room. He spent a lot of time in here, sweating out his hemorrhoids and wondering what to do next. The tiny white hexagonal tiles and the louvered doors gave the agony of his visits a film noir quality. He didn't understand friendship. If you couldn't get beyond talking, what was the point?

On his way back, he noticed that the temp had put on lipstick and was looking up at him; the CMO analyst raised her eyebrows at him in disdain. He felt like he spent his days surfing through other people's expectations and disappointments. Everybody wanted something. Men too—look at Billy Friedman. Nothing was ever enough.

Kiki lived three blocks from his office in a white brick high-rise with her three-year-old son and an enormous vegetable juicer. She'd been a model. Now she was a photographers' rep. When he arrived for lunch, she was in a leotard and tights. He sat on the carpet next to her dressing table.

"This couple moved into an apartment," she told the phone, "and a feng shui practitioner told them the walls weren't parallel. They went in, like a coffin. The feng shui guy says, Move, or you're gonna die. So, they didn't do anything. And like five days later? Their Toyota flies off the road into a gorge. Dead." She was 39, divorced from a Belgian businessman who was late with the checks.

"I ate my gun," Tor burst in screaming, climbing onto her lap. She kissed the top of his white blond head and got off the phone. Vince wondered what a child of his would look like.

Vince and Tor sat on the carpet watching Kiki put on makeup, passing a large plastic truck between them until Tor got his finger stuck in the dump mechanism and started to shriek. Vince fled to the living room while Kiki dealt with it in the bathroom. He'd need at least three days with lawyers in Mexico City next week.

The screaming subsided. He walked back in. "Why do you live here?" he asked, kissing her bare shoulder. Tor stormed out. "Not that I'm not grateful for the convenience."

"It's rent controlled," she said, brushing on powder. Kiki was much sexier than either Laura or Renée, although they rarely had sex, and that was fine with him. He enjoyed looking at her. The slight pouches under her eyes that drove her to leg lifts were lovely. He knelt next to her and she pulled him into a hug.

"You are so young," she said. They stayed like that for a minute. He *was* young. He looked at the sunlight on a patch of blue carpet and wondered if a triple net bond lease was enforceable in Mexico. She had a partial view of the Chrysler Building. Did she have the younger sister in med school or the younger brother in Hollywood?

On his way back to the office, Vince dodged psychotics, watch vendors, office workers, and throngs of Christmas shoppers. A small crowd was watching a cartoon on a TV inside a store window. Several drifted towards him with cups outstretched. Why stop seeing Kiki?

No, but she has a dog

Justine limped into her apartment and immediately called her mother to get it over with. All through college and law school, Justine's mother called her four times a day. Justine spoke to her three times out of four, and felt bad when she dodged the fourth call. Lately, Justine spoke to her mother once a day, and Alma, her secretary, spoke to Justine's mother at least twice a day.

Carol wasn't home, thank God. Then she felt guilty. It was Friday: her mother was in Bedford. As she dialed, Justine imagined Carol Anne Kaminsky Schiff Dunlap in a red sweatsuit ensemble, squinting through her tiny half glasses at the Metamucil label, her gold mule slippers clacking over the quarry tiles in the kitchen. Her tears were on the verge of spilling over when Carol picked up.

"Darling! How's Phoenix?"

Justine picked up her knitting and began a row of purl. "My meeting went over. I'm taking a different flight." She hadn't washed her hands yet. She was shaking.

"I can't believe they're letting you go for a whole weekend. Did you have to pledge your firstborn to the firm?"

Justine breathed. "It's a good thing—the plane I was supposed to be on crashed into Jamaica Bay."

"Holy cow."

Justine thought of adding, "And I met a nice guy," but let it sit. "How's the pooch."

"Adorable. I was setting up for cocktails and I forgot about her. She ate a whole pint of pâté."

"What? Please watch her."

"I wanted you at this party. Who does she think she is, a wedding three days before Christmas. Families should be together."

"We're not Christian, Mom. I hate to break it to you."

"That's hardly the point. Now, I want you to call me the minute you get there."

"My every minute is programmed."

"So give me your number and I'll take my chances."

Justine felt hot. "I don't know the number."

"What's the name of the hotel?"

This was exactly the sort of conversation she thought she wouldn't be having anymore after her near-death experience. She stopped holding her breath and began a row of knit. "Mom? I'll be fine. I'll miss you and I'll call you when I get back."

"All right, dear."

She continued knitting. So it was that easy. She hung up.

She called Allison Baraniak to say she couldn't make her wedding because she'd broken her ankle in a plane crash. They exchanged formula phrases about the tenuousness of life and hung up. She hadn't yet looked in the mirror. She was sitting around in her damp, torn, dirty suit, postponing a shower for some reason. The place was strangely still without the dog. Should she confess to the crash so that she could have her around? She experienced shooting pains throughout her body as she struggled to peel off her suit. There was no way she could walk the dog.

The phone rang. It was Ilana Doisneau, the number three rainmaker at Packer Breebis, the most senior of the four female partners and the chair of the Banking Group. She knew all about the crash, and had it on authority that WorldWide would be blaming it on engine failure, and using Cunningham Pazer Landau for litigation. How Ilana knew that Justine was on the plane was anybody's guess.

"Now, you MUST see my orthopedist," Ilana insisted in her whiskey baritone boom, and Justine heard the electronic personal organizer beeping. "And when you're ready, I want you to meet my physical therapist, Jerome. He loves me. LOVES me. I helped him get out of his lease and he is just THE MOST delicious tomato. You'll love him."

Ilana sounded dissatisfied when Justine said good-bye. She probably needed something. Clearly it could wait till Monday or she would have pushed it.

Justine decided to call her father, whom she hadn't spoken to in about five months. He was out, according to Angelique, his new wife, teaching Chloe how to ride her bike without training wheels. Angelique wasn't really new, having been married to her father for something like ten years now. Angelique was at least 38 by now, if Chloe didn't need training wheels.

Things filtered through her tangled head in the shower. While the plane was smashing across the ground, the previous day had flashed before her eyes, including the petty disputes over a noncompete clause in a purchase letter. She'd arrived home that night at 10:45 to a trail of coffee grinds and chewed-up used tampons leading from the kitchen into the living room. The dog had gazed up at her guiltily. She ate cold Mu Shu Chicken with the TV on and the sound off, the dog right next to her, agitating for food.

This was her life. Justine sat in the shower and let the water beat down on her and collect. If she'd known she was going to die the following day, would she have given Stella more food? Given the proofreading to someone else? So she could do what? What would she have done instead? She emerged from the shower weak and rubbery.

The phone rang. She limped to the couch.

It was Farlowe. "Was that your plane?"

She told him the story, minus Barry Cantor and vomiting.

"Well, you can't dance," he said impatiently. "So skip the wedding."

"I'm going tomorrow morning. Early," she added, lest he find an opening. The tears on his desk felt like five years ago.

"So I guess you're not coming in tonight."

She shut her eyes. This was another conversation she thought she wouldn't be having after her near-death experience. "No."

There was a pause. Neither of them was used to her letting him down. She pictured him at his desk, picking toffee out of his enormous yellow teeth. "Well," he said doubtfully. "I guess you might meet someone at the wedding."

"Yeah, like the bride, whom I haven't seen in four years."

She hung up, and burst into tears on her couch. Who cared. Who really cared. She might have died. And then what. What would they say at her funeral? She always came in when they needed her? She was among the top-five-billing associates six years in a row? She always carried a pocketbook that matched her shoes? Her life was really just a near-life experience. She blew her nose.

About a month ago, Justine had attended the wedding of Heather Pincus, a girl she'd ridden horses with at the Holly Bridle Stables. At 12, Heather had been in love with her horse. In the ladies' room, during the bouquet toss, Justine found Courtney Blanchard lounging on a sofa, drinking red wine and smoking a thin brown cigarette. At Spence, Courtney had pushed Justine down some steps. Justine still had the scars on her knee.

Courtney looked Justine over in the mirror and said, "The only single women left are hiding from the bouquet."

"I thought you were engaged." What Justine had heard was that Courtney was living in Cobble Hill with a shoe salesman she'd met at an N.A. meeting, and was temping to pay her rent while she wrote screenplays.

"Oh, *engaged* to be engaged," Courtney said, and finished off her wine. "When we finally decide to do it we'll be so old, I'll be a bride and a widow the same year." She poured herself another glass from a bottle on the floor. "Did you hear? Charlotte McPherson just came back from Nepal. She meditated for a year after her sister died. Now she's doing PR for the Sanitation Department and living in Hoboken." She pointed to an empty glass.

"Is she seeing anyone?" Justine picked up the glass and Courtney poured her some wine.

"No, but she has a dog. You should've come to the reunion. It was such a revelation," Courtney said, throwing a leg over the arm of the sofa. "Christina Moretti, the one with the nightbrace, is booking talent on a talk show in LA and running a victims' rights group. Divorced. Ellen Haberman is a sex therapist."

"Ellen Haberman is a sex therapist?"

Courtney lit another cigarette, rotating her foot. "Chessie Stringwell lost about 500 pounds and is working for CBS in San Francisco. Her girlfriend—yes, didn't you hear? I always knew. Her girlfriend runs Democratic campaigns. They don't eat white flour or sugar, or anything with sulfites."

Courtney rested her cigarette in an ashtray, stepping on Justine's foot in the process, and gave Justine an uppercut to the cheek while apologizing. Courtney then dumped her purse out on the vanity. Filthy tubes and compacts cascaded in all directions.

Justine took another mouthful of wine. "And Jocelyn Van Der Geest?" The biggest bitch at Spence.

"She married a German industrialist."

"What does that mean, German industrialist?"

"I lied—he's Swiss," Courtney said, pulling a dark brown lipstick across her mouth. "I don't know what he does—his family is loaded and they have a gorgeous chalet on Lake Geneva." She pressed her lips together. "She showed me pictures, making little comments in French, and when we parted, listen, *she blew me a kiss*." Courtney blew Justine a kiss.

"She did not."

"She did." Courtney blotted her lips with tissue and blew Justine another kiss. "She's got three blond children, and the 9-year-old is like a world-class skiing champion." She blew another kiss. "And you?"

Justine wanted to get out of the ladies' room. "I live here." She put the glass down and walked over thick carpet to the door. "I'm a lawyer. I have a dog."

"Seeing anyone?"

"No."

"What about taking a class?"

It would be so easy to get psychotic if she stayed single and grew old. It was only later at home, watching CNN and drinking salad dressing, that Justine remembered that at the age of 12, Courtney Blanchard had actually wanted to be a horse.

Justine touched her ankle experimentally. She looked around her living room. If she wasn't going into the office tonight, what would she do instead? She didn't drink. She didn't smoke. She didn't do drugs. She wasn't seeing anyone. She didn't want to read. She didn't want music or TV. There was nothing to do. What kind of life was this? Who could she call. She didn't want to talk about the crash. She didn't want to talk about anything else, either. Could she call Barry Cantor if she didn't want to talk? It was so rare for her to be attracted to anyone.

She was starving. She dragged herself to the desk and looked him up in the phone book. She dialed the number, forgetting whether she liked him enough to be nervous.

"You have successfully reached the number you have dialed," a male machine said. "If you want to leave a message, we can't stop you."

"Hello." She paused. "Justine Schiff." She wasn't sure if she wanted him to be there. It might be an anticlimax now.

He picked up. "Hi," he said warmly. "How's that shower?"

She was positive now that she wanted to see him. "Wet."

"I see."

"Over."

"I see." The apartment was completely still. She waited for him to speak. He said, "Getting ready to start on the steak?"

"I'm starving," she said. "When are you coming over."

"Now."

She laughed. "How do you like your steak?"

"Well done. You're cooking?"

"Certainly not."

"Shall I bring anything?"

"Just you. But move it. I might be in a different mood when you get here."

"I just left."

She ordered dinner. She tried to recall his face. He had the air of someone about to tell a joke. Would he sleep over. Maybe she should clean. The hell with it. She might have been killed.

The house phone rang shortly, and Barry Cantor came in kissing. He kissed well. She liked the way he kissed. His arms wrapped around her nicely. There was something very dramatic about him, with the widow's peak, and slanted black eyebrows. Moreover, she wasn't aware of any awkwardness or disappointment. He immediately took apart the sofa and set her up with her leg elevated on cushions. He was kneeling on the floor next to her, sucking on her lower lip when the house phone rang.

"My purse is on that chair," she said.

"Let me take care of this," he said, rising. "I got some money from my roommate. He owed me."

He was at least 35 years old. "You have a roommate?"

"At the moment, yes."

"Are you gay?"

He looked at her in surprise. "No." He bent down to brush her mouth with his. "Do I look gay?"

"No, but," she said. "You never know."

All sorts of psychotics flew first class. He was clearly Jewish, but what did that mean? He could be anybody. So what he was in a suit—she knew a Marshall Scholar at McKinsey who'd had unprotected sex with a personal trainer *after* the woman told him she had genital herpes. Yesterday, she'd behaved like a toddler in front of a senior member of the Partnership Committee. Today, she was ready to let a total stranger enter her naked body. She had lost all control over her life.

The doorbell rang. She lay back and let him deal with it. He joked with the delivery boy. There was apparently no one he didn't need to talk to. She didn't owe him anything. She'd been in a plane crash. He began puttering around the kitchen. His red sweater passed back and forth as he set up the table. He tripped.

"What's this?" He held up one of Stella's toys.

"It's a rawhide shoe," she said. "For chewing."

"You chew rawhide?"

He was very funny, in a way. "I have a dog."

He looked around the empty apartment. "I see," he said, and made kissing noises. "Here, doggie." He pretended to greet and pet an invisible dog. How perverted could such a man be.

The phone rang just as they sat down to the table. He smiled calmly and began to take apart his baked potato.

"Farlowe just called me with some real live work that you turned down, you sissy, just because your plane crashed," her colleague Harriet Lazarus told the machine. "Now, I can't believe you're going to risk life and limb twice for Allison Baraniak. So call me."

"Allison Baraniak, the maniac from Scottsdale?" he asked.

"You know her?"

"I think I dated her."

"You're kidding."

"At Wharton, very briefly," he said, and waved his hand dismissively. "Not my type."

"I know her from college," she tested.

"So you went to Williams," he said, looking her up and down. "So thank God I don't have to worry you're going to bludgeon me in my sleep." He was watching her with an amused expression.

She drew in the sour cream with the tines of her fork. "Eat your dinner," she said, to change the subject.

He pulled her onto his lap. She sat facing him and they fed each other pieces of steak between kisses. She wasn't thinking about where it was going to lead. "There's something very nice about this," she said, feeling like a child.

"Tell me something," he said, clasping his hands behind her back. "Tell me about your family."

She was half-asleep. "When I was 9," she said, "my father got into bed and didn't get out for a year and a half."

"Jesu."

She leaned against him. "Why did I tell you that." She must have been completely out of control—she didn't even care.

"Because you're strangely attracted to me and you trust me."

"Yes, but why," she said, stretching her arms out.

"We shared a bonding, near-death experience."

"Yeah," she yawned, "but I trusted you before that."

"So you did see me on line."

"I saw you, and then I saw you seeing me." She rested with her chin over his shoulder. "And then you pretended that you hadn't seen me, so I knew something would happen."

There was another long kiss and he looked directly at her with sharp, amused black eyes. "I think I'm full for now, you?"

"Fine," she said, exhausted. He picked her up, and—showing not even the slightest discomfort or strain—carried her into the bedroom. He put her down on the bed and lay on top of her.

"I can't believe this." She stretched her good leg out long. Did she want to tell her children that she got into bed with their father the day she met him? "I don't even know you."

"Yes you do." He rolled off and faced her.

"No, I don't."

"Well I know you." He began nosing around her stomach. "You're the lady who gave me the Wash'n Dri when I threw up."

"Beautiful," she said, and let her mind slide.

Chapter 3

He came from a broken home

Barry was awake before 6. He felt like he'd been run over by a
tank. He was bruised, he was alive, he was in bed with a real woman.
He hadn't even known her 24 hours yet. He squeezed her rear end
and she grunted sweetly, lost in sleep. Who was she? She would never
be this unfamiliar again. He began to kiss her.

"I'm not a morning person," she said in a cracked voice, turned
away from him, and went back to sleep. In his entire life, he'd never
been so attracted by a neck.

She must have been spending a fortune in rent. Neat closets, not
many books. Would she like his apartment? The famous pocketbook
was sitting on the coffee table, on top of the *Wall Street Journal*. Her
datebook was unreadable, streaked with the scum of Jamaica Bay. She
was knitting something. On the bulletin board by her phone were
five take-out menus and a Reagan pin.

He was seized by the idea that he had to run around the reservoir.

He dressed quickly, before the impulse passed. He composed a brief note, put it on his pillow, squeezed her sleeping shoulder, took her keys, and went out.

The *Post* lay in front of her door. She read the *Post* and the *Journal* but not the *Times?* He informed the doorman he'd be back in an hour, please let him up without buzzing, so as not to wake Ms. Schiff.

The doorman cocked an eyebrow. "You friend of Leona?"

"I beg your pardon?"

"17C." He smoothed down his mustache as he smiled. "Everybody call her Leona. She like things done"—he clapped his hands like an imperious diva.

"I know what you mean," Barry said reflexively, and got into a cab feeling awful: he'd betrayed his wife from a previous life pretending to kid around with her doorman.

He walked into his apartment triumphant. What a miracle the previous day had been! He fell into a reverie about the kiss, the crash, the phone call, the steak, sweeping her off her feet and onto her bed. But the erotic flow was interrupted by the doorman clapping.

There were three messages pulsing with increasing degrees of anxiety from his mother. When he'd called her the night before and told her he wasn't coming to Miami and why, she'd seemed unusually calm. No doubt she was having a delayed reaction, enhanced by telling her sister, Sylvia, who had made panic her life's work. Clearly Sylvia had worked herself and Rose into a froth of hysteria over dinner. They were probably speechless with alarm when he hadn't picked up the phone, and hadn't slept all night. By now they'd found out that the crashing plane had been going to Phoenix, and Rose would pelt him with questions he had no interest in answering. He wasn't calling back so fast.

There was only one other lunatic at the reservoir. The orange sunlight breaking out over the steel blue water and biscuity buildings of Fifth Avenue made Barry feel like life could be painfully beautiful, but was more often ridiculous drudgery, and he had to throw himself into it knowing that. He needed a new goal. He hadn't lived through this to go back to salad dressing as usual.

She was beautiful! He thought of the toast he would give Justine at their wedding: "I don't think many of you know that I had kissed Justine before I even knew her name." To keep it PG-13, he'd omit the vomiting, and the climax of the previous evening. He tripped on a root, and landed on his hands.

"And the next day, I went out running and I fell flat on my face," he added. "I just couldn't see straight."

It was freezing, and his joints were aching. She voted for Reagan?

After a long shower, he put up water for coffee, leaned against his granite counter, and stretched. Soon, he'd have an intelligent woman sitting on his sofa, sleeping in his bed. She'd gone to Harvard Law School. The way she'd handled WorldWide Airlines was frightening; he wanted her on his team.

Vince shuffled into the kitchen in a robe, his hair nearly vertical. She had a one-bedroom on East 76th Street facing water. Vince sat down at the table, blinking. Barry chomped on Cheerios out of the box. She was a lawyer—a choice that spoke of a lack of imagination in a man, but was something else for a woman. Vince began picking a scab on his arm.

Vince was so fucking cinematic—even picking a scab he looked good. Wouldn't Justine prefer someone like Vince?

He wanted his apartment back. "What are your plans," he asked.

Vince yawned. "I thought I'd read the paper."

"No. Have you found an apartment?"

"Well, I hadn't really looked," Vince said, surprised.

"I think you'd better look," he said.

It sounded cold. But he didn't owe Vince an explanation.

The slimy doorman gave Barry a cocky salute, and he snitted about it in the elevator. He let himself in with her keys. Justine Leslie Schiff, Esq., 32, was asleep in a green T-shirt facing away from him. The note he'd written her was gone.

He was terrified.

She was probably looking for someone with more hair. He came from a broken home. It would take her less than two meals to find out that his father lived on a powerboat with an Albanian cleaning lady and watched at least six hours of C-SPAN a day. There was bankruptcy and diabetes in his family, and tacky, tacky relatives in Florida and on the Island.

On the other hand, C-SPAN was better than the track; deep-sea fishing was good fun in decent weather. His mother owned and ran her own business, and he, Barry, ran national brands that had become, under his stewardship, category leaders. He lived on West End Avenue, and faced water. Okay, a slice of water. Anyway: Justine was flat-chested, and subscribed to the *Post*. But it probably didn't matter, if everything else was in place, as it seemed to be. He did deserve a girlfriend. He took his clothes off and crawled into bed with her.

She rustled. She opened her eyes.

"Hi," he whispered.

She turned towards him, pushed him over onto his other side, slung her arm around his stomach, and pressed herself into him. There was something very nice about this.

Bruises bloomed like plums on her foot and ankle. Attempts to locate an orthopedist were fruitless. "I'll have to go to the hospital," she said, kissing him dismissively.

"I wouldn't miss it for the world," he said, watching her pack a bag with a bottle of water, underpants, socks, something in Tupperware, a knitting project. Her cheeks were always flushed with color, he noticed—day and night, indoors and out. It wasn't a tan or embarrassment; it must have been fabulous circulation. He noticed something else he'd been attracted to immediately: a strange activity going on behind her face, like the fluttering of the big board at Penn Station as the trains come and go. What was she thinking about?

She smiled mysteriously and kissed him on the mouth. He felt like he was about to break out of prison.

Any minute now

At the hospital, Barry was attentive and flirtatious. It was touching how he rose to prod the nurses. Justine couldn't help it: she thought about the wedding. It could happen. He was clever, he seemed honest, he wore a suit. If the mingling continued along the lines of last night and she still wanted to talk to him after a month— a big if, but it could happen—why not marry him?

Spangly holiday decorations made the emergency room even more depressing. They were sitting in the middle of a harsh lemon disinfectant smell. There were car races on a hanging television. Every bleeding person who came in was ignored and then given forms to fill out.

"What about that couple," she whispered. "I think he beats her. Watch. She won't look at him."

"I just want you to know," Barry said, nosing in her ear, "I would never beat you unless you really deserved it."

Justine was enjoying herself immensely. In spite of her crushing pain and the misery around them. After an hour, Barry went out for something to eat. Almost immediately her name was called. An orderly pushed her wheelchair through a maze of halls to the radiation department in a different building. She knitted furiously. She wasn't sure if her mother would like him. Or was that the old thinking. About twenty minutes later, Barry rounded the corner with a brown bag. He'd found her. He was a genius.

He'd gotten milk shakes and offered her vanilla or chocolate. She felt like a houseguest at the kitchen table, with an old friend to catch up with and the whole weekend ahead.

"In one day, Ms. Schiff, I've seen you in a lot of extreme situations," he whispered. "I've been in contact with most of your fluids."

She had a searing cold pain from drinking the shake too fast. She pressed her hand to her eye. Jewish doctors were paged over the loudspeaker.

"Listen, Barry, last night was sort of an exception."

"Oh?" he asked, as a flock of nurses in pink uniforms passed by.

"I don't usually just do this sort of thing."

"Well, there was something about the way you asked me to put on two coats of latex."

"Shh!" She looked at him. He was completely there. She couldn't remember the last time she'd had a man's complete attention. She didn't even know she liked vanilla shakes.

An elderly man with ashy naked limbs sticking out of his gown was wheeled on a gurney and parked in front of them. "This is the strangest date I've ever had," she whispered, and he picked up her hand.

Someone called her name. She was wheeled into a dark room alone.

After her ankle—chipped and sprained, not broken—was bandaged, she was given a lesson on crutches and insurance forms to sign. They went straight home. Nothing had really gone wrong yet. He was still interesting. They spent some time comparing bruises. She took a bath with her foot hanging over the side. He sat and watched. If he thought she was fat, he didn't mention it. They read the Sunday parts of the Saturday paper. It was good to do something separately, but in the same room.

At 6, the phone rang. It was Farlowe.

"Listen, I need your help," he started. She sat up. How did he know she was home? She'd told him she was going to Phoenix. "Galsworthy Paper. In Atlanta, bidding for Fitzsimmons Chemical in Richmond."

She should never pick up the phone.

"It's only a couple hundred million or so, but the client is going to be sold in the next few years, and I don't want him to get used to dealing with any other lawyers."

If she didn't take this, her partnership was in the toilet.

"His legal department will draft the bid letter, and do the mark-up on the contract," he promised. "He just wants you to look over their shoulder. I specifically recommended you."

Justine agreed to take on the deal, called the new client, and held the receiver away from her head as he introduced himself. George Underhill Galsworthy IV, but he'd be honored if she called him Cricket. He transferred her to his General Counsel, who had faxed her the relevant material by the time the pizza had been delivered.

She looked over the fax while they ate. Galsworthy's people hadn't done any due diligence, and they wanted to make the bid the day after Christmas. Since they had pretty much no information about the company, they wanted a contract that protected them against everything. She decided not to panic. She called the weekend Librarian for annual reports, quarterly reports, and proxy statements from Fitzsimmons Chemical.

Barry Cantor ate his pizza and watched her, amused. There was something about him that rang bells somewhere. She imagined him with more hair and was still stumped. After dinner, she put *The Sound of Music* on the VCR. He spent a full five minutes teasing her that her remote controls were encased in Ziploc bags. They didn't even make it through "How Do You Solve a Problem Like Maria" before he turned it off.

"I can't make love with nuns singing," he explained, and bounced back into bed. If nothing else happened, it would be perfect. That night, she slept like a big rock in a cave during a week of heavy rain.

On Monday night, Justine waited for Barry in the bar of a noisy seafood place he'd chosen. It was two days before Christmas, and some businessmen from out of town were getting barking drunk. She limped to a corner near the coat check because she felt nervous and exposed. She had a yeast infection already from the weekend.

Everything had looked exactly the same when she hopped into the office that morning at 10. Farlowe came out of his office when he saw her struggling with bags and crutches.

"I'm assuming everything's fine," he said, waving his arm from his waist over his head, to indicate her entire condition. As usual, he'd been billing time since 8:30, having read the *Times*, the *Journal*, and the *New York Law Journal* on the train in from Ridgefield.

She really needed to sit and have coffee first. "Of course. But listen, they don't want me to supervise, they want me to do everything, and they want me to do it now. They're messengering over the CEO's notes this morning."

"Well, don't you messenger back. We spend too much on messengers. Fax everything," he raved. "Put those bicycle hooligans out of business." When his eldest son was hired by IBM, Farlowe had sold him one of his old suits. Justine wasn't going to argue with him.

"What do you make of the CEO," she asked.

"Stuck-up Southern trash," he growled. "He has a company. I'm supposed to be impressed? I had an earful of his grits on Friday."

"Listen, they haven't done any due diligence."

"Well, do what you have to do."

"I'm going to need help. May I have Nicky?"

"Ask him."

Nicky Lukasch was a shy second-year associate whom Justine often relied on. He'd spent the weekend at the printer, working on an initial public offering. He agreed to take on the assignment after he went home for a shower. Floyd the office boy brought in a yard-high stack of Fitzsimmons documents. She had to wade through these by Thursday.

At 11:00 A.M., she received a call from Barry Cantor. She almost burst into song. The conversation could have gone on and on if Alma hadn't buzzed her that Driggs wanted her urgently. It suddenly seemed very important to Justine that Barry drive her to the Department of Motor Vehicles, even though she had six months left to renew her license. He asked when it would be convenient. She smiled. They made plans for dinner that night.

Barry had bobbed on the edge of her consciousness as she met with Driggs, a tiny, fidgety partner who was responsible for a large chunk of the firm's $12 million securities practice. He rarely showed any sign that she'd completed the work, much less that she'd done a good job.

"Schiff: you're going to Cincinnati," he began, looking at his watch.

"Okay," she pulled her datebook out.

"No, I mean now. Alma's got your ticket."

She brought her crutches to his attention.

"Schiff, if you can go to Phoenix, you can go to Cincinnati." He had a lean, selfish face. According to Nicky, Driggs stood three feet from the urinal, hands on hips, and fired away.

"I didn't go to Phoenix, and I'm working full-time this week on a matter for Farlowe," she said, pointing to her stack. "I'm terribly sorry."

He left irritated. Harriet Lazarus poked her head in. "What happened?"

"He called," Justine said, proud of Barry.

"Amazing. But I meant the crash. The ankle?"

"I mean, he said he'd call, and he called."

"Astonishing," Harriet said, nodding at passing associates.

Harriet and Justine had joined Packer Breebis on the same day six years and three months ago. Harriet had been on track until the word leaked about her boyfriend. By the time she'd become engaged, Driggs had Harriet mired in an endless stream of underwritings where her input was limited to choosing the height of the typeface on the tombstone in the *Journal*. Harriet spoke of Driggs in tones of rage and helplessness. She was in free-fall now, expected to find another job and stop taking up space. There was no B list at Packer Breebis.

"Harriet: this man said he would call at 11, and he called at 11," Justine warned. "I think I have to marry him."

"I'll be right with you," Harriet called outside. Inside, she stage-whispered, "You don't have to marry him."

"But maybe I want to marry him."

"It's a phone call. What's the matter with you. Are you on painkillers?"

Ever since Harriet got married, talking to her was like waving from a great distance.

Ilana Doisneau cruised by in a bottle green Escada suit with deafening gold jewelry. She dipped into Justine's office to inspect the ankle, and discuss her own kneecap break, her sciatica, her physical therapist, and the drop WorldWide had taken that morning on the NYSE. Her gold hair was shellacked back into a tiny ponytail neatly held by a bottle green velvet bow. She was of a certain age, but there was nothing about her that hadn't been altered into an ageless, shiny smoothness.

As usual, the schmooze was just an aperitif. Ilana needed an employment agreement done ASAP. "Noah himself asked for you," Ilana said proudly. Noah Clurman was a charming former tennis star who controlled a number of companies. Ilana, though in the Banking Group, hoarded all his corporate work and strictly controlled access to him. "I know you're up to your neck in everything," Ilana boomed, "but it won't take much time. Thanks, you're a DARLING."

She swung out, leaving behind a cloud of Rive Gauche. "No" was never an option with Ilana. Justine knocked back some Tab and called Mitch Boorman, a third-year who'd worked with her on the initial public offering for Noah's venture capital group in June.

Nicky Lukasch came in and sat down awkwardly on her sofa. He was outrageously tall and thin, with fawn-colored hair, a long, equine face, and a vertical scar that split his upper lip into two unequal, puffy halves. If you didn't know him, you might think it sinister.

"Check out the last few chemical deals we did," Justine said, polishing off a Danish. Nicky nodded, eyes glazed behind his glasses. "What are the things we always want to know about. Confirm their patents," she said, and he blew his nose into a napkin. "If they expire in two years, this company'll be worth a dollar fifty. Don't bother with Dristan. Call your doctor for an antibiotic."

"I don't have a doctor," he said, flushed and unhappy.

"How is that possible? You're 27 years old."

"Twenty-six. I don't get sick."

Mitch came in with chapped lips and a red nose.

"Do you have a doctor?" Mitch nodded, blowing his nose into a neat white handkerchief. He was 28 and had a child-wife. "The two of you call Mitch's doctor for erythromycin." They gave her half-lidded stares. "Find out about the Durham subsidiary. Make sure we can get the lease to the land," she insisted, and Nicky wrote it down on a yellow pad. "Get better, both of you. Nicky, you're going to Richmond tomorrow. Mitch, I need your notes on Noah."

Justine spent the rest of the day immersed in the Fitzsimmons Chemical Co., while the central air whooshed steadily through her office, and protected her from the chaos, the traffic, the ferocious gaiety, and the relentless crowds outside. She loved the central air.

A woman with big frosted hair stepped on Justine's good foot on her way to the pandemonium at the bar. Justine wondered if Barry thought this was a great place. She'd slept with him before she knew him well enough to see something she didn't like. That would happen any minute now. She could feel it in the air.

At 8:30, Barry appeared, big and lively. She was glad to see him. He began by sucking on her fingers.

"Hey!"

"Oh, sorry! Aren't you 3A?" He gasped. "I thought so," he said, and began sucking again. She wasn't sure if she liked it. This was public. Not that she'd know anyone here.

He asked her about her day and she told him about Noah Clurman's contract.

"It should have been done a month ago. We have people who are great at it, but I've done all his corporate work, so they wanted me," she said, and he looked down at the bread. "It's flattering, I suppose."

He nodded politely. She probably made more money than he did. That would be a problem for him. She told him about the structure of the firm, how women were on a different track.

"Yeah, yeah, yeah," he said. He was always joking.

"I'm serious," she said, and Barry made a serious face. "If you're a single man and you want to get married, it's Good luck, Charlie. If you're a single woman and you want to get married, it's Good-bye, Susie."

"So you want to get married," he said, smiling like a wolf.

This flustered her. She felt like she was sitting on his hands. "Male lawyers with wives are providing for their families," she continued, "whereas female lawyers with husbands are just shopping for baby clothes. And it doesn't matter how—"

"So you want children," he interrupted, and the waiter arrived. Barry began joshing with him, pulling out a pen and drawing something on the table paper. One of her exes—Donald Albrecht, the banker from Boston who fondled his cat in a way that made her uncomfortable—had had a pencil thing. But that wasn't what was familiar about Barry.

The waiter left. "So why do you have a roommate," she asked.

"I don't usually." He sipped his wine. "I've been looking for a good excuse to throw him out."

"The excuse is that it's your apartment."

"I know," he said, far away.

She hated the weak sound of it. "And you're sure you're not involved with him romantically?"

He smirked. "My roommate is heterosexual in 3-D."

"What does that mean?"

"He's seeing three women. At once."

She froze, mid-chew. "What's his name," she said, but it had locked into place. It was over already. The celery lay in her mouth like wet mesh. She couldn't swallow it, she couldn't chew it, and she would retch completely if she removed it with her napkin. She forced herself to chew and swallow.

"Oh, no," Barry said, in a defeated way. "You're not *that* Justine?"

Seafood appeared.

"What did he tell you," she said, wondering whose opinion she cared about. She hadn't even known that Vince *had* a roommate.

"Nothing. I just heard you on the answering machine once." He looked older. "What happened? Or do I want to know."

Justine was exhausted and annoyed. "Let's get this out of the way, shall we? He and I had an interlude." She leaned back on the banquette. "I wouldn't even call it an episode."

"I can't believe it," he said slowly, loosening an oyster. "I thought you were intelligent."

She decided to ignore that. "I'm sorry you live with him."

He drank his oyster down. "It's a temp—wait a minute," he interrupted himself. "He lives with ME. It's MY apartment."

What were the odds of this? "You shouldn't eat that."

"Why?"

"Contamination."

Barry Cantor sucked down another oyster, watching her spitefully. She should have gone to Cincinnati.

"We're making two stops," Justine said as she got into the cab, and wondered what Barry would tell Vince. At her building, she got her crutches organized, and stepped out on the curb.

The blood rushed through her leg. She was weak. It had been such a nice weekend. She turned around. The cab was gone. Well of course—she'd sent him away. She was ashamed that Barry had risen slightly in her estimation because of the connection to Vince.

Chapter 4

He took her number

Vince had met Justine in September, at a benefit. She wasn't the most attractive woman in the world, but she was a human being getting on with her life. He didn't give her a line, he just took her number. She seemed embarrassed.

He called her.

At dinner she was tired but cheerful. Justine was the sort he would have passed over a few years ago, Vince thought, even last year. She reminded him of the older sister of a childhood friend in Amagansett—you knew where you stood with her, and she was fun to tease. He dropped her off at a financial printer's office at 10:30. Justine would be fun to tease.

On the other hand, his schedule was full enough.

❖

Come talk to me

Every part of Justine's body wanted to say hello to Vince. In addition to everything else, he'd been emitting some kind of aftershave all evening. The man was a five-alarm fire.

She walked into the printer's. Roxy, the first-year associate whom everyone wanted to shtup, was there with Mitch; pages had just been sent back with revisions. Mitch was discussing how his child-wife got back at him when she was mad: she swept the floor and put the dirt under the covers in his bed.

"You have separate beds?" Roxy asked, smirking.

"Well, for sleeping," he clarified. "I thrash around a lot."

Justine had no patience for this kind of nonsense now. All she wanted was to be alone to think about Vince. Had he had a good time, or had he just been pretending to have a good time.

It became apparent they were in for an all-nighter. This caused much grousing from Roxy.

"I mean I get up at dawn, and I get home at 9 if I'm lucky," she pouted. She was a perfect size 4 and she probably didn't even exercise. "There's never any time to have fun."

They decided to order in Japanese. Justine declined, having just eaten Japanese.

"You mean, you had a date and you came *here* afterwards?" Roxy asked, incredulously. "*Why?*"

Justine leveled a look at this, this . . . starlet, and wondered whether she was ever this stupid as a first-year. Maybe Vince wouldn't call her. He was so cool, not a doubt in the world. In all likelihood, she would become captivated by that confidence, and what if he ever lost it?

Three weeks later, when she was deeply immersed in a flurry of 10-K's on another case, he called. He chatted with ease and asked her out to the movies.

Justine stared out the window, afraid to smile. She flew through the rest of the 10-K's and hit the gym. Vince was fluent in Japanese and German, played the piano and dressed like an Italian architect— how could she possibly keep someone like that happy? She climbed 119 floors on the stair machine, trying not to compare her body to those around her.

Second Date

Vince took Justine out again in October. She was overdressed, but he forgave her: she was trying. She seemed to be trying very hard. My mother would like this girl, he thought as he ate a sundae. Justine leaned forward on her elbows and watched him eat. She was nice looking, but the birthmark between her nose and mouth was a mistake. Keeping it was some kind of perverted vanity.

It would be good to be with one woman. It would be a risk. But he was ready. He was sick of the confusion whenever he picked up the phone. He kept glancing at her mouth—there was a slack, fleshy look about it that annoyed him. On the other hand, how did he know it would be good with her? He didn't have to decide anything right now.

She took a taste of his ice cream.

Her mouth was repulsive and the mole was a disfigurement. He announced that he was seeing three women. Her face opened wide. She began to laugh, holding the heel of her hand to her forehead.

"I guess you think this makes me undesirable," he said.

At this, she almost fell off her chair. She was laughing uncontrollably, and some spit escaped. People started looking over. She gathered herself up and sighed, "Oh, I know how to pick them, that's for sure."

"Well, I don't want to see three women."

She began a new round of snorting. "So why bother?"

"Because I don't want to see any one of them exclusively."

"Do you want to see anybody exclusively?"

"Yes," he said, looking at her directly. "I want something completely different." The one thing he had to say about himself was that he was honest.

She wiped under her eyes with a napkin. She leaned forward. "Sounds like you're much too busy." She cackled on her way to the back of the café. He wondered again about seeing a shrink. Kiki said she'd gotten to the root of her problem. Vince didn't want to get to the root of his problem, he just wanted to solve it.

Justine was punchy when she returned. She expressed surprise and delight at how clean the ladies' room had been; this struck him as an unbelievably Jewish thing to say. "You look so rested," she teased. "How do you manage it all?"

Vince excused himself. He called Renée, who agreed to meet him at her apartment in an hour. He hung up feeling ridiculous: he was in no mood to get undressed, and he didn't like talking to Renée. Justine paid, since he'd forgotten his wallet. He was dropping her at her office on a Saturday at 5:30, so how much of a princess could she actually be? As she jumped out of the cab, he said he'd call her. She gave him money for the ride.

And then he felt stupid. Did he like her or not? He liked her fine. Could he like anybody more than that? He didn't know much about her. But what was to know? He was positive she wasn't seeing anyone; she was probably slightly repressed, having gone to Spence. She was over 30, so she was probably feverish to get married. She'd probably had offers but no one appropriate, and thus she was delighted to meet him, and now disappointed. The laughing was weird. Still, there was something decent about her.

☢

The walls were upholstered

Shortly after Vince moved in in September, Barry had been invited to dinner at the Anspachers' apartment on Fifth Avenue. When the
elevator opened, a man in a tuxedo asked him what he wanted to
drink. Just one apartment per floor, and the elevator opened up right
in the middle of it. A very well done woman in a shocking pink dress
swooped towards him with arms outstretched. There was a highly
attuned shine to her, as if she'd been in an adjacent room for twenty minutes anticipating his arrival.

"I'm Cassie Anspacher," she said with a beautiful smile, and he
felt something fitting into place—of course Vince's mother would be
gorgeous in a meticulous, matronly way. He shook her cold slim
hand, noticing the perfectly fixed silver blond helmet hair. She
hooked her arm through his, releasing serious perfume, and shep-
herded him into an enormous room overlooking the park where
older women in dark dresses perched on yellow silk chairs.

"I emm Wince's fazza's cousin Helena," said a woman sitting
beneath a small Matisse. She nodded at him in a courtly way.

"I emm Andrew's frent from shkool," said another woman, sitting
beneath a large Manet, her gold earrings trembling.

Someone in a black-and-white uniform paused in front of him
with a silver tray of beautiful things. Barry took a salmon canapé and
looked around. The windows had curtains, balloon shades, and
valances. The walls were upholstered. There were blue-and-white
Chinese plates and silver tchochkes on every table.

"Tessie!" Vince had arrived. Barry was shocked at how glad he was
to see him.

"Wince!" Tessie glowed, and Vince snuggled up to her; Barry had
seen Vince in action, but fondling a dowager!

Everyone stopped and looked over at the door. "Zhat iss Wince's
fazha," a woman said, and he turned around. Andrew Anspacher had

the same Beatles '65 haircut as Vince, on a head that was at least two sizes too big for his stiff skinny body.

"Wince's fazza und muzza vere encaged at mein haus," the beaded woman under the Matisse said with a twinkle.

"Is that so?"

Andrew Anspacher, the irascible media mogul, arrived in front of Barry and held out a big bony, knobby red hand for him to shake. He said combatively, "Work at Maplewood Acres?"

"Yes, sir." Andrew Anspacher had no shoulders.

"Volney treat you well?"

"He's on our board, but I don't know the man—"

"He's a bastard," Andrew said, looking to the right of Barry's head. Barry laughed in surprise. "He and I go way back. The army. Smart man. Bastard."

Barry didn't know what to say, so he complimented the Matisse. Andrew narrowed his eyes. For a moment Barry was afraid he was going to be asked to date the painting, but Andrew just took hold of Barry's elbow in a pointy grip and marched him rapidly down a hall of photos—himself with the mayor, the former mayor, the governor, the president, the football broadcaster—into a dark, wood-paneled library, also overlooking the park.

"This is my new favorite." Mr. Andrew pointed to a Picasso drawing in which at least two people were copulating. What do you say in such a situation—"Nice tits"?

"Wow. My sister is an artist," Barry said, and wondered why. He never talked about her, or even thought about her much.

"Who's her dealer?"

"She doesn't have one yet."

Andrew's face contorted in an expression of nausea, as if Barry, or his sister—or both—had done something unpleasant. His head lolled on top of his body as if it would fall off. Vince strolled in and Barry marveled again at how glad he was to see him. Vince shook his father's hand formally.

"How's your tennis?" Andrew asked Vince.

"I play squash, you know that."

"Well then you're a fool," Andrew said with distaste.

"He plays with me," Barry said.

"Then you're a bigger fool even than he is," Andrew said.

Barry laughed. He was kidding—wasn't he?

Cassie darted into the room like a shocking pink bird. "Dinner is served." She hooked Vince by one arm and Barry by the other and swooped them into another perfect room with 14-foot ceilings and significant moldings. There were two big round tables set with gold flatware and place cards. He found himself seated next to a blond girl with important jewelry.

"Elizabeth," she said, not shaking his hand. "Vince's sister."

"Vince: I didn't know you had a sister. Did you just get one?" Vince ignored him.

She told him she was in radio. "Where?" he asked, to be polite.

"Anspacher," Elizabeth Anspacher said, as if he were mentally retarded.

After a soup course, men in uniforms went around the table with silver platters of slim lamb chops, green beans, and rice. Each guest served himself with tongs. The trembling woman talked about Paris. Barry's heart turned down wistfully—these people were so foreign, so at home anywhere; he would never live in Paris, Rome, or Buenos Aires. He'd never be James Bond or even Steve Moskowitz, a Dartmouth roommate who'd landed a job with a textile group in Antwerp.

But as they spoke—of somebody's daughter applying to college, of somebody's father passing away—he realized that it was probably just the same people dressed up for Friday-night dinner, only the living room had been in Paris. They probably talked about the same things and told the new person, "Wince's fazza vas encaged at mein haus." Barry didn't want to live here, but it certainly was interesting.

Vince suddenly came to life. "If you could choose," he said to the table at large, "would you prefer to die in a fire or by falling off a cliff?" Everyone ignored him. There was some satisfaction in this.

After dinner, everyone sat down in chairs that had been arranged, as if by elves, to face a grand piano that Barry hadn't even noticed at cocktails. Andrew strode in, sat impatiently, and began pounding gracefully, his big red fingers scrambling over the keys. Andrew Anspacher was frightening. It was as if he'd taken all the oxygen in the room. Vince sat on the couch, arms hooked with one of the dowagers, expression unreadable.

Vince still owed him rent, Barry remembered, looking at the crystal chandelier. Later, when he returned to his own shabby lobby, Barry figured Vince could probably afford to buy the entire building.

Seething

The day after her second date with Vince, Justine sat at her desk chastising herself for wanting him to call. Of course he had three girlfriends. He'd gone to Harvard and Stanford, his father was a self-made zillionaire, he looked like a soap opera actor—why shouldn't he be an operator? Justine was so tired. She wanted to kiss his swollen mouth. She was seething with frustration, operating without any information. Did any of those women speak Japanese?

At home, she moved things from tables to shelves. Stella followed her around, bumping into her and sliming her calves with her wet nose. The whole thing was ridiculous. Vince was a nut. He told pretentious stories. He didn't ask her a single question about herself.

She lay horizontally across her bed. Six years on the partnership track had gone by, like that. She had sweated, toiled, canceled dates, missed life. People she knew were on their second husbands, their third careers, their fourth children. She had begun to settle. She was thickening, solidifying, going south. Alone.

There was nothing that would cheer her up except Vince—not even a phone call from him would sate her. So she went back to the office, got behind her desk, and proofread through the night. The air in the office was always cool, and constantly refreshing itself. She always felt thinner, more alert in the office. Her productivity was directly tied to the central air.

At 9:30 in the morning, Justine knocked on Roberta Silverman's door.

"Enter," Roberta called. She was on the floor, doing back exercises in her gray tweed suit, one of three outfits that Justine knew about. As an associate, Roberta had often been asked to clean up her act. Now that she co-chaired the department with Farlowe and brought in well over $3 million in corporate business, and had the ear of everyone from the CEO of Pacific Telephone to the Minolta repairman, there had been an unconscious collective decision to let Roberta be herself. She was called "a character," "a pisser," or "a lawyer's lawyer."

Justine sunk into Roberta's sofa. "He's not calling me."

"Who is this schmuck?" Roberta called in outrage from the floor. "There must be something wrong with him."

Roberta had never married, had been disappointed too many times to count, had been steeping in disgust for quite some time. Privately, Justine thought Roberta could make her romantic and corporate lives easier if she would only do something about her hair, which she wore like tangled foliage mashed underfoot. But Roberta had no vanity and less patience. She was pushing 50; at what point do you just give up?

Roberta rose slowly to a sitting position, a wrinkled mess on the floor. "Hey," she whispered, and leaned in with a wink and a head toss, as if she were selling drugs on a street corner. "Wanna put together the definitive trader's manual on derivatives for First New York?"

None of her deals was particularly active. "I'd love to."

"Why don't you come over tonight," Roberta offered, falling

heavily into her chair. She needed to lose weight. "I rented *Rear Window*. We can call in from Big Wok and catch up."

"Thanks, I'd love to, but I made plans," Justine lied, retreating to her office. Roberta was always trying to get her to see her apartment; Justine was always declining. It wasn't that she thought it an improper invitation, although there were rumors about Roberta. Of course there were. There were the same rumors about Justine. Either you were seeing a man, and so you weren't serious, or you weren't, and so you were desperate, frigid, or gay. Justine felt guilty, but she had so little free time, and she found Roberta profoundly depressing outside the office.

A week later, Vince Anspacher called to chat. He was traveling, he couldn't make plans. Well, at least he had the courtesy to string her along. Justine closed her door and called Harriet, knitting her office sweater. Harriet told her that if she didn't think she was beautiful enough for him, she should never let him know it.

Vince called again. He couldn't talk, he was on his way to Tokyo. Would she like to have dinner a week from Friday? He'd get back to her early next week.

That night, Nicky Lukasch asked her to a movie. She was in such flux she agreed to go. But she was irritated the entire film, worrying that he might touch her, and furious that he wasn't Vince. Nicky was quiet and intelligent and had a mild crush on her, but it wasn't the same thing as watching a man who moved like water.

Plans

Vince called Justine on Friday at 5 to make plans for dinner that night.

She said she'd thought the dinner was off since he hadn't called.

Vince despised women like this.

"I am calling," he said, carefully. "This is the call." Dinner was dinner; why did every last meal have to be planned in advance like some kind of event of state?

"I like plans," she said.

"So make plans. What are we doing?"

Could we order right away?

Barry sat with a martini in one hand and the remote control in the other, feeling pummeled and bruised from the crash. On Friday, he'd met his wife. By Monday, it was over. You couldn't say he'd wasted any time on this. Justine had a life before him: fine. But this was a bad joke. Was there anyone who Anspacher *hadn't* lain with? At 11:45, he went to bed pissed off. Subconsciously, he'd been waiting for Vince to come home. For what, to beat him up? He'd forgotten: the prince was in Palm Beach.

Barry abandoned the sloppy swirl of enforced gaiety in Marketing on Christmas Eve, and stopped by the lab to visit Dan Roh, a dour chemist who'd called him with a new product. The black-topped tables of the lab reminded him of his father futzing around in the kitchen with a beaker, a ruler, and an eyedropper, inventing a miracle process that took the cholesterol out of fried chicken.

Roh dropped a red lozenge onto a white lab plate and Barry tasted it. Tart, chewy, not too sweet. "It's the raspberry jam formula," Roh said, standing up straight in his white coat, "cooked longer and spun into a denser shape."

Roh was a genius; he'd reduced the Lite dressings to less than one gram of fat. "No kidding. No sugar?"

"Corn syrup. You could do any shape you wanted. We have the technology," he said importantly.

Barry assumed Roh wasn't joking, since Roh was Korean. Then he felt small-minded. "You have the technology, Spock! Fabulous!"

Roh stared back patiently. Of course he hadn't been kidding. The man was a brilliant molecular chemist. He wasn't some crank pretending to be a scientist so he didn't have to sell menswear. "Could you make enough for a focus group?"

"Give me two weeks," Roh said, carefully slipping the candies into an envelope. "By then I'll have an apricot formula."

Barry pondered sugar-free chewy candy while he waited for the elevator. The doors opened, and Jack Slaymaker, the National Sales VP, got off as Barry got on.

"Barry, my boy!" he shouted, and launched into a colorful account of the drinking at the Anaheim sales conference, holding the impatient doors. "Hey, listen," Slaymaker said, coming to the point as the elevator alarm began to honk. "I need a little excitement in drive period two. What can you give me?"

"We're planning eight percent to the trade," Barry said.

"Gracias! I need all the help I can get. Hey," he transitioned smoothly into a tone of formal sentiment, "all the best to you and yours in the spirit of the holiday season."

Yeah, yeah. Barry backed up against the wall and closed his eyes as the doors shut. Christmas Muzak irradiated the elevator. He smelled fresh warm towels and froze. It seemed to be coming from a short fat woman in her 50's whom he'd never seen. He closed his eyes again and inhaled. He wanted to bury his head in this smell. When she got off, he almost ran after her. Only a trace of the smell lingered. When the doors opened on his floor, it was gone.

Christmas came and went. He had friends. He could have seen them. It was fine not to. They'd all complained loudly about having to leave the city, and then resurfaced in Westchester and Fairfield counties like self-satisfied cats stretching in a patch of sunshine. They took the position that he should come to them, and sit around playing peekaboo with their toddlers and discussing their patio renovations. Which was fine, if you were in the mood. This year, he wasn't.

Barry had left three messages with Justine and she hadn't called back. Clearly, they experienced time differently, but he bet even money she hadn't played it that way with Vince. What was she doing over Christmas? Surely even Packer Breebis let her off on Christmas Day.

Pippa arrived on New Year's Eve wearing flowered tights, platform combat boots, and an enormous tatty sweater. She looked like she just didn't know any better. He wanted to take her shopping. She dumped her fraying book bag on the sofa and pivoted back out: she had to pick up some last-minute ingredients. He accompanied her. He had nothing better to do.

"Al Simms," he began, automatically noting the Maplewood Jams gathering dust on the bottom shelf at Barzini's.

"Stan Hubbard," Pippa shot back.

"Hank Crawford." It was a game they'd developed, Generic Giants of Jazz Geography.

Pippa bent low to pull a jar of Peggy's Pickles off the bottom shelf. His heart turned over. "Why did you pick those?"

"These are great," she said, and he clapped his hands to his chest. "We always had these. This is your product?"

"Was." The indignity. "It was like running a front," he said, pointing out the crooked label. "People think it's a little family in the Berkshires with barrels in the basement."

"It isn't?" She tossed a box of Cheerios into the cart.

"No, Maplewood Mexico rolls these out by the millions."

"So what went wrong?"

"Nothing. We're buying the food arm of an Austrian conglomerate, and this is one of their brands." Barry pointed to the gleaming rows of Schlegel's Sours, which sprawled, as usual, over four feet of eye-level shelf space. "My so-called superiors think we shouldn't compete with ourselves."

"Poor Peggy," she said, and went off in search of something.

He drifted to the checkout line. That morning, when Rheinecker had okayed the commercial for the national launch of Caesar With Bacon, Barry had made one last try for Peggy's Pickles.

"The loyalty!" he begged, his face hot.

Rheinecker peered over his steel frames, unmoved. "Caesar will keep you plenty busy," he said condescendingly.

Barry had walked out, feeling pissed off and acutely Jewish for some reason. Another year had passed. At his Wharton tenth-year reunion, Barry was stunned to find quite a few classmates bouncing from job to job, flitting across the corporate landscape with real freedom. He'd plighted his troth with this damn company, and what if it didn't work out?

Pippa returned with a stray Cheerio stuck to her sweater; Barry paid and they walked back home down 89th Street. He liked her trotting along beside him, her head glowing municipal hazard orange. Was he falling in love with her, or did he just want to stay out past dark playing catch with her?

Back at home, a guy Pippa's age took the elevator up with them and rang the Divorcée's bell.

"Company?" Barry called snidely at her closing door.

"Shh," Pippa said.

"Hey, babe, whatever gets you through the night," he called.

How could he even consider that mindless, shriveled Divorcée? Still, the Divorcée had a date on New Year's. Barry had decided to keep things platonic with Pippa; she was a cute kid and a great cook.

Over dinner, she told him that her favorite Beatle was George, that she'd developed the crush based on the dreamy cowboy in the grass photo on the back of *Rubber Soul*, that the record was played and the picture was referred to so frequently in her house that the jacket had to be taped on three sides. He was in such a swoon over her home-made ravioli that he almost forgot about Justine.

Until the conversation turned to Vince, as if Vince were the fundamental issue, the common denominator, and all conversations would naturally come back to him in the end, like gravity.

"Why do we have to talk about him," he said, annoyed.

"I'm sorry," Pippa said huffily, "but isn't it a health hazard?" She was wiping down the counters.

"Of course it is."

"I mean, don't you think he'll lose his soul?"

"If he has one. I'm sure I'll lose my mind first."

She looked up, surprised. "Sorry," she said quickly, ending the discussion with a sponge toss from across the room that landed neatly in the sink. "Basket," she said calmly.

Pippa looked like Raggedy Ann. Barry wanted to stay up late watching the ball drop with her. She declined the invitation: she had three parties to go to, she told him. Well, of course she did. Where was Justine on New Year's Eve? She clearly had things to do. Who was she doing them with?

When Pippa finished cleaning, she didn't exactly leave. She was standing there awkwardly, and he realized he owed her money. He got into bed at 9:45; he read about Churchill's first period of public disfavor and chronic depression. He was asleep by 10:15.

The first Monday in January, Barry sat with people from the ad agency behind a one-way window in the basement of the Paramus Mall. They watched the most enthusiastic series of focus groups that any one of them had ever seen. Thirty separate kids in all three age categories went wild over Dan Roh's fruit lozenges. Boys and girls asked for candy in the shape of monkeys, snakes, and lizards.

Barry gave Iris Galashoff and her assistant, Paul Catalieri, a lift back to the city. He loved the agency people, and he knew it was mutual—he was the lone mensch at Maplewood, the only one who even went to the movies anymore.

"Lizard Licks," Iris suggested. She was his direct peer at Friedkin MacKenna DeFeo, and they spent a lot of time together and on the phone. "They could come in a little plastic collectable in the shape of a lizard."

"Chimpanzee Chews," Barry said.

"Let me tell you the news about Chimpanzee Chews," Paul chanted. He was 25 and had the makings of a very slick yes-man.

"Fruity Friends," Iris suggested. She was very self-possessed, athletic, and asexual, but always in a dress.

"Fruity Friends?" Barry said skeptically.

"All right, Fruitniks," she said. "And the tag line'll be, 'And your mom can't object because they're good for ya.' "

"Won't they see through that?" Paul asked.

"With dudes on skateboards rapping at them?" Barry said.

"I love it!" Paul enthused. "Rap hits Maplewood Acres."

Barry did like his job. He bounded back into his office, making a gently obscene gesture at his secretary, Donna Callabrese.

"How's it hangin', Barry?" she asked with a bleary smile.

"It salutes you, Donna." Donna wore too much makeup and doused herself in a very uncomplicated perfume. She was 24, had been engaged three times, and lived with her mother in Nyack.

He called Emily in and asked her to work out some numbers for fruit candy and dried fruit snacks. "Do them national, regional, and get the age breakdown. Thanks."

"Woah ho ho," she said, her eyes narrowed. "What is all this? Where is this coming from?"

"Me," Barry said tersely. "Your boss." Just a moment ago he'd been on top of the world with a fun new product; now he was tetchy and pissed off. Why did he let this bitch get to him?

He closed his door, and tried Justine again. He got through to her, finally. To get things going, he told her about the Emily problem.

"And you're sure it's not you," she said dryly.

His foot dropped. "Well, thanks for that vote of confidence, Justine. Maybe we should just skip dinner and start avoiding each other immediately."

She didn't laugh. "I can't talk now."

"Okay," he said, wanting to start over. He took a breath and invited her to dinner at his apartment. "Just us," he said carefully. "My roommate will be away—"

She wasn't listening to him, he could hear her keyboard pattering away.

"Look, if you're working," he said, "we can talk later."

"I'll be working later too. Let's just make plans now." She began outlining her schedule for the next two weeks.

She was putting him off, but was it for good, or just for now? "Well. There's nothing more seductive than a woman whose plans don't include you."

She gave a brief laugh, and then sighed heavily. "Friday. Near my office. On the late side, say 9 o'clock. And it would have to be quick."

Was this good-bye then?

Maybe Justine wasn't who he thought she was. If so, he promised himself to get out of it immediately. He'd known right away with Cynthia, and that lasted for five years. From now on, the clock was ticking. If it wasn't right, he'd slap the bell: next? Barry wanted to make a new mistake.

Barry dove straight into the candy project. He worked all day in his office with the door closed, and all night, spread out over his dining-room table. He felt like he was in business school again, racing against the clock. It was laughable that this was as high as he aimed after a brush with death. But wasn't it all the same—scuba, Talmud study, chewy candy? Anything could be a structure for one's energy.

On Friday morning, bright and early, he messengered a package to Iris Galashoff and her superiors at Friedkin MacKenna DeFeo, and hand-delivered smart blue folders to Eberhart, Rheinecker, Plast, and Hearne, and to Teriakis, the VP for Research and Development. He spent the rest of the day planning promotions for Caesar With Bacon.

After work, Barry went to the gym and did a full circuit of the machines, but skipped the free weights; he had nothing to prove. He was looking forward to telling Justine about the focus group, discussing the irrelevance of Anspacher over a bottle of red wine, and spending the weekend together doing nothing.

At home, killing time, he did his best with what was left of his hair. He felt the bottom dropping out, and all his confidence flushed away. What was she doing with him?

Vince appeared, dressed for lawn tennis. He made himself a Scotch, sat down in his regular spot, and turned on The Weather Channel. This was the first Barry had seen of him in a week.

"You have to find a new place to live. Now."

Vince raised a mild eyebrow. "Really."

Barry tried to maintain a neutral tone. "It's just that I'm seeing someone new, and it would be awkward if you're around."

"What's her name?"

"Justine."

"Justine Schiff?"

"Mm hm." Somebody screamed somewhere.

"Wow." Vince paused, and smiled, looking up at the ceiling. Barry wanted to smash his face. Did Vince ding Justine, or the other way around? "What a great idea. I never would have thought of her for you, but now that you mention it, what a great idea."

Meaning what? Barry almost gave him a departure date, but he didn't want things to be ugly as well as awkward. "You still owe me rent," he said, on his way to his girlfriend, simultaneously pleased and annoyed that he hadn't lost his temper.

At a restaurant around the corner from her office, Barry picked out

Justine's shiny, intense head immediately. An excitement spasmed in his chest. She was in a black suit, bent over some work, oblivious to everything. There was something magnificent about her concentration. Why wasn't she in a booth in the back?

As he kissed her red cheek, she calmly placed her papers in a clean manila folder, inserting the folder into a brown portfolio, sticking that into a big black bag on the banquette. She kept the cellular phone on the table.

"Justine!"

"Yes?" she said, like a doctor's receptionist, turning to him again with neutral eyes. Why?

"Here we are!" He had to calm down. She gave him a sly glance along her straight black lashes, and his heart turned over again, exposing a fresh area of anxiety.

Justine waved a waiter over. "Could we order right away."

"I'll be right back with your drinks and I'll take your order then. I'm Sean, by the way."

"We're in a rush," Justine said firmly. She moved the cell phone from the left side of her plate to the right.

"Rush rush rush—what a woman, hey, Sean?" The waiter left.

She looked up and then beyond him. "Hey, Dennis," she said.

"My name is Barry," he said, but she was already shaking hands with a guy and chattering about someone they knew together. Barry shook the guy's hand and waited for it to be over.

Justine's face was drained of expression when she turned back to him. There was a pause. Was this the woman who sat on his lap for steak on Friday and pizza on Saturday and muffins on Sunday morning? Had the crash even happened?

"So," she said. "How's that problematic employee?"

"Emily," Barry said, relieved she was talking. "Talk about attitude." As he was about to launch into the story, Justine greeted a puckish-looking guy in his 30's and an older woman with a massive chin system. This must be the company cafeteria. She introduced Barry, and joked with them. Who was this guy, now? They continued to speak in office dialect; if he spoke up, it would just extend the time these people were eating up on his already very short date with Justine. So he didn't say anything.

But he felt stupid, sitting there. It wasn't fair. Her face lit up for them. They knew her. He probably should have gotten to know her first, but he wasn't good at that. He never knew where to put himself while the getting to know you was going on. Neither, apparently, did Justine. This made him sick.

Finally, they moved on. "That may have been the ugliest woman I've ever seen," he said.

Justine stared at him coldly. "She doesn't speak ill of you. We have to order now," she told the waiter as he arrived with his pad. "I'll have the chicken. Absolutely plain. No sauce."

"Make sure you suck all the taste out of it," Barry instructed the waiter. "If that meat comes with any taste at all, we're sending it right back."

Justine closed her eyes and smiled.

"Chicken, dry," the waiter said, laughing. "And you?"

"I'll have the salmon. Wet," he said, and Sean left.

Barry held his hand out to her, but she didn't take it. Was this a kiss-off dinner? "I am not at liberty here," she said, her eyes gesturing to the walls and air.

"Why are you mad at me?"

"I'm not. But Vince was fairly recent, and now it's weird."

"You're making it much weirder than it has to be. How recent?"

"I can't talk about this now." Her face was closed off.

"I've asked him to move out."

"Well, that's a step."

The food came, and Justine asked the waiter for Dijon mustard, mayonnaise, and a cup to mix them in. "So that's your angle," Barry said. The waiter laughed. Sean would remember him if he came back. He felt better about the place. He began to tell her the history of his apartment renovation, but the coffee came immediately, and before he'd even gotten to the firing of the first architect, she said she had to go.

He hated this restaurant! "Is it always like this?"

She sighed. "Pretty much."

"Don't you feel like you're missing something?"

"Yeah, but it'll all be out on video soon and I'll fall asleep to it anyway." She was actually signaling for the check. "If I worked somewhere in-house, I'd have a normal life."

"So why don't you."

"I'm too junior at this point to get a job that would interest me. I'd take an enormous pay cut. I've just always operated on the assumption that I had to make partner, and then afterwards, if I wanted, then I could go elsewhere." She put on a scarf.

"You're really very conventional."

"Oh yes," she said, as if this were beyond obvious.

He smiled. "Why?"

"I don't know," she said, putting on her coat. This was a very strange, preliminary conversation to be having, considering.

He'd forgotten about the crutches—he couldn't even hold her hand crossing the street. She planted a fast kiss on his cheek and went inside to do her lawyerly things. He watched her slow diagonal progress across the lobby until she disappeared.

It was Friday night. He was alone on a concrete slab in front of a black office building in a freezing cold wind. He thought they'd be regulars by now. He felt cheated.

One-shot deal

On his way to his fourth date with Justine, Vince nearly collided with a tractor shovel full of dirt. He stood there, stupefied. There was dirt right there underneath. You'd think there'd be half a mile of pipes and wires between Third Avenue and The Earth. He waited as the tractor reversed, slightly hypnotized by the beeping. He hadn't so much as reached for Justine's hand yet, and he wondered what he was waiting for.

That morning, at his desk, he'd kneaded the Play-Doh Pippa had given him as a nail-biting deterrent. A year ago he would have gone through the whole routine with Justine out of boredom. He'd gotten himself into a lot of unlikely situations that way.

Any restrictions he might impose on his other situations would be artificial: nobody was moving, nobody was married, nobody was going off to war. Everybody was just a phone call away. He bit his nails. They tasted of Play-Doh. He wondered if the red tasted like the blue. He opened the red drum. It smelled the same. When Claudia came in he had his nose in the canister.

"You are so weird," she said, throwing a fax at him. Her crush had turned to grudge. It was usually just a matter of time.

Justine was waiting for him in front of the restaurant. The expectation on her face when she saw him nearly winded him.

"Vince Anspacher," she said as they sat down, dragging out his last name, dwelling on it.

"I suppose you want to meet my father," he said.

"I've met your father," she said, matter-of-factly. "In the Vista Hotel."

"Is this a regular arrangement?"

"One-shot deal," she said. "A client of mine was trying to get him interested in a new venture. He wasn't interested."

Vince played with his watch for a while. He felt 6 years old. This woman had done business with his father. The meat was too rare, but he didn't send it back. Enough waiting.

He took her home. Both Justine and a ceiling-mounted camera

watched him in her elevator. When she opened the door, a barking spaniel lunged at him, getting hair on his suit, sliming his hands. Living with an animal was incomprehensible. Justine looked up expectantly. He removed his jacket. She blinked rapidly and took it, smiling with her head down—she was embarrassed.

He led her to the bathroom, and began washing her hands with his hands.

"Vince." She was breathing heavily. "It's alarming that there isn't anybody you don't get along with."

"I don't get along with too many people."

"You're seeing three women," she said, in a voice that meant both he and she were crazy.

"Yeah. Well, that's three out of how many millions of women," he said, drying their hands with a towel.

"Oh, I can't believe you." She pulled away, not amused.

"Come here." He put his head on her shoulder and pulled her into him by the waist. "I'd better go," he said, watching her.

"That's not fair."

"I'll go if you want me to." He meant this. He didn't need more trouble. He was only slightly aroused. He could go.

"I don't want you to," she said, putting a few of her fingers on his mouth lightly.

He relaxed, and kissed a finger. "Then it's not a problem."

She looked him in the eye. "It's a big problem."

"So I'll go."

She was all over him then, and completely available, and it was too late anyway. He'd known since he'd met her that it was just a matter of time.

Afterwards, picking sand out of his eyes in the cab home, he realized he had no idea whether her last name was her father's or her stepfather's, and he didn't know her well enough to care. He had to go to London on Thursday. He was nauseated thinking about how he would fit her in. She was flat-chested, with thick thighs and a big behind. She didn't say anything when he left. He just wanted to sleep. Did he care about anyone, or even know anyone? Or was it just repeated exposure?

Chapter 5

How about lunch?

Justine rose reluctantly at 9. The crash seemed more like a movie she'd seen a few years ago than an event that just two weeks ago had ripped her out of the sky and flung her into a freezing swamp. Her palms were blistered, the crutches were a nightmare, and another blizzard was predicted. Vince Anspacher was back in frame. In general, it felt like garbage had been delivered instead of picked up.

Justine refused to succumb to fear on the flight to Atlanta. She tried the biofeedback, but arguing on the plane phone with Feinman, Dingle, O'Shaughnessey about the restricted stock provision clause in Noah's management contract was really more distracting as well as more efficient. At the Galsworthy Paper headquarters, George Underhill Galsworthy IV held out a hand, meaty palm up, as if asking her to dance. He was a beefy Southerner with big red jowls and bloodshot eyes. He dominated his board like a charismatic general.

When she got back that evening, the Partnerships had been announced: Dennis Delaney and Harry Chu had made partner. Bobby Weiler (white, male, top-10-billing associate and all-around nice guy, passed up last year and given a nonbinding pat on the back) had been passed up again. If Bobby Weiler wasn't partnership material, then no one was safe. Maybe she should start walking now, while she still had some market value. Justine went to talk to Roberta.

"He came in at the last minute and read me the riot act," Roberta said of Dennis Delaney.

"You didn't stick up for Dennis?" Justine asked, aghast.

"Not initially," Roberta said sheepishly behind her coffee, and put her feet up on her desk. She'd stepped on gum in her flats. Men would tell each other such things. Justine pointed out the gum, and watched, a little disgusted, while Roberta hacked away at it, first with a token, then with a paper clip, and finally a small screwdriver that she fished out of her noisy drawer.

"Why not?"

"It's nothing in particular," Roberta said, organizing the shreds of gray gum into a pile on a coffee-stained napkin. "But I didn't go to bat for him in the way I'll go to bat for you."

Well, there. But still.

"He reminds me of Charlie Quinty, the guy down the hall that everyone cried on," Roberta digressed, putting her shoe back on. "Sweet guy. Wasn't gay. We all thought later that he might have been, but he wasn't. Got married later in life, nice guy."

"And Bobby Weiler?"

"Well, yes: Bobby should have made it. No question. But *somebody* had to go," she said, taking off her big red glasses and rubbing her eyes. "It's sad, but that's the way it is."

Justine dropped her time sheets off on Alma's desk. A few days before Christmas, by special messenger, Carol had sent Alma an absurdly expensive scarf from Yves Saint Laurent, and Justine couldn't do anything about it. Alma had worn the scarf every day since then. Everyone asked her where she got it and she said, "Carol Dunlap, Justine's mother," with a reverence bordering on awe. Justine wanted to yank the scarf off her neck and send it through the shredder.

Alma dealt pink slips in front of her. "Barry, Barry, Barry! Aren't you going to call him?" she said, excitedly. "He's a live wire!" Now that was a Carol Anne Kaminsky Schiff Dunlap expression if Justine had ever heard one. She'd call him when she was good and ready.

Justine limped into her office and turned her full attention to Fitzsimmons Chemical. The Galsworthy board had reluctantly agreed that a more thorough due diligence was necessary. She had Mitch doing debt, and Nicky doing corporate documents. She spent all day sifting through vendor contracts, periodically appeasing the client, sucking down Tab after Tab.

Nicky knocked and came in. "I think you should look at this." Nicky Lukasch had no small talk. She liked this about him.

She read his changes and nodded. "Fine. What's their litigation clause," she asked, settling into her chair. He shuffled through pages and read it.

"Too vague," she said, as Ilana and her Rive Gauche made a theatrical entrance.

"Jus-TINE. Did you call my physical therapist, Jerome?"

Didn't Ilana have better things to worry about? "I will, Ilana, it's too soon."

"I told him about you." She pointed her finger at Justine accusingly, and her jewelry rattled. "I told him ALL ABOUT YOU! So it's too early for physical therapy, but you should call my orthopedist. He's very used to giving second opinions, and he doesn't take it personally. Just call him."

Justine promised she would. Ilana lingered, poised in Justine's chair like a highly colored, magnificent butterfly. What did Ilana want, and why did she want it of Justine?

"Where are we with the depositions," Justine asked Nicky.

"The beginning of nowhere. Why are we taking them one by one?" he said, standing up to pace. "Why don't we have them all in here at once and get three court reporters?"

"Because Mortie's shtupping Helen," Ilana boomed, "so no one can hire any other court reporters."

"I don't like gossip," Nicky said with quiet dignity, as if he'd been asked for the record.

"Well, then you must be sitting on some fabulous secrets," Ilana laughed. "It's always the wallflowers who are the biggest exhibitionists, you know."

The scar stood out white as Nicky blushed along the length of his face. "I'd better get back to work," he said.

"Calm down," Ilana commanded, and turned the hot bright light of her full attention on him. "Nicky: Tell me all about you. Where do you live? Where do you get your shirts? Who's taking care of you?"

The kid looked like he might implode. "You can interrogate him another time," Justine promised, and stood up. Ilana winked at both of them like a vaudevillian, and pivoted gracefully away.

"By the way, Nicky," she popped her head back in, "I have an article coming up in the *Business Lawyer*. Want to help?"

"Um, sure," he said, looking trapped and foolish.

Ilana vanished.

"That woman," he whispered, looking ill. "It has to stop."

"That's nothing," Justine said, amused. "She keeps insisting I call her breast doctor. Just a consultation, to talk about implants. Three or four times, she's mentioned it."

"That's sort of harassment, isn't it?"

Justine shrugged. "The woman can get any Republican senator on the phone in two minutes," she said. "I think she has a crush on you."

Nicky ducked behind her copy of the *Delaware Litigation Reporter* as Farlowe stuck his head in. "Stop," he pleaded.

"What's the matter," Farlowe shouted. "Can't handle a dried-up old fruit like Ilana?"

Nicky darted away with the air of an unhappy greyhound, and Farlowe remained standing impatiently, shaking the change in his pocket. "Well?"

"Some of their contracts aren't assignable," she reported, "but most of those expire in six months so we're okay. Looks like a good fit."

"Think so?" he asked dryly.

"Yes, I do," she said, annoyed. If he didn't trust her judgment, then why give her the case. She went back to the contracts. The client, a total stranger, had trusted her with his company instantly. But after more than six years of good work for Farlowe, she still had to start every day pretty much from zero with him.

She hit the bottom of the box at 11:30, stitched together a summary, and arrived home at 12:15, grateful that her mother still had the dog. She crawled into bed. Wouldn't it be easier to just not get involved with Barry. She was already involved. She had visions of Barry and Vince discussing her body over breakfast and she wanted to throw up.

A month after the Vince episode petered out, Justine had reluctantly agreed to a blind drink with a friend of Harriet's husband. "So, tell me about your sexual fantasies," the bond salesman had asked her, before the drinks had even arrived. She'd been correct to dislike him over the phone.

Later, as the dog dragged her up First Avenue, Justine had wondered what sexual fantasies were—she couldn't be sure if she had them. She noticed too late that Stella was enjoying a barbecue chicken dinner on the curb.

"Stop that." She yanked the leash. Periodically, Justine had warm thoughts about a thin-lipped conservative economist who wrote a newspaper column in a very courtly fashion. He'd take her out for a long, gossipy lunch in an old-fashioned Washington hotel. He'd shake her hand with warm eye contact and offer to write her a great recommendation. Was this a sexual fantasy?

While she removed her eye makeup in the bathroom, she heard a baby's blood-stilling scream and the sound of rushing water. She'd been standing in this exact spot when Vince had leaned into her and slowly washed her hands in warm water; he was pressing her into the sink, passing his lips over her neck, and she was just on the very verge of smelling his aftershave again when she had to exhale.

The wailing intensified—was the baby upstairs, next door, downstairs? Stella retched on the rug. Justine got out her accident kit and cleaned. How dare Vince not call her. This wasn't bad manners, this was contempt.

Nicky leaned awkwardly on Justine's threshold the following morning and asked her how things were going and did she want to have lunch, or how about dinner, or dinner tomorrow? Or lunch?

She was almost 32 years old: she didn't have time for dinner, or even lunch, that wasn't leading to something else. She felt the slinky, silky arms of passivity draping around her protectively. Wouldn't she rather go home, do the hand wash, do the bills, get into bed with a pint of coffee ice cream and watch *How to Steal a Million?*

Of course she would; this was why she was the only one she knew who hadn't even come close to marriage. Although she had been engaged, to Rob Principe, her boyfriend and study partner in law school, who had proposed after two years of near constant companionship and shared ambitions around the clock. When he confessed, out of a clear blue sky, that his real dream was to open up a self-sufficient, ecologically sound resort hotel in the Maldives, she'd put an immediate stop to it. She had no patience for this kind of thinking.

It took a very long time to get to know a man, and then you found out you didn't even like him. Nicky was a very nice guy, but not a romantic possibility. So why even get started. She smiled apologetically, and pleaded too much work for dinner, or even lunch.

Justine took off her makeup that night and heard the baby screaming again in the rushing water. Were they torturing the child or just bathing it? They were in the ocean. His face was briny, the water was perfect. His hands were on her waist. She went to bed and cried. Someone like Vince should have to spend eighteen months in a room alone, watching bad TV and drying out.

Justine decided to seek advice from her colleagues the next morning. Roberta was leaning on Ilana's threshold, her black-and-white hair bouncing out into the air in tight, snaking waves from her forehead. Ilana was sitting behind her desk looking as groomed as an anchorwoman and twice as accessorized. Justine bit into a Danish. Her fat suits were tight.

"So call him," Roberta suggested.

"Under no circumstances call him!" Ilana commanded from her desk.

Justine didn't understand how Ilana existed on Sutton Place in a plurality of fur coats, club memberships, serious jewelry, and admirers, while Roberta was eking out an existence on East 16th Street, alone, depressed, unaffiliated. She was probably investing, brilliantly.

"Why can't she call him?" Roberta said, cleaning her fingernails with a coffee stirrer. Roberta had a lovely smile and a striking nose and could have been quite attractive, but did absolutely nothing about it. "It's just a phone call."

"If it's just a phone call, then he can make it," Ilana said, majestically sweeping imaginary lint off her navy Prada jacket. Ilana wasn't pretty, but she was shiny, and she did all the things that made you look. Farlowe once said, "It took me eight months to figure out how ugly Ilana is."

"She has every right to make that call," Roberta insisted.

Ilana tapped her spotless leather blotter with a hard, long, red-lac-quered nail. "Why should she have to?"

Justine agreed with Ilana, but she wanted to talk to Vince badly. "I need to see him!" she shouted in frustration. "What do I do?"

"I must have missed that day, when they told you how to get a man," Roberta rasped. "But isn't there an office downtown?"

"Yes, it's next to the DMV," Ilana said, powdering her white face. "That's where you go to pick up your husband."

Justine smiled. "He's waiting for you there?"

"Yep," Ilana said, applying candy apple red lipstick with a gold lip brush.

"Maybe this guy is seeing somebody," Roberta suggested.

Justine was too ashamed to go into the details. She wandered back into her office and sat down heavily, feeling disappointed and over-weight.

Justine had a disturbing thought. Her friend Jenny Kravcek, with whom she no longer had anything in common other than the fact that neither of them was married, had had a so-so blind date with a travel agent. Two days later, he was in a car crash, and he called and asked to stay with her. Three days after that, Justine had eaten dinner with the two of them. She'd been repulsed by his demeanor, his con-versation, his looks, and his table manners. "If this week goes well," the travel agent had said, licking his fingers, "I plan to ask Jenny to marry me." And Jenny had smiled weakly.

Was that what happened? You went on bad dates till you just couldn't take it anymore, *and then you MARRIED one of them?*

Everyone was married, everyone. The dim, the bovine, the nasty. Girls who smelled. The biggest bitches at Spence had found their mates and were going about the business of their lives, taking vacations, reproducing themselves. Of course there were exceptions—Ilana, Roberta. But pretty much, after a certain age, people came in pairs. It didn't solve your problems, but it gave you new ones to think about.

Occasionally, Justine had to have lunch with her old friends when they ventured in from out of town. The husbands flirted with her in a chaste, gentlemanly way, almost as if they'd been prompted by their wives, her friends, who pitied her singlehood and thought, There but for the grace of God, and wrote the whole event off as an act of charity. It was meaningless. She knew interest when she smelled it: her college roommate's husband, whose lively systems shut down almost audibly when Justine was around. She'd once spent an elevator ride with him in a storm of electrically charged silence—he couldn't even look at her.

Justine's lights went out. She waved her hands over her head to acti-vate them again. Farlowe had convinced the Partnership that they would save money by hooking the lights up to a motion sensor with a timer. So she'd been perfectly still for four minutes.

Alma buzzed her. Carol on the phone.

"You know, Howard Klenz faints from you," her mother began.

Justine tore the wrapper off an Almond Joy with her teeth. "Isn't he a grandfather by now?"

"He's 47, Justine. He's a good man. I gave him your number but I told him that I'd work on you."

She bit into the candy. "Not interested."

"If you didn't work so late you might be interested."

Carol thought a great job was working for a man who thought you were such a knockout that he married you and then you would-n't have to work anymore.

"I don't think so," Justine said, chewing. She was too exhausted to go through another round of pointless socializing. But Howard Klenz couldn't possibly be the answer.

Vince was the only living man that she actually knew who interested her. That had to count for something. Although, their one episode of physical contact had not, in point of fact, been good at all. But that took time. His situation was bizarre. Her interest in him was bizarre. But at least it was interest. Before she could change her mind, she dialed his number with a shaking hand to invite him to dinner. Or lunch.

Vince answered his own phone. He was running out the door, on his way to Tokyo, and he'd definitely call her when he returned. He'd have oodles of time then. In a small tight voice, she wished him a good trip.

With a single stroke, she hung up the phone, knocked her head on her desk lamp, and sent her can of Tab flying, leaving pools of brown water puckering her papers.

Oh! She thought she'd made her last embarrassing mistake, but no: there was always a new disgrace. Oodles of time, oodles. He was a jerk. He had three girlfriends. Why was she wasting her time on this arrogant airhead.

Alma came in. "Howard Klenz!"

She picked up the phone. Alma lingered, coyly. Justine dipped her head and raised her eyebrows.

"Isn't he the guy who faints from you?"

"Get out of here," Justine said, as pleasantly as she could. When the door was closed, she said, "Hi, Howard."

"Justine!" His optimism made her feel ashamed. "Maybe we could have lunch sometime," he said. "No pressure, just friendly-like? How's Thursday? Next week?"

"Howard, I'm sorry. It would be awkward, I would dread it—"

"You would dread it!"

"No, I mean, I'd worry about it and I have so much work—"

She should have taken a cue from the pro. She should have been on her way to Tokyo. She waded through documents until 10, went home, watched *Mary Tyler Moore*, and ate mayonnaise on crackers. Her 32nd birthday was coming up. She was peaking, alone. She would wilt, wither, decay, and rot.

Perhaps the real fantasy was to be whisked away to a Swiss clinic and drugged while specialists removed unwanted facial and body hair permanently. Four months of diet and exercise, and then a train to Paris to pick out a wedding dress in *taille* 38. Was that all she wanted? Who was she marrying? Why did he have no dialogue?

Justine drank some salad dressing and got back into bed. She saw Vince striding into a party, sleek and European-looking. He saw her. There was an extended period of gazing, and then he came over. No, it was a summer wedding on a patio. He walked out. He saw her. She saw him. There was significant eye contact. She was wearing a sleeveless turquoise Thai silk shift with matching slingbacks. He had no dialogue. Who was he? She had no idea. Was this a sexual fantasy? There was no sex in her sexual fantasies.

It was the second Saturday in January. Nicky was waiting for her in the conference room with a Fresca and Fig Newtons. He was touching, but too young, too tall, too accommodating, and too quiet. And anyway, she was seeing Barry. Right?

The conference call began:

"There are too many marks on the page," the Galsworthy legal department said of the bid letter.

Justine squinted. "What does that mean?"

"You have all these arrows, balloons, riders," said the General Counsel. "I can see them looking at this letter and saying, 'These people, we can't even negotiate with them.' "

"Look, Fitzsimmons is a sophisticated company," she said. "We could change one word and create a problem of magnitude. Here, we've made a lot of little changes that don't amount to much. You honestly think they don't know the difference?"

"We want to present a clean face," said a new person. "But don't lose the substance."

The call ended. "This is ridiculous," she said.

. . .

At home, Justine paged through the New York Law Journal in a trance. The Vince episode was so far away now. The intensity and futility of it were strange. She imagined going to Barry's apartment in a nice black suit. Vince would be stunned.

"I'm on my way to Tokyo," he'd say, breezing by.

"Have a nice trip," she'd call. She played this through several times, with variations. But Vince kept going to Tokyo. She tried to imagine him watching her with Barry, but it didn't work—he kept getting phone calls and tossing good-byes. Even in her fantasy, Vince wasn't interested.

She took a shower and shaved her legs. Barry was the better man, but did she want to pursue it? He was quick, he was interested, there was always another joke coming. On the other hand, the jokes weren't always funny. She should continue seeing other people.

What other people.

Wild children raised by wolves

Barry anguished at his desk: he felt like he was on probation. He wanted a slew of plans that he could count on. Every time he hung up the phone he wanted to call her back and do it over.

Meanwhile, Vince showed no signs of leaving. Barry wanted a messy fight, slammed doors, and no more Vince. It was outrageous. Barry wouldn't have spent an extra hour in a place he wasn't wanted.

Hearne stopped by Barry's office with the blue Lizard Licks folder held aloft in triumph. "This thing is gonna blow the roof off the house!" he enthused, and walked off. Barry smiled.

The phone rang. "Hello, I'm calling from Kenosha?" a woman began—the classic opening gambit from an irate consumer. "And I have a real problem with your labeling?" Consumer interaction could either be a pain in the ass or a revelation; once he'd opened a letter and found a tooth inside. But his assistant had arrived; Barry put the woman on hold.

"Some bitch from Kenosha wants to rant about labels," he told Emily. "Talk to her and then get in here."

Miss King glared at him. All your business relationships should bear the stamp of character. He should do something about the Emily situation. But what?

Plast called Barry in after lunch. "Well, I enjoyed my reading here," he said, pushing the Lizard Licks folder to the side of his desk without opening it. "But I don't think it's a real volume opportunity. The margins aren't good enough. It's only twenty-eight profit."

"Excuse me, twenty-eight *point seven nine* profit."

"Maplewood policy is thirty-two," Plast said smugly.

"Hey, William? You know how John D. Rockefeller got his start? He bought rock candy by the rock, and sold it to his siblings by the piece. At a profit. I don't know if it was thirty-two percent profit—"

"We don't know from kids, Barry," he said in a singsong way. "We have no products like this and no history to work from."

"So we start here with this here product."

"It's a cute idear, but a fly ball." Plast had clearly spent the weekend looking for the right sporting metaphor. He pushed aside the folder. "Plus, the fruit bits concept apparently went through Jam already. Greg and Rich ruled it out. Now this," Plast said, pointing to the fill-in-the-blanks Garlic Dijon memo that Barry had coughed up at 2 A.M. in contempt, "this is fabulous."

Typical.

Barry mulled this over later in the lab, tasting a new flavor, lemon raspberry. So Roh had approached the Jam guys first. Well, it was their formula, after all. But he'd come to Barry next: he knew a maverick when he saw one.

Jack Slaymaker stuck his big red face into Barry's office in the late afternoon. "You little snake! I can't wait to go to Kroger with varmints, bwah!"

"You may have to—the House of Lords won't go for it."

"Stand your ground," Slaymaker shouted. "You and your funny little kid product."

At 5, Rheinecker's secretary asked Barry to stop by, and he trotted down the hall. He sat in a guest chair, while the big man made notes in the margins of something and ignored him. Barry examined the photos on the wall: a stone house, assorted boats and kids, his wife, Judy, a trim, athletic once-blonde with serious bone structure and a glacial stare. The big man himself was there, looking very much like Bobby Kennedy, probably because all the photos were taken on a sailboat in a stiff wind.

Rheinecker tossed his work aside. "What have you been doing, Cantor?" he accused, picking up the blue folder.

"I thought I'd help build profits, up the price per share. That okay with you, sire?" Why did he still bother? They didn't like his jokes, they never had.

"Mr. Cantor," Rheinecker said, unamused. He didn't like people who wore belts, people who ate Chinese food, people who used ballpoints, people who talked too much. Barry knew this because Rheinecker wore suspenders, wouldn't touch Chinese, used fountain pens, and kept his own counsel.

Teriakis, capo of R & D, stalked in, harassed, with the shiny blue folder. "What are you spending your time on this for?" He drove in every day over the Tappan Zee Bridge with an ax to grind and a bone to pick. Barry tried to stay out of his way.

"You're right. Shall I take Kool-Aid at noon?" He should just stop.

He switched gears. "Look. I haven't been playing hooky. Caesar With Bacon is steaming right along. This idea just grabbed me. The response in focus group was astonishing. The kids went gaga."

"Well, you'd better get a presentation ready," Teriakis said spitefully. "You want to do it now, or after the Caesar launch?"

A foot wedged firmly in the door. "Now."

"It's a very interesting proposition," Rheinecker said, concluding on a cautious upnote. "But don't forget Caesar."

"I will be like Caesar's wife!"

Better and better! Barry twirled out to share the triumph with Roh.

"Sympathy for the Devil" came over the radio as Barry fought psychotics in traffic on the West Side Highway. The Stones were a damn good band to listen to, but he couldn't watch them without getting nauseated. New York City was out of control. The density was causing violent behavior. If forty percent of the people who lived here didn't live here, and ninety percent of the people who didn't live here but worked here, didn't work here, this could be a livable city. He'd be the one to decide who had to go.

When he opened his front door, Barry saw Vince's shoes on his rug and wanted to punch his lights out. Even more annoying than his ongoing presence was the fact that Barry had asked Vince to stay in the first place. Why? On some level, he'd wanted to impress him. He gave the door a big knock.

Vince opened the door a crack and peeked out.

"I want you to leave," he said.

"I know," Vince said. Now how could Barry respond to that? "I've been sick," he said, like a 12-year-old who hadn't done his homework. "I'm going to London tomorrow and I'll get on it first thing when I get back."

Go live at the Plaza, your highness, he wanted to say. But it made no sense to antagonize Vince.

. . .

Barry met Justine at an Italian restaurant she'd chosen. Dinner was noisy, crowded, rushed, and unsatisfying. It was unclear whether he was coming back after, and the tension was killing him. They hadn't kissed since she'd told him about Vince. Almost two weeks. It was frighteningly cold, with moonlight. They picked their way over the ice in silence. She was off her crutches.

At her corner, she said, "Would you like to meet my dog?"

About time. Upstairs, a silly-looking dog with wild popping eyes lunged at them in a whirling frenzy when they walked in.

"Woah, Simba," he said, as the crazed animal scratched his thighs as it flew by. "May I use the little girls' room?" he asked, and she tossed him an unamused look; it wasn't like he didn't know where it was.

In the bathroom, an explosion of bras, underpants, and stockings hung from the towel rods and the shower curtain. "Hey, it looks like a delicatessen in here," he called out to her. No response. Would she ask him to sleep over on a school night?

Justine wordlessly walked into the bathroom as he walked out of it, and the bouncy dog followed her in, red tail waving. Justine blocked the dog's path. "Go play with Barry," she said softly to the dog, and looked up at him.

He inhaled slowly. It was the first time she'd said his name. It sounded very intimate. It sounded like a couple of years' worth of long weekend afternoons spent indoors.

It had to work out with Justine.

When the door closed, the dog jumped up on the couch next to him and panted at him with terrible breath. "Hello, stinky doggie," he said. He held onto her ears and she looked up at him with wet brown eyes. "Do you want to play?" She laid her chin on his thigh. He petted her bulbous little forehead. "Oh, Stella wants to play with Barry, yes," he said, and she rolled on her back. "Yes, Stella." He began stroking her white stomach, and she gazed at him, entranced. "You like Barry." She squirmed happily. "Oh, yes. Barry is a good man. Tell Justine. Good with his hands."

Justine reappeared. "Off the couch."

Both he and the dog stood up. Justine wordlessly handed him his coat and put hers on again.

Downstairs, when the dog began to produce, Justine pulled on a pair of surgical gloves.

"Wow," he said. She smiled at him in a masterful fashion and made a Styrofoam cup and a tongue depressor appear. She bent at the waist as if bowing, and with a flourish, she tapped the turds into the cup with the tongue depressor. She threw out the cup, carefully removing the gloves without touching the outsides. "Aren't you being a little anal about this?"

"If I am it's entirely appropriate," she said primly.

Enough pleasantries. "So. Are we going to talk about this?"

"No," she said without looking at him. But she walked into her building without stopping him from following her.

"No talking," he said hopefully.

Upstairs, they took off their coats. Justine had a bump on the top of her nose that made her face impossibly, tragically beautiful. He pulled her to him by the arms and pressed his mouth to hers. She kissed slowly with eyes closed. After a moment, she pulled him backwards, still kissing, into the bedroom. They fell awkwardly on the bed. While he took off his shoes, she turned over. He took off her shoes. He took off his shirt. He pressed himself up against her, completely aroused. Stella was digging somewhere. Justine was breathing slowly, ignoring him.

Justine was asleep.

What kind of behavior was this? Let's say she didn't want to do anything right now. Okay! Still, she should either invite him under the covers, or ask him to leave. He wanted to get on top of her and run his face over her body. Was she faking it? He stared at her intently. Had she fallen asleep on Vince? The idea of Justine with that beach boy— he wanted to bite someone's ear off.

He'd let her sleep for 20 minutes, and then wake her up. He sat on the loveseat across from the bed with Stella, who accepted his caresses with a languorous look. She began licking his hand steadily. She rolled over to have her tummy scratched. She writhed in a possessed way.

He was making out with the dog.

Justine began to snore. This kind of disregard gave him hives. He wanted to bite her! He left in disgust. At home, Vince's shoes were still on the rug. Barry almost punched a wall. The dog was the best part of the evening.

Barry drove to work in a fury the next morning. He played *The White Album*. Paul could rock, certainly, but there was often an element of role-playing (e.g., "Helter Skelter," "Kansas City," "Back in the U.S.S.R."). John *was* the rocker (e.g., "Twist and Shout," "Revolution I"), without the wink, the camp. On the other hand, who could maintain the energy level of "Helter Skelter?"

He waited as long as he could, and then he called her. It was 9:35.

"Sleep well?"

"I'm so sorry. I didn't mean to conk out on you. I'm about four months behind on sleep. Let me make it up to you. Tonight."

At 5 she canceled. This was ridiculous. There were plenty of women out there who could be interested in him. And this woman had fucked his roommate: *she* should be calling *him*. He flipped through *Regional Bottler's Monthly* in frustration and despair. He received statistics on fruit snacks from Merle in the Library. What about Merle? A possibility. A redheaded possibility, excited about his product. The hell with Justine. Really. Wild children raised by wolves were better-mannered than this.

Contributions

Pippa had sex with Zack as often as she saw him and that was fine, getting better. But everything else was a problem. He ridiculed her for being afraid of his boa, would only play music that she hadn't heard before, and had nothing but disdain for her bosses and her roommates. He gave money to everyone on the street, and turned to her each time.

"I always say, there but for the grace of God," he said, as if to a child.

It was cold on the street. "So you believe in God?"

"What a question! It's Friday night, relax!" Zack stopped in front of the next man with a cup, shook his hand, gave him a $5 bill, and said, "Have a good meal, my man."

She wanted to go to a movie, but Zack didn't have any money left, and this struck her as preposterous. Still, Zack had helped the homeless and she hadn't. So she paid for the movie and dinner. They saw *The Man Who Loved Women*, which was the most interesting film that she had ever seen in her entire life. On the way home, Zack spent ten minutes riffing on how bad it was, and another ten on the short, nightmarish life of a calf before it was butchered so her degenerate employers could have Veal Marsala.

"Enough!" she shouted, giving him a token. "They eat meat, and so do I."

"Fine," he said, thrusting his hips through the turnstile. They watched a man making the rounds with *Street News*. Zack gave the man a dollar, and looked up at her expectantly. "If you gave some money from your princes to someone who needed it—"

"I actually need it." Where had this dollar come from?

"Turning into a real conservative, aren't you?"

"Look, I'm really tired of defending what I do," she shouted over the din as the express roared by. "I think you need a vegetarian who wants to listen to your speeches."

"What speeches," he said, annoyed.

They got off at 110th, and were hit with a blast of air that smelled like dirty feet. They walked to her building in silence. He asked if he could come upstairs. She said no.

"Fine," he said, and walked away, skidding slightly on a sheet of ice.

That night, she stripped her hair with a peroxide kit. She couldn't decide if it was the best thing she'd ever done, or an awful mistake that would take years of her life to fix.

Chapter 6

Getting to know you

It was the first week of February. Justine was sitting in Mitch's office discussing employee benefits for Noah Clurman's new chain of frozen yogurt franchises when the phone rang. "For you," Mitch said, giving her the receiver.

"Alma says you're looking like dreck and that men call you and you don't call back."

"That's it." Justine hung up and hopped into Harriet's office. "I'll trade you Alma for Bob."

Harriet clapped her hands together hopefully. "Are you sure?" Harriet hated Bob because he was a sculptor first and a secretary almost parenthetically.

"Positive," Justine said. "Please, now."

They called the office manager. Ten minutes later, Alma took her belongings around the corner on a red cafeteria tray, with Carol's fuchsia scarf flying behind her like a flag. Bob, who was 23 and had gray hair, arrived with a tattered copy of the *Voice* in unclean hands. He announced he was ill and took the afternoon off.

So Justine answered her own phone when it rang. "I hear Harriet's expecting!" her mother said excitedly.

"What?"

"Who's Barry?"

"You may not call here anymore," Justine said, and hung up.

As she dropped her time sheets on Bob's desk, Farlowe pulled her aside.

"I'm no gossip," he said low, "but did you hear that Ms. Lazarus is with child?"

"Everyone knows? She didn't say a word to me."

He shrugged: not his field, female things, office intrigues. "I suppose she'll be wanting to spend time with the offspring," he said, delighted: Harriet was deadwood to Farlowe.

"You're asking me? Apparently I'm not even on her mailing list anymore."

After a quick call to Feinman, Dingle, O'Shaughnessey to ensure a cap on Noah Clurman's severance obligations, Justine picked up a Tab and went to see Harriet. She wasn't in her office; she was in the little lounge off the ladies' room, where a group of secretaries and paralegals regularly ate lunch and gossiped.

"You look surprisingly calm for a woman with something living inside her body," Justine said.

Harriet smiled as if nothing was out of the ordinary. "We were just discussing Retin-A," she said, eating pasta salad with her feet up.

Alma was perched on the other couch. "Oh, don't talk to me about Retin-A," Alma said, like a tough old bird. "I've been using it ten years."

"Alma," Harriet said, intrigued, "How old are you?"

"Forty-one."

"Forty-one!" Harriet said. She and Justine looked at each other. "Alma, honey, you don't look 27." It was true.

"Thank you. But I'm 41." She seemed almost upset about it.

"Just exactly how pregnant are you," Justine asked.

"Five months," Harriet said, unbothered.

With a feeling of unease, Justine left them chatting. Harriet was eating with the support staff in the bathroom?

A year ago, Justine had had a pregnancy scare. While anxiously awaiting her period and the final signatures on a complicated asset deal, she'd played Tetras, first repeatedly, and then continuously, for two weeks straight, and had caused herself carpal tunnel syndrome. The day after the wire transfer, her period arrived, she was put in a soft cast, and she went into Harriet's office to talk.

"You had a pregnancy scare?" Harriet said in disbelief. "YOU?"

Justine rested the hand on Harriet's desk. "I don't like the way you said that. What does that mean—'YOU?' "

"I mean," Harriet laughed, "good! You're not pregnant. Our coffee table is two weeks late—I don't know what to do."

Justine worked most of Saturday, and met Barry at the Baronet. He was joking grandly with people on line. When he saw her, he shouted, "I met her in a crashing plane!" and grabbed her shoulders and kissed her deeply in the mouth. In front of the people. She resisted, but he had her locked in. She wanted to scream. When he let her come up for air, she held her temper. But this had to be addressed. Now.

At the seats, he carried on about his favorite deaths in the movie this was the sequel to, not noticing her irritation.

"Listen," she said, when he'd settled himself. "I don't like what you just did."

"What did I just do?"

"Kissed me in front of those people. Like that."

He looked like someone had just taken away a plate of food he was about to eat. His face hardened, as if he were about to yell or hit. Outraged, he shouted: "I can't kiss you?"

"Sh! I'm very affectionate," she said low. "In private."

He ate popcorn continuously, staring straight ahead.

"Come on, Barry, I'm not cheesecake."

Not looking at her, he said, "Some women want to be told they're attractive."

"You can always tell me I'm attractive."

"You're attractive," he said, as if he were handing her some batteries.

"Thanks."

There was a long pause, during which they watched Hollywood trivia on the screen. He would get infantile in an argument. It was good to stop it now before it turned into one. She hooked her arm through his as the lights dimmed. He gasped in mock outrage and pushed her away. She gave up.

He pulled her back. "Okay. Fight's over. C'mere, Frosty."

It was a buddy movie with guns, explosions, high-speed car chases, and naked women. It was a complete waste of time. Barry laughed hysterically and glanced at her constantly to make sure she was laughing. This annoyed her. He was in high spirits afterwards as he walked her back to the office. It was the best movie he had ever seen.

Upstairs, she got a call from the CFO of Galsworthy Paper. "I'm sorry to bother you," he said, sounding embarrassed. "I was talking to someone I can't name, who said he overheard a certain person I work for discussing the bid at his golf club."

Justine felt hot. "Cricket was bragging? Are you kidding me?"

"He's real excited about the stock rising. I was wondering if you could maybe speak to him."

"You bet your life I will," she said and hung up. She called her client at home to read him the riot act.

"Miss Schiff," Galsworthy said, his voice drenched in forty-eight years of Jack Daniel's, chewing tobacco, and getting his own way. "Calm yourself."

At 6, she took a cab to Barry's. He lived too far uptown. But a nice old building. Dingy hallways. She hadn't been prepared for how tasteful the apartment was. She felt as if she hadn't been quite fair with him.

"You like it?" he asked. "Top of the line, all of it," he said, strutting around. The phone rang. "Check it out." He waved his hand, picked up the phone, and disappeared behind a door.

She sat on the sofa. She should have been researching Farlowe's article, "Fiduciary Responsibilities in Change of Control Transactions: Recent Developments in Delaware Law." But she was exhausted. It was nice just to sit. It was nice to be in a man's apartment on a Saturday night. She closed her eyes and breathed in.

There was a key in the door.

Should she hide? That was ridiculous. Vince had been notified about her.

Vince took his coat off, and stopped when he saw her.

"Let's get this over with," she said sarcastically.

"Justine." He grasped her hand like an elderly professor. He looked young, thin, and sick. She barely knew him. It was embarrassing to be reminded of this.

He poured her a drink without asking her, sat down on the couch next to her, and leaned in to clink glasses. Had he always been this smooth and fatuous?

Drinking with Vince Anspacher in Barry Cantor's apartment was probably the stupidest thing she could be doing. Barry would explode when he found them. He had a real temper, she was noticing. But the Scotch was a pretty color in the heavy glass and she drank some. She didn't even like Scotch. Vince's head was tipped back on the sofa. She almost asked him what it was he didn't like about her.

Vince stared up at the ceiling. "So you prefer Barry to me."

He was kidding. Right? "I wasn't aware you were available."

"I know," he said, seriously. "I wasn't, really." He smiled up at her from beneath his streaky blond bangs, and in an instant, it was clear: Vince Anspacher had never made a decision, never mind a difficult decision. He would always have options, he would always do the easiest thing, he would always be bored.

Barry arrived and stood in front of them. Barry was in a different category.

"You gotta go," Barry said, smiling dangerously. She really liked Barry.

"I'm going." Vince picked up a book on the coffee table and walked. He had skinny wrists and sticklike forearms. It just wasn't attractive. "Good to see you, Justine," he said, saluting her from the foyer with his Scotch glass.

Barry stood until they heard his door shut. Then he dropped into the sofa, squeezed her hand, and looked at her closely. "I can't get him to leave," Barry whispered savagely.

"He hasn't found a place?"

"I don't even know if he's looking. And he misses all my subtle hints, like when I say, 'Leave.' Should I cut up his suits?"

Vince reappeared: "Do you have an extra umbrella?"

"No."

"Could I borrow your umbrella?"

"No," Barry said with exaggerated patience.

"Oh." There was a silence.

"Do you think you can get an umbrella delivered?"

They stared at him.

"Well. It isn't really raining anyway." Vince approached them, took another book off the coffee table, and walked away again.

What on earth had she been thinking? "This is a beautiful place," she whispered to Barry as she kissed him. "Let's go to my house."

Justine woke up the next morning with a boyfriend in her bed. He was so calm and solid, she almost shivered. They drove to LaGuardia in a snowstorm. She'd been afraid he might turn the baggage pick-up into a reunion, but he was quiet.

Being back at the airport made her angry again. People were picking through glasses cases, wallets, and paperbacks that were splayed out all over the floor. There was something obscene about it. They found the luggage soon enough, but her files could have been any-where—it looked like a landfill.

"Leave it?" Barry asked, and she nodded.

They had to walk down two flights of stairs with their bags. "Welcome to New York!" a sign proclaimed.

"What the hell kind of planning is this?" she seethed. "What if we were older, or if we had medical problems."

"Here, let me take that," Barry offered.

"That's sweet of you, but not the point," she puffed.

A crowd was milling around, blocking the exit. Every other city in the world tried to make itself accessible. This city encouraged chaos, inconvenience, danger. There was a quarter-mile walk to the car. The Port Authority should be sued separately.

She seized an Almond Joy from her bag, and bit into it, trembling. She was furious.

"It's bad enough they crash the plane," she spat. "But then they hold your bags for two months 'investigating,' and then they give you no notice, and they make you come back here, and still you have to schlep up and down stairs? This is grounds for a class action suit. I never heard of such bullshit!"

She stopped. "What are you laughing at?"

"I've never heard you speak like this."

"Well, how long have you known me, mister."

"I'm so happy our plane crashed," he said in the car, interrupting the flow of her anger. "I never would have met you."

The annoyance was dissolving into a feverish nausea. She was sweating in the car. She felt as bad as she had the day of the crash.

"I don't think I've ever been this happy," he said, taking her gloved hand. On automatic, she opened her door, walked a few feet, and threw up next to a red hatchback with a ski rack. This was awful. She felt sick enough to die.

"Are you all right?" Barry jumped out and handed her a bottle of water and some Kleenex from her bag. "My poor darling."

She rinsed her mouth and began to cry. He opened the door and they got into the back seat. She tried to rest. It was too difficult to cry. Her head was splitting. They sat a while. He held her head. She had a boyfriend who was holding her head.

"I must say, you've got to stop throwing up every time I tell you I'm glad I met you," he said, and she tried not to laugh because it made her dizzy. "A guy could get offended."

The stop-and-start traffic made everything much worse. Justine couldn't stop thinking about revolting and awkward episodes with men in her past. If she were married, all the surreal phone calls and mortifying moments with her clothes off would be meaningless. She'd have a clean slate. But every one came back at her like shelves crashing down, one book hitting her head after the other as they inched their way onto the TriBoro and she prayed she wouldn't throw up again.

Barry put her into bed. It was a hot little nap and she drooled. She woke up ashamed. Justine stretched her arm out and he handed her a glass of water just beyond her reach. It was nice that he was taking care of her. Not that she needed to be taken care of.

She drank and lay back. Barry, from the very beginning, had tried very hard. No one in recent memory had tried *at all*. No one even looked at her anymore. He was so friendly. She knew so little about him. She needed time to absorb him into her system.

"Who was your first girlfriend?"

"Ellen," he said, sliding into bed with her.

"What was she like?"

He propped himself up against the headboard. "We were 14—what was to know? She had nice handwriting?"

"Ellen who?"

"Ellen Haberman."

Amazing. "I played jacks with her! Did you hear?"

"What?"

"She's a sex therapist."

He laughed very loud. She draped herself across his chest and stomach. She was very glad he was there. She fell asleep without meaning to. When she woke up, he was holding onto her lightly, looking around. She felt like a protected animal.

Who were these people?

Vince was sitting above a steaming plate at a macrobiotic restaurant in the Village. His stomach was churning.

"I've got a rags-to-riches show coming up," Renée said between tiny bites of mealy bread. "What about your dad?"

"Never." She'd asked him before and he'd told her no.

"Well, I'm not giving up on Papa."

Vince tuned her out and faced his plate. The idea of it was nice, health food, but it looked so gray and damp. Renée wrote something in her fat, soiled, crowded date-address book.

"You should get another book," he said. "That's a mess."

"Who cares," she said, writing something down in the book.

Vince stared at her. "You're left-handed!"

"Of course," she said simply.

He stared at her, astounded. He had known her a year. It was as if he had just discovered that she had monkey blood. "How could I have missed that?"

She stared back.

He dropped her home and went to the video store. In Foreign, he saw a tall woman in a leather jacket who looked familiar. By the time he reached her, he remembered why. He said hello. She said hello. She went back to reading the video box.

"Didn't we go on a date during the Gulf War?"

She turned. "Yes," she said, and went back to the box.

"I remember because I wanted to be home watching TV."

"Thanks," she said, and walked towards Classics.

He was too honest. He should probably be charming and make it up to her, but in truth, he didn't care, and he couldn't pretend he did anymore. She knew he didn't care, and she didn't care. But now it was awkward: he wanted to look around, and this woman wasn't leaving. He left feeling unsettled.

When he walked into the apartment, Barry was standing in the middle of the living room. Barry stared at him. He stared back.

Who *were* these people? He was surrounded by strangers. He waited in his room until Barry's door closed, then slipped out for some Scotch. He got into bed; it felt like he'd tripped but hadn't landed yet. He socked back the Scotch and got a nice, familiar flooding in his face.

The following morning, he went to The Commodore, a luxury high-rise on 55th Street. A blond agent chattered nonstop about the quality of the tenants as she showed him four different apartments. He was about to tell her he'd get back to her when he realized that if he didn't decide now, he'd never do it. He signed a one-year lease on a one-bedroom on the 37th floor and joined the health club, for an extra fee. He didn't have any furniture. He'd call his mother. They could make a day of it. She would love the new apartment.

They did a poll

Malcolm Forbes's father once said he'd never met a rich man's son who was worth a damn. Barry remembered this the morning Vince left. He'd moved in with some extraordinary luggage, and now it had resurfaced.

"Well, good luck," Barry said, thinking, Go to hell, selfish airhead prick. But Barry had barely known him when he invited him to stay, and hadn't given him a departure date. Live and learn.

Still: you don't have to be happy about it. Eat my exhaust fumes, Barry thought as he cruised out.

Winter sunshine was scattering tiny crescent scales of light over the Hudson. He should plan an outing with Justine. They needed to do something different, a trip to Hyde Park, perhaps. It haunted Barry: all those women in love with FDR, living with him in the White House. And he was paralyzed from the waist down—*including?* They never actually came right out and said it.

He spent the day preparing his Lizard Licks presentation to the Council. That night, Justine arrived, her beautiful face flushed red and yellow like a nectarine. It would be her first dinner and sleepover at his home. He introduced his girlfriend to his chef.

"How do you do," Justine said with rapid disinterest, gave her coat to Pippa, and walked back to the bedroom.

This was not the reaction he had expected.

Pippa put the coat on the couch. Barry hung the coat in the closet. He wanted the two of them to hit it off. Maybe Justine could help Pippa. Give her fashion advice, tell her where to go to be washed, plucked, painted, and sprayed. But when Justine emerged a few minutes later, she looked tired.

"Well, I felt real bad all day," Pippa said, peeling garlic.

He went to work with the corkscrew. "Why?"

"A guy came up to me and asked me for money," Pippa said.

"This was the first time?" Justine interrupted, an eyebrow lifting skyward.

"Of course not," Pippa said, running leaves of romaine under the tap. "But he said he was a diabetic and he needed $2.69 for insulin. I gave him $2, and I felt bad. It was just 69 cents. I mean, either I believed him or I didn't," she said, tearing the lettuce. "If I believed him, I should have given him the whole thing. If I didn't, I shouldn't have given him anything."

The cork emerged; he poured three glasses of wine.

"Most of those people are crack addicts," Justine said with authority, putting her feet up on a chair.

"He didn't look like that. He said he lived in the neighborhood, and he would pay me back."

"It's not your problem. That man should get a job."

Barry didn't like the way she said that. "Maybe he was laid off. And he can't find a job, and he never thought it would get this bad, but today he was down to his last batch of insulin."

"If he were laid off, he'd get unemployment," Justine insisted. "And the insulin would be part of his . . . *arrangement* with the government."

"Maybe he was laid off before he could qualify for unemployment, and now no one's hiring and he doesn't have the right skills for a new job."

"So, what, we should pay to retrain this guy for a job that doesn't exist?" Justine took a carrot off a platter. "Because labor is just cheaper in Honduras and Thailand."

Pippa set a cup of dip in front of Justine, who dipped her carrot without thanking Pippa. "Did you peel these?"

"No, I washed them. Most of the vitamins are in the skin."

"Really," Justine said, unconvinced.

Barry watched Justine's mouth. "What Justine means," he said to

Pippa, "is that most of the people asking for money are mentally ill—they need psychiatric help."

"They're mentally ill because of crack," Justine said, her big mouth wrapping around the carrot stick. She sounded like a 48-year-old housewife from Roslyn.

"Not all of them."

Pippa said, "Cassoulet?"

They sat down. He poured more wine. He toasted to a new phase in the life of the apartment, and formally welcomed Justine. She turned to Pippa. "Are you a chef?"

"Well, I've taken cooking classes, and I've worked in restaurants, but I don't have a degree."

"Well I suppose you don't need a degree to be a good cook," Justine said, tasting the food carefully.

"Henry Ford said the minute you deal with an expert, everything becomes impossible," Barry told the women. "They're too familiar with the reasons why things *can't* be done."

"Yes, but. You can only really do one thing well," Justine said firmly. "Two, tops."

Barry felt hot. "That's un-American!"

"It's true."

He couldn't marry Justine. He looked at her cautious mouth trying to find a reason to dislike Pippa's food and he hated her.

"Why do you have to be good at it?" Pippa asked, as if she really wanted to know.

He laughed. "You can tell she was raised on a commune," he said, and squeezed Pippa's neck playfully. She squirmed away.

Justine sat up straight. "You were raised on a commune?"

"In Vermont. We grew our own food, we had our own school. But it fell apart after about five years. Personalities."

"What a strange way to raise children."

"No stranger than raising them here," he said, surprised at how limited she seemed.

Pippa said, "My friend Daria's sister?" Barry looked up and saw Justine looking down. "They just had a baby. And they're moving upstate because the schools are better there."

"I would never send a child to public school," Justine said, adamant and smug. She was an alien.

"What Justine means is that public schools are not safe in New York," Barry explained to Pippa. "But something has to be done, it's disgraceful."

"What should be done? Shall we throw money at it? Money won't make those people raise their children properly."

Those people? He had fallen in love with a Young Republican? How was that possible?

After dinner, Barry performed his Lizard Licks pitch. Pippa applauded. Justine told him to keep his hands above his waist and not to clear his throat too often. Pippa left.

As they prepared for bed, Barry searched for clues he might have missed. Maybe it was a family thing, a tradition. Moynihan once said that in his district, people were baptized Catholics but born Democrats. She'd had formative years in Westchester and at Spence. She probably didn't like eating with the help. She probably didn't want to go to Hyde Park.

"Most people don't agree with you about the street people," she called from the bathroom, where she was doing something that involved running water for fifteen minutes straight. "They don't say what they really think because it doesn't sound nice."

He pulled the bedspread back fast. "You know this for a fact." He felt like he was arguing with his father.

"They did a poll."

"The opinion poll is the worst thing to hit this country in thirty years! It's mind control masquerading as information." He arranged the pillows and sat back. "Instead of telling you what the candidate stands for, they tell you what thirty-seven percent of the American people think he stands for."

"Don't you think the American people know what he stands for?"

"The American people don't know jack shit. They know what the idiots on TV tell them."

She emerged in a white nightgown. "You're such an elitist," she said, smiling as she wiped her wet red face with a towel.

He didn't want her in his bed. "Opinion polls lead to lemming-like behavior." She was rummaging through her bag. She found a bottle and went back into the bathroom. "Plus! Thirty-seven percent of Americans is a crock of shit," he called after her indignantly. "Which Americans? Nobody ever asked MY opinion."

"Yeah, let's make a law about it," she said, looking at him in the mirror condescendingly. "From now on, it's a misdemeanor to ask more than three Americans in a row what they think about something, and it's a felony to report it."

He wasn't sure he wanted to see her again.

When she turned off the bathroom light, he said, "I just want to know: did you ask him to wear two condoms?"

She gave him an unamused look. "Give it up."

"You haven't said anything about the Lizard Licks."

"How is a focus group different from an opinion poll," she asked, climbing into bed. She clearly made more money than he did, but how much more? He wasn't sure he wanted to know.

"You know," he said carefully, "I was really excited about you." He turned off the desk lamp. "Don't let's fuck it up."

Her voice was foreign from the bed. "Must we agree on everything?"

"No." He got back in. "As long as I don't have to hear your ridiculous opinions, it's okay if we don't agree."

She laughed. She poked and prodded him until he gave her a kiss on the forehead. But he wasn't going any further, and he told her so. "Suit yourself," she said, turning over, tucking her knees under, and falling asleep within two minutes of settling in. This was their first sleepover in his apartment. How could she do that? And so sure of herself! They did an opinion poll, and that proved it. HE was an elitist.

He couldn't go to sleep like this. He had a presentation tomorrow! He pressed himself against her until she rolled over, cranky and peeved. He silenced her with insistent sucking. After a while, she stopped kvetching and gave in.

Republican!

Rheinecker's dry gaze from the foot of the table made Barry feel overdone, like he'd spent too much on his tie. He wouldn't do jokes. He'd keep his hands above his waist, and think before he answered questions. This was a walk-through; if they weren't up for it, why would they ask for a formal report?

"If you have kids or were ever a kid yourself, you know that candy is central in the life of a child," he began as casually as he could, while Emily disgustedly passed out the Lizard Licks samples to the Council members. This had been an argument, of course: she wasn't a waitress, she wanted him to know.

"Here's candy that even a mother could love: all-natural, sweetened completely by fruit preserves. Oh, and corn syrup," he added nonchalantly, and got a chuckle. "Try one," he said, surprised that they hadn't. Everyone opened their envelopes and chewed. He felt a warm wave of solid support from Hearne, who'd come in at 7:30 to coach him through a final dress rehearsal.

"The market's theoretically crowded," Barry said, projecting the stats on the screen, "but it's patchy: very few products are distributed with any kind of consistency."

Except for the chewing, there was utter silence as he went through his multitude of charts. The numbers spoke; he'd done his research.

"This is not one of Maplewood's traditional areas," he concluded, nodding at Plast. "But we're so strong in distribution, and the figures show an enormous demand."

There was silence. Eberhart said, "I like this."

Barry thought he'd heard wrong.

"Let's do it," Eberhart said. "Any objections?"

There was more silence. "So we'll get test plans from you at next week's meeting?" Teriakis said impatiently. Teriakis—stocky, sweaty lunk that he was—was married to a party girl with mall hair thirteen years his junior.

Barry stood up. "There is something else to consider."

"Yes?" Rheinecker asked, as if he expected a minor point of procedure.

"General Mills, among our other good friends, is much bigger in the kid business," Barry said, feeling hot in his face. "If we test this, they can pick it up in Minneapolis or wherever and go national within three weeks, and beat us to the punch."

Hearne nodded slowly. Plast looked like he had been socked in the mouth.

"So what are you saying?" Teriakis said testily. He was equal parts naked ambition, naked irritation, and naked disdain.

"No test market. We go national immediately or we don't go."

He loved the murmuring hush this bald statement caused. Someone whistled, like he'd hit a line drive way back. Plast looked utterly betrayed. Hearne was beaming at him.

Eberhart drummed his fingernails. "Well? Any objections?"

"Yes." Plast said regretfully. "We don't have anything like this, and we don't have real data. I think going without a test is a big mistake."

"I think Barry's right," Hearne piped up. God bless John Hearne. "If we wait a year we might as well not do it."

Rheinecker asked, "Anybody else?"

No one responded. "Do the marketing plan," Eberhart said to Barry. "Figure out how much we're talking. We'll meet next week."

Hearne shook his hand and patted him on the back proudly as they walked out. "Big man with a new brand!"

Barry called Justine. She was in a meeting with a client.

So he went down to schmooze with Hearne. "Maybe I'm Amazed" was being piped softly into the elevator. Not the Muzak version, the real version—the live version. What did that mean? Barry thought about Paul. Lately, no one compared the new material with the Beatles, or pre-"Londontown" Wings. Still: Paul knew the difference. At any moment "Let It Be" or "Maybe I'm Amazed" might come over the radio to mock his current work. On the other hand, if you were tapped into genius at all, why should it matter how long it lasted, or if every song wasn't a masterpiece? And if the song truly was a masterpiece, could it be debased by being played at a discreet volume in an elevator?

Chapter 7

Uptown Express

Pippa cut up a pair of fishnets for a headband, but she still looked like a freak. It was snowing constantly. An embankment of ice had ringed their building for weeks, collecting soot, newspapers, and dog turds. Daria had a new boyfriend, Brian, who lounged around their apartment all day smoking pot, taking Ecstasy, and calling 976 numbers. He irritated Pippa in every conceivable way.

She decided not to register for classes. What was the point? She'd stopped thinking about law school. When considering her future, instead of vacillating endlessly, she just scolded herself for not knowing what to do. Vince had moved out. At the very least, she'd be working fewer hours. She might be out a job entirely: Justine wasn't keen on her. There were three issues: a job for now, a summer job, and the rest of her life.

At the Career Services Office, Pippa asked to see the architecture school binder. While she was signing for it, she asked for the government internships binder as well.

"Wait," the librarian said, her face hardening. "You want to see architecture schools and *government?*" The woman pulled the binder back.

"Yes," Pippa said. "Government internships in DC."

Several heads perked up at the tables nearby. The Career Services librarian blinked at Pippa's hair, and bit her lip. "Do you have an appointment with a career advisor?"

"I just want to look at the binders. See what's out there." And she tried to take the architecture school binder at least.

The librarian inhaled, blinked, put a cautionary dry white hand on the binder, and inclined her head slightly. "I think you should see a counselor at Health Services." Everyone in the room was watching now. "Do you know where the Health Services Office is?"

Pippa pushed the binder at her and stalked out, furious, feeling all the good students (who knew exactly which position they'd occupy in exactly which company ten years from now) watching her leave. She smoked furiously.

At a temp agency on East 41st Street, a woman in a dark suit looked her over and told her not to waste her time taking the WordPerfect test—most of their clients were Wall Street brokerage houses with a serious dress code. Pippa took the No. 6 train to Houston, and walked down the icy Bowery sidewalks, passing restaurant supply, lighting supply, blanketed bodies. Steam was escaping around manholes.

In a market on Elizabeth Street, long, almost penile bamboo shoots rested in a tray of water next to black fish staring up dead through shaved ice. There were barrels of bark, bottles of murky solution, and hairy brown strings in plastic bags. Someone in the back gathered up to spit. She held her breath, waiting. At Sloan's, the supermarket closest to Barry, things were shrink-wrapped and pasted with stickers. Here, there were wings, gills, skin, hair, and teeth.

They weighed animals in a hanging scale that swayed when the door opened.

Pippa bought a bag of the strings to investigate, light soy sauce, hoisin sauce, and a chicken, which an elderly Chinese man wrapped in brown paper. Had he killed it in the alley? The bottles clanked against her shins as she walked west. On Canal Street, she bought a tiny automated marine that was crawling across the snow with a machine gun. She'd give it to Barry for his birthday.

She took the No.1 to 14th Street, ran across the platform, and nabbed the last seat on the Uptown Express. A tall man stood directly in front of her, holding on to the strap. She noticed, almost immediately, that his fly was undone.

"XYZ," she almost said, but thought better of it. The subway was not a place to be light with people. She wondered whether the chicken was leaking. As the train left the stop, a penis rose out of the man's fly like a separate alive thing.

She couldn't believe it. It was about two feet away. The woman on her left had her head down in a crossword. On her right, a guy in a handyman's uniform with shiny black hair like a pelt was staring straight ahead. The woman next to him was reading a textbook. And this guy with the penis was blocking the people across the way. She had thrown her newspaper away. She took the marine out to read the box. But it was in Chinese.

He was staring at the ads above her. She wasn't sure if he knew. How could he not know? The penis had by now partially crept out of the jeans, and she wondered what to do. She couldn't get up without touching him. The train slowed down. She had a raw chicken in her book bag—what if she died here?

The train stopped altogether. There was an explosion of static on the PA system to explain why. Barry said the trouble with public transportation wasn't the transportation, it was the public. What would he say about this? Finally, they moved.

As the train slowed down at 72nd, the guy was jostled, and the whole erect penis jumped out into the open air. He covered it fast with his jacket and fled, knocking over an old man. The woman still had her head in the crossword, the handyman was still staring straight ahead.

Hey! Did you see that? she wanted to say, but she didn't. She switched back to the local and went directly to register for classes with the chicken.

When Daria came home with Brian, Pippa jumped up to greet them. "You're not going to believe this," she said, and rapidly told them the whole story, realizing too late that they hadn't even taken off their coats yet.

Daria burst into high, breathy laughter. "That is the funniest thing I've ever heard."

"It wasn't funny."

"It wasn't funny," Brian imitated her. Pippa realized they might be high. Brian's cheeks were deep pink and he seemed angry.

"I didn't feel in danger or anything then, but I do now." She pulled Daria into a corner and whispered, "Is it any different from my thinking about sex with people on the subway?"

"Yes," Daria said firmly. "He took it out. Was he black?"

"Why do you ask?"

"Did you get turned on?" Brian asked coldly.

"Shut up, Bri," Daria said. "So did you say anything?"

"Like what? What could I have said?"

"'Put that back?'" Brian said, and unzipped his fly.

She slammed out of the house with the chicken. What was she upset about? It wasn't as if she hadn't seen one before. At Barry's, she turned on C-SPAN. Some Texan was yodeling about the budget in an empty chamber so she flipped between Oprah and MTV, and got angrier and angrier at the amount of implied sex and actual female flesh she was seeing. The only safe place was the Food Channel.

Barry and Justine arrived at 7:30 and sat down at the table. Justine was looking very formal, elegant, and annoyed.

"I was flashed on the subway," Pippa said.

"You're kidding," Barry said, spreading his napkin on his lap. "How terrible for you."

"Why terrible," Justine said impatiently. "I get flashed all the time, Barry." She turned to Pippa. "Was he black?"

"Why is that everyone's first question?"

"Maybe you shouldn't take the subway," Justine said, digging into the salad.

How could she not take the subway? Justine was in a light brown suit with a black collar and light brown pumps with black pilgrim buckles that matched the outfit perfectly.

"I love your shoes," Pippa said. "May I ask how much they were?" Not that she could walk in heels like that, or wear them in the snow.

"Three hundred dollars," Justine said briskly. "Worth it."

Sometimes Pippa didn't know whether she was rooting for or against them.

The loneliness of obsession

The Council had approved a September national launch for Lizard Licks; Barry's work life was a revolving door of resentful congratulations. Eberhart himself had made a special trip down to say, "We should have had a kid division ten years ago." Barry would begin reporting directly to Rheinecker.

Barry dialed Justine, and was put on hold by Bob the male secretary. He glanced over the business section of the *Times*. Justine usually undressed him immediately. Then he'd lie there while she hung up each item of her ensemble neatly.

"Come to bed," he'd warn, every time.

"In a minute," she'd say, smoothing pleats.

"Justine."

"Coming!" she would call, doing a flying leap into the bed. Everything always began on this cold and violent note. And since they'd graduated from condoms (somehow without a blood test, probably because of his pathetic history since 1984), she'd disappear again at a crucial moment, to run water endlessly in the bathroom. She'd come back with freezing cold hands. This was when they had sex. Often, they didn't—she was tired, she was cranky, she had a yeast infection.

Bob came back on: Justine would call him later. This happened every morning. He hated the pattern that had developed.

Hearne poked his head in. "Listen: Jean's folks are coming into town the eighth, so we won't be using the house. Would you be interested in a weekend in Vermont?"

Before he had a chance to get too excited, he called Justine. "It's not urgent, but it's timely," he told Bob the male secretary, who put him on hold. Justine came on.

"So they have a fireplace and the mountain is fifteen minutes away and I thought we could go whenever you can get out on that Friday," he said, trying to sound casual. "How does that grab you?"

There was a silence, and then she said warmly, "By the rear end, actually," and he felt physically lighter.

He was beginning to tell her something intimate when she said, "Gotta go." He hung up feeling frustrated again. Packer Breebis owned ninety-eight percent of Justine. On the other hand, she'd said yes. He ran out and bought *Fodor's New England*. He called for lift tickets and dinner reservations. She would cancel at the last minute.

That afternoon, the Friedkin MacKenna DeFeo people were waiting in the media room, looking spicy, exotic, and hot. Barry began the meeting: "We see Lizard Licks as a fun, high-energy product for kids."

"Until we test," Rheinecker interrupted, "it's Fruit Bits."

"Fruit Bits," Barry said, trying not to sound sarcastic. "We want to target the older kids, but we'll bridge the ages with young music, a unique shape, a fun name."

"Nifty," said Len Lefkowitz, the Creative Director, chewing a candy. "Hey, kids! Tangy, chewy, with a burst of . . ."

"So you want to alienate women 18 to 54," Rheinecker said, as if he were debating with a child. "The majority of consumers."

Had Barry missed something? "This is the kid division."

"When we have a kid product," Rheinecker said casually, "there will be a kid division. There's more volume in moms."

Moms! "Moms don't buy candy."

Rheinecker peered at him over steel frames. "That's not what your research shows," he said. The bastard was using his numbers against him. "All-natural is a crucial point of difference. A fruit strategy fits in nicely with our image, what we do best."

Barry was roiling internally. It *wasn't* all natural. It was candy. "Candy is America." He stood firm. "It's what we stand for—instant gratification, unnecessary expenditure, empty calories. Sugar! So let's call it candy, and have fun with it."

"Fruit Nibbles," Len rambled, eyes wide open. "Fribbles. All-Natural Fruit in a Nibble."

"Acoustic guitar," said the new art director.

"Kid on a swing," said the new copywriter.

"Kid on a *tire*, swinging over a sunlit lake," Len extemporized. "The Snack Moms Love."

Barry's heart dropped very low. "Oh, I'm getting cavities just listening to this. Look, moms buy Honey Dijon Ranch at the drop of a salad fork. But they won't buy candy without a specific request. We'll have to target the kids, so they'll drive their moms crazy. We could have a main brand, let's call it Lizard Licks—"

"Nobody over the age of five is going to ask for Lizard Licks," Rheinecker said derisively. Everyone laughed.

"Whatever name you want," Barry continued, "and then a kid qualifier. Fruit Bits, and Lizard Fruit Bits. Separate campaigns, neither group knows from the other."

Why was he always the most enthusiastic person in the room?

"A line extension," Rheinecker chided him for overreaching.

"Remember that focus group at Christmas?"

"That was phenomenal," Iris backed him up. About time. "The kids went wild. And reptiles are very big now."

"A two-track campaign—"

"Confuses people unnecessarily and costs twice as much," Rheinecker concluded, squinting in distaste. "We're getting nowhere. Set up a focus group."

Barry didn't expect the rapport he'd had with Hearne, or the access he'd had with Plast. But he'd hoped—in addition to getting closer to the aorta of power—that he'd learn something from Rheinecker. But the most gracious sovereign wasn't in the mood to teach.

Barry tried to concentrate back at his desk. *Fodor's New England* only listed the big tourist spots. He wanted to call her, but he stopped himself. He was sick of walking on eggs with Justine! He wanted to relax already. He wanted to graze. If they were planning a vacation together, she could damn well meet his mother.

Bob the male secretary put him on hold.

"What," she said, too busy.

Through clenched teeth, he said, "I want you to meet my mom."

"Okay, set it up." She was hustling him off the phone.

"Fine," he said, and hung up peeved.

He caught sight of the autumn leaves on the cover of *Fodor's New England* and laughed. He was so fucking neurotic.

On Thursday night, Barry's doorbell rang. His mother walked in looking crumpled and exhausted, a thatch of white hair standing straight up. It was disappointing that she hadn't made an effort.

"They've screwed up the inventory," Rose said, big and busty and emphatic. "Everything. If I hadn't checked it myself I would have been caught short." She picked up the phone and left his number on two answering machines. She pinched her creases, and sat down on the sofa heavily, beads clacking. "I just might retire."

"And do what. Go to Florida, to die?"

"No, to live." She scooped up some dip with a carrot.

"To turn into a vegetable like your sister, Sylvia? Take a vacation, Rose."

"I did," she said, crunching carrots noisily. "I went to Florida. You missed it—it was beautiful. It was easy."

The bell rang. "When has easy ever been good?" he asked.

"Easy is looking better all the time," she called.

It was only Karen and Carlos. Barry kissed his sister, who still had, at 31, the pinched, overserious look of a child gymnast. She'd been an alien since the 7th grade anorexia. Carlos stood at least a foot taller; his blond curls and suntanned face glowed with health, as if he'd siphoned all the life and color out of her food. Carlos was a furniture refinisher, ostensibly Argentine. Karen's previous male roommate had been an Australian dog walker—another direct personal insult. They were wearing the same earring, left ear—did this mean they were they engaged?

The bell rang. Justine rushed in, apologizing, wearing a bright blue suit that he didn't like at all. After the introductions, he sat his mother at the other end of the table, with Justine and Pippa on his left, Karen and Carlos on his right.

Justine looked at Pippa, opened and shut her mouth, and then sat down. "How long have you been in business?" she asked Rose.

"It feels like 150 years," Rose said. They would get along great. "My father started in Misses' Dresses, 1936. It's been interfacing since 1958, right after I started."

"My mother is thinking of letting the unions drive her into a Florida retirement," he explained to Justine. "A big mistake."

"My grandmother did Florida for a year," Justine said sweetly. "She came back. I think she missed us."

"Well, that's a factor," Rose said, face bent to the soup with her eyes closed.

Justine turned to Karen. "I hear that you're an artist."

Karen nodded, stirring her minestrone obsessively. Her hands were filthy. Karen enjoyed being awkward and misunderstood.

"Do you have a gallery?"

"I've shown in galleries, schools, restaurants," Karen said, spoon clenched. "No place specific, though." Fairly polished, for Karen. She was eyeing Justine jealously. Yeah, take a look: see how real women dress. Barry couldn't imagine Karen in bed with Carlos—Karen in bed with anyone, come to think of it. She used to chase him around the house to squeeze his zits; he suspected she enjoyed the work. There was something evangelical about the whole process.

Rose wasn't really interacting anymore, her mind perhaps on the imbeciles who worked for her. Her face remained in the heavy-lidded expression of struggle. She looked like Lyndon Johnson. He should have introduced Rose to his intended ten years ago, when she had the energy to care.

Conversation splintered. He and Justine chatted with Rose about her ongoing union problems while Karen and Pippa discussed Brooklyn and Carlos chowed down on the lamb. Carlos had given him a preposterous cabinet for his birthday last year, an electric blue thing that tottered on teeny tiny skinny legs and clashed with everything Barry owned. No doubt they would ask where it was, and Barry would have to lie and say that he broke it and it was in the shop.

Rose labored to the phone, stabbed the buttons, spoke briefly, grunted in frustration, and hung up. So much went on behind her face. You'd think you were watching Brando brooding over whether to turn his brother in. Pippa brought out angel food cake.

"They don't spend even one third as much on the women," Karen said to Pippa about something, and Barry responded reflexively, "Oh, get off your soapbox."

Karen looked at Carlos, and Carlos put his fork down.

"We must go," he said, and they got their paint-spattered coats.

Proving, of course, that Barry couldn't spend any time with his family without someone getting offended, usually Karen. Was Karen molested? Was Karen raped? She wasn't nearly attractive enough. Was Karen hit on the head as a child? Had he done it?

Rose decided to leave too. "But you didn't have any of your cake," Barry tried. "We made it special for you."

"I'm dying for a cigarette," Rose said. "They'll give me a lift in their van."

"Their van is a *nightmare*," he whispered, and Karen glared at him. He could honestly say there was nothing that she did that didn't irritate him. It was probably mutual.

When they'd gone, Justine disappeared into the back. Well, at least they hadn't mentioned the cabinet.

"Karen is impressive," Pippa enthused, her hair a cartoon yellow in the track lights. "She's got her own priorities."

"No, she's just being pious and difficult," Barry said, checking his widow's peak. It was still there. "It's what they cling to in the absence of clean clothing and hot water. If I were living like them, I'd believe all that bullshit too."

She did a plié to put a pot away. "Your mom liked Justine."

"Really?" She nodded. He wanted to believe her.

When Pippa finished cleaning up, she threw on her leather jacket and wordlessly handed him the Steely Dan disc he'd loaned her as part of his ongoing campaign to broaden her, musically. Did the lack of comment signify she thought he was an old fart trying to turn her on to Lawrence Welk? He gave her a hug good-bye. She wasn't wearing a bra. Her loose breasts pressed against his chest pleasantly.

"Now, how many different colors do you have in your hair," he said, about to browse through her roots to count.

She pulled away. "Night, Barry," she said, patting his cheek like a grandmother and walking out on her black platform combat boots. Women were so weird. He went into the bedroom; water was running in the bathroom. He kicked off his shoes.

"Well?" he asked his girlfriend. "It went better than I thought."

"Ye of little faith," Justine called from the sink. He draped his pants on the chair, kicked his underpants into the corner, got under the covers naked, and sat propped up.

"You look just like your mom, you know." She emerged from the bathroom fully dressed with her shoes on, and the day came tumbling down.

He grabbed her by the waist. "Where are you going."

"I have a dog." She could care less about him.

"Invite me over. I'll walk her."

No response. Why was it always like this? He wrapped his arms around her waist, and her hands fell on his shoulders and stayed there. "My mother loved you, I could tell."

"That's nice." She accepted caresses with her eyes closed.

"Comere." He pulled her down on the bed.

"Barry, I need to sleep."

"Am I even a top-three priority in your life?" She gave him a look of fatigue and disgust. "Why are you looking at me like that, like we've been over this a thousand times. I'm the new guy, remember?"

"I'm sorry. It's been a long day."

He hated her.

"All right already, come over if you want."

"What a lovely invitation."

"Don't give me this."

"Look, do what you have to do," he said, putting his pants on. "Just don't expect me to be delighted about it."

They kissed while she waited for the elevator. It was irritating the way she closed her eyes all the time, when he was kissing or making love to her, like he could have been anyone.

Why was obsession never mutual?

See you later

Early Friday morning, Justine sat in her office, contemplating an unexpected offer: Betsy DeNatale—her old mentor, a partner at Packer Breebis until she'd joined the Bush campaign—had called to tell her that Whitman Sklar was looking for a senior attorney. Justine thanked her, and said she'd consider the offer. It was flattering, but she wasn't about to throw away her seniority for a nonequity partnership in a shop that saw a tiny fraction of what Packer Breebis handled.

She went to visit Ilana at noon.

"Jus-TINE," she boomed in her cultivated voice. "You MUST see my dressmaker, Mrs. Pasquisi. She loves me. LOVES ME. I got her granddaughter into Dalton. Well, find the time, darling. I'm a pro and I am telling you, you'll go so much farther if you show a little more leg. I'm not talking mini, I'm saying just above the knee. Like mine, see?"

Ilana kicked her legs up to show off her pale white well-turned calves in French stockings. Ilana's beaus were all rich, bald, middle-aged men she met at Republican fund-raisers. By the way Ilana bragged about them, Justine doubted that there was any physical component to these liaisons.

"Noah Clurman has at least four affiliate transactions with the company he's buying," Justine said firmly, "and several other board members also have some involvement."

"Yes? And?" She raised a penciled-in eyebrow derisively.

"You're not surprised?"

Ilana leveled a half-lidded look at her. "Why should I be surprised?"

"Well. We can't have that." If Justine hadn't brought it up, would Ilana have let it slide?

"I guess not. So tell him."

"How."

"Smile a lot," Ilana said, smiling brilliantly, showing all her resculpted teeth. The face work was really undetectable. You knew she'd done it, but there were no traces.

"Over the phone?"

"All right. You piss him off, and I'll smooth it over. Call me as soon as you hang up."

Barry perched on the edge of her tub, watching, intrigued, as she put on under-eye concealer. "I'm really looking forward to Vermont," he said.

"Oh, me too, sweetie, but don't say it too loud." Stella was leaning into the toilet to drink. "Stop that," Justine swatted her down.

The phone rang, and she let the machine pick up. "Whatsa story, darlin," Galsworthy's voice oozed from the machine. "I'm worried about my little birdie."

"Who the fuck is that?"

"The client from Atlanta," she said, putting on lipstick. "Out of control, and probably three sheets to the wind."

She ignored the message and went out—an actual date on a Saturday night.

The middle-aged couple in front of them on line at the Beekman were discussing the congressman accused of molesting the 12-year-old daughter of his wife's business partner.

"Oh, what's the problem—12 is old enough," Barry said loud.

"Stop it," Justine warned, low.

After a shocked pause, the woman asked her husband, "How was he even in contact with her?"

The husband said, "They said he picked her up at school."

"Hey, man," Barry sang, "if there's grass on the infield, I say: play ball."

The woman turned to see who was talking like this. Justine wanted to fall through the floor. The woman took a good look at her: what was she doing with this jerk?

Not a bad question. While he got popcorn and she chose seats, Justine wondered where these atrocious lapses of taste came from. How could someone who kissed so beautifully be such a vulgarian? That morning, for example, she'd awakened to him kneeling next to the bed, wearing a flamboyant bathrobe like an aging movie star. He was kissing her hand and looking at her like he didn't know what to do for her first. Was his sweetness in private enough to outweigh these bizarre displays in public?

Already she was thinking: death, divorce. Death was really the best, because it left all parties blameless, if lonely, with happy memories. She would marry Barry Cantor, and he would die young. Young enough that she would find a second husband one-two-six. She was strangely unworried about finding a second husband. The first husband was the problem. By the time he came back with popcorn, people had dispersed. Still: she had to say something.

"You can't talk like that. You embarrassed me."

"Oh, lighten up," he said, passing her a soda.

"You embarrassed yourself."

"I'm sure that's my business." It would be a messy divorce.

The movie was wonderful. It was a complicated love story in Edwardian London, with sets and costumes and china. He complained the whole way to dinner. When the miso soup arrived, Barry held the waiter by the arm and shouted, "Waiter, someone sneezed in my soup!"

Everyone in the restaurant turned to look at them.

Why was he doing this? "It's fine," she said to the waiter.

"It is NOT fine!" he shouted holding up the cube of tofu.

"Somebody sneezed big white chunks into this, look at it!" Some people were laughing nervously. Justine wanted to make him disappear. What was wrong with him? The waiter left, smirking. She drank the steamy soup from the bowl with her eyes closed. The warm, wet air around her nose and mouth made her feel like a sleepy child. She finished the soup and put the bowl down.

The scene was over, and there he was. He was looking dark and handsome. It was touching that he'd put on a jacket to take her to a movie. He was watching her with eyes half-closed. She loved this slouchy look, when the day and the wine showed up around his puffy eyes. Nothing had lasted more than six weeks in four years.

So she didn't say anything more about it.

Back at home, the dog had thrown up on the corner of the rug and Galsworthy had left a message on the machine: "Where you, Justine? You outta town? I must speak to you. Urgent business."

Barry said heatedly, "What the hell is his problem?"

"Want to hear something weird?" She folded her pants on a hanger. "He asked me what church I belonged to."

"Oh, that's a Southern thing," he said authoritatively. "It's just being sociable. The way people here ask you which gym you go to, and what's your rent."

"Well, I didn't tell him."

"Afraid he'd show up in your lobby in sheets? I could beat him up for you. I bet I'm taller."

She smoothed his eyebrows. "Yes, and so much stronger, too."

Before she thought about it too much, she called the client. He answered loose and wet: "Justine. I was worried."

"I'm fine. The work is on schedule. I was out with my fiancé."

"You—"

"Get some sleep," she said briskly. "Let's talk tomorrow." She hung up and went into the kitchen for the accident kit.

"Fiancé?" Barry asked with quiet amusement, too smart to make a very big point of it.

"Yeah," she said, flushing slightly. "It's a Southern thing. You're fair game unless you're betrothed."

Barry hooked Stella on the leash. "I'll take her out."

"What a nice guy you are," she said, feeling bad for having killed and divorced him. The dog was in love with him. She gave him the cups and gloves.

"No." He opened his wallet. "I have some stuff here."

"What, cash-machine receipts? Are you out of your mind?" She pressed the cups and tongue depressors into his hands.

She cleaned the carpet and called the office: Nicky said there was nothing for her to do until he and Mitch finished, probably at around noon the next day. She put *The Sound of Music* on the VCR, skipping ahead to "Sixteen Going on Seventeen."

Barry returned, and cavorted with the dog. "I can't believe it," he said in disgust, sitting down. "This again?"

"Oh, please, this is the first movie I ever saw, and it would make me so happy."

"Imagine if your first movie had been *Total Recall*. You and I might even be able to talk."

"Shut up. Liesl is in love."

"With a Nazi," he said, and turned it off when the song had finished. He pulled her hand. "Come lie down."

They got into bed. The phone rang. The machine picked up.

"Hi, you," the client said. "I need to talk to you."

Barry threw the covers off. "Shall I give him a piece of my mind?"

"No, I'll deal with this." She picked up the phone. "Cricket. I'm turning off my phone. Good night." She hung up.

She yanked the wire from the jack. The phone rang in the living room. She yanked the wire from the jack in the living room. Vulgarian or not, it was good to have Barry there. If he hadn't been, she would have spent the night worrying about this.

She slipped back into bed. She wasn't anxious, she wasn't full, she wasn't frustrated or disappointed. She felt as if she was in the right place at the right time with the right company.

They woke up early and went to her gym. He was in an expansive mood. She feared he would embarrass her anew. But whereas all the men were wearing obscene spandex outfits, grunting like pigs and making faces, Barry was not. He traveled from one machine to the other in sweatpants, positively low-key. Barry, who was never low-key about anything. He could surprise her.

"See you later," she said, kissing him good-bye.

It was nice to say that. She'd forgotten how essentially content she was in domestic situations.

The firm was its usual Sunday self. Nicky and Mitch swung into her office. Sick, subdued, in casual clothes, they looked like bored but obedient high school boys on the debate team. They looked her up and down: she hadn't showered, and she was still in her tights. Well, yes, she was now having a life. They should just get used to it. Some people had lives, after all.

She began reviewing Mitch's riders. "See you later" assumed that there was an agreed-upon place where the seeing would be done, and that it was agreed upon beforehand that both parties were amenable to being seen, and that there was no need to plan or ask or wonder or worry. There was something very relaxing about that.

She had a good feeling about Barry. It wasn't excitement, or obsession. It was just . . . nice. Like she'd moved into a bigger apartment, and now there was a place for everything, and space to get more things.

Suddenly, Justine felt like a big long chat when she got to Packer Breebis on Monday morning. She went into Harriet's office, but

Harriet wasn't there. She was in the lounge off the ladies' room eating chocolate.

Justine sat down on the opposite sofa. "Let me give you an update."

"Are you coming with me to Saks for Retin-A?" Harriet asked.

"No. Listen. He's decisive," she said, delighted about it. "We're going to Vermont. He got books. He made reservations."

"That's what you need," Harriet said, rising with a hairbrush. She was really showing now. "Someone who'll meet you halfway."

Barry met her more than halfway. Barry took care of everything—transportation, reservations, conversation. Vince, for example, just showed up.

"He's very charming," Justine said, ready with examples.

Harriet was almost out the door. "Enjoy it while it lasts," she called.

At the recruiting event that night, Roberta darted over to Justine at the first opportunity and pulled her aside.

"All right, come on. Who is he?"

Justine smiled and lowered her voice. "A nice guy!"

Roberta cracked her knuckles one by one. "Good in bed?"

"Yes."

"Finally! Old enough to vote and drink?"

"He's 34."

"Excellent. Employed?"

"Product manager at Maplewood Acres Food."

"Perfect! Jewish?"

"Yes."

"Unbelievable. Old girlfriend still in the picture?"

"Nope!"

Roberta's jaw dropped. "Not possible."

"Single, unhappily, for a long time. Can't get enough of me! Can you believe it?"

"Wow! When do I meet him?"

Justine could see Barry pulling a tofu stunt in front of the partnership. "Well, soon."

"Problem?"

"Sometimes . . . he's just not good in public."

"So?" Roberta picked two pigs-in-blankets off a tray. "How often will you be in public?"

The following morning, Justine, Mitch, and Nicky and the bankers from Fosdale Cleat discussed the term sheet in the conference room. Cricket waltzed in an hour late, big and red.

"Good news!" he said. "I called Butch Fitzsimmons, and I made a bid of 220. My people said I could've gotten away with less, but I just want this thing settled so I can call it mine."

There was a stunned silence. Everyone stared at him.

Cricket continued, amused and determined. "We'll sell the plastics and pesticides, and just keep the paper treatments."

In the middle of all of this, the lights went out.

"We're just a bunch of working stiffs here," Mitch joked, waving his hands over his head to turn them on again.

All three bankers were on the floor, holding their heads. "Jesus," one said breathlessly, brushing his suit. "That was almost as scary as your bid."

"What a bunch of sissies," Cricket shouted, amused.

Justine halted the conference for a private meeting. The client agreed, but insisted on conducting it over lunch.

They left the lawyers and bankers gossiping in the conference room, and Galsworthy took her in a ridiculous white limousine to an absurdly expensive restaurant for a serious lunch with courses. He'd be paying for everyone idling in the conference room, too.

As they sat down, Justine saw Rhoda Weisenblatt and Connie

Tischler, her mother's friends and golf partners, across the room. She prayed they wouldn't come over.

"I'll have my friend Jack Daniel's on the rocks," Galsworthy told the unimpressed French waiter. "And the lady?"

"The lady will have her friend iced tea," she said firmly.

"Oh, come on now. Live it up a little."

"That bid was foolhardy."

"I like Fosdale Cleat," he said, ignoring her point with a worldly toss of his hand. "They've done good work in chemicals before." When the drink came, he swirled the ice with his index finger, and sucked it suggestively. This man was out of control.

"That bid was too high, too soon," she insisted. "Your stockholders could sue you."

"My wife's in love with Billy Ray Cyrus."

"Who?"

He hooted. "So, what do you and your fiancé do together. May I ask. I mean no indiscretion or disrespect."

Would Farlowe sit and take this? "As your lawyer, it is my job to advise you. You're behaving irrationally. We haven't finished the due diligence. I wanted tax, antitrust, and environmental Partners to sign off on this first."

"Oh, why this endless bullshit, Justine," he said, his big teeth tearing through shrimp. "I know this company. I do business with them. Somebody else gonna come and snatch it up."

She heard her name being screamed. Her stomach dropped.

"We thought that was you!" Connie called, in rapid approach.

"Darling," Rhoda screamed across the room. "Your skin looks gorgeous!"

Someone should spank this ridiculous woman. "Good to see you," Justine said primly. "I'd love to chat, but this is a working lunch." She turned back to her client, furious with everyone.

"Well then, we won't bother you!" Connie sang, and pretended to hustle Rhoda out. But Rhoda wasn't moving. She was giving Cricket the twice-over. He was enjoying it. He stood up, pulled the napkin from his collar, and introduced himself, easygoing and natural. He understood these women.

"We were just discussing this woman's fiancé," he told them offhandedly.

"Fiancé!" Connie trembled with excitement. "What fiancé?"

Rhoda looked unconvinced. "Carol never said a word."

"Is that so," Cricket said, with a big, rich, sticky laugh.

"Justine?" Rhoda insinuated.

Justine folded her hands, and waited for this to be over. Everyone else had left their small towns—why hadn't she? She should have moved far away long ago.

"Good to see you," she said dryly, sipping iced tea.

The women minced out, brimming with intrigue and frustration. Galsworthy watched them go.

"Well." He knocked back his drink and chewed some ice. "Your skin *does* look gorgeous."

At three o'clock, she was sitting in Farlowe's office watching him eat his homemade lunch: tuna fish with onions on Wonder with tomato. When she told him about the bid, he stopped eating.

"He took you to *La Casque?*" he asked, outraged. "To talk about *Billy Ray who?*" He chewed with his face in his hands.

"He drinks," she suggested.

"Well, Schiff, I drink. But you're never gonna get a seventy-five-dollar lunch out of me—I don't care HOW many I've put away." She laughed: Farlowe disdained those who spent money to go out for tuna fish sandwiches.

"He called me at home on Saturday night completely soused."

"In the middle of a meeting with Fosdale Cleat!" He knocked his forehead with the heel of his hand, and then waved her away dismissively. Unlike other men his age, he didn't want to be charmed or entertained. He didn't need to complain about his wife.

In the hall, she heard her name being paged over the loudspeaker: "Justine Schiff: Your mother on two! She's getting her color done after her nails, so you can't call her back, Justine Schiff!"

The entire firm had heard that. Two partners, three associates, and a paralegal turned to look her over. Other than not being Alma, Bob had no saving graces.

"I hate that snotty kid who answers your phone," her mother shouted over hair dryers. "Alma misses you. She hates Harriet."

"This had better be an emergency."

"Who are you engaged to, may I ask?"

"No one. It's none of your business."

"You're right. As your mother, I really should wait to read the announcement in the *Times*. Is this the one who's taking you to Vermont?"

"No one is *taking me* anywhere."

"Okay, so you're *going* to Vermont. As a fiancée?"

"I. Am. Not. Engaged."

"Okay, so as a what? As a girlfriend?"

"No, Mom, as a locksmith. This is inappropriate. Good-bye."

She hung up and called Bob into her office to read him the riot act.

"She said it was urgent," Bob said, not even pretending to hide the smirk. "Who was I to decide that it wasn't?"

"Listen to me," she began, wondering what she could possibly threaten him with. He seemed to want to lose his job.

Just then, Nicky ran in, sweating. In 1987, *Virginia Magazine* had done a piece on the top-five polluters in the state. Fitzsimmons had ranked third. Justine called Farlowe.

"How did you miss that?" Farlowe bellowed at her, and called Louise Brody, the most senior Environmental Partner, a good friend of Roberta's. Nicky set up an immediate conference call.

"I'm real worried about the nursery school," the Galsworthy General Counsel said slowly.

Justine had a terrible feeling. "What nursery school."

"We got a nursery school on an old Fitzsimmons property just outside Richmond, where they used to put bins of stuff."

"Oh, my God," Justine gasped.

"Let's just buy the school," Cricket said testily. He'd called in from his suite at the Plaza Athenée.

"It doesn't matter," Justine said. "You're still liable for the damage, and anything that's happened to the kids."

"They look fine," Cricket said, relaxed. "I drove by the other day, checked it out."

"You didn't," Justine said, feeling unsteady again. "Tell me you didn't talk to anybody."

"A pretty teacher."

"Oh, my God. No. You didn't tell her who you were."

"Course I did! Sweet girl, smart as a whip."

"Are you blind!" Farlowe said. "Do you not see fifteen years of litigation? A parade of maimed and sickly children suing you?"

"I say forget the stock deal," Louise said, delicate and peppery in her late 40's. "We do an asset deal, limit the liability. Sell off eighty percent of the assets—"

"Is this even worth buying," Justine asked.

"Come on, people," Cricket barked. "I want this. The whole point is that it's cheap and easy, and right next door."

"There's nothing cheap and easy about a class action suit when you take on debt to buy toxic waste," Louise warned.

"Those assholes have no right to tell me jack shit—excuse me, ladies. If we got a bidding war, it's not worth my while."

That ended the call. Justine was working out toxic tort scenarios with Louise and Farlowe when Nicky ran in at 5.

"The stockholders have filed a class action suit!"

"Finally," Farlowe said. "Someone's awake in Georgia."

Justine thought of Barry's hopeful face, hot chocolate by the fire. "Well, that kills my weekend," she sighed.

"Anything exciting?" Farlowe asked.

"Skiing. Vermont."

He looked displeased.

She'd done it again. The brilliant protégé thing actually depended on her being a neutered person. All she wanted was a weekend! Barry would be crushed.

"So the same cast, then," Farlowe dismissed them. "Go do it."

"No, Mitch will be away this weekend," Nicky piped up. "It's his wife's birthday vacation. She's 24."

"That's not old enough to need a vacation," Justine said.

"What do you want me to do first," Nicky said, as he followed her out.

"Schiff!" Farlowe called. "There's a fax in Vermont. Boorman can cancel his wife's birthday. You take your long weekend."

Long weekend? She'd be in free-fall by Wednesday, with the rest of her life to ski. "No. I'll do it."

There it went. It wasn't possible to just do the work. Being a maniac was part of the job. This was what she was paid for, paid a lot of money for. She even liked the work—plenty of people didn't. Who was she to complain?

When Barry came over that night, she was so glad to see him she stayed draped over him a long time without moving. After a while, he said, "Could I take my jacket off? It'll only take a second."

"I'm so sorry," she said. "I was so looking forward to it."

"Never mind," he said, beyond disappointed. "I knew it would happen. Even as I was asking you, I knew it. Why do you do this?"

It was a simple question. She couldn't even remember.

Chapter 8

Baby teeth

Barry felt very adult about the way he'd absorbed the Vermont disappointment. He'd given up on seeing Justine during the week; he was working late, focusing on his new brand to the exclusion of all else. He felt compliant. Sometimes there was virtue in just showing up, living your limited routine, and crossing things off your list. Nothing fancy. Not every day was like the second side of *Abbey Road*.

He received a call one afternoon from Rheinecker's secretary: his immediate presence was requested. Barry sauntered down to the big man's office. Eberhart and Teriakis were sitting in the chairs, alert and expectant. There was something in the air.

No one spoke.

"You're firing me for press leaks," he tried.

Silence.

"Dress code violations?"

Silence.

"She said she was 18, I swear!"

"We've been rethinking Fruit Bits," Rheinecker coasted by with phony brightness. "We don't think it's a kid product."

"No kids! Aw, man!"

"Kids is down the road apiece," Eberhart said, his little fingers cracking his little knuckles. "We've already got a bunch of these all-natural products. We got dried apricots, mixed nuts, apple chips, and carob balls," he rattled off. "Why not throw in Fruit Bits and make a new division. Natural Snacks."

Everyone was looking at Barry. He had to think. "Yeah, okay. Restage with transparent packet design, a snappy-looking floor rack. We could break into the goddamn health-food chains! Those self-righteous bastards—"

"Want to run the group?" Eberhart asked. "You and John?"

Rheinecker said, "And how about a raise?"

Barry looked around. "Well, that would be helpful."

"Ten thousand okay?" Rheinecker said impatiently.

"Am I supposed to haggle?"

A fleeting flash of horror passed over Rheinecker's face and was replaced by a smile of frozen granite. "Come back tomorrow morning and we'll discuss it."

Eberhart and Teriakis continued to sit.

"Is that it?" Barry was mistrustful of the tight smiles.

"That's it," Rheinecker said over his glasses.

"Well, bye then," he said, and walked out. He'd never even seen the carob balls.

There was traffic on the Sprain Parkway. He went to Justine's, took off her clothes, made love to her, ordered in Japanese, and sat staring while CNN played and her mother left an endless message on the machine. He had a raise, a promotion, a new product line, a regular girlfriend. He felt like a cartoon character who continues to run long after he's left the cliff. He had to retool. Regroup, rethink. Suddenly, he was in a strange apartment with a woman who was ironing naked. How had this happened?

Barry took a cab to Justine's grandmother's on East 53rd Street. A very small, dark girl—14?—in a black uniform smiled up as if impressed by his height. The floors, walls, and ceilings were paved in white carpet. The child-maid (legal?) brought him to a white door and wordlessly left him there.

He knocked. Justine opened the door and kissed his cheek. She looked beautiful and subdued, like a good girl visiting her grandmother. In a queen-sized adjustable bed was a tiny lady with a Day-Glo green headband in flossy white hair.

"Call me Miriam," the lady commanded, and drank hungrily from a small carton of two percent milk. A napkin was attached to her sweatshirt with hairpins.

He and Justine sat down together on a white loveseat by the side of the bed. "Well, what do you think?" Miriam asked, smiling at him like an 18-year-old.

About what? "I don't know what I think anymore."

"My teeth!" The woman was smiling ferociously. He leaned over to look. "My wittle baby teeth. The big ones never came."

They were beautiful little teeth—tiny, boxy, sharp, and fine. "I have never seen anything quite like this. Justine, come and look at your grandmother's teeth."

"She knows all about them," Miriam said grudgingly, fussing with her pillows. "So let me tell you about this date I had."

"You had a date?"

"My husband, Lou, died sixteen years ago."

"Nana goes out a lot," Justine said proudly.

"So we went out for dinner. Italian. In the neighborhood. We came home. He slept over. Oh yes," Miriam continued, slightly flustered. "Does that shock you? It shocked your mother, let me tell you.

But Herman is a learned man," she said, impressed. "Schooled in things."

There was a long pause. What things? Miriam fiddled with three or four enormous rings on her fingers.

"Then I don't hear from him." Miriam looked at him accusingly. "Is this a gentleman?"

"I don't think so," he said.

"Two days I don't hear from him. Three days. Four days." Miriam rearranged her pillows. She opened a bottle of pills with shaky hands, took one out in soft, slippery fingers. She put the cap back on. She put the pill in her mouth. She washed the pill down, making a terrible, anguished face. She sighed.

The suspense was killing him.

"FIVE DAYS LATER, I get a call from Lois Sapperstein: did you hear? Herman." She raised a hand slightly and let it fall. "Dropped dead. A heart attack." She took another swig of milk.

"That's no excuse not to call," he said, and Miriam laughed so hard she spat out her milk. "He should have called. But in the event of illness or death, his son has 24 hours to call."

Miriam's laugh trailed into a terrible cough. "I love this guy you found, Justine!"

A redheaded woman in an extremely well matched green and black outfit bustled in on four-inch heels. She stood in front of him. "I've heard absolutely nothing about you," she said, tossing her head. She was wearing a lot of serious gold jewelry.

He stood and shook her hand. Justine's mother gave him the twice-over, looked him in the eye, and said, "Is he married?"

"I'm not married," he said, more amused than indignant.

Carol clucked impatiently. "Not you: your boss!"

What? "Very." Her face betrayed nothing about what was coming next. "With three children," he added.

"Get along with him?" she asked, watching him closely, massaging her mother's feet behind her back.

"I wouldn't go that far."

Her eyes were weirdly beautiful, a murky green. She must have been ravishing when she was young. She still looked good; she clearly spent a lot of time working at it.

"So I hear you have a place in Vermont?"

Justine gave him a dire look that said, Give her details, and I'll never speak to you again. "No," he said, feeling duplicitous, although he was speaking the truth.

"I thought you had a house. No?" Justine stared at her steadily, like a teenager, and her mother rolled her eyes in disgust.

Teenage Justine! He could see her: a frustrated Spence girl in an uptight little kilt and rebellious yellow socks at Baskin-Robbins. Carol patted Miriam and shouted, "Okay, you want to get your act together?"

He and Justine went into the white living room. Carol sang from the bedroom, "Muffin muffin muffin face!"

Justine turned to him like a helpless lamb tangled up in vines. "What the hell am I going to do with her?"

"Muffin face, muffin face, who's the best in all the place?"

"It's kind of cute," he ventured, and her face stiffened.

"Only gwown-ups in here," she sang in a baby voice.

"Ketzela, go help her do her hair," Carol said impatiently, as if Justine should have been doing it already. Justine stomped off, and Carol took her place on the couch. She opened a photo album on the coffee table. "That's Aunt Esther. From Philadelphia. She died at 24."

"Of what?"

"Fever. That's my father. That's Uncle Saul, and Cousin Ricky, who threw my skate key into the upstairs toilet, and Aunt Blanche, and Blanche's sister, Frieda, and Frieda's husband, Joe. He invented television long before they even had programs."

"Sounds lonely," he said.

She smiled at him. "And Blanche's daughter Tatiana, the fairy princess, who performed *Swan Lake* at every party. Christ, was she an irritant." Justine's mother had fallen into a slight Tri-State accent: fee-vah, dawta, Uncle Sawl. "And here's Justine. On Halloween. She alternated. One year Cinderella, the next year, princess. Cinderella, princess."

Little Justine at Rye Playland. On a horse she looked like a snotty little bitch. He turned back to the Cinderella Justine. She was a beautiful child. She was an only child. There was a torn photo. "That was Justine's father," Carol said, pointing to a remaining pant leg with a long red nail. "The man was a lunatic. You have no idea what I put up with. None."

Justine in a cap and gown. "I told her: work in a law firm. You go to law school to meet a law student. But if you want a partner, work at a law firm. But she had to be a lawyer herself. Hey," she looked him up and down again. "How did you two meet?"

There was a high, cracked shriek, and Justine came running out. "Consuela!" Carol screamed, and the child trotted out of the kitchen; Carol sighed and went back into the bedroom.

"What happened?" he asked, standing up.

"You don't want to know," Justine said darkly, next to him.

That was definitely true. She then surprised him with a very wet, open kiss and a lovely squeeze on his rear end. "They'll be a while," she said, softly massaging the backs of his thighs.

"Not that long," he said, but they continued to kiss with ardor beneath the blinding track lights. He adored her.

In the restaurant, Carol immediately began a scene.

"We specifically asked for that table," she said imperiously, pointing to where a nice family was minding their own business, eating dinner. "Where's Lorenzo?"

They stood by the door waiting for the magical Lorenzo to make the nice family disappear. He hated people like this. Just sit down and eat the fucking dinner. Lorenzo apologized for the gross miscarriage of justice. Carol agreed to sit, for now, in the back, but only because her mother was so frail; she said this next to Miriam, who showed no signs of hearing it. They sat in the back, primed to leave. He didn't like Carol at all. He wasn't sure what to do about it.

Justine's stepfather, Gene Dunlap, arrived, looking the way Justine had described him: a portly cigar smoker who'd stopped talking several years earlier. Gene shook Barry's hand lamely, and quietly ordered a Gibson.

"We're not sitting here," Carol announced to him loudly, and the surrounding tables again listened to their plight. Lorenzo summoned them, and everyone watched as they made slow progress—Miriam was the leader of the pack—to the front, where the good people were.

When they were settled, people they knew arrived. There were kisses and pleasantries. "Do you know my daughter, Justine?"

"No, but we've heard so much about you," a woman with ink black hair and white lipstick enthused. "Howayadolling."

"And THIS . . ." Carol proclaimed, with import, "is Barry Cantor." They looked him over and nodded approvingly. When the couple pushed on, Miriam said loudly, "She looks disgusting."

"Can you believe that hair?" Carol agreed.

"She's got three grown daughters—how dare she wear long hair."

Carol was pleased and alert. "And BLACK! Ridiculous." She began grousing about the service. Justine seemed in acute discomfort.

"Well, if they never come, Justine can feed us all," he said. "She's got a chicken in her pocketbook."

"Wise guy," Justine said, with some affection.

"What," Carol said, eager to get in on the joke.

"And ratatouille, in a special Ziploc bag, and she'll heat it up for you, right there, in her purse."

"You want her to cook?" Carol looked at him sharply, with disapproval. There was something very strange about Carol's eyes. He'd be having mother-in-law problems.

"I hear you have horses," he said to Gene.

"Mm," Gene said, a wet, unlit cigar in his mouth.

Okay. So Barry turned to Miriam. "I hear you did Florida."

"Uch. Years ago," Nana said eagerly. She was suddenly stroking his wrist with soft, slippery fingers. He wanted to flee. "Awful. Beautiful weather, of course. But I couldn't stand it." He felt bad for her, but very disgusted. "All those alta cockers in Bermudas with their ugly veiny legs stickin' out. So I came back, but everybody here had moved there. Or died."

"My mother is considering Florida," he said, picking up his glass to shed her hand. He was a coward. "I think she's crazy."

Miriam piped up again. "Listen: Leona Klein found a fella."

"Mother, Charlie died four months ago," Carol snapped. "You're getting senile."

"I am TELLING you! A fella she went to high school with. He read her husband's obituary, and came to the funeral. They've been seeing each other ever since. They're living together."

"Huh," Carol said. "Well, I never heard of that."

"That sort of thing always happened to her," Miriam said jealously. "Always in the right place, at the right time."

"Maybe you should print Lou's obituary again," he suggested.

Miriam and Justine laughed. Carol didn't think it was so funny. Salads arrived; Carol immediately sent hers back because there was something insurmountably wrong with it.

Justine said, "Did I tell you Barry works in Tarrytown?"

"You didn't tell me anything about him," Carol said, with pursed lips. "And you're so touchy I'm afraid to ask him anything, now that he's here."

"Oh, ask me, ask me." He smiled at Carol.

He was expecting another meteor from left field, like "Is he married," but he was even more shocked when she leaned in and whispered, "How do you tell a WASP?" She began to giggle.

"Mother," Justine warned.

Carol was laughing so hard now she couldn't speak. "He's the one," she managed, "who steps . . . out of the shower . . . to . . ." She collapsed in laughter. Miriam and Gene chewed, not looking at her.

Justine said sharply, "If you can't say it, then you shouldn't tell the joke."

"Urinate!" she said, as the waiter placed a new salad in front of her. "OK, Teenie? Urinate!"

Gene continued to crunch slowly through his salad, almost as if he were watching the dinner with the sound off.

"And why are you telling that at the table," Justine accused.

Carol fixed her weird green eyes on him. "Do you have brothers or sisters?"

"One sister," he said. "She's an artist."

Carol smiled. "That's nice for a girl."

There was a noise from Justine that made him laugh.

After the good-byes, Barry and Justine walked up First Avenue. She sighed. "Well. There they are."

"They love you," he said, putting his arm around her.

"Listen: if ever I get like that, just shoot me, okay?"

"Well, I don't think she'll be playing The Sands anytime soon," he said, wondering if Carol was merely embarrassing or actually psychotic.

"Just shoot me, okay?"

He took her hand and put it in his pocket. "Miriam slept with Herman on the first date?"

"I don't even want to think about it," Justine shivered.

He'd slept with Justine on the first date. Of course, it hadn't killed him.

☢

Intimate Apparel

Justine, Nicky, and Mitch spent seven frenzied days on Galsworthy-Fitzsimmons damage control. Justine went to Delaware for the injunction hearing and then joined Mitch and Nicky in Richmond to work out a strictly worded asset deal for a lower price. At 2 A.M. the eighth day, they received verbal agreement from the stockholders' counsel that the new deal would avert the suit.

The following morning, Justine lay on her side, waking up slowly in the cold blue light. The dog stretched, padded over, and put her paws on the edge of the bed. Justine played with Stella's ears a while. There was a key in the lock. The dog ran out, barking.

"Who is it!" she called, tense, furious, and afraid.

"Muffin! Sh, down, Stella. It's only me."

This had to stop. Barry had gone half an hour ago, but what if he hadn't? Carol marched in in a black mink coat.

"I wanted to make sure that I caught you."

"You caught me," Justine said, and lay back down.

"Check it out," Carol said, unveiling a black denim suit slashed in all directions by gold zippers. "I saw this, and I thought of you!" She tossed it on the blanket over Justine's legs, took off her coat, and sat on the sofa, waiting. She looked garish and overdone this early in the day. "Well, try it on."

"I don't like you coming in here in the morning."

"When else are you available?" Carol removed a container of coffee from a brown bag and said slyly, "Should I have brought it to the office?" She carefully peeled the lid off.

The cold zippers cut into her naked stomach, and it was hard to breathe. It was something the 19-year-old companion of a Greek shipping magnate might wear to draw up a prenuptial. "I couldn't possibly wear this."

Carol was offended. "Why not? You look gorgeous."

"Too flashy." It was an outfit Alma would love.

"So?" Her mother took a swallow of coffee. "You might meet someone who would take interest in you."

"It's hard to believe that we're even slightly related."

"Look, I got it wholesale, and I can't return it."

Justine took the skirt off. "Carol. Don't buy me things you can't return. Don't come here at 8 in the morning."

"Thank you Mommy for the lovely gift," Carol said, miffed.

"Thank you Mommy for the lovely gift." It would hang in the back of her closet like a reproach.

"Okay, I'll get out of your hair," her mother chirped.

Justine went into the bathroom and shut the door. Then she felt bad. Why would she shut the door on her mother. Did her mother think she wasn't saying good-bye? When she finished peeing, she opened the door. Carol emerged from the closet fuming.

"You're walking around in schmattes! Looking old and dowdy."

Justine looked at her pouchy face in the mirror. Had Carol seen his shirts in the closet? She agreed to go shopping at lunch.

"Why don't you take the suit," Justine suggested. "It would look great on you."

"Oh no: it's WAY too big on me," her mother said.

After spending the morning setting up a tax-free corporation for a drug rehab center (pro bono work for one of Roberta's causes), she read Nicky's work, translated Mitch's into English, dropped time sheets on Bob's desk, and went to the ladies' room. She bumped into Harriet, who was coming out of the lounge with a tweedy impression on her cheek. They exchanged a wordless glance of mutual incomprehension.

While Nicky drafted the credit agreement, Justine met her mother at Bloomingdale's. They found a black suit and a beige dress, and moved on to Intimate Apparel. Justine took ten pairs of white underpants into the dressing room. Carol followed her in. The mink coat took up half the room.

Her mother watched her calmly from the mirror. Justine left her jacket on and tried on the underpants over her panty hose. "So?" Carol's eyes were shining and she was bursting.

"Things are good," Justine said, stepping out of the underpants. It was cramped, and she was hot. The hell with her mother. She peeled off her panty hose and underpants, and tried them on again. They fit.

"Yeah?" Carol nodded eagerly, waiting for more. "And?"

Justine put on another pair. They fit. "And what."

"Oh, Teenie! Come on! You haven't introduced me to a guy in five years. This must be serious. How often do you see him?"

"Well, you know my schedule. Hardly ever."

"Men have needs," her mother twittered, and Justine cringed as she put her foot through another leg hole. Carol always seemed to be speaking to her from the mirror in a ladies' locker room during a country club dance in 1960. "Oh, TELL me," Carol begged, as she applied a smile of Burgundy Bonanza.

"No." She couldn't avoid her rear end in the three-way mirror. Whatever. This was who she was. This was what she weighed.

"Oh, come on," Carol said impatiently. "We're adults here. Miriam tells me all about her sex life and I don't want to hear it. You, I want to hear."

And who else wanted to hear this in the next fitting room? "I don't want to hear about hers, I don't want to hear about yours, and I'm not telling you about mine." She dropped a nightgown on her mother's lap. "That I'm taking."

"You've gotta be kidding," Carol said with disgust. "You finally got a man and you're buying plaid flannel? I never heard of such nonsense."

"If he wants to see me, he can take it off."

"Here," Carol said, waving a tiny white silk camisole at her like a handkerchief. "Try this on."

"Sorry." Her mother thought she needed this to get Barry excited.

This was probably the sort of thing she wore to get Gene excited. Did Gene even have the equipment? "And by the way," she said, "you may not barge into my home whenever it suits you."

"Oh, well I knew he wasn't going to be there."

"How."

"Because I talked to you last night at 10 from the office."

"Oh, really. So you knew."

Carol's face drained. "I would never have come over if I thought he was there!" She put a hand on Justine's arm, astonished. "You have to know that. How embarrassing—was he—"

"That's. Not. The Point. Go." She pushed her mother out of the room. While she yanked on her panty hose, she saw the black mink hair through the down-slanting louvers of the door, waiting. This made her hot. When she emerged, her mother's face lit up. Carol trailed behind, rocking racks of bras with the coat.

"Darling, I think you have to grow your hair," she announced to the world. All sorts of people looked up. "Men don't like short hair."

Justine dropped everything on the counter. "Which men?" If she was a serious person, what was she doing here anyway?

"It's true—think how stunning this little number would look with your hair long," Carol said, shaking the camisole. "I'm not saying to the waist, just to here," she said, her hand grazing Justine's collarbone. Justine flinched and turned her head.

Her mother's eyes flashed. "What's the matter with you?"

"Mother. Stop making a scene."

"I'm making a scene? I am?"

"Sh!"

A saleswoman arrived and opened up the cash register with a key. She pointed to the underpants. "Is that it?"

"And the flannel nightgown."

Her mother grunted, threw the camisole on the floor, and pivoted away. Justine picked it up, keeping the mink in her sights. What would she do if her mother stormed out—run after her? The hell with her. Carol was flipping through bras in a fury. Hangers were flying. Women were moving away from her. She returned, clicking her tongue and pouting like a teenage actress.

"I bumped into Anne Cray," Justine said, to change the mood.

"Really? How is she—she was always such a winner."

"She's running an abortion clinic in Midtown and spending weekends at a yoga retreat in the Catskills."

"Oh, well," her mother said, unimpressed with Anne's life. She fingered the camisole. "So she became a geek."

"You don't even know what a geek is," Justine said, handing her credit card to the saleswoman. "Anyway, she's married."

"Well, so? You could be married. If I were a man in my 40's, for example, I'd think you were a real peach. I'd want you to come up to my country house for the weekend."

She swung around. "Mother, WHAT is your problem?"

"She's taking this too!" Carol shouted, dropping the camisole over the dirty register recklessly.

"No, I'm not taking that."

"Yes, she is. My treat." Her mother pulled out her credit card with an aggressive smile.

"I'll be with you in a minute," the saleswoman said, slowly shooting a laser at each pair of underpants.

"That doesn't fit," Justine insisted.

"How do you know, you didn't even try it on."

This felt very familiar, all of a sudden. "I don't want it."

"I want you to have it," Carol declared, head up, the coat over her shoulders like a coronation cape.

"I Don't Want It. Thank you." What did she expect, shopping for intimate apparel with her mother? Why did she always agree to this? "Why don't YOU take it?"

Carol waved away the idea, the Gene diamond flashing in the track lights. "I'm just saying," she lowered her voice theatrically. "These young guys. They don't know what they want."

"What are you saying, that *Barry* doesn't know what he wants? Barry isn't that young."

"I didn't say that," Carol said, waving her Visa.

"Barry doesn't have a country house," Justine said, signing the receipt. "Is that it?"

The saleswoman asked, "You want that or not?"

"No," Justine said firmly, and felt guilty. "No thank you."

"Darling," her mother warbled, near tears, "I just want you to fall in love with someone wonderful."

Justine ignored the hand she held out. "Mother. *The EMOTION*." She picked up the bag of underpants and swung out towards the Down escalator. Her mother followed.

At 10, Justine left Mitch to finish his riders on the new asset deal and went home. There was a message from Ilana: Noah Clurman thought Justine would make the most fantastic partner. Could Justine call her very first thing in the morning—there was another matter that she thought might suit Justine.

So Ilana knew about the Whitman Sklar offer. *How?* Ilana was like an aging starlet, brimming with schemes and favors, meticulously groomed. No: Ilana was like Carol with a job. Justine left her door unlocked and jumped into the shower.

When she emerged, Barry was waiting for her on the sofa with Stella. "You look tired, sweetie," she said, dripping on him as she kissed him hello.

He watched her dry herself. "Why are you doing it like that?" He pulled her to him by the legs, and smoothed the towel over her thigh slowly, like a stripteaser.

"Because I was drying my legs, not putting on a show." She went back to the bathroom and put on the big robe.

He followed her. "Why wouldn't you want to turn me on?"

"Are you attracted to me, or do you need a show?"

He looked at her closely. "Why are you always mad at me?"

"Because you always make me mad," she turned. "Yeah, *you*." She went to see if there were any leftovers, wondering what she was mad about.

As she dragged on her panty hose the next morning, she noticed Barry's underpants—dirty—on the floor by the bed. She looked at them. He was long gone. Just shut up and put them in the laundry bag, she thought. No big deal. But that would set a precedent. So she threw them out. Previously, she'd thought: what if it didn't work out with Barry. Now she thought: what if it did?

Kneel

On Thursday night, Vince stopped off at Kiki's after work. He sat on the floor and watched while she tried on outfits and modeled them with the very fluid runway walk he'd seen her use in restaurants.

"I like the velvet pants with the sweater," he offered.

She spun around. "Look, Vince: this is not day care."

He was stunned by her tone.

She was shaking slightly. "I have a date, for Chrissake!"

"Look," he stood up. "This is getting ridiculous."

"I AGREE!" she said with force, tripping over shoes in her path. She opened the front door and he walked through it.

Back at his apartment, he called Pippa and asked her to start cooking for him.

At the end of the week, he went to the proctologist. After 45 minutes in a waiting room overflowing with standing and reclining people, he was sent to an exam room with its own bathroom. An intelligent-looking Philippine woman in hospital green came to give him an enema. For some reason, he was sure she wasn't a nurse, but she wasn't yet a doctor. Maybe a med student.

The doctor arrived ten minutes later. "What do you do?" he asked as he snapped on gloves.

"I'm an investment banker."

"I'm impressed. Kneel."

The irony was lost as the doctor tilted the bench so his rear end was up in the air. Who becomes a proctologist?

When the doctor had gone, the assistant leaned against the counter and asked him a series of astonishing questions. "Any accidents? Cancer in the family?" and a horror settled in his chest. She put his answers in a tiny hand-held computer and then gave him another enema. Nearby, the end of a coiled black hose was dripping black oil on the floor.

"What's that for?"

"This is the camera." She pulled it out to show him. It was a long, thin tube attached to a TV and control board. She swabbed the end of it and slipped out of the room discreetly. The second enema began to take effect. What was this bright young woman doing dispensing enemas and cleaning the camera?

When the doctor returned, they tilted him upside down again. As they stuck the tube in, the assistant patted his backside gently. It wasn't sexual, and it wasn't condescending. It was just a reassuring pat. The doctor was patting him too. That was nice of them. Initially, he watched the TV: it came on in color! It looked like an episode of *Nova*—how pink and cavernous he was inside. But the tube was going up so fast he got dizzy. When he felt it snaking into his intestines, he stopped watching. It was way up there now. They continued to pat him.

After all this, the doctor told him he had hemorrhoids. He recommended the messy over-the-counter stuff that didn't help. The doctor wanted to track stool samples over time—they'd give him a kit to send them through the mail.

He paid his bill shakily, took a taxi home, and got into bed quietly. His intestines shuddered and groaned all night long. He looked at the kit. Send stool samples through the mail?

Chapter 9

Molds

It was like getting on a moving train: Barry now had five new products instead of one. The days were an aerobic whirlwind of back-to-back meetings with International, Quality Control, Operations, Sales, the ad agency, the foreign subsidiaries of the ad agency, the package designer, working till 11 every night.

On Friday night, Barry fought the remains of the St. Patrick's Day traffic to meet Justine at an Italian place near her apartment. When he sat down, he realized with a shock that all he really wanted was to be home alone watching the Knicks.

"I need a new assistant," he said, tearing the bread.

"It's important to be able to work with anyone," Justine said, buttering both sides of her bread in a self-satisfied way.

"The point is, we need excitement, a sense of team."

"The point is to launch a new brand," she said, like a mean teacher. "That's why they call it work, not fun."

"Well, not all of us are being paid enough that we can hate our work and the people we work with and not care," he said, and one of her perfectly sculpted dense black eyebrows shot up.

"What are you saying, that you don't like your work?"

Was Justine just a detail person, mindlessly competent? She'd gone to Harvard. He shouldn't forget that. Interesting: she let him forget that. She wasn't one of those people who never get over having gone to Harvard.

Anyway. "I think the Admiral may be right. Americans don't want to take the responsibility for eating candy. And they don't like food that's good for them. They want crap that they can *pretend* is health food. They don't care if you know. Just don't remind them. Rheinecker's even more cynical than I am. Candy, masquerading as health food. Like Disney."

"I love Disney."

She also had lousy taste in music, and sang along with the cheesiest, most irritating pop songs on the radio. When the pasta arrived, they actually had an argument about the capital gains tax.

They were back at her apartment early. He read the Churchill biography. She knitted. What was she thinking about? To just sit and make knots in yarn—what a waste of time.

"I think you should read this book."

"Put it on my night table, I'll get to it."

"No you won't." Even Vince read.

"Oh, give me a break, Barry. I'm wiped out."

"You should take that job at Whitman Sklar. The hours couldn't possibly be worse than what you have now."

"I'd be taking a huge pay cut."

"How much?"

"Forty thousand. The combination of salary and bonus would only be 140 a year. I could get them to 145, clearly—"

"Wait a minute. You make $180,000 a year?"

He had known, of course, but somehow to have a number

attached to it: he was flabbergasted. Even if she took the pay cut and he got his raise—the acid indigestion was overwhelming. Justine looked like she wanted to be smug, but was holding back.

"I don't think we should talk about this anymore," he said.

They got dressed to walk the dog. On 78th Street, they crossed to avoid a man sifting through bags of garbage. Stella lunged towards a sheepdog. Justine yanked the leash.

"She just wants to make friends. Why won't you let her?"

"Because I am not interested in that mangy dog," she said, like an uptight librarian. "Or its excrement."

"You can't stop her from yearning," he said, thinking she'd be a real strict mom, and not liking the idea. They turned to go back. Now garbage was scattered all over the sidewalk. The dog browsed through the trash and Justine yanked her away roughly.

"Those filthy people."

"You can't blame him."

"Yes, I can. The garbage was in bags, and now it's on the street," she said, self-righteously. "He did it, I blame him."

"He's eating out of the garbage. He's at the very nadir of his life," he whispered. "Have some sympathy."

"Oh, I don't hold him responsible for his terrible, dysfunctional family. The incest, the alcoholic father, the beatings he got in prison," she raved. "Just the garbage."

"You're a hard woman."

"Why? If he isn't responsible, then he shouldn't be walking around. He should be in a facility where he's taken care of."

"You don't care about him, you just want the street clean."

"Yes, I do—but that doesn't mean I don't care. I have my causes. I read to the blind. I do pro bono work all the time."

He really hated her at that moment.

"I think you think you're more liberal than you really are."

When did she read to the blind. "Well, I'm more liberal than you want me to be."

"What do I care how liberal you are?" she said, her brown eyes gleaming, the president of the Williams Young Republicans, ready to debate. "No: this is you. It's like that book. You're worried that you don't read enough. And so I should read more, my heart should bleed more."

While she called her office, he read the sports section and stayed out of her way. He was reminded of a day he'd spent in Larchmont with his friend Jacob and his wife, Lucy. They each carried on separate, simultaneous conversations with Barry, between picking up Lego pieces and washing bottles, while their children caromed off the walls and the cat licked his balls on top of the armoire. They ignored each other carefully, like people in a hot climate without air-conditioning. And this noncombative indifference was the best marriage he'd seen among his friends. Justine turned off her light and got into a sleeping position.

If he didn't do something immediately, she'd fall asleep before his very eyes. Very slowly, he ran his hand over her rump.

"Stop," she said resentfully.

What was the point of having a girlfriend if he never got to see her, and when he did he couldn't shtup her? "Please."

She sat up on an elbow. "You know, before you met me, Barry, you hadn't had sex in over a year," she said, sounding crass.

"So?"

She heaved herself out of bed and stalked to the bathroom. "So, even if we had sex once a month," she called, "it would still be a serious net gain for you." She came back and sat on the bed with her back to him, with a strange white thing in her cupped hand.

For a moment, he deluded himself that this was some new kind of contraceptive. He put his chin in the curve of her neck, and peeked over her shoulder. "What's that?"

"Bleaching molds." She inserted the enormous white thing into her mouth, and turned around smiling like a monkey.

It was horrifying. "You look like an experiment! Take it out!"

She popped it out of her mouth, and poured a clear, ammonia-smelling liquid into the recesses. "Look. If you're going to sleep in my bed, and go spelunking in my body, you can damn well know that I'm bleaching my teeth. Occasionally, when I remember."

"Please, your teeth are beautiful." He hugged her from behind while she fiddled with the things. "White. Like pearls of the sea!" She ignored him. "Don't do it! Don't put them on!"

She put them on again.

"Take them off."

She shook her head.

He tried to take them from her mouth, but it was like wrestling with Stella when she'd found food on the street. Her fists were pushing against his chest. He grabbed her hands, and pinned them back. She planted her feet in his ribs and she shoved, knocking him clear across the bed. He hit his head on the closet door on his way down to the ground.

She spat out the molds and stood up, her face red with fury. "Get out of here."

He explored the back of his head in the cab home: a lump was forming.

He thought having a girlfriend would solve his problems?

List

At the Practicing Law Institute Conference at the Santa Fe Radisson, Justine spent an afternoon in a seminar on the "T Plus Three" trading rules. During refreshment breaks it became evident that everyone was married, and most of them were on something: Covey Technique, Pritikin, tinctures, Total Quality Management. Justine feigned fascination. On day two, Roberta would present "The Implications of GATT for Cross-Border Mergers," for which Justine had done the research. They would spend the entire weekend with name tags on. She did this at least twice a year and it had never struck her as absurd until now.

Justine sat on a sofa and read gossip in the *American Lawyer* while Andes highlands music washed over the lobby lounge and people pointed at carved wooden coyotes in the glass cases and screamed, "*We have to have it!*" Barry hadn't called since the fight. Just because this had started didn't mean it had to continue.

"If I see one more turquoise necklace I am going to throw up," Roberta bellowed as she sat down next to Justine. She'd spent the day in the spa. Justine wished she'd done the same. When she was a partner, she could do that sort of thing.

"You look fabulous," Justine said.

"I have been waxed," Roberta cooed. "I have been bleached. I have had my hair conditioned, shaped, colored, blown-dry, and moussed into place. Check out the nails," she waved at Justine. "Also the toes. My face was steamed, squeezed, and moisturized. I am moist!" she shouted, smiling at passing men. "Notice also how the bag matches the shoes, and how I've got both earrings on at the same time."

"You look stunning."

"This . . . is as good as it gets," Roberta sang resentfully. "So all I want to know now is . . . who do I have to fuck to get fucked around here!" She was wearing her name tag on her crotch.

"Maybe there'll be someone at our table tonight," Justine said, realizing how ridiculous that sounded, how deluded and pathetic. This could be the rest of her life.

Justine called in for her messages before the dinner. Barry had called. About time. She quickly called him back. "Mr. Cantor," she began.

"Ms. Schiff," he responded. "I would like to make an appointment to talk to you."

"Okay! Have your girl call my boy."

They made a date.

· · ·

Justine arrived at Barry's and he gave her a businesslike peck on the cheek, as if there had been no fight—or anything else—between them.

"Clark Coleman," someone called.

Pippa was standing in the kitchen with a huge cleaver raised, head down. The table was set for three. What had this girl been doing all day that she didn't have dinner ready?

"Chuck Baxter," he shouted back.

Pippa gave a sly, victorious smile. "Bill Clinton."

"Oh! Brilliant!" he shouted, and they did a high-five in the kitchen. The whole point of having a chef was not having to wait. And they always waited. Justine had a toxic waste dump on her hands.

"Hey, you watch those women comics last night? It was fantastic!" Pippa was skinny and busty and 21 years old—why would Barry mind waiting for dinner?

"Gyno jokes," Barry said with a disdain that Justine took personally.

"Marian Koslowski was hilarious."

"Oh, she is one YOO-gly woman," Barry said with enthusiasm.

"What does that have to do with anything," Justine snapped, and he ignored her. He was swilling his beer, looking at Pippa.

"If it were a guy you'd say he was funny," Pippa said.

"She's a skank. She's a woof." He barked.

"Barry, we have eyes," Pippa stated. "That's just unkind."

Unkind! Why hadn't Justine thought of that? Unkind led to other things she was thinking, like self-elevating, misogynistic, and infantile. But unkind was the kindest of these.

"You have to stop it," Justine said.

"The two of you," he said, belching outrageously. "Bunch of dykes." He strutted to the back of the house. This was contempt:

ignoring her, talking like a truck driver, drinking beer from the bottle, using his cook to make her feel old.

Pippa gave her a wink. It was presumptuous. So was her sitting at the table. Justine would have been perfectly happy to eat out. Of course, then there were restaurant scenes to deal with.

"He says these things, but I don't think he means them," Pippa said, stretching up her skinny white arms. "You can't take him seriously. If I did, I'd have to quit."

"Why don't you?"

"I need the money. And I don't believe he means it."

While the coffee was dripping, Justine pulled Barry aside. "We need to talk."

"Okay, let's go," he said, and walked towards the back hall.

"I am not having this discussion on a bed," she said, low.

His eyes closed and opened. "Okay, well, she'll be done soon."

"No! I have an environmental disaster—"

"All right, all right!" He went into the kitchen. "You'll never believe this, but Justine wants to do the pots."

"I'm almost done." Pippa was washing her face in the sink.

"Go," he said, pushing Pippa out of the kitchen.

Pippa gave Justine a fresh look as she hoisted her ratty backpack on her shoulder and swung out of the apartment, sarcastically calling, "Bye!"

The door slammed. A cook was a good idea when Barry was roving, but it wasn't working now.

There was a lot of air in between them, and a week of not speaking. The sofa was comfortable. She didn't want to fight.

"Wait," he said, and went into the kitchen. He came back with two mugs of coffee. "Shoot," he said.

It was nice that he brought her coffee, and that he knew how she liked it, and that he liked his coffee the same way. It was 9:30. She didn't want to go back to the office. "I missed you."

He grunted. She leaned into him and squeezed his waist. He moaned in pain.

"Careful," he said, and pulled up his shirt. There was a purple-and-yellow bruise the size of a matchbook. "Look what you did."

"I'm sorry," she said, and kissed the bruise and laid her head on his chest. She was comfortable. She forgot why she'd been so mad that night. She forgot why she'd been mad half an hour ago. He began touching her knee, moving up her thigh. He was going to try to take off her clothing. Idiot.

"There are things that we have to discuss," she said, untangling herself, sitting up now. "Let's see."

"You have a list?" He was astounded, outraged. "Let me see that." He snatched the paper out of her hand. "You *typed* it?" He was up on his knees next to her, towering over her. Would this turn into wrestling again?

"Wait," he said. "Did *you* type this, or did Bob?"

"I did! What do you think. Now, let me speak." He settled back down in a normal sitting position. "You can be very funny, but sometimes you cross the line into bad taste."

"I have no defense, Your Honor. I am merely a poor jester, trying to give pleasure to the court—"

"Oh, cut the crap. I wanted to shoot you at the movies."

He nodded as if he were her bored teenage son. As if she had no sense of humor. "Well, what do you want me to say?"

"That you'll behave yourself in public," she said, and added, "and keep the misogyny to yourself when you're with me."

"Misogyny! I worship the fucking ground you walk on, bitch."

"Listen to yourself."

"What?" he shouted, hands out. He swiped the list from her hand, holding it high when she tried to get it back. He read: "Two. Phone calls." He looked up. "I can't call you?"

"No, but you have to understand that when I'm at the office, my time is not my own. You can't make me feel guilty."

"No, but I can try."

"Stop trying."

"Fuck you," he said, his face thick and beefy.

"Language." She wished she had her knitting with her.

"Three," he read. "Frequency." He looked at her as if the word were foreign.

"I have to go," she said, and smoothed up her panty hose.

"Frequency," he said, grabbing her hand and holding his thumb to a point on her wrist.

"Ow! What are you doing? Stop it! This is violence!" He dug his thumb in harder. "I am not here to service you!"

He let go her arm. "Is that what it is?"

She found her shoes under the table. "It is when I don't want to and you make me feel like I've violated your warranty."

"I see. Four. Waiters."

She would tell him once and for all. "You want to leave every restaurant with the waiter saying, 'That was the funniest man I ever met.' Why can't we just have dinner? You have to have everyone saying, 'Wow, what a guy.' "

He picked up the newspaper and sat down in the far armchair. He looked at her blankly. She was on a roll, but now wasn't the time to bring up Pippa.

"Okay, I think you can leave now." He pretended to read.

"I'm going, I'm going. You're being infantile."

"Put it in a memo, Justine," he said, taking a swallow of coffee. He looked exactly like his mother.

It was cold in her office. She kept her coat on, and went through Mitch's litigation riders, feeling Barry's pique all the way across town. She had been right to bring these things up.

She called him. "You want me to apologize. I will not."

"Neither will I," he said petulantly.

"So the hell with you."

At midnight, she bumped into Dennis Delaney in the stacks of Federal Court Reporters the firm kept for Judgment Day, when Westlaw and Lexis went dark. "Hey, Partner."

"Tell me again why I wanted to do this," he asked wearily.

"Because now you're a grownup," she said brightly. She was looking forward to this. "You don't have to impress anyone."

"That's not true." Dennis smiled in fatigue. Dennis was married. Of course he was. All the nice guys were married by 27, 30 tops.

"Think really carefully before you jump into this," he advised her. "It's all the pressure, plus. I can't very well tell a client, Let me discuss this with the partner and get back to you. I'm the partner! They expect me to know! My matters are the last ones staffed, and I never get someone like you. I get Roxy." Roxy, who'd had a much-discussed fling with the head of Tax. "I might as well do it myself," he grumbled and moved on.

Maybe Roberta was right about Dennis. Maybe he was missing some drive.

No messages

Barry didn't need Justine to remind him that he was a fool. Every time he drove to the gym, he saw a sign that said "Fiedler's Flowers," and remembered sitting next to someone named Fiedler at a wedding, and asking, "Hey, are you related to that bitch on the City Council?"

"That's my wife," the fellow had said dryly.

"When's it due?" he'd once asked a pretty woman on the bus. "Due?"

"Your baby." He'd pointed to her stomach, and the woman's face became congested. He wanted to throw himself off the moving bus. There was always something triggering a mortifying memory. Why did anyone speak to him anymore?

But that was who he was. Deal with it, or get out of town.

He didn't call Justine. Justine didn't call him. Did she count up all the time she spent with him and calculate how much she could have been billing?

On a blustery Thursday morning in late March, Barry bought an extra cup of coffee and went directly in to see Hearne.

"Mr. Fruits and Nuts!" Hearne greeted him with delight and thanked him for the coffee.

"Bro, how much do you make a year as a department head?"

"Don't get me into this," Hearne said and took a sip.

"I was offered ten thousand more." Hearne breathed in, but his expression stayed the same. "Does that come close to you?"

"Closer. Not close. Not in the range."

"That bastard." Barry let out a Carol. "Thinks he can throw me a little bone and I'll perform, like a trained seal."

"It's a huge bone," Hearne said as his phone rang. "He's calling you up to the majors." When he picked up, his smile faded into morose exhaustion. "Look, I'll call you back," he said bitterly, and hung up.

"How's Jean?"

Hearne gave a complicated sigh. He'd moved back with his wife, after a very depressing period during which he'd lived in a brick box across from the KFC in Ossining and hadn't slept.

Barry didn't want to hear about another marriage gone bad. "What should I do?"

"Tell John you want what every other group head gets."

Still in his coat, Barry cruised in to see Rheinecker, whose grapefruit face was shining pink from the Cereal Convention in Palm Springs.

"I run a group. It's a small group, but it's a group. I want to be paid what group heads get paid."

Rheinecker gave him the granite look over the glasses.

"If I'm taking on the responsibility, I should be rewarded accordingly. Ten thousand is nice, but it's not even close."

"We'll talk about this later," Rheinecker said abruptly.

"I mean it, your highness." He cruised out.

"Hello Goodbye" was a classic Paul song: conflict without mess. It was circular, episodic, and ultimately solved nothing. Not for the first time, Barry wondered how he would approach the Natural Snack group if it were his own company. He had too many roots to watch out for at Maplewood Acres.

The first Monday in April, in the depths of the Paramus Mall, Barry sat drinking overboiled coffee with Iris, watching through the one-way window as bus drivers, beeper salesmen, and word-processing temps revealed intimate details about their purchasing habits for $50 and a sandwich. After a series of questions, during which it was determined that most of them watched seven or more hours of TV a day and didn't read a newspaper, they were finally given the product on paper plates.

Six out of ten said they liked it, six out of ten said they'd buy it. Six out of ten said that Fruity Friends and Lizard Licks were stupid names.

"Democracy is so disappointing," Barry said, stretching.

Iris smirked. She had a mole on her neck. He always tried to sit on the other side of her so he didn't have to look at it. He thought she'd been divorced, because there was no mention of a man, but she lived in New Jersey in a house.

The moderator asked about the idea of animals. "You gotta be shittin' me," one refrigerator repairman said, looking directly at Barry through the one-way window. "Snake candy?"

"Look. His wife beat him up last night," Barry said, tapping on the glass. "See how dented he looks?"

"Don't!" gasped the coordinator. "They don't know you're here."

"Like hell they don't," he turned to her. "That guy practically winked at me. I bet he does this once a week."

"Well, I don't know what to tell you," the coordinator said in a high, breathy voice, clearly flustered. "Why are you doing this if you don't believe in the process?"

"He believes in the process when it proves him right," Iris said, and he gave her a courtly nod. Smart cookie, Iris, if a little difficult. On the other hand, Ms. Schiff made Elizabeth II look easy.

"Nobody wants snakes, lizards, gators, or chimps," Iris read from her yellow pad. "For shape, they prefer lozenges, caplets, pillows, or flowers."

"Sounds like the fucking hospital," he said, and she smirked again.

Iris seemed strangely satisfied; Barry wanted to know why. If he could figure out Iris, he might understand Justine. Maybe a bad marriage, the absence of which made her relieved. Well, that couldn't last long. Justine wasn't satisfied. Justine, in her own stationary way, was as restless as he was. He liked that she had an edge. On the other hand, he had marks from Justine's edge. Literally.

He got home at 9:30. There were no messages. He wasn't calling her. Pippa's pot roast was waiting in the oven. He sat down and ate without tasting. They should call the candy Cleverettes, and sell them to tired, frustrated grown-ups as a cure for loneliness and low self-esteem.

Somewhere in his closet was a T-shirt that one of the frats came out with his junior year at Dartmouth. It was a drawing of the ideal woman: she was three feet tall, toothless, and had a flat head so you could rest your beer on it while she went to work on you.

Go to your room

Vince had been summoned to his father's office. It was unclear why. The usual faces plus some new ones greeted him with affection, resentment, and awe. Vince looked at the Corot behind the desk while his father spat information at someone on the phone. A scared young man with a Federal Express envelope came in. Andrew ripped it open, glanced through some papers, signed twice, and threw it at the messenger, who left running.

There was tension.

Vince said, "I know what this is about."

Andrew looked at him poker-faced. "*What* is this about."

"You're worried." He tried to sound bright, jokey.

"I never worry." His father stuck a pipe between his teeth.

"You want to know my plans."

"I could care less about your plans."

"Oh." Vince smoothed down his tie.

"Your firm is folding within the next four months," Andrew said, sucking the pipe without lighting it. "Aware of that?"

"Well, I didn't know for sure. How do you know that?"

His father lit a match, made a disgusted face, and waved the question away. He puffed impatiently, making sharp whistling sounds. "Look, what you do is your business," he said, holding the pipe by the bowl. "I just thought you should know."

"So I should probably get out while I can, you mean."

"You're 30 years old. Do what you want. If you don't want to do anything, that's also an option. Plenty people don't."

Vince wished his father would say what he meant. Go to your room. Or something like that. His father said, "I received a call from a Renée Mellentine. Said she was a friend of yours."

"Oh."

"Should I give her a job?"

"No. Absolutely not."

"Well, that's about it," his father said, and stood up.

He called his mother from a pay phone in the lobby. She was at the hairdresser's. He called Pippa. She was out. He bought a pack of Merits from the concession stand in the lobby and lit one, sitting on the cold lip of the fountain in front of the Anspacher Building.

Chapter 10

Sorry

Everything had hit the fan on April 1. Apparently, the Fitzsimmons board had ignored a second suitor—a group with experience turning around troubled chemical companies. The Fitzsimmons shareholders promptly filed a class action suit. Everyone would have the weekend off while the bankers tried to find more cash and the second suitor took advantage of the equal access.

Justine went home exhausted. Her apartment looked empty and alien. The dog was with her mother. Barry hadn't called. The Churchill book was on the night table. She leafed through it, looking at the pictures. She should read more, he was right.

When she woke up, it was 6:30. She listened to the news, showered, shaved her legs, bleached her mustache, and tweezed her eyebrows. She heated soup and turned on *The Sound of Music*.

Julie Andrews, as Maria, was running down a leafy lane, swinging her guitar case, singing "I Have Confidence in Me." Justine had joined Packer Breebis like Maria had joined the Von Trapp household, kicking up her heels and swinging her guitar. She'd be leaving soon like Eleanor Parker, the Baroness: older, world-weary, used-up. Was Packer Breebis the convent? Was Barry Cantor Baron Von Trapp? How many times had she seen this movie?

She did a row of purl. The list was a tactical error. She saw that. It had been two weeks. She missed his noise. It was 7:45. She could be there in twenty minutes.

His doorman let her up without checking. As she waited in front of his door, she suddenly felt nervous. It hadn't even occurred to her that he might not be alone. She barely knew him.

Barry opened the door. He was in his movie star bathrobe, holding a glass of milk, looking amused and in no way surprised to see her. She felt a rush of relief.

"I meant everything I said and more," she warned.

"Care for a glass of milk?" he asked, stepping aside.

"Yes." He walked into the kitchen as she tossed her coat on the couch.

"Shot of cream, or straight up?" he called, his back to her.

"Oh, whatever," she said, and grabbed him from behind.

He turned around, and gave her a long kiss. She leaned into him—he was a handsome man. Better yet: he was handsome to her, but probably not to most women. It was so important now that she be with him, and in a regular way. Was this biological, or was he really right for her?

He'd been reading comic books in bed. She probably wouldn't have to worry about him philandering later in life. He was so awkward, so magnificent, so amusing. She had such an uncomplicated sensation of desire. If she could just stop him from talking, she could reach this state sooner and more often.

After a particularly sweaty and intense bout of sex, he turned to her and said, "While you still like me again, I think you should meet my father."

"Okay, set it up."

"Do I get to meet your father?"

She was exhausted by the very idea. "I suppose you'll have to."

The phone rang. Barry picked it up. He gave her a look and hand-ed her the receiver.

It was Driggs. "I need you to come in."

She remained calm. "How did you get this number?"

"I have friends in low places," he said, presumably referring to Bob. "But you should always have your cell phone on. I have a mat-ter for your attention—"

"I have several other things that are active right now," she inter-rupted, before he could dump it in her lap.

"I can tell, by the way you're burning the midnight oil."

She was among the five top-billing associates again this quarter. She didn't have to take this. "I'm terribly sorry," she said, doing her best impression of Ilana, "but if you need to staff this now you'll have to find someone else."

Driggs hung up without saying good-bye. Barry looked at her. "Is there a problem when you say no?"

"Not if you're legitimately busy and can show it."

"If you say no often enough, will they stop calling you?"

"No. They just want to get the thing staffed, so if you say no once, they immediately call you on the next thing, thinking, How could she say no to me again?"

"So he'll call you with something tomorrow."

"Probably," she yawned.

When she awakened the next morning at 7, his back was to her and she turned over and settled in behind him, and began breathing with him. It felt like she had achieved, after a long period of real difficul-ty, a state that was ultimately not very complicated at all, as if she were sitting on a porch swing, swaying lightly, dressed correctly for a cool September evening. She could push off at any time. She fell asleep again pressed up against him.

Wife, mistress

Things were very different in Barry's bathroom. There had been an explosion of personal-care products, Plexiglas organizers, and cotton pads. Of course, Justine had at least three sets of everything, so the fact that she'd arrived with a suitcase on a Saturday night probably didn't mean much. She'd taken over Karen's old room, unpacking in a swirl of cleaner's plastic. He read the Nielsens for dried fruit, staying out of her way.

"Let's take a bath," she said, taking off her shirt. She was walking around naked all the time now. The cellulite wasn't too bad, but then again, Cynthia had set the standard, with the most massive, hunking clumps of cottage cheese he'd ever seen.

She was exuberant about his tub. "For this alone I'd move here," she said, up to her neck in bubbles. "Not that you asked."

He pulled her forward and lowered himself in behind her. Water sloshed over the side.

"Baba," she said, after they got settled.

"Jujube." He lay motionless, exhausted, his legs too hot and his chest too cold. "What about the dog?"

"My mother has the dog until Tuesday."

"Does that mean sleepovers tonight and tomorrow?"

"Why not?"

"Because you know I love Stella," he told the back of her head. "She could stay here. No problem. Pippa could walk her."

"Pippa," she said darkly, and he laughed. An argument they were avoiding.

"Tell me the truth," he said, the tops of his wet arms cooling in the air. "It's the tub, right?"

"Oh, no, sweetness, it's you," she said.

But he'd been kidding. He felt cold. She turned around and kissed him flush on the mouth. Would he ever kiss her and not feel like she was about to leave? And yet, he was going to be seeing her every night until Tuesday. What more did he want?

On Wednesday morning, he arrived in his office to find a group of people looking at the six-foot display stand he'd ordered in the shape of a tree, with snack packs dangling from branches like pieces of fruit. The thing was so quirky, Barry almost kissed someone.

"This is just . . . the cat's pajamas!" he enthused.

"It does say hello," Emily said, circling it cautiously. She'd just returned from a week off to study for the midwife midterms.

"It says, Hello Gorgeous, take me home!" Donna said.

Barry took a pack of nuts off the tree. The packs were long cylinders instead of the usual square pouches. The colors were bright and flat—fuchsia, green, and Tang orange—with black cartoon outlines of leafy vines surrounding a clear window onto the product. The design had the spirit and the exact colors of his favorite bathing suit of all time. He'd worn it and won the Intermediate Medley at Camp Raponda, and afterwards, when he'd made out with Melissa Ravitsky in the canoe shed.

Barry dragged Rheinecker away from his desk to show him.

"Fabulous," Rheinecker said, smiling as he circled the tree, weighing an apricot pack in his hand. Barry had never seen Rheinecker excited about anything. "It's beautiful. Do a focus group with the old package and the revamped old package."

"Why waste that money when we know we love the package?"

"I know, just do it. We need data on sizes and prices too."

Rheinecker continued to throw him. Probably because, unlike

Plast—who measured each new piece of information against his belief in family, white sugar, and God—Rheinecker had no ideology. He didn't go by the book: he went by the numbers.

"What about a collectible canister," Barry suggested off the top of his head. "Same vertical proportions."

Rheinecker brightened. "Great idea!"

Don't look now, but you've got your boss excited. Back in his office, Barry smiled at his tree. Life was looking up.

That night, when he came home, Stella jumped all over him. Justine kissed him ardently. Pippa had dinner ready. The meal was delicious, the conversation light, and afterwards, Justine worked, Pippa did dishes, and he read about dried apricots, the dog panting peacefully at his feet.

He entertained the thought of two women: wife, mistress. He wasn't sure what kind of a wife Pippa would be. But he was almost positive Justine would make a fantastic mistress, although he wasn't sure why. It had something to do with the Republican thing. Certain areas remained forbidden—she'd probably get a big charge out of being naughty.

Still, what would she do as a mistress that she wasn't doing now, as a girlfriend, or later, as a wife? Anal sex? He wasn't even sure he wanted anal sex. And with regular sex, she wanted it when she wanted it, and when she didn't, she wanted him in a different state.

This depressed him. Soon he'd be 35, out of his prime, and raising children, which was such a noisy, messy, thankless thing, and then deteriorating into middle age, forgetting his glasses, succumbing to bone loss, prostate problems, and bad smells.

There was always Pippa. He went into the kitchen for another cup of coffee. She was doing pots and pans with rubber gloves. Her hair was greasy, her face was broken out, and she smelled like Brillo. He went back to the dried apricots, depressed further. When you can't

even get a kick out of the idea of having an affair—Lord! He was getting old. Doors were closing.

He looked over at the ever-focused Justine. "Maybe we should live
overseas."

"Eh."

"What about a vacation."

She looked up, intrigued. "Okay, where."

"Morocco!"

"Forget about it."

"China?"

"Barry."

"You know, getting you to do anything is like pulling monkeys
out of a corner."

She ignored this.

They went to sleep without touching, and he was outraged the
next morning to find himself singing "Edelweiss" while rounding
the Riverdale curves on the Henry Hudson Parkway.

Thursday, Barry flew to Minneapolis and back to give Caesar With
Bacon a rousing send-off at the sales conference. This was important:
the item that got the best pitch at the conference usually ended up
selling off the shelves. Bizarre. You'd think you couldn't bullshit a
bullshitter. But no: these sales guys, they wanted to be sold. Barry's
Roman parody got a few laughs, but it didn't bring the house down
the way it should have, the way "The Raspberry Peppercorn Hip Hop
Dancers" had the year before.

Slaymaker patted him on the back in the lobby of the convention
center like a New Age therapist/priest. "No panic, no tears, Barry,"
he soothed, winking at the next guy he wanted to talk to. "The
Fruity Friends will knock 'em dead."

This didn't cheer him.

The last time Barry had seen his father, Ira Cantor had been ranting about "New York Views," a call-in talk show on AM from which he'd been blacklisted for abusive language. This was where Barry came from; he wanted Justine to know it. When his father arrived, he shook Justine's hand, gave Barry a white plastic bag, went directly to the TV, and turned on CNN loud. News rocked the apartment. Nice.

"Dad!" Barry shouted. "You can watch at home. Meet Justine."

"Look in there," his father said, gesturing to the plastic bag. "I got you lager, very special. From the Netherlands, very rare, difficult to find."

Barry took the bag; the bottles clinked. "Thanks, Dad."

"My treat, really." Ira by now looked like a dandelion gone to seed—a gray 'fro on top of a pale, thin, rubbery stalk. Katerina came in like the Lusitania, in a tight jersey outfit that showed her enormous boobs and massive two-part stomach. Her yellow hair was in a turban and she was wearing garish Balkan makeup. What would Justine think of the gold teeth?

"So I hear you live on a boat," Justine said. "A sailboat?"

"Whaddayou, kidding?" Ira started up. "Do I look like a cheapskate to you? Do I? No. I have a 30-foot cabin cruiser."

Katerina made a calm, exhausted, what-can-you-do-with-him face. Dish. This was his father's dish. It was hard to imagine.

Justine asked, "Is that big?"

Ira considered this. "There are bigger. Plenty smaller, though. We have cable. It beats everything." He told a long, pointless story about a rogue boat that sailed downriver without a driver. "There were warnings on the radio. It was coming right at us, fast. Just missed us. By that much. Sailboat, my ass!"

Katerina said, "Strenge, teddible."

If Justine thought they were bizarre, she didn't let on. She asked about fish and boat people. She was really trying.

"Want to see what I've done with the place, Dad?"

Ira ignored him. But Katerina took the tour, her mouth fixed in an impressed expression, stroking the drapes and weighing the tchochkes in her hand. She was probably calculating the price of everything. "Nice, Berry, wery nice." She had a calm, catlike look. "I'd not mind living here."

"Don't even think about it, schnecken."

She laughed uproariously. "I even clean for you," she said jauntily. She had quite a sense of humor. She'd have to, living with Ira, cable or no. Why was he so small-minded about her? This was America. So she was once a cleaning lady.

"How much it cost?"

He sighed, disappointed. "More than I expected."

"But you're okay, not in trouble?"

"No, no trouble," he said, and felt a wave of warmth for her. This woman was married to his father: she thought she was going to have to pay for it.

She pointed to Justine's clothes in the closet. "You merry the girlfriend?"

"I hope so, Katerina."

"Yes. Is no good to live alone."

"It sucks," he agreed.

She became merry again. "It socks, Berry!"

His father's dish was flirting with him. They had a quick and lively volley of Ping-Pong. She was strangely light on her feet for such a big-assed dumpling. Back in the living room, Ira had the TV turned to C-SPAN.

Pippa was spooning soup into bowls. "I watch C-SPAN," she told Ira.

"Ever call in?" She shook her head. "You gotta call in. It's our station. I called in," Ira said, with edgy satisfaction.

Barry had everyone sit down at the table.

Ira continued: "I told that C-SPAN guy: I am sick and tired of our army dealing with the VERMIN in every last CESSPOOL of a third world country. Let them all kill each other—really! Whoever wins is the winner," he said, pouring himself a glass of lager on a tilt. "Let them figure out how to feed their own savages. Why do we have to do it?"

"I completely agree with you," Justine said, smiling slyly.

Barry began his soup. "Wait till he gets going."

"And in this country? When people lock themselves in a house and say they're gonna blow themselves up? I say, GO RIGHT AHEAD: who are we to stop you!"

Justine laughed. She probably wouldn't hold Ira against Barry generally; she'd save him for a big argument.

"Let them KILL THEMSELVES!" Ira shouted, spoon in fist. "Let them kill their CHILDREN. Really! The kids are CARRIERS! Better to kill them now," he nodded. "Save the state a lot of money later."

"Wait till he starts on federal subsidies for boat owners," Barry said, sipping the lager, which was bitter.

Ira turned on the TV again. Shots rang out. "I just have to see this one thing," he insisted, and sat back down and chewed on a bone. A British voice gave facts about Sarajevo. "Historically, the rape in Bosnia is gonna be seen as a good thing," Ira said.

Pippa looked like she might choke.

"They should intermate," he went on, "so the ethnic distinctions are blurred. See, if they're all related to each other, they're not gonna want to kill each other."

"Wanna bet," Barry said.

"You know," Justine offered, when they were brushing their teeth later, "most people have an uncle like that stashed away. Crazy Uncle Ira. For you, it's your father."

Barry got into bed. How was he going to take that? He wasn't proud about Ira, but he'd held his tongue about Carol, after all.

She put cream on her eyelids. "When did he go bankrupt?"

"Look, he's my father. He's not my favorite subject."

"No, no, no," she said quickly, "I'm just curious."

She jumped into bed. "Did I ever tell you the hide-and-seek story?" She stuck her freezing feet between his limbs to warm up. "I was about 8. My father hid, and we looked. My mother and I. We looked, and looked. Looked and looked. Three hours later, we were still looking. Five hours later, he called. From Philadelphia. Now it's funny, but at the time . . ."

They were lying side by side, facing up.

"My father once walked right past me on the street. He didn't recognize me."

"That's nothing," she said. "My mother sucks her thumb."

"I can't believe it! But it makes perfect sense."

"Just wait till you meet my father," she warned.

"Hey! Set it up!" He snuggled in with her and they chatted about nonsense. This was the first time he'd been with a woman where he didn't have an escape plan. He honestly couldn't see it ending.

Nostalgia

Vince's new pad was in a swanky, ice black tower, and the lobby was so immense and austere that every time she'd come here, Pippa felt slovenly. She put on lipstick in the mirrored elevator and pulled up her tights. Surely the doorman was watching her. She gave the camera a regal nod of recognition, like Glenda Jackson gave George Segal from the top of a red London bus in *A Touch of Class*.

Vince was still too good-looking. His apartment looked like an airport lounge. This was her fourth visit and he hadn't paid her yet; tonight she'd have to mention it.

"I've been thinking about applying to this summer architecture program," she told him through the pass-through as she washed vegetables. "It's in Rome."

"Mm," he said, on another planet. "Got any cigarettes?"

"Sure—in my bag."

"Would you bring them to me—I'm zonked."

Lazy little brat. She dried her hands, got the pack, and threw them at him.

"Menthol!" he said, disgusted.

She sliced the fennel vertically. "Look—take it or leave it, that's what I smoke."

"Okay." He lit a cigarette in the dark. She dumped the fennel into a pan with olive oil and shoved it in the oven. "This is like"—he held his breath, and exhaled—"inhaling a lake."

She began reading about menhirs. There was something weird and majestic about a single stone standing alone in a field. It was such a relief to be in classes again, it wasn't funny.

"Every single person in my studio class knew from day one that they wanted to be an architect," she told Vince as they sat down to dinner.

His head was tilted up, as if he were sunbathing. He wasn't eating. "So you think you're too old?"

"No, but I've got a lot of catching up to do."

"Never mind. You'll get out of school, and there won't be any jobs. You'll have plenty of time to develop."

"Thanks. You're really inspiring."

"I'll be out of a job myself soon." He did a cheers parabola with his Scotch, took a big swig, and made a face.

"Oh, I'm so sorry," she said. He hadn't paid her because he didn't have the money. He came from a wealthy family, but he probably didn't have enough to cover it all. "What are you gonna do, or shouldn't I ask?"

"You can ask. I have no idea."

He wouldn't be needing her to cook anymore. They finished dinner in silence.

While the coffee dripped, she washed pans, making a note to pick up some Brillo. But then, she wouldn't be coming again.

He was suddenly alert, shuffling a deck of cards. "Gin?"

"Sure," she said, rinsing the pan, feeling a kind of reprieve. They sat at the table and he dealt out cards.

"I'm smoking again," Vince said, enthusiastic all of a sudden. "I love it! We have to stick together," he said, his hand on her arm, and she wondered why all of a sudden he was trying to be charming with her. "They're passing laws against us."

He slapped down a hand of gin, and poured himself another cup of espresso. "I almost stepped on someone at the ATM today. You know, this city is beyond the control of even God," he said unhappily. "It's so depressing—why do we live here anymore?"

It was late, and she was bored with this conversation. She put on her sneakers and stood. "Um, you owe me for five nights."

"Do you want cash?" He stood up, looking drunk and tired.

"Whatever. I don't take credit cards."

He went into the bedroom and came out counting bills. "I'll have to owe you the last $35."

"Write me a check. I won't cash it till you tell me."

He stood in front of her, looking like a wreck. His eyes shut. "I'm so tired."

"Okay. Don't worry about it."

He put his head on her shoulder. In a moment they were locked in a long hug, which was interesting, because all the strangeness that had built up disappeared.

She slid her jacket off and snuggled in. His body surprised her—he was shorter than she'd expected—not more than an inch or so taller. But his loud breath in her ear made her nostalgic for a time when he was all the way across the room and she didn't know him yet.

He held her away with his hands on her shoulders, looking at her intently. "I can't do this anymore. You have to go."

"Wait. You just started this a minute ago. Now you're kicking me out?"

"Well, if you stay," he whined, "I'll have to get into bed with you and I can't do that!"

"Okay," she said. But nobody moved.

It wasn't like she had a boyfriend or anything. Nothing else was going on. He was gorgeous. She'd liked him once. He seemed interested in her. She put her head on his shoulder and pressed lightly against his stomach. The dishwasher rumbled and sighed.

"This tension is good," he said. "It's forcing me to think."

"Yeah? What are you thinking about?"

"Your breasts."

"You're a tease."

"Don't you think we should stop here," he whispered, eyes closed. "I mean, it would be awkward if things didn't work out."

"Oh, things wouldn't work out."

"I'm glad you agree. Yeah, you gotta go," he said earnestly, but still stood there with his hands on her behind.

It wasn't fair, to be excited and then dismissed. She tried to kiss him, but he jerked his head away. This wasn't flattering.

The hell with him. She walked out, rounded the corner, and poked the elevator button. She didn't want to get involved with him. She didn't want to work for him, but could she afford not to? The elevator was taking forever. You couldn't make a real exit in a New York apartment building. Was she cooking next Tuesday? She went back and rang the bell for clarification.

He opened the door, pulled her in, and pressed her up against the wall. Very soon, they were in bed thrashing around on dark sheets. He didn't kiss her, and he buried his head in her neck when she tried to kiss him. Things went very quickly, and there was no talking. He had condoms right there by the bed. Pretty soon everything stopped. He lay face up, eyes closed.

It was cold. Traffic noises filled the room. He got under the covers and rolled away from her. She wasn't sure what to do. She stood by the window and smoked her last cigarette. There was something menacing about being up so high at night; planes were flying by, and so much was going on—it wasn't restful. In the windows of the building opposite, two naked people were cavorting.

"Holy cow. Vince. Look: one down, two windows over."

"Oh, yeah," he yawned. "Every night. I watch them, they watch me. That's life in Midtown."

Thirty-seven stories high, she heard a garbage truck beeping as it backed up. "I don't like the idea of people watching me."

His eyes were closed. "The light was off."

It was clear he didn't want her sleeping over. She dressed, and kissed his head.

"I'm asleep," he said.

She let herself out. Had she just screwed herself out of a job?

He didn't want to talk

In the morning, Vince found one of Pippa's hairs in his sink and almost threw up.

A low-level depression had settled over Mingus Resnick like smog. Everyone—including Resnick—was trying to get the other foot out the door. Claudia stood in front of his desk.

"I wanted to tell you," she said abruptly. "I got a new job. It's at Parnassus. Way downtown, but the pay's the same."

"Good for you, Claudia." They hadn't discussed it, but he'd assumed she'd be coming with him. But of course, he wasn't going anywhere. "Will you hold my calls?"

He closed the door. He sat at his desk, and felt a warm wave of sleep rising. He fought it. He would do one more letter, and then he could sleep. His stomach was grinding. He lay on the sofa and felt like he'd let himself down. He lay, but didn't sleep, for half an hour, anticipating being startled by a knock.

The phone rang. "I just want to tell you," Pippa said before he had a chance to say hello, "that I think you're great. But it would be a big mistake to continue this and I'm sorry to say this over the phone. You were right in the first place."

"Okay," he laughed, relieved. "Would you still cook for me, though?"

"Well, we'd have to work out a regular schedule. You're a little too informal for me."

"Okay. Come tonight. I owe you money anyway."

"I'm sorry. I have work."

"I've got a lot of reading myself," he said, wondering if he even wanted her over. "We can work together." He never should have started it with Pippa—why was he continuing it?

On his way home, he picked up the new P. D. James and a bottle of Scotch. When Pippa showed up, he was annoyed with her. She knew damn well he couldn't digest corn. And, she brought a can of soup.

"Campbell's?"

"I didn't have time."

"What am I paying you for?

"That's a good question, Vince," she said fast. "And *are* you paying me, that's another good question."

"I can't eat corn."

"Stop whining!" she hissed, very nasty.

The whole idea of Pippa was not having to worry about food. But now he had to worry about Pippa, so what was the difference? What did she want? He smoked one of her menthols. People always expected too much. Why had he insisted on her coming?

He jumped up, alarmed. "You opened the window?"

She didn't look up from her book. "It's spring."

"I have central air." He banged the window shut. "Don't *ever* open the windows. Things fly in and lay eggs in the furniture."

"Oh, come on," she said, still reading.

"And everything gets coated in soot."

He opened the book to the acknowledgments.

Pippa was drawing something, curled up on the sofa in her tights.

"So, are you going to Rome?"

She shrugged, pretending to be deep in her book.

"You must. Maybe I'll go with you." He rose, and sat down next to her feet. "Andiamo."

"Well, I don't know if you're allowed," she said, flustered. "I think you'd have to apply separately."

He took her hand and pulled her to him to give her a hug. She resisted. Her textbook slid onto the floor with a thud.

"I thought we went through this," she said.

"You're just so sweet. I'm allowed to say that, right?"

"I'm not ready for the kind of friendship you want."

"How do you know what I want?" He stood up quickly. It made him dizzy. "I don't know what I want."

She took this in as if he hadn't said it. "Okay. But you still owe me money." She went back to her reading.

He seized his wallet from his jacket pocket. "Here." He shook everything out over the coffee table. "Take it. Really. Take your fucking money."

She scooped up her books and papers, and counted out bills. She'd probably been calculating what he owed her all this time. She stormed out barefoot, carrying her shoes and her jacket, slamming the door. The door bounced back open.

He lunged forward to close the door, and barked his shin on the edge of the coffee table. The glass of Scotch flew off the table and landed on the carpet, splashing over his credit cards and rolling till it hit the wall.

He shut the door. He limped back into the apartment.

He shouldn't call anyone. Not drink too much. Not watch TV. See what happened. He should read something. In Los Angeles, he'd been on a reading jag. Book after book. He'd read on his terrace. Things had gone well there. He sat down with the book.

He didn't want to read!

He ran down the hall; when he turned the corner, Pippa was boarding the elevator.

"Wait!" He threw his arm against the elevator door. It made a loud buckling noise and she gave him a look like he was out of his mind. An attractive woman with dark red lipstick was standing at the back of the elevator. "Hi," he said.

"What." She was making him do it in front of the woman.

"I need to talk to you. Come back in. I'm sorry."

"You can call me tomorrow. I have to work now." She stood back in the elevator and pushed a button. The woman behind her looked at him indifferently. The door shut.

He opened the new Scotch and poured himself a glass, sitting on the sofa and flipping through the channels. He stuck on a talk show for some reason. He was suddenly aware that he was watching The Swamp Thing, from the old neighborhood. The panel topic was people who compulsively mutilate themselves. The man was sitting next to a woman whose eyes looked beaten shut. Her breasts were heavy and uneven—had she hurt herself there? He shivered, and drained the Scotch. His focus was fading.

The Swamp Thing said in a pompous voice with a thick New York accent, "I can't do it unless I know she's listening."

He needed a whole new situation. He had no idea where to find it or how to look.

Chapter 11

St. Regis

In late April, Justine completed a tender offer for a U.S. brokerage firm on behalf of a French bank. She was seeing Barry regularly and the word was out, firm-wide. She was considering a draft of a merchandising contract for Noah Clurman's basketball team when Nicky came in and shut the door.

"I just had a little talk with Driggs," he said, shivering. "It went like this: Lukasch, I'd like you to work on this deal. Well, I'd love to, Driggs, but I'm so busy with three other matters. That's funny, Lukasch, because I was talking to Justine, and—Justine Schiff—and she said that you weren't really contributing. I don't know, Lukasch, I'm sort of out of touch, would you say that's accurate?'"

Driggs got into fights on the golf course. He sat on the boards of all his institutions, and started trouble at every meeting. He sent around memos complaining about coffee filter theft and berated his wife in front of people at cocktail parties.

Justine marched into his office.

"I'm glad you're here, Justine," he said mildly. "I want you to work on this deal."

The fact that he was now using her first name meant that she was on probation.

"I hear you told Nicky that I said he wasn't contributing."

"I never said that." His remaining brown hair lay across his head like strips of bacon. "In fact, Lukasch told me that you haven't been pulling your weight, looking over his work. That he felt exposed, Justine, and had to deal with clients directly since your, uh, romantic involvement."

She looked at Driggs sharply. He had to know that she knew that he was lying. Apparently, he didn't care. He had the upper hand.

"This is a hot new deal—you should be flattered I'm asking you. And you got nothing else going on."

She hated his freckled face. Nothing else going on? The hot new deal was a $10.7 billion stock swap in a three-way merger of public utility companies in Florida. She took the deal and left feeling sick.

"Just wait till you hear this," she said, and gave Nicky the update.

"I'd . . . never . . . ," he said, haltingly. "say that about you."

"Of course not," she said, dialing Amanda McBride, a third-year with a good attitude. "He's a prick and we're never going to work for him again. We'll finish this up one-two-six and get off that liar's list. How's that?"

Amanda came in ready to work. "We're going to be really low-key, and really careful," she told them both in a low voice. "You will not discuss this with, or be overheard discussing this by, anyone at this firm, *especially Ilana*. Don't discuss this with *each other, except over the phone in whispers*," she whispered. "We can't have rumors hitting the market."

They smiled at her, amused. By the end of the day, quietly, they'd secured a $200 million breakup fee and options to all three parties to purchase shares in the others if the deal failed to close. This sort of thing used to set her blood racing. Now she didn't really care. All she wanted was to lie down and sleep for a week.

. . .

On Saturday at noon, Justine left Amanda and Nicky working on the merger agreement, and walked west towards the final parental introduction scene. She felt the familiar mix of chill and sweat, hope and dread. Would her father be heavy, and how heavy. Two years ago he'd put on at least 50 pounds, and he'd sat over his stomach like an upset bear, looking dull, slow, beyond reach. Last year, he was thinner, sharper, stepped up, impatient. The conversation was quick and chancy then, like getting on a bike that was too tall for you.

Barry was sitting on a sofa in the lobby of the St. Regis, people-watching, looking like he was about to tell a joke. "They're late," he said, relaxed and unbothered.

"She probably misplaced what's left of her mind."

"So it'll be a while," he offered.

"It's so tiny," she whispered. "It could be anywhere."

Barry meowed quietly, holding her hand. He had a way of ducking his head and nodding with eyes raised, like a child who'd been laughing so hard he'd begun to cough. Thank God for Barry.

They emerged from the elevator. Alex Schiff was in a powder blue sweater and powder blue corduroy pants. Angelique Schiff was in a pink sweater and pink leggings, with overdone makeup and obscenely swollen lips.

"I've heard only good things." Her father shook Barry's hand.

"From Justine?" Barry exclaimed in mock astonishment.

"Wise guy," Justine said, and they walked into the dining room.

Angelique whispered to her, "Are you having a fight?"

"No," Justine said, already annoyed.

Everyone in the lobby gazed at Angelique for two seconds too long; the bee-stung mouth was a freakish magnet. It didn't seem to prevent her from speaking. Her father found this attractive?

Angelique ordered for her father, and her father talked for Angelique. He was dropping names as if they should be impressed. "I got Jake

Kalman involved," he told Barry, importantly. Involved in what? Who was Jake Kalman? "He told me he'd never do multi-use. Ha!"

Barry nodded diplomatically, pushing eggs onto his toast.

"So I said, Just give me ten minutes of your time. Just ten minutes. Then, if you're still not interested, go your own way, no pressure." Her father thumped the table with his hand. "What do you think happened?"

Barry said, "I don't know—what?"

"I sat him down," Alex said. "I said, Start your watch. So I do my spiel. And after five minutes, he says to me, Stop. I see what you mean. I'm with you all the way. There's no catch."

"Great," Justine said.

Her father held up a finger to her. "So I say, You call yourself a businessman?" he continued, putting Equal in his tea. "There's always a catch! He says to me, Your ten minutes are up!" Angelique burst into laughter. "He's quite a guy, that Jake."

"Yeah," Angelique said knowingly. "Jake's something else."

Justine was on her second bagel with Nova.

"He's his own man," her father elucidated. "You can agree or disagree, but you have to respect him for being his own man."

They were talking about people. They praised these people for being themselves. Who else would they be? Had he always been like this? She was reaching for a third bagel but stopped. They had a child. The man she used to follow around was gone.

Her father was asking Barry questions about marketing. Barry answered him directly, intelligently, without shtick. Barry was so solidly himself she squeezed his thigh.

"So tell me about life in Palm Springs," he asked Angelique.

"My life?" She blushed. "Oh, nothing. I mean, I'm a mom, and I take care of the house and stuff. I shop a lot."

"She shops a lot," her father confirmed.

"I love consumers," Barry said. "Buy many natural snacks?"

"You mean, like, no-pesticide apples?"

"Oh, you are my dream customer! Do you buy at a supermarket or a health-food store? Do you care about artificial sweeteners? What about carob—do you think it's a good-tasting alternative?"

"That's what I love about New York," Angelique said to her in the ladies' room later. "We have such interesting conversations when we come here." Her stepmother traced her bloated lips with a brown pencil. "People in general, but you especially."

The compliment annoyed her. "What do you talk about in LA?"

"Oh, the gym," she said. "What SPF are you using. That kind of stuff." Angelique was wearing brand-new pink gingham sneakers with pink laces, and a pink leather watch. Carol had nothing on Angelique in the matching department. "What a great guy!"

Justine gave a false smile. It was none of her business. Still, he was a great guy.

"So?" Angelique insinuated, fluffing her hair.

She hated this, people cornering her like this. "So what?"

"So, good," Angelique backed off. "I'm glad."

"How's Chloe?" Half sister.

"She's a little doll." She pulled out the photos.

They walked out together. Did people think they were friends, on a double date? Barry and her father were standing outside, apparently getting along fine.

"When do we get you for a real meal?" Alex asked.

"Well, Barry and I have to work," she said firmly.

"We have no idea where to eat." They were standing there in their baby clothes, having just eaten, planning the next meal. Their passivity irked her.

"What about The Stage? We used to race down the Hutchinson River Parkway for pastrami at 10 at night," she told Barry.

"We have him on Dr. Ornish," Angelique whispered.

"And remember when you had to have that specific camera, there was only one place to get it, on 45th Street! And we raced down the Hutch! It was urgent! And the place was closed."

Angelique looked older all of a sudden.

"Well, what about a cultural event then," her father asked, as if he hadn't slammed his hand in the car door when he found out the camera store was closed. "You pick it, Teenie, you know all the things to do around here."

This was New York. Alex Schiff was at a loss for something to do? It wasn't like he'd grown up in Missouri. "Why don't you go to a museum or something," she suggested. "I'd take you, but my time is not my own this weekend."

"I guess that means we go shopping, honey," Angelique said, and smiled sadly.

"I can understand how easy it would be to hate her," Barry said as they walked up Fifth in a light mist. It was almost warm enough to wear just a jacket.

Justine wasn't in the mood to trash her stepmother, or explain how her father used to be different. "Who, Collagen Barbie? I don't hate her."

"You know, as shiksa second wives go, I think your father definitely did better than mine."

A cab slammed into a limo and everyone got out to abuse each other. How could her father spend his time with a woman with a mouth the size of a lemon who needed everything broken down into small pieces and explained several times. How could her mother spend her time with a cigar smoker who never spoke unless addressed directly and then throttled. She must have been suppressing something in order to sustain interest in Barry.

But why was she so cynical? Barry would probably do anything for her. She felt lucky. They walked into the park.

"So we're not going out with them again?"

"Enough! We have lunch, they want dinner. If we had dinner, they'd want breakfast. You met them, they met you: the end."

"Whatever you say, Frosty. But I think he came to see you. He really wants to spend time with you."

"It's a little late in the game."

Justine sat in her office, feeling baffled and overweight. Even the sweet breeze of the central air wasn't helping. They had locked in the three-way stock swap in six days, and they had done most of it over the phone while another group made hostile bids from Chicago. The hostile bidder would be challenging in Delaware Chancery Court, but the deal was done. Even Driggs was pleased.

She wanted to be somewhere else. Was this even worth it? Dennis Delaney told her that between taxes and the capital contribution, his monthly draw as a partner was less than what he made as an eighth-year associate. And he had to hustle to bring in business.

Driggs dropped by and made a big point of looking both ways.

"Partners on this floor don't usually work on weekends, do they," he said smugly, and meandered, not waiting for a response. He'd billed 3,590 hours last year and made sure everyone knew it. His kids were probably better off at the boarding schools he'd shipped them to at the first opportunity.

Justine was on partner track. It was what she planned around, how she measured time, the way she was going to leave her mark on the world. This was a dangerous time to start resenting her work.

Corporate wives

Barry felt a rush of exaltation in his chest on his way to his garage in the morning. The sky was clear, the air was cool but promising.

This was one of those moments when he was excited just to be alive and walking to the garage. The garage! Life was beautiful.

There was a round-robin of focus groups at the Passaic Mall, and Barry spent a morning basking in the glow of approval for the perky new package. He skipped out to his car, and blasted *Let It Be* on the turnpike triumphantly. He could almost hear the sound of people who currently disapproved of him complimenting his judgment and strategy in the very near future; momentum was building. The Founder's Day banquet at the Waldorf was coming up. People at the Acres treated it like the prom. For years he'd had no one to take, and then he'd cringed at the idea of taking Cynthia. He was ashamed about it, but there it was. And then years of nobody again. He'd invited Justine on Tuesday without a second thought.

You could probably make a go of it with anyone. Look at all the arranged marriages through the ages. Look at his history with Cynthia, a woman he really wasn't attracted to. Cynthia was five years of his life—five years of dissonance and guilt—but he honestly couldn't say he was unhappy. You could probably find something nice about anyone, if you had to, and that was probably what most marriages were about.

But he was naturally attracted to Justine—without trying. He was completely engrossed in her, he thought about her constantly, with deep appreciation. That had to mean something. He was afraid to tell her. What if she was just making a go of it?

The bounding B section of "Two of Us," came on, interrupting his fears. These men were alchemists. And everything hung on John, Paul, and George meeting as teenagers and bonding during the dank, sleazy, violent nocturne of Hamburg. You couldn't plan that, or replicate the exquisite confluence of events. It was Destiny.

He felt Destiny with Justine. Was it Destiny for her, or just Company?

. . .

Back at the office, Barry returned a call from Emil Dienst in International. "We have a conflict with the graphics and colors for the Natural Snacks line," Emil said. "There's a very popular German chocolate with these exact colors and similar graphics."

"It's not chocolate."

"It's carob, and it's sold in the snack area. We can't use that design."

"Well, you have your own budget on this—use it. Send me some of those chocolates. I'd like to see them."

Five minutes later, Rheinecker called him. "What was going through your mind? Telling Dienst how to use his budget."

"I merely told him—"

"If you so much as raise an eyebrow at International, I will string you up and hang you from the yardarm."

Well, so much for the era of good feelings. "They don't want me poking into their business? Fine. I won't," he said, throwing his red rubber ball against the wall. "They shouldn't come poking into mine. That's the American design."

"We'll see," his boss said.

Meanwhile, Caesar With Bacon was limping in the Midwest, falling in the Northeast, and dive-bombing in the South. Barry's stewardship was in question. Like an idiot, he hadn't pushed his raise with Rheinecker before the launch; now it was almost a guaranteed no.

The phone was ringing when they got home from dinner that night. It was Karen. Rose had apparently been so irate about an hour-long wait in the doctor's office that she'd gone into a violent rage and had to be sent to the hospital.

"It's blood pressure and chest pains," Karen said quietly.

"Chest pains!" Justine was somewhere, in the bathroom, probably. Barry, speechless, felt a vibration in his own chest.

It was almost 9 when they got to his mother's. Rose answered the door slowly, in a pink bathrobe and slippers, looking like herself, but much worse.

"Well, if you have to get sick," he ventured, kissing her cheek, "the doctor's is the place to do it."

Rose sat down in the armchair with her feet up on the coffee table. Her ankles and insteps were like relief maps, with a network of veins—thick, blue and gnarly, thin, red and wiry. He looked away.

"So what were you at the doctor's for to begin with?"

"My health," she said disgustedly, and picked up a cup of tea in a shaking hand. When had she started shaking?

"I don't blame you for getting mad," Justine said. "Nobody has the right to make you wait an hour."

"There may be another strike," Karen said, carefully, looking thin and translucent. Karen drank too much skim milk.

"A strike, a canceled order, a lost shipment," Rose ranted.

Justine asked, "What happened to the retirement plan."

Rose shrugged slowly, her face thick with irritation. She looked terrible without makeup.

"Why don't you just sell it," he asked.

"Because I've finally figured out how to run it," she said, suddenly loud. "See—people are expensive," she ticked things off on her swollen fingers. "They have salaries, they have medical benefits, they get sick, they use the phone, they steal the scissors and toilet paper. They take up space, they waste time, they make mistakes. They go on strike." Everyone watched Rose as she brought the cup to her pale lips and sipped. "Fire EVERYBODY. That's the answer."

Maybe his parents had more in common than not.

.   .   .

"You should go into the business," Karen said later as they barreled down the FDR. It was a clear, warm, gorgeous night.

"That's right, taken in like the idiot nephew who screws everything up, who they have to take in, because he's family."

"I broke up with Carlos," Karen announced with a random recklessness that sounded just like his father.

"You're kidding!" he said, getting into the slow flow to the Brooklyn Bridge. "When?"

"I'm never gonna meet anybody else," she began to cry. "He's gonna find somebody in two minutes."

"Men always do," Justine said, passing her some Kleenex.

"My own bitter personal experience proves you both wrong."

"I'll be alone for the rest of my life," Karen sobbed.

"You'll meet someone," Justine said, passing her a bottle of Evian. "It may take a while, and it'll be terrible." She was so matter-of-fact, it chilled him. "But there's no other way."

He looked at her sharply. "What?"

"I'm not talking about you," Justine said. "Relax."

There was silence as they trundled across the grooves of the bridge. Karen was holding the bottle and looking out the window waifishly. He just couldn't take it when she did the victim thing. "So get out there. Do something. Take a course."

"I am. It's a seminar at NYU in environmental racism."

Barry took the Cadman Plaza exit. "In what?"

She stared out at Brooklyn. "You wouldn't understand."

"That's for sure," he said, and he put his hand out. Justine took it. In the rearview, he saw Karen recoil. Hey, just because she was miserable didn't mean that they had to be.

On her street, there were broken saints on the dry gray lawns and empty lots of abandoned car parts and garbage. "Why not get out of here," he said, pulling up in front of the decrepit, crusty garage she lived in. "Live like a human being."

"Fuck off," she said, and slammed out. She hadn't thanked him for the ride, or Justine for the water, or said good-bye.

"You could be a little more sympathetic," Justine said. "It's not like you were so happy when you were in her position."

"Are you telling me I'm happy now?"

"Aren't you," she asked, surprised.

Barry pulled over, and put the car in park. He held her hand, and considered the strange little fingers and the thumb that looked like a toe.

"Very," he said, and kissed his intended slowly. He was happy. It wasn't the galloping happiness that bounces around and makes a mess, but the seeping happiness that spreads calmly and doesn't need a full-time caretaker. Part of him wanted to ask her to marry him now. The other part wanted to live through a full year of seasons with her. Just to be sure.

"I'm so glad you were here tonight," he said sincerely, and the whole car was vibrated with the latest bad music as a low-slung car careened by on its way between felonies.

Emily threw something at him as he rounded the corner. It was a pack of German chocolates. He examined it closely.

"Aw, man!" he shouted. "Totally different."

He went down to shmooze with Hearne.

"I never said that," Hearne spat into the phone with quiet fury, waving Barry in. "I'm getting off now. No. I'm hanging up."

Barry looked at his hands. Hearne was a good man. A good man who was trapped in a life he didn't like anymore. Which was more frightening: the idea of never finding a soul mate, or the idea that Hearne thought Jean was IT when he married her?

Hearne wasn't hanging up. Barry mouthed to Hearne that he'd catch him later, and walked back to his office depressed.

Jack Slaymaker arrived, coughing sclerotically. "I hear you're taking on the German brass," he said, clearing phlegm.

"I demand to know your sources!"

"I got a mole at the Turkish consulate." He picked up a pack of the apricots. "I'd love to peddle this. And they'll be lining up around the block for the snack tree, trust me. Fight for it."

At 6 o'clock, on his way to the men's room to clean up before driving to the banquet, Barry saw a frosted blonde in blue sequins lingering in the hall.

"Oh, fudge," she said. It was Kimberly Eberhart, with the new breasts on display, front and center. She was trying to do up her belt, but the two-inch white false nails were in the way. "Would you be a doll and fix this for me?"

He checked out the freckled cleavage on his way down to the belt. She knew it. She wanted people to look. That's why she had them out on a tray.

"You're crippled," he said, doing up the belt without lingering unduly.

"I know, isn't it ridiculous," she laughed, slinking off towards her husband's office.

He'd met Kimberly Eberhart at least three times a year for the past three years, at various company functions, and each time she pretended they'd never met. So she was the CEO's wife; so what? What had she ever done? She wasn't young, she wasn't beautiful, and the teeth, the hair, the nails, and the chest were false.

Justine had never mentioned silicone. Unfortunately, Barry could honestly say that small-breasted women were his type, in that he always ended up with them. In point of fact, the only serious chest he'd ever encountered up close and personal had belonged to Melissa Ravitsky, at Camp Raponda. That really had been his lucky bathing suit. Melissa Ravitsky was twenty-two years ago.

He'd been dating for twenty-two years! *Would it never end?*

· · ·

When Barry arrived at the Waldorf, Rheinecker and Teriakis were standing belly to belly at the bar. There were awkward, hearty hellos. What bullshit: as if they hadn't just seen each other an hour earlier, as if they'd really be hanging out and socializing if they didn't work together.

Barry ended the phony festive tone. "Jack Slaymaker says that he'd break records with our gorgeous new package and tree."

"He's a *salesman*, Cantor." Teriakis rolled his eyes in disgust, lapping up his gin.

"He doesn't bullshit me."

"He's a *brilliant* salesman," Rheinecker insisted. "It's what we pay him for."

"He wouldn't lie to me. We're friends."

Judy Rheinecker joined them, a sturdy, windblown woman who looked like she could fix a drain from under the sink. This was what turned His Lordship on.

"First of all, he's not lying," Rheinecker said. "He's exaggerating. He gets you excited, you give him more promo money. It makes his job easier. And secondly, you're not friends."

Barry saw Justine's sleek black head gliding through the room, and excused himself. He couldn't get to her fast enough.

"I missed you so much last night," she whispered, and his whole body curled in yearning for her.

"Come meet the family," he said, kissing her gratefully, barely noticing the excitement this generated among some randy Sales guys. He started her off with the Plasts; when he returned with her drink, Justine was deep in conversation with Hearne and Rheinecker about fiber optics. Justine was a high-powered shmoozer—why was he surprised?

"Wow," Hearne said, sidling by. "I bet you never thought you'd be glad to be in a plane crash."

"I know, it's weird."

Mary Plast gave him a nosy smile. "So this is serious," she whispered, blushing violently.

Hell—he was blushing himself. He felt as if he were at a 7th grade dance. "Yeah, I think it is," he said, watching his boss in rapt conversation with his girlfriend. Ricki Teriakis and her hair entered in an obscene red dress, and jumped in on their conversation, flirting with Rheinecker and ignoring Justine.

Eberhart and Wife II came by, and Kimberly Eberhart shook Barry's hand with her two-inch talons as if she'd never seen him before, had never met him before, hadn't asked him to dress her an hour ago. She accepted compliments and giggled.

What a bunch of corporate bimbos.

"Kimberly Eberhart is a hood ornament!" Barry said later, when they were gossiping in a speeding taxi.

Justine had her head on his shoulder. "I thought you liked your chicks stacked and shiny," she yawned. He adored her.

"None of those bitches compares to you," he said, proud and out of sorts. "What were you talking about with Rheinecker?"

She put her arms around his waist. "Oh, Jonah Broadbent."

"The Pentagon guy?"

"Former. Now he's doing cargo deals with a client of mine."

"Influence peddler. Ethics violator."

"What's he supposed to do," she asked playfully. "Go to med school?"

"Is that all you talked about? That whole time?"

"Oh, that, fiber optics, what on earth I could possibly see in you. You know, like that."

Justine had no idea how funny she was. How much more time did he need? As they turned on 76th Street, he looked into her eyes. "Do you perceive me more as a John, or a Paul?"

"What?"

"See at the Acres, I'm a John, but deep down, I really think they're wrong, I'm a Paul. I'm cheeky, but I do care."

"Wait. John Rheinecker? What are you talking about?"

He dropped her hand. "What planet did you grow up on?"

The next day, Barry sat in Rheinecker's guest chair. When His Highness got off the phone, Barry was looking at a photo of a flushed teenager on top of a horse. "That's Kelly," Rheinecker said. "She'll be 17 next week. John, Jr. is 14," he pointed to a boy with a lacrosse stick. "And Talbot's 11," he pointed to a healthy child of indeterminate sex in a kayak. His kids were as neatly spaced as his teeth.

"Look," Barry said. "We've already paid for this design. A new design would be just as much."

"We've got the revamped old apricot design."

"You said yes to this design."

Rheinecker shook his head.

"Yes! You did. Do I have to issue minutes to our meetings?"

"I said yes *pending*," Rheinecker said, not really mad.

"Come on: look how elegant, accessible, whimsical, and appetizing this is." Barry held up the pack of nuts. "How could you kill this?"

"You're not such a bad salesman yourself," Rheinecker sighed. "I enjoyed speaking with Ms. Schiff, by the way," he added, looking at him differently. This was annoying in one way, and gratifying in another. Of course, no one at Maplewood Acres would be truly convinced he wasn't gay until he produced children. Children that looked like him.

Back in his office, he looked at his fruit tree with amazement. What would Cantor-Schiff children look like?

Chapter 12

See how they run

Pippa woke up feeling rotten. She made tea, and decided to stop drinking, start exercising, and eliminate things that ate up her time to no purpose. She wasn't going to see Vince again, in any capacity. Vince was bad news.

The phone rang. It was him. "I'm really sorry," he said.

"Yeah, yeah." She poured a bowl of cereal.

"This is just a really bad time," he gave a strained laugh. "Let me take you out tonight."

Well, nothing else was going on. She said yes. Immediately he pissed her off: he didn't want to see the Truffaut movie, which was playing one night only. They went round and round.

"Look," she said finally. "I'm going to the 7:30 show. If you want to come, fine. If not, too bad." She hoped he'd say no.

"Well, if you put it that way. Why don't you pick me up at my place first," he said calmly. "It's more convenient for me."

"Well, it's less convenient for me. I'll meet you there."

She hung up, peeved, and brought her cereal to the table.

Something ran behind the stove. Cheerios and milk went flying. She ran into the living room screaming.

This was ridiculous. She'd just been startled.

Daria in her yellow Indian dress ran in. "What? What?"

"Something just scooted across that wall," she said, walking cautiously into the kitchen and stepping up onto a chair. "I think a mouse."

"Ay! Ay!" Daria jumped up on the other chair. "Where is it?"

They were both up on kitchen chairs, like Ethel and Lucy.

"Daria! I can't believe you got a nose ring!"

"I told you I was going to. Look, you have to deal with this—"

"I'm fine with this. He just surprised me, really." Pippa stepped down off the chair. There was cereal and milk all over the floor. "At home, we just chase them into the yard."

"In New York, that's aiding and abetting. Two to five, minimum."

There was a scrambling noise behind the stove. Daria began whimpering. Pippa shot back into the living room and called the first exterminator listed.

"How's next Thursday?" he asked.

"You've got to be kidding."

There was a loud, rich scream from the kitchen. Daria ran in, emitting a high-pitched exhale, like a steam whistle; a gray rat the size of an adult shoe ran in after her, scrabbling along the baseboards. They watched from the sofa, paralyzed, as it vanished into the front hall closet. Pippa bounded over, slammed the door shut, and bounded back.

Daria let loose a stream of hysterical Italian. Pippa called two more places before AAA Metropolitan Pest Control, who said they'd send someone right over.

Downstairs, they dressed on the hood of a car in the cold, bright street.

"Whatever it costs," Daria said, pulling on a jacket, "we pay it. My mother will foot this bill, no problem."

She'd missed Daria. She wanted to ask her advice about Vince. She wanted to yell at her about Brian. She wanted to spend the day with her shopping downtown. "What's new?"

"Not much," Daria said, as if they'd spoken yesterday. "You?"

Pippa found herself talking about Vince. Daria listened, lacing up her boots. She didn't tell Daria he'd thrown his wallet at her. "Why do you think he wouldn't kiss me?"

"Isn't that the weirdest? A guy is in you up to the hilt and gets flipped out from kissing," Daria said. "What was it like?"

"Well, we only did it, or tried to, once. I'm also theoretically working for him."

"Wait," Daria shook her head, blinking her eyes impatiently. "You had a perfect situation there. No panty hose, good money, neat apartment. You screwed up everything! Why?"

"It just happened," she said. But she wasn't so sure she'd characterize what she'd done as screwing up everything.

Daria made impatient rolling movements with her hands. "Back up. What do you mean tried to do it?"

"Well, I don't think things were really working."

"His things or your things?"

"My things? What do I know if my things are working or not?"

"It takes a long time," Daria said, kind of sadly, but also kind of smugly, brushing her blue-black hair in the sunshine. "I've got anthro ten minutes ago—can you handle this? I'll owe you big." Daria's straight thick long black hair swung side to side as she strode across Broadway against the light.

Pippa hated her, suddenly.

The exterminator arrived in a corroded van. He was fat and red-faced in enormous work boots and big dirty silver gloves.

"I'm Glenn. I do this for a living. You want me to hit your roach-es too?"

"What the hell," she said, wanting him to do a good job.

He strolled through the rooms as if he were thinking of renting the apartment. He shone a light inside the coat closet and assured her there was nothing lurking. "But you got another Hudson River crossing here," he said, showing her a hole in the wall to Benita's room the size of a football. Under the kitchen table he showed her a hole the size of a tennis ball.

"We've been eating here all this time!"

"And these guys've been dancing in and out, right under your nose," he said, blocking the hole up with a box of tea bags. She would throw them out. Everything had to go. She began stuffing food into a garbage bag: cereal, crackers, potato chips.

Glenn took off the gloves and threw a clattering sack on the table. "How's two in each room?" He opened the fridge.

"What are you looking for? Oh, cheese?"

"This'll do," he said cheerfully, opening Benita's peanut butter jar and sticking a dirty red finger inside. He stroked his finger over each trap, smiling to himself. He left to lay the traps, and she followed him. In Benita's room, he pulled an open Entenmann's box from under the bed.

"You're living with fucking geniuses here."

There was a clap, and then a scraping sound coming from the kitchen; he bolted and she followed him. A wild-eyed rat—smaller and darker than the first one—was thrashing around the floor attached to the trap. It was spurting blood, biting its own tail with long, thin, sharp, wet yellow teeth. She cringed on the threshold. Glenn stomped on the head with an enormous work boot.

"Die, muthafucka," he said calmly. There was a whipping noise, and then a liquid crunch. "Dead," he said.

He used Daria's spatula to flip the smashed rat into a black garbage bag. Pippa shivered. He dislodged the rat, and threw the trap on the floor. "Oh my God," she said, as he tossed the spatula into the sink, and stuck his finger in the peanut butter to rebait the trap. The bag sat in a smear of blood.

"Get ready. These guys is never widows or orphans," he said, replacing the trap.

He sprayed the baseboards and inside the cabinets with pesticide from a big tin canister. He stopped everything. "I could use a glass of water," he announced.

"Please, could you just take it out of the apartment?" she asked, pointing to the rat bag. "I'll get you water."

He dropped the bag into a red drum marked Hazardous Waste and took it out to the stairs, leaving tracks of blood and milk in a waffle pattern on the floor. She brought him a glass of water, dripping Pine Sol from the kitchen to the front door on her way. The exterminator drank, watching her.

"Would you just check the front closet again? I don't think the one you trapped was the one I saw before."

"Listen, you're gonna have to deal with it eventually."

"Please."

He opened the door, squatted down, and said, "Holy shit!"

"What!"

He roared with laughter, pulling out an enormous, phallic-look-ing wooden bong, two feet tall. It had to be Brian's. "It's not mine," she said, cringing as he wrapped his mouth around the mouthpiece and pretended to take a hit.

He smiled up at her. "Yeah, right." He rose. "Any rodent hangin' out in here would be too wasted to give you trouble."

"Please, could you just look."

He squatted down and turned on his flashlight. "Holy shit!"

"What!"

"Nothing! Absolutely nothing except your coats."

.   .   .

Pippa called Vermont collect from Barry's. The rumble and whine of pottery wheels behind her mother's voice made her a little homesick.

"Well, if you think you did the right thing, that's what counts," Serena said doubtfully.

"It would have come back, or gone into another apartment. That's aiding and abetting in New York; two to five, minimum."

"You've gotten awfully callous," Serena said. "We've always had mice—"

"You have no idea what I'm talking about," Pippa shouted, surprised at how strong it came out.

"Well, darling, you did kill a living thing."

"No: the exterminator killed a diseased rat with teeth. You sit up there passing judgment—you have no idea. I can't talk to you."

She hung up, furious. Daria's mother wouldn't second-guess her. Anybody in New York would understand. She turned on the radio. On every station, people were shouting at each other. It was too much. She got into Vince's old bed and took a nap.

When she woke up, it was 4:30. She wandered through the rooms, looking out at blue sky, water tanks, the crenelated tops of apartment buildings, white steam drifting from strange chimney tentacles. A blimp glided by overhead. It was spring. Life was sweet. She drank jasmine tea and read about Iranian mud dwellings.

Barry came in. She had never been so glad to see anyone in her life.

He gave her a huge hug. "What's the matter, Peeps?" She wished she were seeing him instead of Vince.

"We have rats." She felt very shaky.

"Yikes! Look, if you want to stay here till you get it sorted out, you're more than welcome."

She wanted to cry. "You're such a nice guy, Barry."

He laughed loud and mighty. Sometimes she really felt that he liked her better than Justine. This made her happy.

"You'll take care of it. Hey, check out my nifty new package," he said, tossing her a pack of nuts. "Stay for dinner. We can go out—whatever you want. Justine isn't coming till 10."

Would she ever have believed both of them would be asking her out to dinner? Not that there was anything to it. "I'm seeing Vince tonight."

"Seeing," he paused, unbuttoning his shirtsleeves.

"Seeing."

He took a deep breath and said, "Young lady—"

"Yes, Dad?"

"You're out of your mind." He looked pissed off.

"Thanks. It's over already." She kind of wanted to tell him.

He slapped the counter. "No fucking way!"

"It was sort of over before it started."

He raised an eyebrow. "How soon before it started?"

Vince was late. A woman in front of Film Forum went into a spasm of loud psychotic ranting. For a moment, the street paused, and considered her. Then everyone on line went back to their business again. Vince showed up and apologized indifferently. Clearly he was late on purpose.

Stolen Kisses was lighter than air. Was she looking for Jean-Pierre Léaud, or did she feel just like him? She glanced over at Vince. He was smelling his fingers. Something had to give. She needed to find someone who was at least slightly more together than she was.

Was it something I said?

Barry sat in the media room apprehensively; Friedkin MacKenna DeFeo were presenting their preliminary animatic. He still hadn't been formally promoted, or appropriately raised.

"We're gonna run through this once without music," Len Lefkowitz said. "And then, forgive me, I'll sing. It's acoustic guitar, but since I don't play, you'll have to imagine it."

Iris started up the VCR. The animation showed a healthy twenty-something woman with roses in her cheeks wearing a plaid shirt and shorts of a chaste length. She climbed up a hillside calling, "Come on, Lucky!" and a golden retriever bounded up after her. She smiled, and patted the dog. She reached the top of a peak in her hiking boots, triumphantly looked down at the wildflowers on the hillside, dropped her knapsack to rest on a rock. Taking a pack of Fruit Breaks (the zany new name, approved by four focus groups) out of her shirt pocket, she chewed radiantly in the sunshine, the dog smiling at her feet. "And then in voice-over, the tag line—'All the sunshine goodness you've come to expect from Maplewood Acres Natural Preserves, in a bite-sized fruit treat. You deserve a Fruit Break.' "

Iris added, " 'Try all the delicious Natural Snacks from Maplewood Acres,' with the group beauty shot."

Iris replayed the tape. Len sang tunelessly, "It's a special kind of morning, it's a special kind of day. You put yourself in all you do, in a very special way . . . Have a Fruit Break, and taste that special goodness, that special sunshine goodness, from Maplewood Acres . . . straight to you!"

"Beautiful, Len," Iris said, kidding around.

"This could be a spot for oatmeal," Barry said. "Or gum, or laxatives, or life insurance."

"It's appropriate for our target," Rheinecker said tersely.

"Our target audience listens to The Stones. This looks like a 4-H bake sale." No one responded. "Look, have you seen this exciting package?" Barry tossed a couple of packs out. "Can't we match that somehow?"

"I like it," Emily ventured, and was universally ignored.

"Do a focus group," his boss said dismissively. "And get me those gross rating point figures for daytime."

"'Please?'" Barry ventured sweetly.

Rheinecker cast back a look like a midnight sky full of thunder-clouds.

The ad people sat around the table like frightened children, col-lectively holding their breath.

The day before his big presentation, Barry sat with his feet up on Hearne's desk. "He's running this like it's a bargain basement!"

"So what," Hearne said impatiently.

"So, I'm starting to feel like Cinderella."

"Look, it's just a snack, and you're just taking it to market. It's not going to solve obesity or cancer. If he thinks you should go with a jam tie-in and keep the old pack, I'm sure he has reasons. He's not new to this, remember?"

Since when was Hearne so impatient? "Oh, holiest of holies, Susie Strudel," Barry said dryly. Hearne was now part of the prob-lem; he probably shouldn't confide in him anymore. "What's new?"

"We're having a retail backlash in the frozen novelty desserts. Don't ask why. I don't know why. How's Justine?"

Justine was the best thing that had ever happened to him. "Fine," Barry smiled, but didn't elaborate.

Rheinecker was on the phone, but waved Barry in when he stopped by for a final chat. He put his hand over the mouthpiece and instructed, "You may show the package and the tree, but emphasize that there will be changes in colors and graphics."

Emily walked in and sat in the second chair.

"Global standardization is beyond ludicrous," Barry said, feeling hot in the face. "It's insanity."

"Do it," Rheinecker said impatiently.

"What do you mean, do it," he said, feeling pissed off and acutely Jewish for some reason.

"Do as I tell you," Rheinecker barked, and Emily shrank from both of them. "Your group is on a short leash."

He wanted to hit the man. "Why? Explain that."

"Because these brands have been dying for years, and it's enough. They're going to have to hold their own."

"Of course they will, with the snazzy new package."

"The foreign subsidiaries are already shelling out for the floorstand and the initial promo. Understand?" Rheinecker said, as if Barry were retarded. "The less we spend, the more we profit?"

"That includes my salary, doesn't it," he said. "Twenty-five percent less across the board, including my salary?"

"That has yet to be decided," Rheinecker said.

"Bullshit," Barry said, and Emily's jaw dropped. "You've already decided. You're micro-managing me and insulting me with this fractional salary so that I'll leave and then you can take credit for the whole fucking thing."

"Watch it, sailor."

"You're the sailor. You've got the boat. All I'm asking for is parity with the other group heads. That's it."

He pivoted and walked out. Emily, meanwhile, was already sitting on Donna's desk, giving her the play by play. "It was like a testosterone demonstration," she enthused.

"Shut up and put the Snack Tree in the fucking conference room," Barry said, and went to the men's room fuming. He was going to go to the mat for this thing.

The following morning, Eberhart started the Council meeting on time even though some seats were empty. Barry sat in his chair on the periphery through three presentations as if he had swallowed a bird. Rheinecker avoided eye contact.

When the time came, Barry did an announcement about the group as a whole, and then gave Emily the floor. She strode up to the podium, cleared her throat, and then delivered, without notes, the entire speech from memory, pausing at the appropriate spots, keeping her hands above her waist. Polished, clean, no nerves, no sweat. Astonishing. When the questions came, they were more related to the group at large, so Barry got up and did his shtick for apricots, apple chips, carob balls, and mixed nuts.

He put on the acetate with the old apricot package and the update side by side.

"Here's the old package and the update, which came in third and second, respectively, in focus groups. And this," he tossed out the new packages to the table, "is what came in first."

He caught something under the surface, some ripple of communication between Rheinecker and Teriakis.

"There must be a way of getting past this impasse. Look at the difference." He held up the German chocolates and the carob pack. No one said anything. "Different size, different category."

"We want a global design for this," Teriakis said. It wasn't even his department.

"Why? Every brand has variations internationally. Why are you holding this one to an abstract standard?"

"Can't you keep the design and just change the colors?" Hearne asked.

Traitor. Barry motioned to Emily to bring out the tree.

"Then we'd have a conflict with Canadian apricots, or French plantains. Look, there's always some kind of variation. If the Germans don't want to pay for their own wrapper, then they can just opt out of the floorstand."

"There's nothing really wrong with the revamped old apricot package," Plast said.

"That earth-tone burlap crap is old. It's been done to death for natural products. Which is probably why these brands have been limping along close to the floor for two decades. Why restage a tired old brand with a tired old look?"

"The Council thinks you can find a way," Teriakis said.

Who was he—The Godfather?

Barry was feeling huffy. Nobody was responding to the tree. "Well, if we change the colors, will the French mind? They can handle a little reality, perhaps?" Emily was standing by the tree, stock-still. "Oh, here's the Maplewood Acres Natural Snack Center; take a look."

There was a hush and a lot of appreciative noises. These people were sheep.

"This is the deluxe version—the supermarket model won't have the auto doorlocks and racing stripes, but you get the idea. The fruit hangs from the tree."

"I doubt the foreign offices will go for a floorstand," Rheinecker said.

"Then the Germans can spend the extra five bucks to have the colors on their package changed."

"Will somebody please tell me what is the big deal about this package?" Eberhart demanded.

"The big deal is that I was told to restage this group. Package People outdid themselves with this brilliant, gorgeous design, and this committee wants to trash it for something that looks like last week's oatmeal, all because the Germans are too cheap to change the colors on their pack."

Eberhart turned to Emily. "What do you think about the package?"

Why was he asking her?

"I like it," she said lightly. "But the revamped old package isn't a tragedy. The floorstand will throw everything into relief and make rows of anything look good."

"You give me a group to run and then you don't let me run it," Barry said, beyond angry now. "This committee routinely sucks all the life out of everything I propose."

"Now, Cantor," Eberhart said.

"And this is candy—fool yourselves if you want to, but this thing is about as all natural as your wife's new chest, sir."

There was a weird moment when everyone looked at him blankly and then looked down. Had he said that?

Eberhart looked up. "What?"

He felt like he was playing stadium tennis and had just flung his racket across the net. "I'm sorry. That was out of line. I'm just saying, this candy—"

"Step out," Teriakis said. "Apologize and step out."

"For what? I am trying to run this group, and all I get is second guesses, and impossible standards. You aren't even listening." He deliberately avoided looking at Hearne.

"We're listening now," Eberhart said dryly. "You have my undivided attention. What is it?"

"This is the best package I've seen in a long time." As he said this, he realized he had lost his job.

"That's it?" Eberhart said, calm, incredulous, unimpressed.

"We should go with this package." He'd lost his job because the package reminded him of his lucky bathing suit.

"Okay. I've heard enough about the package," Eberhart said irascibly. "You can go now. If we have any questions, we'll ask John or Emily. Let's move on."

Barry picked up his pad and his acetates and went out of the room carefully, a high-pitched humming vibrating in his head. He wandered back across the empty floor to his office. It looked barren without the tree. What had he done? Mortification and despair.

Hearne ran in, slamming the door behind him. "You lunatic moron! You pulled a fucking Tobias! I can't believe you! Why?" Hearne had red blotches on his cheeks. "Who cares about the fucking package?"

It was more than just the package, but he couldn't think about it now. "I don't know."

. . .

He drove carefully over the speed bump and out of the parking lot, as if they were watching him. Once out of sight he blasted *Sgt. Pepper*, and then turned it down. He wasn't 13 anymore. "A Day in the Life" was the perfect distillation of the separate Beatle essences. The verses were John—dreamy, ambiguous, possibly drug-induced, trying very hard to shock. The B section was Paul—jaunty, bright, domestic, trying very hard to please. The final note was pure John, as anti-social as you could get.

Barry hadn't even hit his target—he'd go to bed every night for the rest of his life kicking himself. He had no beef with Eberhart! It wasn't even a good line. On the other hand, he couldn't remember what Gary Tobias had said. It was the music, not the lyrics, that people remembered, that had lent Tobias's name to furious, ranting insubordination.

At home, he wandered around, bewildered and depressed. Justine was coming at 8:30. It was now 2:05, and he had no idea what to do. He opened the refrigerator. The dog jumped on his legs.

The phone rang. It was Hearne. "I think if you sent out your résumé now, before this gets around, you might be okay."

"I've been beating myself up about it. But then I remembered that nobody remembers *what* Tobias said, just the way he said it."

"Oh, I remember. He told Rheinecker, 'You puny little taskmaster, you snotty son of a bitch.'"

"You remembered that?" The dog looked at him disdainfully. Even Tobias had hit his mark. "Do you think if I apologized to Eberhart—"

"You *must*! But even so, you've got no future here."

"Did anybody say anything later?"

"Not a single word. It was so British. And later, in the hall, Rheinecker asked me the same exact thing about vegetarian entrées that he'd asked me yesterday. As if nothing had happened."

He had to get out of the house. He put the leash on the dog, who danced around, delighted. The Divorcée got on the elevator, looking like she'd spent all day adorning herself. She slinked towards Broadway in her heels, all dressed up and nowhere to go. Like him, in his suit, at 2:35, unemployed.

The dog stopped at a tree. He realized that he'd forgotten bags.

"I ran out of bags," he said to a doorman. "Do you have a newspaper?" The guy shrugged, indifferent to his plight. "Not even a fucking catalogue?"

Barry picked a Burger King wrapper out of a garbage can, praying it didn't have dogshit on it already. Justine was right about so many things.

What was he going to tell Justine?

They continued down West End in gorgeous sunshine. He had nowhere to go, and it was not a magic feeling. At Collegiate, Barry stood outside the red gate, watching the kids in the narrow yard playing handball, trading baseball cards, and bashing each other in the face. He had an ancient memory of his mother picking him up after school once, saying, "If you're an idiot when you're 14, you'll be an idiot when you're 40."

He should visit his mother. But what would he say to her?

Chapter 13

I told you so

The day the utilities deal closed, Justine left the office early and walked up Park Avenue in the lush, warm air in a new green dress. The stock swap had been all over the news, and her name had been mentioned in the *American Lawyer*. Tulips were blooming in the center islands. She was practically living with Barry, at his house. The streets were alive with everyone going home in the gorgeous May sunshine. Barry had suggested a real vacation, and this time nothing would stop her.

At home, Justine packed up her entire spring-summer wardrobe, including shoes and bags. Every wedding she'd ever attended had seemed like science fiction: very nice, but completely irrelevant. It had nothing to do with her. But these things didn't seem so alien now. Anything could happen.

She took a cab across the luscious, blooming park. The West Side was beautiful. She used her new key. "It's your roommate," she called, kicking off her heels, "with her entire closet."

Barry was sitting on the couch looking like a very awkward teenager. He didn't get up. She sat down next to him. He put his head on her chest quietly.

Something had happened.

"What," she said, and he got up and walked around, sharply turning his head, making an impatient clicking noise with his tongue. Someone died. His mother? "What?"

"I did something really stupid today."

"Okay," she said, and felt a hole opening up underneath her. It could be anything. She had no idea what he was capable of.

"I think I got myself fired."

"For what?"

"Well, I insulted Eberhart."

"You what?"

"They were chucking the package. They were being so fucking RIGID and infuriating! I couldn't stand it anymore!"

She knew his mouth would get him into trouble one day. "So you insulted the CEO?" He paced around. "What did you say?"

He put his head on the wall. "I don't want to go into it."

"What happened after that?"

"I don't want to talk about it."

She hadn't unpacked. She could just take it back, all packed up. No, she couldn't. "Where's the dog?"

He pointed to the chair, where the dog was trembling under towels. "She's recovering. I gave her a bath."

"Let's go," she said, and put her pumps back on.

They went to the first place they saw and sat at a table in the window. He ordered like a normal person, without a scene.

His face looked sharper and more forward-thrusting than usual. He drank wine recklessly, watching the street. "Hey, do us a favor and shave once in a while," he said of a woman passing by outside.

It was always something with Barry. She suddenly saw him at

15—gangly, with too much energy, usually in trouble, his mouth blue with braces. There was something very affecting about this. He was in constant conflict with himself. He slid down sighing and rested his head back a moment. He watched her with an exhausted expression. She felt an electrical current connecting her face to his face. This was weird. It wasn't just affection or good sex or someone to eat with. She was in love with him. This was very upsetting. People don't self-destruct without a reason.

The food came. "When are you going to apologize."

"Apologize!" The sleepy look was gone, and he was up and barking again. "Why should I apologize?" He was such an infant. "I mean, I'll apologize for the insult. Absolutely. But I will not apologize for standing my ground." He was raving now, clutching his fork. He was a very handsome man.

Now she was really sick. She was in love with the stupid loudmouth Barry, too?

"All right. So you were long due to get out of there. It's amazing you lasted as long as you did," she said, and his face relaxed a bit. "What's wrong with waiting until *after* you've found another job to insult the CEO?"

"Don't," he said, embarrassed. He dug into his salad with such fury that a leaf landed on her new green dress. He put the fork down. "I am so sorry." She ignored the hand he held out to her, and dipped her napkin in water. How had this happened?

Back at the apartment, Justine had no idea what to do. She wished somebody else was there—Pippa even. She wanted to spank him. Was he psychotic?

The phone rang. Barry looked up fearfully.

"Pick it up," she said. He did.

"It's for you," he said, and handed her the phone. What now? "I'll be in the shower." He dragged himself out like a repentant child.

"Now remember Frieda's daughter Linda?" Miriam said, gearing up for a story. "A Very Lovely Girl."

Justine sighed. "She was the dancer, right?"

"No that was her sister Stacy, the showgirl. Big scandal. Big. She didn't tell Frieda and Joe. But she was dancing in a nightclub. She ran off with a gambler. Eloped. Her parents found her on the Baltimore Line. They had the marriage annulled. She was underage. Then she met a Wonderful Guy. Had two kids. Like a normal person. He was a tax specialist. Crazy about her. She didn't deserve it. And then she met a guy from Australia. And went to Reno for a divorce. Then she moved to California, to be with the Australian. Always had a fella, that Stacy."

The woman had lost her mind. "And?"

"Now Linda, she went to Mount Holyoke and married a Doctor. A good one. Solid practice, very well respected in the Community. A Gastroenterologist. And he left her for her best friend. So she went to get a license to sell real estate—you know that course. Your mother took that course. *And what do you think happened?*"

Miriam paused. The dog rolled over, still damp.

"What happened, Nana."

"She met an Italian. At the real estate course. Like a contractor. Like that. So they got married. They live somewhere out on the Island, very Italian. So who do you think your mother bumped into at The Garden? Linda and the Italian, happy ending."

Why had Miriam called with this tonight? "And?"

"And nothing. So maybe you're right. You could get married to the best person on paper and it could be terrible. People marry all sorts of people and it's not the end of their life." Barry came out again, pink and clean, his hair combed into tracks. "Did I tell you that oncologist I had? I fired him. He thought he was some hot stuff, that charlatan."

Barry patted the dog with a towel. Justine felt guilty. "Nana. I love you. I have to go."

"Okay, darling. You keep me posted." She hung up.

Barry and Stella looked at her: What would she do?

"I brought all my stuff," she said.

"The irony is not lost on me," he said, and took her suitcases into Vince's old room. He put the bags on the bed and sat down on the floor, knees up, back against the bed. It was her room now, her closet. She had to put everything away.

She sat down next to him. "What are you going to do?"

He leaned into her. "I have no idea."

He pushed her back onto the floor. In a moment he was on top of her with his full weight. He was very heavy. He might cry. How long could she hold her breath like this?

The next morning, she tried on her pink suit from four years ago, a size 10, and it fit. Barry was waiting for her at the table. Usually he was gone already. He'd made breakfast.

"What are you doing today?" she asked.

"I thought I'd get my nails done and go to the bridge club."

She wouldn't respond to this. "Enjoy yourself," she said, and picked up her bag.

He ran ahead of her and stood against the door. "What's wrong with my coffee?"

"Stop it." She kissed him briefly, and walked out.

"You can't just leave me here." Barry stood at the door like a punished child who wanted to come out and play.

Justine smoothed his forehead. "I wish I had advice for you," she said. "But you'll do okay." She got into the elevator.

It was early, and she was in a terrific mood, in spite of him. She decided to walk. She was fitting into thin clothes, Fosdale Cleat had found a serious buyer for one of the Fitzsimmons subsidiaries, the sky was a perfect blue. It might be a good thing, what had happened. If he got his act together now, he might never pull a stunt like this again. He should just figure it out and get another job. Soon.

"Harriet had a baby, she wants you to know," Bob said without interest as she walked into her office.

"What kind of baby!"

"White, I assume," he said, walking out.

She called Mount Sinai. "What kind of baby?"

"A boy, 8.1, vaginal," Harriet whispered. "We're deadlocked on the name. He likes Harry. I like Henry. We may have to call him Jason. I have to go," she said, and hung up.

Bob walked in, excited. "Your dad's on the phone! I mean, I talk to HER all day long, but suddenly I feel so much closer to you, Justine." Bob's days were numbered.

It had been a month and a half since they'd had lunch the four of them. Why was he calling now?

"I called to rave," her father said. "Great guy!"

"Yeah, he is," she said, wondering what the great guy was up to. Probably playing handball in the bedroom, eating cereal out of the box.

"So?" he insinuated.

This was a nightmare. "So I have no further statements on this topic at this time," she told him.

Justine went directly to Roberta's office, but she wasn't there. On a hunch, she went downstairs and found her smoking in front of the building with the head of the ad agency on 17, the receptionist of the European publishers on 31, and some of the Packer Breebis maintenance staff. Justine nodded to her, and Roberta excused herself; they went to sit on a concrete wall facing Park Avenue. Roberta had recruited Justine as a summer associate eight years ago; they'd had many talks on this wall.

Roberta angled her face to the sun and closed her eyes. "Okay, let's hear it."

"Barry lost his job."

"Well, at least he's got his health," she yawned.

"Roberta!"

"I'm sorry, you're right, tell me about it. It was too good to be true, the whole thing from the very beginning, wasn't it?"

When Justine arrived at Barry's at 7:30, he was on the sofa watching TV.

He would become his father. She'd be left with all the adult tasks, the way his mother had been. The way her mother had been. It *was only Friday*. She had to get the hell out of there.

She ducked out, but he saw her. "I forgot milk," she called.

He jumped up. "I'll come with you."

"No, I'll just be a minute." She caught the elevator. He rushed out and jumped on just in time. He kissed her up against the wall. She felt hot. Trapped. Upset. She hated this dark dingy elevator. She had to get out. There was a whole weekend ahead.

The problem was the dog. The dog was living there, and Pippa was walking her in the afternoon. She couldn't ask him to keep the dog if she wasn't around. She walked ahead through the lobby. She could cancel Pippa and reinstate her old dog walker.

"What's Pippa's number," she asked, as they hit the street.

"Why?"

The air was fresh, but he was right on top of her, grabbing her arm. She needed to breathe. She disengaged from his arm, ostensibly to write down the number, but really to walk free. How on earth had she thought this man was going to be a partner? She must have been in a crashing plane. "I may need her, coming up."

"Oh, yeah?" He was being friendly and upbeat. "What for?"

He'd probably had a terrible day. He was petrified. He needed someone to hold his head. All she wanted was to be sitting alone in front of her air conditioner, knitting. "I was thinking of having a party," she lied, looking at a tree in almost obscene blossom to avoid his eyes. "I thought she might cater it."

"Oh, she'd love that." He stood directly in front of her, smiling down at her, as they waited for a light that wouldn't change. "You know, Pippa really looks up to you, it would be such a vote of confidence for her—"

"Barry, I can't be here now!"

He breathed in. He was horrified.

"It's just tonight! I'm suffocating." Traffic was whizzing by. "Tomorrow, I'll come over and we'll talk."

"Okay, but what about now?"

"Oh, God, don't make me eat dinner!" She almost walked into a car.

Now what?

Barry went upstairs alone, feeling an icy wind blowing through a ragged hole in the center of his body. This was intolerable. There must be some drug that knocked you out instantly. He wanted to wake up when it was all over. Quaaludes? He was allergic to aspirin, penicillin, and sulfur drugs; he'd surely die trying anything more complicated than Tylenol.

He took a shower. He called Golden Dragon Wok. He held the dog in his arms like a baby. He waited. They should go away—have a nice vacation, come back with a sense of purpose. He did deserve a vacation. One stray remark didn't negate years of solid work. It was taking an enormous amount of energy not to call her. He dialed her number, but hung up before it rang. How could he go away? He had to think about money. He had no idea how much he had left—he'd been living without counting for some time. Henry Ford said that money didn't change men, it just unmasked them. If somebody was selfish or arrogant or greedy originally, money brought it out, was all. On the other hand, Henry Ford was an anti-Semitic bastard.

Golden Dragon Wok delivered, and he made sure to give the guy a good tip. He turned on the TV.

Okay. What was the worst that could happen? He might not get a comparable job at a comparable company. So? The *problem* was the company. The dog was sitting as if for a portrait, shifting her gaze between him and the food, hoping he'd take pity on her. Ten years of experience and an MBA from Wharton—how could he not get a job? He had to make sure he didn't take just any job. He finished the egg roll and looked for something on TV. Stella lunged at the food.

"Get out of there," he batted the dog away. She sat on the arm-chair, piqued. Justine had just left her without thinking.

Justine was going to walk—he should brace himself for that. He cleaned up. He took a bath. He needed something to do next.

He called in the morning. "I want to see you," he warned.

She let out an impatient sigh. "I have to work today."

"So when are you coming over?"

"I don't know. When I'm finished."

"Well, ballpark, so I can be home for you."

"I have a key," she said. Why did she always miss the point?

"I'm flipping out, Justine! I know you are too, but this isn't help-ing me."

"I know, sweetie. Go to the library. Do research."

"On what?"

"Employment."

He went out. What was the point of a girlfriend if she gave you assignments, like a teacher. He came back—it was Saturday. Throngs of people were everywhere with sporting equipment and lovers in the perfect high spring weather. He didn't want to run into anyone he knew. He sat the dog on his lap and called Pippa.

"I feel really stupid. What should I do?"

"Run around the reservoir."

"You're brilliant! Will you come with me?"

"Can't." Everyone had important things to do. "Since you're home," she said, in a deal-making tone, "can you walk the dog this week? I could really use all the time I can find."

"Finals? Why don't you come over here to study? No rats, no psycho-killer boyfriends. It's quiet, you wouldn't have to cook."

"Are you going to be there?"

"Yes."

"Forget it then. I'll get nothing done."

Everyone was disgusted with him. He opened the refrigerator and polished off the rest of the beef with black bean sauce. He roamed through the apartment. What was he waiting for? For Rheinecker to fire him?

He turned on the computer and began a letter. You rigid, anal bastard, he thought.

He wrote: "Dear John." Hey, a Dear John letter. Enough fun. He had to write to the offended party and to Rheinecker. Rheinecker first.

"It causes me great pain—" Fuck that. "It should come as no surprise to you that I have been frustrated for quite some time at the rigidity of your policies. I wonder what I am being paid for, since you have actively prevented me from doing my job."

He wouldn't send it. Christ, just the idea of printing it out gave him hives. He had to resign, or they would fire him. In the end, it was the same thing. He wouldn't get a reference, and he'd been there ten years. Legend had it that it was easier to go out in a box than to find a food job after the Acres. The infamous Gary Tobias was a deejay in Colorado somewhere.

Which didn't sound half bad. Oh, Justine? I was thinking about deejaying in Colorado. Why not just go to Mexico and sleep on a beach, she'd say. Justine was not a patient person.

He had to move. He revised his résumé and wrote separate, specific cover letters to Dover Soup, Bobbie Brownies, and Harmony Products and mailed them. It was already 3, the day was almost over. He felt like he'd done something. He called to tell Justine.

"Sent them; you mean mailed them," she asked.

"Yes. Why?"

"No reason," she said fast. "I would've faxed them."

He was clenching the phone. "All right, Justine." He hung up, and went back into the kitchen. He looked in the fridge.

He called her back, mad. "It's Saturday, dammit! The janitor would've thrown out a fax, or put it anywhere."

"You're right, okay? Now let me work. I'll see you later."

She finally came over at about 7, and she didn't want to talk. She removed his hands when he tried to touch her. "I'm organizing my closet," she announced, and walked out.

He left her alone and watched the Met game. During a commercial, he went in. She was sitting in a pile of all the old family stuff, wrapping, sponging, boxing, bagging. She upended a box. Out shot extension cords, his catcher's mitt, broken toys.

"Stop," he warned.

She held up the mitt and looked at him.

He stared at her. "Absolutely not."

"I'm not throwing it out. But don't you have another one? We could put them together. In a box. To make space for my stuff."

"There's plenty of room in that closet."

"Why am I doing this?" she asked the room rhetorically. "God knows you've got the time now."

He felt impaled again. She wasn't going to apologize for this, he could tell. They should probably go out and do something distracting. The mirrored closet door had jumped off the track again. He yanked it back onto the groove, catching his toe underneath. He screamed, went hopping, and knocked his head on the dresser. He lay on the bed with both ends throbbing. She came towards him with hands. He waved her away.

"Go!" he seethed through his teeth. "Just go."

She wandered. The floor was still covered with thirty-six years of family debris. It was only Saturday night! This was the longest weekend of his life.

On Monday morning, she went to work. He read the newspaper. His time since the event had been divided between sitting in the apartment and feeling like shit, and going out and feeling like shit. This day looked like more of the same. The waiting was driving him crazy. He called Hearne. Hearne said he'd have to call him back. There was nothing to do. He turned on CNN.

What if the neighbors heard? On the other hand, what did they know? He could be a media critic, working at home. He could be who he was, doing market research on a day off. He did some stomach crunches on the floor.

He could get in shape for real. That's what he would do. Go to the gym every day.

In Tarrytown? Yeah, right.

He had to retool. Think it through. He stood by what he'd done. It was the way he'd done it that was embarrassing. He'd been too hot, too mad. They thought he was unbalanced and violent. He was ashamed.

It was Monday at 9:40, and he couldn't eat lunch yet. He called Justine. Bob took a message in disgust. Did Bob know?

He found the card of a headhunter who'd called him a year ago with something in Baltimore. He called, and made his pitch.

"I just got a *lead* on a job at Maplewood Acres," the headhunter said. There was a pause. "Was that your job?"

Barry had to remind himself to breathe. "Probably."

"Well. Fax me your résumé—I'll see what I can do."

He dressed quickly, deciding not to shave. He took the dog out. It was another heartbreakingly beautiful day. The dog sniffed around the copy store while he faxed to the headhunter.

Back at home, the phone was ringing. "We have a hockey game

tonight with my mother and Gene, remember?" Justine said, pissed off. "You can skip it if you want."

"Do you not want me to come?"

"I didn't say that." She was so far away.

He didn't care if Carol approved of him or not. Still: he had no desire to hear her opinion. "Did you tell her?"

"No," she said emphatically.

"So don't tell her. Or tell her, and I won't go."

"I *hate* hockey—why should I go?"

"Okay, don't go. We can go to a movie."

"We'll go and I won't tell her."

As if there weren't enough dread in his life.

The phone rang. It was Maplewood Acres—someone he'd never heard of. Yvonne in Personnel. His hands began to sweat. To set up an exit interview. Her voice was neutral. She asked him if Friday at 10 would be convenient. As if he had a choice.

"You should probably set aside about an hour and a half, to be safe," she said. He hung up shaking.

To be safe? He'd be strung up, spit-roasted, and eaten alive. And, he had five days to look forward to it!

The phone rang. Pretty busy here, considering he might as well be a dead man. It was Iris, bless her freckled soul! "Iris! I'm so glad to hear from you!"

"Barry, I heard. What are you gonna do?"

"I'm starting a suggestion hotline," he said. "You tell me."

"Get a product," she said seriously. "You're not a company man." He wanted to thank her for the vote of confidence, the only one he'd received. But she was evaporating into her job. "Sorry, I gotta go. Your favorite former assistant is on the other line."

The Midwife was settling into his job: icing on the cake.

Do it yourself: Iris was so smart. He looked in the classifieds under business opportunities. Miracle fish-food formula. Angel needed for kosher catering. Cutting-edge communications device, patent pending. Not that he had money to start anything up. But Iris was right: he wasn't a company man. He was a trailblazer. His mind had been atrophying all this time on the hamster wheel of salad dressing distribution. He'd need a lot of energy to go off-road with a whole new idea. He had so much to do! Did the call mean she liked him, personally?

He went to Barnes & Noble for a marketing book she had suggested. It was vague, celebrational, for amateurs: "You know your customers, you have a product or service that you know serves a real need. You just need to get the information out!"

Christ. He was standing in a bookstore at 11 o'clock on a Monday morning, reading a primer for college kids on how to make money in their spare time selling novelty T-shirts. This was embarrassing. He went back to the apartment and looked at the dog. The exit interview kept popping into his head every time he had a half-relaxed moment.

Hearne finally called him at 5 o'clock. "I'm at a pay phone. Not only are you persona non grata, anyone talking *to* you or *about* you is suspected of treason. And I should tell you, if you try to go to General Foods, or come up with a better salad dressing on your own, they'll sue your ass into the ground."

He shaved and put on a suit for the hockey game, as if he'd come from the office. He hated Carol. He met Justine at the Garden. From her face he could tell that she didn't want to hear anything short of "Honey, I got a better job today, and I start tomorrow morning." Would she be in a bad mood until then?

They walked into the harsh noise of the stadium. The game had started and they were already there, looking like a prosperous Jewish Mom and Dad with strong opinions. Carol greeted him warmly and started swiping at his face with her thumb to get the lipstick off. He leaned away.

"Justine tells me you've been promoted, Barry," Carol shouted at him with wet maroon lips.

"That was a while ago," he said. Justine took his hand

"We should see you more often," Carol nodded and got active: the crowd was shouting. There was a fight down on the ice; Carol was cheering, and Gene was chomping peanuts morosely. Justine took out a bag of carrots. She was barely speaking to him tonight. He felt her feet in the small of his back—her feet, Carol's feet. Get a job, any job, not that job: nothing we'd be ashamed of.

A Bruin was up against the Plexiglass and Carol was yelling, "Hit him! Nail that bastard!"

Carol was a bloodthirsty marauding hun. She'd skate right over his face and not look back. Justine wasn't paying attention to him. She was ashamed of him. She was proud of her mother. The woman hadn't worked a day in her life, but he, *he* was dirt. Barry was chilled through to the core.

He leaned into her and said, "I want to leave."

"No." She didn't look at him. "Just wait until intermission, okay? I'll come with you."

"I want to go now."

"Fine. Go."

This was excruciating. They stayed till the first intermission, said good-bye, took a taxi uptown without speaking, and went to sleep separately in the same bed.

On Wednesday morning, he was awakened by a phone call from Burlingame Claris White, the company lawyers. He was forbidden to work for any direct competitors. Moreover, he was forbidden from working on any category that he had ever worked on at Maplewood Acres for five years. Furthermore, he was forbidden from working for any of Maplewood Acres' subsidiaries, vendors, contractors, or agencies ever. Additionally, he was forbidden from working on any product in any category in which Maplewood Acres was currently represented, or might be represented, for five years. If he tried any of this, he would be sued. They would be sending over some papers forthwith that needed his immediate signature.

He needed a lawyer. He was living with one. He was strangely calm. There were other things to sell besides food. He called the headhunter. "I'd like to expand the search. Doesn't have to be food. Probably shouldn't be food."

"What's your story again? Okay, fax me your résumé."

Friday finally came. As if he hadn't had enough time, he was late. He swung into his old space in the lot. Rex, the security guard he used to kibitz with, made him sign in, relinquish his driver's license, and wear a visitor's badge. Barry wanted to take the stairs, to avoid see-ing too many people. But being back here was weird enough with-out getting into trouble with security. Waiting alone for the eleva-tor—feeling more guilty than he actually was—was a very familiar feeling.

Slaymaker got into the elevator right after him with two salesmen.

"Hey!" Barry said, glad to see a friendly face.

Slaymaker nodded cordially, and went on talking as if he weren't there. Being too enthusiastic in an elevator with somebody cutting him off was also strangely familiar. Rheinecker had been correct: Slaymaker wasn't his friend.

Everyone in Personnel had tweezed their eyebrows into straight lines. Why? He was brought into a blank room where he was given a clipboard and some forms to fill out. Eventually, an overly made-up woman came in with a folder and shut the door.

"Am I allowed to see my old boss?"

"Of course. Now this is for our tax purposes," she said, and pro-duced a multipage governmental form. "I've indicated where you should sign with the yellow arrows. Now your COBRA—"

"I flew off the handle, but the principle was sound."

"I don't want to know about it," she said with a straight face. The pores on her nose were enormous. "Now, Cobra. Your health will be covered until you secure another position—"

"Have they filled the job yet?"

"—and that includes part-time work or full-time work that doesn't have health. Now we need you to fill out a waiver—"

After submitting his ID card and electronic passkey, and receiving a check (they counted Self-Immolation Thursday as a half-day), he went back to his old floor feeling resigned.

Teriakis and a bunch of suits acknowledged him by turning inward as a pack. So be it. He gave Donna a half-salute.

"Well, you look like you're walking fine, what with ya foot in ya mouth an' all," she said, with a cocky nod.

She was just a smart-aleck kid; he didn't hang around for further proof that their bond had never been more than small talk.

Eberhart's secretary nodded at him, but didn't stop him.

He walked in talking. "I wanted to say how sorry I was," Barry said, without an ounce of embarrassment or nervousness. He really was sorry.

"Accepted," the little man said tersely, signing things behind his enormous desk as if Barry weren't there.

"I feel weird," Barry said.

"You are weird," Eberhart said, glancing up. "It's a shame, because these snacks are really exciting, and you were doing a fine job with the group."

Was he offering him his job back? Unlikely.

Eberhart continued signing things. Barry excused himself, said good-bye softly, and walked quickly down the hall to Rheinecker. With each step, he felt lighter.

"Close the door," Rheinecker said with acid.

The tree was in the corner. Mocking him.

"You are so stupid," Rheinecker began.

"You're probably right," Barry said with fatigue. He didn't want to be chewed out. He'd apologized to the offended party. He wasn't going to apologize for doing his job. "I want the tree."

"You can't have it."

"Why? You didn't like the package, and you're not going to use the tree. It would just sit here." He was almost weightless now.

"I *did* like the package," Rheinecker said, almost savagely. "We didn't use it because there was a conflict. Are you an infant?"

It was lighter than air here, now there was no structure between them. "Look, I apologized to Eberhart—"

"You son of a bitch."

"Language."

"You stupid son of a bitch," Rheinecker yelled. "If you'd just played ball, you could've written your own ticket."

"Bullshit."

Was this what he'd come for? Rheinecker was all over the place. A vein pulsed on his temple, and his neck was getting striated and red. "Look, no one here is going to help you. Forget about working in Food. Ever. And if I were you," he threatened, finger pointed, "I wouldn't ask Hearne for a reference. You'd be putting him in a very awkward situation."

There was no real reason to stick around for more abuse.

"Okay, well, bye," he said, and held his hand out. Rheinecker took it on reflex; they were both disgusted. Bizarre custom, when what you really wanted to do was deck the prick.

Well, okay, that was over. But when he walked into his office, he was flooded with despair. This was a good job. He sat down in his desk chair. He felt heavier than he'd ever felt before.

Emily had her cubicle packed up in boxes; clearly she was just waiting for him to evacuate. Plast was watching from the far corner of the floor. He wouldn't dare come in. It was useful, being a pariah. Barry started throwing things into a shopping bag.

"Hi," Plast said at the door. His forehead was an unreadable scramble. His hands were in his pockets, and he was leaning up against the wall. "I don't know what to say to you."

"Me neither."

"What are you going to do?"

"I have no idea. I'm in touch with a headhunter."

"Ray Badger? Don't bother. Think about the agency side," he said carefully. "None of our agencies could ever hire you, but there are others."

"That's good advice."

"Or think about cosmetics. There's a more creative approach."

"Thank you." Barry felt well and truly awful now. "It was good working with you," he said, wondering if that was a guilt-driven lie, or if he just hadn't recognized it at the time. They shook hands. Plast left him alone again in his mess.

Miss Emily King walked in, closed the door, and sat down with arms crossed. The only thing missing.

"Wow," she said. The mouse-faced midwife was going to rub his nose in it.

Get out. "What."

"I just wanted to let you know," she said seriously, "I was really impressed with what you did. That took real guts."

Well, that took the cake. He should have had something clever to say, but he didn't. "I gotta go," he said, and walked out with his pathetic little shopping bag.

The complete lack of concern on the faces as he walked out of the building would probably stay with him for the rest of his life. He returned his visitor's pass, and got into the car.

Now what?

Chapter 14

Provenance

Two weeks after the Mingus Resnick folding announcement in the *Wall Street Journal*, Vince was invited for a final interview at Gruber-Stenck. "You just have to impress a few chieftains," Rick Erlich said, friendly and encouraging. "That shouldn't be too hard, given your provenance, your résumé, and your natural charm."

Erlich steered him to an older man with lidless eyes and one or two white hairs sticking out of a liver-spotted scalp. "Jarvis," the man said, not smiling. He was the managing partner.

Erlich disappeared. Vince followed Jarvis into his office. He was wearing thick-soled brown shoes. The overheads were off. A desk lamp threw a yellow glow on a bare desk with a neat but old-looking blotter. There were no pictures of Jarvis with important figures. There were no papers or bulletin boards. It was all in this man's head.

Jarvis looked at him with unblinking eyes, as if to say, So?

Vince began to sweat. This had to end soon. "I'm very glad to meet you, sir. This is quite an institution you run."

Jarvis sat back in his chair and said, barely moving his lips, "What did you learn from the Van Laer deal?"

"Patience." He tried to smile.

"That's it? You sat and waited?"

Vince hated men like this. He breathed in. "Well, no. We were quite active." Just give me the fucking job and I'll do it for you. Don't make me tell you why I deserve it. "But there was always one more piece of analysis they needed." Jarvis was staring, unmoved. "And between the time we started and the final bid, contracts had expired, new laws were enacted. All the research, all the negotiations had to be done all over again."

Vince had no real talent or skills. This moment right here—his nervous system on red alert and the unimpressed stare—was a distillation of every interview he'd ever had. And he hadn't had many—he usually got the job. Surprise, surprise.

"Why'd it take so long?"

Thank God, a neutral question. "Well, you can't convince people to sell if they don't want to sell."

"Bull," Jarvis said flatly, lacing his fingers in front of him. "Everything is for sale. Everybody has a price. Take your father, for example," he said. "He's got a price. Higher than most people's, sure, but he's got a price."

Vince didn't say anything. He'd stopped asking people who insisted on pulling his father into the conversation how they knew him. He wondered what his own price was. A dollar fifty. No kidding. He'd run out of this room right now for a dollar fifty.

"Thank you for your time," Vince said at the end. Jarvis shook his hand indifferently and went back to do his real work.

Back in Erlich's office, there were papers on the desk and things on the wall and life going on under fluorescent lights. "Do you have anything in the works to bring over here?" Erlich asked expectantly. Vince saw it now: if he pulled in a single deal, Erlich would be disappointed, and Jarvis would be surprised.

"I have solid relationships with a fair number of my clients. Whether they'd follow me elsewhere, I have no idea."

"Your modesty becomes you," Erlich said, and made him a larger offer than he'd expected. He accepted. It was that easy. He'd narrowly escaped something. But maybe not narrowly enough. He knew why he'd been offered the job.

The best time of your life

As usual, in the lush, ripe air of May, Pippa was writing a paper in the stuffy bowels of the library, bursting to escape. Outside, people were playing frisbee and falling in love. Her topic was ziggurats, but her heart wasn't in it. She watched it emerge from the printer, feeling like she'd let herself down. Whatever: she had to get out.

She strolled across campus in the gorgeous air. Everyone was lounging on the steps like a huge herd of sea lions, their big smooth orange limbs shining in the sun. She was through for the year. She headed down Broadway.

Every time she saw Vince, something really embarrassing happened, and it was clear that she would never see him again. She went about her business, convinced of it. And yet, he kept calling her, and she kept going to see him. That was probably the most adult part of the whole thing—that they kept seeing each other, even though everything was a problem. Everything.

She spotted a fantastic pair of black platforms. She bought them instantly, and wore them out of the store, delighted. Two blocks later, the straps were biting into her heels. By the time she got to Barry's, she had ripe blisters. Ridiculous.

Barry was standing in the kitchen in dirty clothes, looking big and unhappy. "I'm trying," he said, gesturing at envelopes, résumés, yellow pads, classifieds.

She sat down to play with the dog. "It's gorgeous out."

"I know!" he paced. "But every time I go out, I think I should be in trying to get a job."

He turned on the TV. A woman's voice said, "And he, he ripped my skirt off, and then he was on top of me, choking me—"

"Do you think the incidence of rape is up," she asked, "or is it just more people are talking about it now."

"They're all lying," he said, zapping Oprah with the remote. The next channel had male bodybuilders in tiny bikinis flexing their muscles in the delighted faces of middle-aged ladies. "Whaddya thinka that!" the host shouted.

"This is the beginning of the end of our civilization," Barry said. The next show had a caller asking a transvestite ex-convict what his father thought of him. Barry turned off the set. "Afternoon TV is the contemporary equivalent of Roman group vomiting." He wandered around, bouncing a Super Ball.

"Speaking of which. I've missed the deadline for Rome."

"Rome is the Eternal City. There is no deadline. Just go."

"You mean by myself?"

"Whatever. Go to Rome, go to Paris. I bet you're sick of hearing it, but this really is the best time of your life."

Her feet were throbbing. "That really depresses me. How can I enjoy myself when I keep thinking I should be doing something else?"

"I know exactly what you mean," he said, his hands gray from newsprint.

. . .

She ate Japanese with Vince in the East Village and they walked in the beautiful air. Her feet were killing her. Everyone had a tattoo or a navel ring, interesting shoes. She was suddenly annoyed with all of it. What did it have to do with anything? You buy new shoes, and they cripple you. Pierce your navel, pierce your nose: it doesn't change what you accomplish in a day.

"I should live down here," Vince said, nodding. "So many interesting people."

"Why do you need to surround yourself with interesting people?" Pippa asked. "Do you feel boring?"

He gazed vacantly. They passed a couple talking rapidly in Greek. The woman was in a ratty fur coat, the man looked a little drunk. He had his arm around her, and she was crying. Something was terribly wrong, but at least they were communicating. Pippa was hit with an overwhelming sadness. Vince was right next to her. She might as well have been alone there.

"You want to go to a movie?" he asked.

She didn't want to go home alone now, but she didn't want to be with him, either. She was lonely when she was with him.

Problem-solving

On June 2, his parents' former anniversary, Barry stood on line at the Unemployment Office in White Plains. Two fat Slavic women with hair growing out of the moles on their faces were bearing down on him from behind. Every time he inched forward to get away from the smell of sweat and root vegetables, they inched forward too. He read the *Times*, and tried to angle himself to prevent them from getting any closer.

This was his fourth week without a job. Justine was wanting sex constantly. He couldn't seem to stop spending money now that he wasn't earning any. His cleaning lady had cried when he let her go; he half expected to see her here on line.

It was finally his turn. He presented himself at the window, leaving the Commissars of the Volga Steel Works behind.

"They aren't going to pay full benefits," the clerk said, after he called up Barry's file on the computer. "They say you were doing substandard work."

"WHAT?"

"They often do that so they don't have to pay full benefits."

Somebody gathered up to spit behind him. "If I was doing substandard work, why did they promote me and give me a raise? Not enough of a raise, but a raise."

"You can contest it. In a hearing."

He went to his gym, fuming. He saw a guy from Quality Control on the StairMaster, so he left.

Driving down 9W—the scenic route; boy, did he ever have the time—he calculated that without full benefits, he could last four months, if he didn't eat much and charged everything. How was he going to keep paying Pippa? At home, he called Justine, who was unavailable, and faxed his résumé to Lady Luxe and Flanders Soap. He made follow-up calls to PomaSil, Clensabar, Rita Doria—still nothing.

Churchill had been down and out for long periods. Of course, it wasn't like Churchill had to fax his résumé around.

He had to plan strategically. His job hadn't been difficult. It had required perhaps thirty percent of his abilities and had taken a lot of time. When was the last time he'd been challenged or fascinated at The Acres?

Barry called Iris. "Maybe nothing is happening because I'm not completely sure I want a job in packaged consumer products," he proposed.

"A friend of mine had a career crisis," Iris said, taking him seriously in a way that Justine didn't. "She got this problem-solving software. It asks you questions and makes a flow chart. The questions are pretty general, but it might get your mind moving." She told him there was a software catalogue that you could order from 24 hours a day that delivered to your home the next day.

He was excited.

"There are a few different programs, so let me tell you what sort of questions to ask," Iris said, and told him things to ask about the graphics. He was impressed. "What sort of questions should I ask" was a great question. Barry felt bad; he hadn't ever given Iris credit.

Suddenly focused, he called the catalogue and asked about the differences between the various brands of problem-solving software.

"What do you mean by problem-solving?" the Catalogue asked.

"Solving," he said, thrown off balance. "Problems. It asks you questions, and they get your mind moving on the problems."

"Personal problems?"

"No, it's work related. Um, it makes a flow chart," Barry said, mortified. He didn't know what he wanted to be when he grew up.

"We've got diagnostics to find what's causing the glitch in your computer," the Catalogue offered. "That's the only thing like that that we have."

Barry hung up the phone and reached for the Sharper Image catalogue. To think: he'd actually believed that with a credit card and an 800 number he could change his life. Iris was a stupid twit. He ate egg salad standing up in the kitchen. He listened to "New York Views" on the radio. He ordered an odometer from the Sharper Image. Training began this afternoon. Three miles a day.

Stella was dragging herself across the rug in a sitting position. "Stop that," he said. "You look silly." She ducked her head as if caught in a compromising position.

He patted his lap and the dog jumped up and stood on his legs. She'd been biting herself, and her rear end looked pretty bad. He wanted to call Justine and tell her, but he couldn't, without bothering her. How come she hadn't called him back?

Justine canceled dinner. She had to work late. She got home at midnight, made love on him, and fell asleep without speaking.

The next morning, Stella was biting her ass. Dragging her ass. He called Justine.

"Barry?" Bob the male secretary asked. "She's out, and she didn't give a number."

For shame. She had her male secretary lying so she didn't have to talk to him? He called VitaCare, DelixCo, and Cecil Harding Products. He was transferred, put on hold, hung up on.

He went to Times Square for an interview with a direct mail group. In the worst way, he didn't want to work in direct mail. The guy was a sleazeball with gold jewelry.

"Look, some of my best friends are crawling on the street," he said, after telling Barry he was impressed with his résumé and had nothing for him.

Bobby Kennedy had been on academic probation at Harvard. Walt Disney had gone bankrupt. These things built character.

Justine arrived that night at 7:30, looking tired. He didn't know what to talk to her about. He couldn't talk about presentations to sales conferences anymore.

"So tell me all about the class action suit," he said as she walked in. "I really want to know."

"Barry, do you mind," she asked. "I want to go to a movie."

"Why don't we rent one."

She spread the paper out on the table. "No, let's go out."

"You just don't want to talk to me."

"I talk to you all the time," she said wearily. "Don't you ever just feel like a movie?" She was standing in her shoes with her bag on her shoulder, pointing to an ad for an action movie. She hated action movies.

"Any movie. You'd rather see any movie than talk to me."

She sat down with her bag and looked at him. "What do you want to talk about, Barry."

"You didn't call me back today."

She inhaled and he could see her teeth clenching.

"Fine!" He stepped on the dog by mistake. "Just go to a movie and forget all about me. I just thought we could talk."

She looked at him in utter exasperation, and then said, very slowly, as if warning a child not to put his hand on a stove, "Well then, why don't you tell me what's on your mind."

"You're always yelling at me. You pay no attention to me."

She dropped her bag, tore off her jacket, threw it across the room, and stalked out, slamming the bedroom door. He decided that it wasn't a good idea to follow her. He stared out the window at the sun setting over a slice of the Hudson. She emerged three minutes later naked under his bathrobe, and pinned him on the sofa, kissing him furiously.

Barry awakened the next morning with a craving for steak, cold sliced steak on French bread with horseradish sauce. He bought a steak at Sloan's and played "I'm a Loser" three times in a row, eating horseradish sauce on bread as he waited for it to cook.

At 2, he had an informational interview at Lady Luxe, the Hair Care People. Nice office in midtown.

"Tell me," the head of personnel said. "You left because of personality differences?"

"Actually, it was a management decision that I disagreed with strongly."

"So you were fired."

"It was mutual," he said, and her eyebrow rose.

She looked at her watch. "But who did what first."

.　　.　　.

Stella's biting was getting out of hand. Barry couldn't get Justine on the phone, so he went to the animal hospital on Amsterdam. He filled out forms as best he could—he knew so little about Stella—and waited with a terrified cat in a box and a dirty white Scottie flailing on a leash. Barry held Stella in his lap—she shouldn't catch anything new.

The door opened, and a sick Akita walked out carefully, clearly miserable. The poor dog had scratched himself until only the mane around his face was left. A tuft here and there, the rest was just raw skin—dry, inflamed-looking naked brown skin. The tail was obscene, just a shriveled-up purplish curl, like a tiny dead snake. The dog looked up at Barry apologetically. He knew he was pathetic. It was the saddest thing Barry had ever seen. He kissed Stella on her warm, bony head.

The vet was a woman about his age, not very attractive, but nice. Looking at her, he realized that he'd never been attracted to any of his girlfriends prior to Justine; they'd all been nice and he'd felt slightly sorry for them. Justine was much too big and competent to feel sorry for. Did she feel sorry for him? The vet was spending time petting hello to Stella. Smart: get the dog's trust. He could always be a vet.

But then she put on rubber gloves to examine the anal area. He could never be a vet. She did some squeezing that made the dog squirm. When she was done, several inch-long, liver-colored cylinders lay on the table.

"Yuck! Worms?" Living in his house?

"Oh, no," she said calmly, rolling the stuff in her gloved palm—it was dense and crumbly. "Her anal glands needed to be expressed."

Stella strutted down Broadway like a new woman, looking up at him gratefully. Maybe he, Barry, had some glands that needed to be expressed.

.   .   .

The next morning, Barry drove to his hearing in White Plains armed with a *scathing*, well-rehearsed speech and Xeroxes of pay stubs, tax returns, and bonus checks. He was ready for those cheesy shysters. After two hours of waiting, the arbitrator asked the Maplewood Acres representative—a skinny guy Barry had never seen or heard of—if the company contested his claim.

"No," the skinny lawyer said, "we do not."

And that was that. The whole thing took a minute and a half.

Barry drove down 9W gnashing his teeth. Once again, he'd worked himself into a lather, and the company had responded with indifference. It felt unfinished—how dare they try to pull that? He turned around and drove to his gym. There was that same guy there from Quality Control. The hell with him. He did half an hour on the bike. On closer inspection, the guy wasn't from Quality Control—of course not, at 11 A.M. Barry vowed to work out daily. Now was the perfect time for a triathlon.

He didn't know how to be with Justine that night; he was still upset about the previous one. As he put the sushi on plates, Justine came up behind him suddenly and nuzzled his back, running her hands across his stomach. Justine was so luscious, so available at that moment; he tried to remember that it was not always so.

"Dinner's here," he said, while she unbuttoned his shirt.

"We can put it in the fridge," she said, turning him around to kiss him deeply, with her hands on his rear end.

He broke away. "Hey, enough."

"What do you mean, enough?"

"I mean, we had sex this morning, and last night. What is going on with you?"

She was very still. "What do you mean, what's going on with me?"

"What happened to the yeast infections?"

She dropped her hands from him and walked away with a look of such hatred he had to hold on to the counter.

"I'm sorry, I just wanted to talk."

"About what," she said, ten feet away.

"About how nobody answers their phone messages!" he said, spilling the soy sauce. "About those bastards trying to get away with saying I did substandard work."

"But they didn't get away with it." She popped a piece of sushi into her mouth. "So what are you throwing yourself for?"

"Och! I can just hear your mother saying that!"

"What does my mother have to do with this?"

"I bet Carol is just thrilled I'm unemployed."

"She feels terrible," Justine said slowly, "as do we all."

"I bet she told you to ditch me." Her mouth curled in a slight smile. "She did, didn't she? Ditch him, he's a loser."

She exhaled loud. "Must we fight now? I had a long day."

"I know! AT THE OFFICE! Rub it in!"

"I work, Barry. I can't help it. Some of us do."

"Bitch."

"I can't talk to you when you're like this," she said, and walked off with her bag.

"Where do you think you're going?"

"Home," she said, hooking the dog on the leash.

"How dare you! You leave that dog here."

"Fine." She let go the leash and walked out. Just like that.

Stella looked at him and then the door, confused. He lay on the floor with her, stroking the pale hair on her stomach and kissing her curly ears. Justine had to give up her apartment. She had to move in with him for good. She couldn't just walk out in the middle of a discussion. The dog licked his nose.

He got up. He ate ravenously, continuously, watching bad television until 2:45, until he had to stagger into bed. He woke up wanting to hunt for matzos, or Easter eggs. It would be relaxing to look for something that was definitely there.

Beyond irritation

It was July 2nd. Barry had been unemployed for three of the seven months Justine had known him. She was sitting on the porch in Bedford, trying to remember what she liked about him. She hadn't told her mother yet, although she'd let Barry believe that she had. Every topic of conversation seemed to touch on the unsaid thing; it hung in the heavy suburban air like an unexploded bomb.

"What are you doing, stuck in the sweaty city the 4th of July?" her mother charged. "He should be taking you to the Hamptons. At least you could go for the day someplace."

Justine was in no mood to defend Barry. She'd worked so hard to absorb him into her system. Now it was anarchy all over again. "Barry is busy today."

Gene put a fat cigar in his brown mouth.

"You finally have a day off and he can't make it?" her mother attacked. Gene lit the cigar.

"Whatever."

"What do you mean, whatever."

"Barry lost his job," she said, just to end the hocking.

"*What?*"

"You heard me." Fine. It was out now.

"Wait, wait," Carol said and went out. Gene's freckled face hung expressionless behind the thick white smoke. Carol marched back in with a fan. "Since when."

"A while."

"I knew something was up! I knew it!" She plugged in the fan and directed it at Gene. "He was fired?"

"He got angry at his boss," Justine said.

"My God, he's an idiot," Carol said, and looked at Gene. He was actively not listening behind the rippling pink tent of the *Financial Times*.

"He has an interview today," Justine said.

Carol looked disgusted. "Well, good. Meredith Zazlowe said she had someone for you, and I said I didn't know where you were at. But now I'll call her back."

"You knew where I was at," Justine said, incensed.

"No, I didn't. What am I, a mind reader?"

Justine drove back to the city in Barry's car, doing isometric clenches. She'd been living very lightly with Barry, trying not to notice much. But now she saw it all. His sister was anorexic. His father had gone into bankruptcy twice. His mother had screaming fights in public. His paternal grandfather walked out one day and never came back. His mother's parents had refused to eat in restaurants—not once in their entire lives, not even on an anniversary. It was terrible, using his car and thinking ill of him.

It was sticky and raining when she picked him up in front of an office building on Second Avenue and 42nd Street. "Well?"

His face was amused. "The sleaze bucket offered me a job!"

"So you took it?"

"Not a chance. Generic brands are a black hole."

Well, why do anything that might make her happy, after all. "But you have other interviews set up."

He looked as if he were going to lash out. "Yes," he hissed.

"Okay." She didn't ask anything else, to avoid a fight.

"Come on, come on!" he said impatiently at every red light.

"How's your mother feeling."

"Fine," he said tonelessly.

They walked home from the garage in foul humidity. The streets were lined with trash. There was something to be said for getting out of town, even if Carol was the one saying it. Piano music spilled out of an open window and filled the street.

"See? People play the piano on the West Side," Barry said proudly. "I bet the windows don't even open on the East Side."

The doorman was rude. The elevator was scary. The hall was dingy. Upstairs, on the coffee table, was the pale green budget ledger she'd brought him last week, empty. Barry was unstable, immature, and had lost much of his hair. Barry was going nowhere.

He flew in with Ping-Pong paddles. "Play."

"No."

"The whole point of living with someone is you have a partner," he bullied. "Come on!"

"Not in the mood."

"Justine! You're so accomplished, you're so intelligent, you're so beautiful. Now pick up the fucking paddle and play."

It was easier than fighting about it. She beat him.

"Another round."

"No."

"Come on."

She played. She enjoyed beating him.

"Three out of five."

She beat him again. He gave up. "Hey, Playland tomorrow?"

"No. I'm visiting Harriet and the baby."

How could he even think about Playland? She took a shower and shaved her legs. When she'd had a month off between taking the bar and starting work, she'd almost lost her mind. When she emerged, Barry was in the bed with the dog. They were growling together, rhythmically. She pushed the dog away, and knocked Barry back against the headboard and bit his stomach. She was furious with him. She wanted to be making plans, already. They had sex.

When she emerged from another shower, he was watching TV.

"Don't look at me like that!" he cried. "It's C-SPAN! I'm not watching *Wheel of Fortune!*"

He had become his father.

. . .

Harriet's second bedroom was decorated in a dinosaur theme.

"My mother's appalled that I'm nursing," Harriet said, fixing up her shirt and yawning. "She thinks I'm doing it because his family thinks it's a sacrament."

"I always thought it would be more fun to breast-feed the husband," Barry said as Justine passed him the infant carefully. Doug was out getting diapers.

"Top of the first for you, Harvey baby," he said, kissing the baby's head and holding him high up in the air.

"Okay, don't give him brain damage," Harriet said, and the baby began to scream.

"I'm sorry! I swear, I didn't do anything!"

"He cries. That's his job," Harriet said, taking him away from Barry. "You have no idea what it's like to live with someone screaming all the time."

"Oh, I don't know about that," Justine said.

Barry marched out, offended.

"Anything new?" Harriet whispered, and Justine shook her head. "How can you stand it?"

"Excuse me?"

"I'm sorry," she said quickly. "It's just, if Doug is home two days in a row, we're at each other's throats."

"By the way," Barry said in the elevator. "I'm growing a beard."

She nodded. "It looks like dirt. I'm going to the office."

"You made the mistake of telling me your case had closed," he accused.

"I have other cases," she said.

They started walking downtown on Lexington, and he veered towards a three-card monte game in the blazing sun.

"Why are you bothering with this." She tried to pull him away. "They have pickpockets here."

"No, I know how this is done."

"Fine." He was an idiot. She walked on.

A bus thundered by, emitting dark gray exhaust in the heat.

"Don't you walk away and leave me like that!"

She continued walking.

"Look, we have to talk," he said, sweating.

"Talking won't change anything."

"You're just embarrassed because of Harriet."

"The hell with Harriet! I don't want to *be* with you."

"You negative, critical—"

"Just. Get. Your act. Together."

"You are *such* a princess!" he shouted, and hit his hand on a lamppost. In broad daylight, half a block from her office. She looked around. Mainly tourists.

"Fine. I'm a princess," she said reasonably. "Show me a nonprincess who wants you unemployed, behaving like an infant."

"Lots of women would love extra time with their boyfriends."

"Oh, yeah, this is about me," she said, crossing the street.

"Okay, so you're not a princess. You're just a bitch."

She threw herself against the revolving door. A couple of days of sulking was understandable. A week of vacation was okay. But this! Upstairs, she checked in with Fosdale Cleat—nothing new. Typical: the one weekend she could have used a crisis situation, and nothing was going on.

The phone rang. "I forgot to tell you," he shouted from a pay phone. "That *woman* at Unemployment gave me a wrong address. She wasn't even smart enough for a job at the post office."

"Sorry to hear it." She hung up and began reading the *New York Law Journal*. The phone rang.

"What would you say to going to the beach tomorrow?"

"No. But you go. It would do you good. Bye."

She turned on her computer. The phone rang. This was pathology. *"What!"*

"What kind of a way is that to answer a phone?"

It was Carol. Nana was in the hospital. She'd had a stroke. She was in New York Hospital, on the 14th floor. If Justine was going to visit, could she check about private nurses for the fourth of July, which was going to be a problem?

The elevator at the hospital took twenty minutes to arrive. The entire building smelled like greasy chicken. There were old people lying on stretchers in the halls. Nana was in a semiprivate room. The woman in the bed by the door had no hair. Nana was being cleaned by a Philippine nurse in plastic gloves.

"Hi, Nana," she said, and walked around to the other side of the bed to see her.

Miriam was staring at nothing. She seemed senseless. But Justine had expected that. The nurse ignored both of them. She was washing Miriam's limp white arm, scrubbing her gray armpit hair. Nana had armpit hair? The nurse turned her over. This exposed gray, loose-fleshed legs and a pendulous stomach. Justine looked away. Nana moaned and held her hand out.

She wasn't senseless? Justine went over to the bed and took her damp hand, looking at the veiny wrists and the swollen fingers. There was an IV in her other hand. Terrible smells.

"She had a bad night," the nurse said, swabbing Nana's toes. "She had to be restrained." Nana roused herself to make a nasty, childish face at the nurse. This was terrible. The nurse tossed the sponge into the bucket of soapy water, and took it away.

The sun was streaming in through the dirty window. Someone was crying in the hall. Nana's eyes were closed. The other woman was either sleeping or dead. Carol wandered in, looking drained and exhausted.

"She was impossible last night," the nurse called. Carol made a nasty face when the nurse's back was turned. Justine looked out the window, not to be part of this.

The doctor walked in and read Nana's chart for a while. "How are you, Miriam?" he shouted. He was younger than Justine.

Nana hissed, looking at the doctor steadily.

"What year is it?"

She bared her teeth, as if she were doing something difficult.

Carol stood on the curtain side of the bed. "When can she come home? I can get a hospital bed set up."

"Well, you have to understand that she's not going to be herself," he said. Nana was looking up at the ceiling. They continued to discuss her deteriorating capacities across the bed. "Speak to the family liaison about your options with nursing homes. But the mental decline—"

"Excuse me," Justine interrupted. "Why don't you talk about that outside."

They looked at her blankly, and went out to the hall.

The family of the other patient came in and whispered behind the curtain. Carol had probably already had an incident with these people. Nana was pushing the remote control to the TV, on and off, on and off. She bared her tiny teeth at Justine.

A person in mint green clothes and a shower cap brought the damp chicken smell into the room with a tray of food. Justine tried not to gag. Carol returned. "Is she eating?"

"We can try," Carol said. "Yesterday she threw food at the nurse, so she's on IV only."

"Crackers," Nana said weakly, and both Justine and her mother went over and shouted encouragement.

"Nana! You're talking!" Justine unwrapped a Saltine and broke a piece off. Miriam looked at her like a grateful animal, and chewed until the cracker was liquefied. Justine couldn't watch.

"Oh, Ma, you're doing great!" Carol smiled, and fed her another cracker. There was suddenly a fecal smell. The nurse threw the covers off Miriam, and pulled out a turquoise bedpan.

"We'll give you your privacy," Carol shouted.

Miriam glared at her angrily, and fought off the nurse.

Justine hurried out to the waiting area. She felt like she'd moved from a sturdy house with good plumbing into a dirty room with a hot plate, where everything was broken.

Chapter 15

Not Catholic

Vince took a plane home from Chicago. New job, new apartment, yes. But he hadn't gained anything by being alone. He'd just been unavailable, and now, coming out of it, nothing had changed. He was impressed with people who had a point. His grandfather had been a tailor. His father started out as a musician, and then went into radio with a specific idea that he wanted executed. His mother's father was a teacher. His mother had wanted a family.

He was fed, clothed, educated, and set free. What was the point? He didn't care about real estate or banking. He didn't really like the people involved. The tinkering with bond issues—well, so what? It wasn't fascinating stuff, and he didn't need the money.

Vince had an apartment. He had a car. Now what was he supposed to do?

. . .

When he got home, Laura was pacing the black granite floor in his lobby, irate.

"I've only been here for two hours," she hissed.

He'd made plans with her two weeks ago, but had completely forgotten.

He began to sweat. "I had no idea you were coming so soon."

"You told me to meet you here. You did! *You.*"

The doorman held his hands out—not his fault.

In the elevator, Laura glowered at him. Had she expected a resumption of things? Vince was pretty sure he didn't want to. It was pointless.

"So this is where you finally park," she said, surveying the living room.

The house phone rang immediately. "Send her up," he told the doorman.

Laura smiled, disgusted. "Well, this should be fun."

"I'm very sorry." He didn't want to see either one of them. He wanted both of them to go.

"I don't even know why I'm here," Pippa announced as she walked in. "Oh. Company," she said sarcastically. She and Laura had met before, and they reintroduced themselves.

"He forgot I was coming," Laura said, doing neck exercises slowly.

"I just got the day wrong," he said, pouring Scotch.

"That's nothing," Pippa said from the sofa. She wasn't leaving either. "He forgot he called me this afternoon for tonight."

"Look, I'm starving," Laura said, and took the Scotch he offered her.

The two of them were very chatty in the cab, and he sat with his head back while his stomach churned and they talked about Vermont. At Wok-o-Matic, he ordered wonton soup without the wontons, and let them choose everything else. They were hitting it off.

"I just turned 34," Laura told Pippa, chewing on some ice. "Do you know what that means?"

"Your clock is ticking?"

"Everybody's clock is ticking," Laura said, and Pippa leaned in. "No, it means that it's too late to have the early disaster marriage. The one that ends so I can turn around six months later and marry the right guy just in time to have kids."

"It's not too late to have kids," Pippa said.

"No, see, it's too late to make a mistake."

"But you're Catholic," he said. "There are no mistakes."

"Of course, I could always become a second wife," Laura said, ignoring him. "If you're the second wife, you're young for the rest of your life."

The food came; too many plates, everything swimming in brown liquid. He couldn't look at it. The two of them dug in, passing plates, adding sauces, and mixing things around with spoons. They asked for chopsticks. They asked for low-sodium soy sauce. They ordered more Diet Coke. Laura probably thought he was a fool. Pippa probably liked Laura better than she liked him.

He blew on a spoonful of soup. "I thought Catholicism was really important to you."

"Some of it," Laura said coldly.

"I thought it was all or nothing."

"If my kids are raised Catholic," she said, trapping a mushroom and popping it in her mouth, "that's all that matters."

"Wait, I thought—"

"WHAT did you think," she said, bored, disgusted. She dumped a load of stringy wet food onto her plate.

"Nothing," he said, switching from soup back to Scotch. "All this time I thought it was a problem that I wasn't Catholic."

She snorted sharply. "No, Vince: the problem with you is that you're you."

The waiter arrived with more food.

"I feel like I'm in a French movie," Pippa said with sudden enthusiasm.

. . .

After dinner, he and Laura watched Pippa walk west on her platform shoes.

"I'll be out of your hair tomorrow," Laura said.

"Stay as long as you like," he said, hailing a cab. What was the difference?

At home, he let Laura get settled in the bedroom and he closed the kitchen doors. He called his mother and announced that he had a new job. She congratulated him, and told him she'd been a little worried about him lately. She couldn't talk—she was on her way to pay a condolence call.

He tried Kiki. Pat Metheny was on the stereo; she was probably putting slides together on the table. It had been months; she probably wouldn't mind him calling.

"What do you do for confusion?"

"Potassium. Deep breathing. Come talk in person," she said over the grinding of the juicer. "Tor is fast asleep."

"I can't," he whispered. "I have company."

"Well then, do your thing."

He called Pippa. "I'm surprised to hear from you," she said.

"Don't pull that on me, I just can't deal right now."

"If you don't want to deal with me, then don't call me," she said impatiently. "This is boring." And she hung up.

He skipped a breath; then he breathed in. He opened the doors. Laura was in the shower. He dialed Pippa's number again.

"I think you need someone younger," she said firmly. "Someone who doesn't know that this is bullshit." She hung up.

This was ridiculous. He just wanted to have a conversation on the phone. He called Renée. He hung up when she answered.

☢

That tone

Barry walked into the crusty din of his mother's factory; a couple of the old guys waved. They'd been working under the ancient, fuzz-dripping pipes since his grandfather's day. Barry had new respect for older people. Not the very old: they were tedious and frightening. But people 40-65, say. Just living that long was a real accomplishment.

When he got to the tiny ugly carpeted hole in the back, his mother was on her knees, pulling fabric samples out of cracks in the wallboard. The whole place was probably held together with asbestos and Popsicle sticks.

"You're looking very pretty." Barry kissed her, and looked at her closely. "Everything under control?"

"This place is a sty. A sty. I never noticed."

Lawrence, her latest in a long string of unacceptable assistants, tilted his chair into the doorless threshold between their desks. "Sol says the silk's delayed," he called.

She slammed her hand on the desk. "Put him on."

"Mommy. Don't get upset."

The phone rang. "Don't jerk me around, Sol," she warned the speaker. "My patience has vanished."

"What patience?" Sol squawked on the other end. "What can I tell you, Rose? It's not my fault."

"Och!" She hit the phone, disconnecting him. "You hear that? You hear that?" She stalked the cubicle, her wobbling heels digging into the dirty carpet. "If ONE more person tells me it's not his fault, he was sideswiped by an ambulance, her husband threw her out the window, the policy doesn't cover between the truck and the warehouse, I am going to SHOOT somebody! I don't NEED this irritation!"

He didn't either. And yet, interfacing had put him through college and business school. Outside, over the din of the machines, someone was coughing up phlegm and spitting.

"You sick of white shoes and civility?" Rose smiled, looking lovely all of a sudden. "Come to Seventh Avenue."

A frail young Chinese woman ran in, frantic. "I can't, I wish, I
sorry!" she cried, and darted away. He worried for her.

"Well?" Lawrence leaned in on the chair. "This is the third time.
What should I do? Fire her? Shoot her?"

"Fire her," she told Lawrence calmly, putting on her jacket. She
turned to Barry. "Lunch?"

He couldn't imagine doing this.

They went to a calm, chic place in Chelsea, with ceiling fans and
attractive people. He was surprised—they usually ate hot dogs with
UPS drivers at a stand-up counter on 36th Street.

"How's the grandmother?" Rose asked.

"Worse and worse. Justine's flipping out."

"I can understand that," she said. She looked like she was going
to ask him another, more personal question, but didn't.

He wished she had. They never talked about anything.

"Why did you marry Daddy?" he asked, after they had ordered.

She looked at him as if she'd never thought about it. She laughed.
"I have no idea. Well, I was 28 years old, already."

The waiter brought iced tea. "Were you ever happy with him?"

"Sure," she said.

He didn't believe it. "Really?"

"Oh, yes. When you guys were little, and we moved into
Manhattan, and we were going to the Island in the summers. That
was fun. Before the first bankruptcy," she said, deadpan.

"Do you have fun now?"

"Fun? What is fun, Barry? I'm 63 years old. Fun is probably over-
stating the case." The usual look returned to her face: life was an
incessant battle, producing—at the very best—constant frustration,
pointless compromises, and the occasional bitter laugh.

The salads came; she told him how she would train him, what he could expect.

"And you'd be the boss," she said, lipstick bleeding onto her chin. "None of that corporate hierarchy that makes you so crazy."

The woman hadn't had a date, as far as he knew, in twenty years. After the divorce there had been a partner named Merv, but they'd had a falling-out over business, and they'd stopped speaking. There were a lot of people his mother wasn't speaking to.

What would she do without the office? And no way was he working for her. As they strolled back to the office, four Hasidim marched purposefully into the Garment Center Synagogue. Barry wished he'd been raised with more Judaism, something solid he could legitimately resent. He wanted to ask his mother what she believed in, finally. How did she get up in the morning and not think about dying?

"Take the damn business, Barry," she said, exasperated. "You could do a lot worse than this. You'd be doing me a favor."

"Sell it, Mommy."

"I don't need the money. I don't like how you're drifting."

"I am NOT drifting."

"Okay," she said. "Look. Don't make up your mind now. Think about it, talk with Justine. You'll let me know."

He kissed her in front of her loading dock and took the subway home. She should run it or sell it. He wasn't going to live like that. He hadn't gone to Wharton for that.

Now he sounded like Carol.

At home, Barry put up water for coffee. Everything before Justine was ridiculous, unnatural. For five years, he suffered an incessant internal debate over Cynthia. He couldn't look at her without disappointment; there wasn't a single thing about her that he didn't want to change; she routinely said things that made him cringe. In truth:

he wanted to be out to dinner with someone else, and he hated himself for it.

Cynthia seemed completely unaware that he was constantly talking himself into her. This made it much worse; he worried that one day, when his guard was down, all the criticism he routinely swallowed would leap out of his mouth and shower her with contempt. He kept getting disgusted, breaking it off, and returning out of loneliness and habit. There was no chemistry with Cynthia, just a cycle of boredom, repulsion, guilt, and pity.

Ms. Schiff, however, was compelling as a person. Since there was chemistry, there were no traits to weigh, only aspects of her person that fascinated him. Her flushed cheeks, her mutant thumbs, her bossy ways: anyone else might find these unattractive, but they moved him. Again, he wondered: was she talking herself into him? Of course, even if there was chemistry, there was always daily friction and bad behavior to erode the attraction. Things were terrible lately. She'd told him she loved him the other night as if she were thanking him for opening a door for her.

He poured the coffee into a thermos, and took a cab to the hospital in the sultry heat. Miriam was looking more delicate, more out of it than ever. She was mewling. The current nurse was nibbling quietly on her lunch. Justine wasn't there, but he saw Carol's gold sunglasses on the foot of the bed. An undetermined period alone in a room with a dying woman and Carol? Oy.

Carol strutted in. "I thought I told you I didn't want you eating in here," she barked at the nurse, who was minding her own business. "She brings in this disgusting Jamaican food," she said loudly as the nurse took her food out. "It stinks up the place."

Barry was horrified. There was nothing to say. Carol was unassailable.

"Last night's nurse, now she was a winner." Carol went into an extended kvetch, while the current nurse returned to take Miriam's pulse. Carol and Alex must have been quite a couple. Justine was so aggressively normal. She must have channeled all the mishegoss into her 90-hour workweeks and color-coded closets.

Justine walked in, looking cool and lovely. He was so glad to see her, he almost lunged.

"How is she," Justine asked, putting her bag on a chair.

"In and out," Carol said. "How are you?"

Justine went to the bed and leaned over. Miriam looked at her without recognition. Last night, Justine had told him she believed that Miriam understood everything, but wasn't trying. Justine poured a cup of coffee and stood neatly by the window.

"Hey, Gene and I are going to Tessio's later," Carol stage-whispered. "Would you two like to join?"

He hated Tessio's. He was delighted when Justine said no.

"There's an operation," Carol said slowly. "But the doctor wants to see how she responds to medication first."

This was bizarre. She had to see that her mother would be better off dead, not lingering. "The doctor isn't hopeful."

"Please don't talk about her condition in front of her," Justine said firmly. "It can't help her to hear that."

"She hears what the doctor wants her to hear," Carol said. Justine closed her eyes and dropped her head, incredulous.

"Hey, how about a walk for Nana?" he suggested.

"What a good idea," Justine said.

The nurse took the sheet off. Miriam's arms were wrapped in canvas.

Justine looked like he felt: in need of a strong drink.

"It's a straightjacket," Carol told them quietly. "She hit the night nurse. She keeps pulling out her IV."

Miriam was unwrapped, and she began fussing. The nurse got her to the edge of the bed and Justine helped her up. They made progress by inches to the door. Justine turned to him and said, "Barry wants to walk you out, Nana."

He took over. Miriam's wrinkled gray arm was like wrought iron.

They walked to the end of the hall, about 10 feet. She was working her lips and drooling.

Each time he turned to go back towards the room she resisted, her mouth in a line, her hairless brows puckered in anger. She was pulling him towards the other end of the hall—20 yards, at least.

He was getting tired from the stooping, the tension. "Come on, Miriam," he shouted, instantly horrified—he was talking to her as if she were a child. "Aren't you tired? I know I am. Let's go back into the room. Okay?" She let him lead her into the room, but she wouldn't go to the bed.

"Sure you don't want to come?" Carol put on lipstick in the guest chair.

"Yeah," Justine said.

He was close to release, but each time he veered towards her bed, the old lady wouldn't go. He looked to the nurse for help, but she just stood by the bed, expressionless.

"She doesn't want us to go," Carol said sadly. "That's what this is about."

Later, at home, Justine sat glazed on the couch. He stood behind her and pressed his hands into her neck to give her a massage. She shrunk away from him and stood up.

Just once, could they be in the same mood at the same time?

"Okay—no hands," he said, and she smiled, but in a complicated way. "Justine. I need to talk to you."

"You want to call me a bitch?"

"No. And I'm sorry about that."

"So?" She stood, waiting.

"Not with you in this humor," he said, and went into the kitchen for some wine.

"Fine." She went into the bedroom for a while. She'd been making career guidance suggestions, and asking follow-up questions.

She clearly expected him to e-mail her a memo within five business days, stating, "I have incorporated your ideas into my new strategy, and can report the following results."

Her not responding to his repeated calling of her name, first straight, and then with sheep bleats, caused anger to rise in him and lodge in his chest and throat.

It was awful: she emerged, ready to go.

"You're going? What am I going to do for dinner?"

"I don't know, Barry, what do you want to do for dinner?"

"Don't use that tone with me."

"Don't use that tone with ME."

"What tone?"

"'What am I going to do for dinner,'" she whined.

He hated the very fiber of her being. "How dare you."

She put a pouch in her bag. "I'm getting out of here before we have a fight about nothing again."

"It's not nothing."

"It IS nothing. It's a bad mood. It'll be over as soon as I'm out the door," she said, swinging her bag over her shoulder. Why was this bag always there at the ready to take her away?

"It'll be over for you when you leave, but not for me."

"It'll be over for you when you rejoin the world." She went to the foyer to put on lipstick.

He seized the bag. He hid it in the bottom drawer near the sink. She came back and looked around. He knew he was grinning.

She got supremely pissed off. "Where is it."

He couldn't keep from laughing. She began pushing him around and pummeling his arms. Finally he opened the drawer.

"In the festering onions? You're sick!" she shouted, hitting the bag to get the onion paper off it. "This is disgusting."

"Oh, lighten up."

"I can't STAND you anymore! I AM GOING!"

"Fine. Go."

She hooked the dog on the leash and slammed out the door.

It was summer! What was all this fighting indoors about? Whatever happened to baking in the sun between bodysurfing and hot dogs? Although, as long as you had to find parking, carry a wallet, and think about skin cancer, you couldn't really have that Endless Summer feeling.

She walked back in. "I don't want to see you for a while," she said, her key still in the door. "If you get your act together you can call me. But not before."

A judicious use of horns never did a band any harm. Chicago knew it. Van Morrison knew it. He wanted to discuss this with someone. No one talked about this anymore. Who *were* his friends?

Chapter 16

Material adverse change

In the last two weeks of August, Justine shuttled between the office, the hospital, and home. There was freedom in this kind of bondage. She hadn't spoken to Barry in two weeks. She couldn't say she missed him. But the silence was odd.

On Friday at noon, Galsworthy Paper signed a letter of exclusivity with a Los Angeles-based bidder for the Fitzsimmons pesticide subsidiary. Galsworthy stock promptly dropped five points. Justine and Mitch set up their laptops in one of the opposing counsel's conference rooms at 8 P.M. The banking group was working in a room nearby. The lead opposing counsel was a Driggs-in-training. Mitch was bouncing his leg up and down, shaking the entire table. They ate pastrami and argued until 2 A.M., and then argued about what time to return the next morning.

The disputes continued over bagels at 9 A.M. By 10 the arbitrageurs were calling. By 11, Farlowe was calling. At noon, the pizza arrived. Cricket's PR agent had to comment on every clause, slowing everything down exponentially. The bankers ordered in for food every three hours. Mitch was caroming off the walls. At 9, she told Farlowe to stop calling, she told Mitch to stop shaking, she told the bankers to stop ordering food. At 10 P.M., she told the PR agent to go home and stay there until she was called back. They worked through the night, and all the next day.

On Sunday night at 10:45, Justine stood up, bloated, exhausted, disgusted. They had to close the deal by midnight, or the stock would plummet again the following morning. The bidders had to do it or lose their exclusive.

"I know you think otherwise," she said, not smiling, "but that which I offered you as our final position? Well, it really is our final position."

In the end, they scrapped everything they'd already drafted, and Justine wrote the whole deal on a single piece of paper with a 30-minute deadline. The respective boards were faxed at 11:35; there were handshakes and signatures at 11:55. Galsworthy had champagne sent up and insisted on doing a five-minute toast over the speakerphone while everyone blinked at each other in contempt and fatigue. What a waste of energy.

She slept until 2 the next day and then dragged herself in. Farlowe had her paged. She went into his office heavily.

"How are you, Schiff?" he said accusingly.

"Okay."

"Just okay? What's the matter with you? Oh, right, Grandma."

"She's not well."

"Uh-huh, uh-huh." He looked at his watch. "I have a new IPO for you. That is, unless your family troubles would interfere."

She used to find the crustiness amusing. Now she was angry. Why did everyone have to accommodate him? So his metabolism was efficient. She was plenty efficient herself, and she wasn't rude.

"The 'family troubles' aren't the problem. I just don't have time now with two active sales going on."

"You finished one of them last night," he tried. "And your other one won't start right away."

She'd just spent an entire weekend locked in a room! She didn't deserve to be treated like a first-year whiner. "I'm sorry, really."

He looked her over and raised a scrambled eyebrow. "Okay." He stood. The undone work lay there between them. "So what am I supposed to do with this?"

That was another thing she couldn't stand: the coy pose of helplessness. It used to work on her: she'd been flattered that he needed her so much. Now she'd outgrown the need to impress him.

"I'm sure you'll find someone," she said.

That night, she couldn't sleep. Assuming Barry got a job and turned back into the good Barry of December through April, Justine thought she could be happy with him. But he'd be making vulgar remarks and flirting with waiters and leaving dirty underwear on the floor. For all of eternity. Was that happily ever after? There was no one else to think about.

She called him, very late. Her room was glowing blue from the digital clock. It felt good to hear him breathe. There were comfortable pauses. This was a critical juncture. She wanted to see him. They made plans. She'd see how she felt then.

The following afternoon, she was sweating. She took off her jacket. Her pulse was 125. That was impossible. She checked it again. The same. Normal, lying-down pulse for Justine was 48, and sitting up in a chair was 55. She was upset. It shouldn't stop her from working. She got down on the floor to calm down.

The door opened. It was Bob. "Lying down on the job?"

She stayed on the floor. "What do you want."

"Mindy needs you to sign off on these agreements."

Her calves were cramping. She caught a typo. These paralegals were a joke. She took an Advil.

Carol called. Miriam had had another stroke.

When Justine got to the hospital, both beds were empty. Carol was flipping violently through all the big thick French magazines. Gene was sitting in a stray wheelchair. He was there, you had to say that for him. They were waiting for Miriam to return from a CAT scan.

"Justine," Carol pleaded, "a woman was raped and murdered on the West Side."

"I am not responsible for every bad thing that happens on the West Side."

"West 86th Street," her mother said. Her face looked like a swollen peach. "I didn't say you were."

"All right, then, Barry isn't responsible for it."

Carol sniffed, unconvinced. "I just don't want you to go through hell," she warbled. Justine got up. If the woman was going to reminisce about Alex Schiff's descent into bipolar disorder, she was leaving. "You were too young to know what I went through." Carol put on lipstick with a shaky hand.

"I don't think the situation is analogous," Justine said.

"I want someone *together* for you. Someone wonderful. You've waited *this* long—why settle?"

She'd been so comfortable talking to Barry on the phone in the dark.

"Nana said that Cousin Linda married a guy who was perfect on paper. And he turned out to be a louse," she said, annoyed and amused to be speaking her mother's language.

"He was *not* perfect on paper," Carol said contemptuously. "He was *always* a louse. He was a salesman at Altman's, and they fired him for stealing gloves. Linda did the real estate, and she met the Italian, who's a nice guy, even if he is Italian. She just got lucky." She looked over at the empty bed as if to scold Miriam for getting the facts wrong.

"And Stacy, the dancer, with the sexy Australian?"

"Not a dancer. Cousin Stacy was a songwriter. She'd gotten one of those groups to record her song. But she took money up front, like an idiot. So, it became a huge hit. And she didn't get a dime—The End. The Australian left her for his physical therapist. The kids were wild. The son stole her jewelry for cocaine. The daughter married a Chinese faith healer. Okay?"

Justine laughed. She loved historical gossip. Nana was the biggest source of it. She didn't want her to die.

"Don't throw yourself away on some nut," Carol pleaded.

Justine went to find Nana on the radiology floor. She recognized a yellow blanket from home on a cart in an empty hallway. Nana was alone and practically naked on the cart. She was breathing raggedly though an oxygen mask. Her eyes were clouded over with a film. She looked alarmed, but Justine wasn't sure if Miriam knew who she was. She didn't make any sign to Justine. She was dying. There were so many tubes, Justine didn't know if it was safe to pull up the blanket. It was freezing cold in this hallway. She was just standing there, embarrassed to be there with this gasping, nearly naked woman, and ashamed that she was embarrassed. She had no idea what to do.

The doctor came by. "Miriam, you must be cold," he said, and pulled the blanket up. He ignored Justine and read Nana's chart. He wheeled her into a dark room. Justine was alone in the hall. She felt wretched. She could have talked to Nana. She could have pulled up the blanket. She should have held her hand.

"It'll be an hour," the doctor said. "Go get some air."

She met Barry in the hospital lobby. He'd shaved and gotten a haircut. He looked nice. Justine felt a little sheepish. They walked into the first coffee shop and Barry ordered without event. At the counter, a guy in a white lab coat dropped a bottle. Green pills scattered on the dirty floor. He gathered them up, put them back in the bottle, put the bottle in his pocket.

"I hope Nana isn't taking anything green," Barry said.

"I missed you," she said, and he took her hands and squeezed. She was shaky. She told him about Miriam on the cart in the hallway.

"Sweetie!" he cried. "Let me be with you!" He came over to her side of the booth and gave her a hug. She loved it when he did that. "You know I'm going to get a job eventually."

"I do?" She blew her nose into her napkin.

"Yes, you do." The waitress brought their sodas. He squeezed her stomach and she flinched, annoyed. How did she know that? Things had only gotten worse.

Barry went back to his side of the booth in frustration. "It's like, you're mad at me all the time."

"It isn't *like* I'm mad at you. I *am* mad at you. *All the time!*" She hadn't been too young to remember. They used to have to drag her father into the shower.

The waitress dumped the cottage cheese in front of him and the sandwich in front of her. "My mother wants me to take over her business," he said, and they switched plates. "But I don't know."

"How many offers have you turned down at this point?"

"Just get a job, any job, doesn't matter what it is."

"Someone is handing you a business. I don't understand how you can say that you'd rather watch TV." There was a black hair in her cottage cheese.

"You wouldn't mind me being a garmento?"

"Well, what do *you* want to do?"

"My mother would die if she didn't have a company to run."

"She wants to retire. I heard her say so."

"Look. I know I have no right to ask you this." He reached out over the plates and glasses and clasped her hand in his.

He was going to propose to her while she was sweating in a sticky coffee shop? Over a chipped plate of cottage cheese with a hair in it? "Don't you dare."

"Okay." He took a breath in. "Definitely no?"

He was! He would have proposed over a chipped plate of cottage cheese with a hair in it. He sighed and she looked out the window at the sweltering vastness of First Avenue. Maybe she should just marry Barry Cantor and call it a life. Who else was there? If he got himself together—would he, though? Her parents had been married for 11 years before her father went off the deep end. Carol wouldn't have walked into it with her eyes open.

"I'm thinking of starting a band," he announced.

"Look, I can't see you anymore. This has to stop."

They went back to her apartment because he had things there. She knew exactly what her life was going to be like from now on: no one to talk to, no one to eat with. The rare free evening spent at the gym. Embarrassing fix-ups. Occasional dates with angry men she didn't like. No sex. Just like last year. It was enough to make you consider relaxing your standards.

The dog ignored her and bounced around Barry. He played with her on the sofa. Enough. "I'll get you a bag," she said.

"I just don't understand this. Don't you need me?"

"For thirty-two years I did just fine. I won't die without you."

"I'd die without you!" he said, clutching her shoulders. Everything was such a drama with him. "And what about your Nana?"

She would not respond to this manipulation. "That is very upsetting," she said, pushing the shopping bag at him. "But it's a separate issue. It shouldn't affect what we have to do."

He held the shopping bag to his stomach and stood still. "You are so fucking clinical. I can't believe it."

"Why?" How dare he use her grandmother like that.

"You have no feelings for me at all."

"That's not true. I have nothing but feelings for you." She went to the kitchen. But there was nothing to do in there. "Bad and good. Feelings." The next man would have all his hair and work longer hours than she did. Starting a band, for God's sake.

"Isn't this negotiable?"

"No. We have to move on. And it has to be a clean break."

He came into the kitchen and began kissing her ardently.

"No."

"Why?" He kissed frantically. "We'll never do it again."

This was maudlin. She wasn't in the mood for big emotion. He would never understand that. He was unstable. He was a fool. Lying around, turning down jobs, watching TV. She disengaged from his mouth in disgust. "I'm sorry, I just can't do this."

"Fine. I'm leaving."

But he wouldn't go! He walked to the bulletin board and pulled off the '84 campaign pin. "I never wanted to ask about this."

"So don't ask," she said, and his eyes flashed. She didn't care. She wanted him out. He stabbed the pin back into the board. He was slightly menacing now.

"Could I take a shower?"

Quit stalling. She exhaled.

"One fucking shower!"

"Go ahead!"

But he came out of the bathroom looking so combed and scalded and pink, she felt different. She'd had some kind of deep peace with Barry. She couldn't dismiss that. Was that love? He was ridiculous, he was charming, he hated himself. She gave him a hug, and he seemed so overwhelmed that she wanted to just marry him and be done with it.

He was shaking his head bitterly, tossing underwear and socks in the shopping bag cavalierly. Just watch: he'd forget the dirty pair on the bathroom floor. She gave him a last hug and almost cried. She wondered how she would phrase it to her mother.

He kissed the dog and walked out without looking.

There they were, the dirty pair, on the bathroom floor, soiled, pathetic, ridiculous. She didn't pick them up. There was more to Barry than dirty underwear, but she didn't want to think about it now. She made herself some tea, organized and cleaned, and noticed them every time she went into the bathroom.

Justine was afraid of what this would do to her face.

It was the night before the closing of the sale of Noah Clurman's sporting-goods chain to a competitor. While waiting to proof some last-minute changes, Justine glanced through the wedding announcements in the *Times*. Miss Eberly Pitts, 21. Miss Jocelyn Grebbins, 23. Who WERE these people? Inez Campbell Nunce, 28. Well, there. Still: 28.

She should never read this section.

Nicky ran into her office, his face in a sweat. "You're not going to believe this, but they say they can't close tomorrow until they've seen some documents."

He handed Justine a list. She looked over the things they wanted, grabbed the phone, and called the other side. "Are you kidding me?" she told the associate impatiently. "A lease for office space in Eau Claire, Wisconsin—less money than I spend on rent? This cannot possibly hold up the closing." She hung up.

"They've had months to do this," Nicky said heatedly. "At 11:30 the night before? It's just unprofessional. It's stupid."

The phone rang. Nicky seized it in his skinny hand. "Put him on speaker," Justine commanded, disgusted.

"How dare you talk to my associate like that," the partner from the buyer's side spluttered over the speaker.

"Ron," Justine said. "You've had four months to ask for anything you wanted. We have been more than cooperative."

"We have every right!" he shouted. "What are you hiding?"

"Ron." She held her temper. "My client can yell at me, and my partner can yell at me. But you cannot yell at me."

"I want the record to show that—"

"What record? There is no record!"

Nicky was smiling. "We'll fax you the documents," she said, "but you know as well as I do that you won't understand them in an hour. You're just covering your asses, which is fine, but you should've done it last month. I'm surprised at you."

"So you're faxing."

"Yes. But if my client doesn't get his money tomorrow by 10 o'clock, I don't think he's interested in waiting till 11."

"Call him."

"I am not calling my client at midnight. We want the money at 10 A.M. We've had other offers, if you recall."

She disconnected him. Nicky gave her a weary, pro forma high-five. This job wasn't even interesting anymore.

Justine spent the closing day waiting for confirmation of the wire transfer with Nicky and some investment bankers. In the morning, there was a mood of ragged relief. By afternoon, everyone was cranky and itching to get on to other things. At 4:30, there was still no word from the bank.

"If you can put a man on the moon and call home from a plane," Nicky said, leaning on the wall to stretch his hamstrings, "you'd think you could transfer money by 3:30." The investment bankers grunted in agreement.

At 5, they were told that the transaction couldn't be found in the computer. At 6, they were told the moneys were not in the Noah Clurman Ltd. account, in the SportPro Equities account, or anywhere else.

Nicky said, "Four hundred million dollars, they lost?"

"Like fun they did," Justine said, dialing the bank. "What the hell is going on here," she bellowed. "Find that money now!" She slammed down the phone. People scattered to take care of other business they could have done at any point in the day had they known. Justine and Nicky waited for the phone to ring.

The money was found at 8; Justine went home and collapsed.

She woke at midnight and walked the dog. She ate mayonnaise sandwiches and watched *Mary Tyler Moore*. This was her life.

Call for success stories

Barry was dreaming. He knew he was dreaming. He knew it was morning. Stella kept eating crap off the street, and he kept hitting her. She kept eating it and he kept hitting her, and she just didn't understand. He woke up in despair.

He looked around the empty humid room. To go to sleep miserable and abject, as he'd been doing for so long, was one thing. But to wake up and have the day already be pointless and yawning ahead like a weedy junk lot next to rusted El tracks with nothing else in sight—this was intolerable.

August had come like sickness. Barry was sick. Everything he did was wrong. He sat in the living room. Then he lay in the bedroom. Then he ate in the kitchen. He went through the rooms this way. The hairballs and rawhide shoes drifting across his floor reminded him of Stella. He missed her.

One morning, he woke up with a completely new idea: he should have some of his sperm frozen.

. . .

His life was fine until he talked to anybody else. Anyone with a job, a wife, a girlfriend, a blind date in their future. He called Karen. She couldn't talk, she was on her way to the dentist.

She had a place to go. He was jealous. He was jealous of his sister's dental appointment.

He'd lost his wallet somewhere. He spent two hours tearing through the apartment looking before realizing that he'd probably left it at the gym. Okay, good, so this week, he would tend to his wallet. The last time he'd done this was after the crash.

He called up the credit card companies, who took the opportunity to advise him about his balance. He went to the DMV for a new driver's license. There, improbably getting out of the subway at Chambers, was Monique, the blind date whose chest he'd obsessed about for six months two years ago. He reintroduced himself. She was on jury duty. He told her he was unemployed, and thinking of starting up his own salad dressing company. She looked at him as if he'd parted his clothing to show her some very special boils. She excused herself and walked off rapidly.

Every time he thought he'd hit his nadir, something else happened and he descended lower still. Well, you can't expect vision from someone not even smart enough to get out of jury duty. He suddenly understood what Karen was doing in Brooklyn.

He called Karen. Her strange little life had some kind of internal logic.

"The power to change is in the present moment," she told him, sounding sure of it.

"What the hell does that mean?"

"I don't know, but I have a headache. Can we talk later?"

He hadn't done anything in the present moment in at least six years. He wasn't good about the present. He wasn't present.

He went to Del-Sport and sold the '53 Yankees and Willie Mays. He could keep himself afloat selling one big card a week. But he'd learn to type before selling Tom Seaver.

Barry listened to "New York Views" and did bicep curls. He shouldn't be doing that. He should be looking though the classifieds. He turned off the radio and took out the paper.

Barry wanted the kind of attention that comes from being chosen for a special top-secret government assignment: physicals, hypnotism, language labs. He didn't even qualify for a waiter's job. He called Rita Doria. There were no openings, they'd received his résumé, they'd get back to him if ever, please don't call anymore.

He should probably go out and get some exercise now, since he wasn't expecting a call. On Riverside Drive, near the Soldier's Tomb, a short, fat, ageless mongoloid girl was tripping along, making farting noises with her mouth, completely unaware. He hurried on, heartbroken for her and the whole world. Things could be so much worse.

And then he saw her wedding ring.

He had occasional thoughts about Cynthia. Two years ago, he'd heard from his friend Jacob that Cynthia had married a Canadian anesthetist she'd met on an escalator in Bloomingdale's. So now, in addition to the sharp, bittersweet memories whenever he was on First Avenue, whenever he ate onions, whenever he heard The Cars, Barry had oblique, abstract thoughts about Cynthia whenever Canada, anesthesia, or Bloomingdale's were mentioned.

But even Cynthia wasn't an option now.

He entertained the thought of bumping into Justine. Accidentally, of course, in front of her office. She had to come in and out of it sometime; he could stake it out. Of course, the building had four exits. But in the morning, she always used the same door, and approached it from Lexington. So he could trap her. But what would he say to her? He had nothing to say.

Upstairs, the phone rang. It was Hearne, calling from a phone at the White Palace in Yonkers. "So, let's hear your news."

"I'm thinking about applying for a lifeguard job," Barry told him. "What do you think?"

There was a pause. "Well, it's none of my business."

"What does that mean, you just don't care?"

"Why ask for my opinion if you don't want to hear it?"

"I don't have to like your opinion."

"You want my support, Barry? You have it. You want to fight with me, you're on your own. Nothing you say makes sense to me."

When he hung up, he was hit with a wave of remorse so total that he had no where to hide. He wanted to go to sleep and wake up when everyone who had ever known him had died. He didn't deserve anything anyone had ever given him.

Should he move to a different city? No, he had to build on top of a fouled nest. There was no fresh start. He watched *Looney Tunes*.

Pippa arrived at 4, looking strong and healthy. She was going to Paris in September; his jealousy was bittersweet. He should just go with her; nothing keeping him here. She gave him the grocery bill. He'd have to sell Ted Williams. He convinced her that she didn't want to try a new recipe for puff pastry—what she really wanted was to watch *The Compleat Beatles* and order in for Chinese. She consented.

"What is it about this?" he said, while the teenage girls at Shea Stadium shrieked behind the chain-link fence in spastic frenzy. "Whenever I see the Beatlemaniacs I want to cry. Why?"

"Adolescent male fantasy is the driving force behind rock," she said, like a think-tank sociologist on NPR. "The fantasy is," she wiped duck sauce off her pointy little face, "you piss in the face of authority and get chicks because of it."

"It works," he nodded, taking some orange chicken from the carton. "Chicks love that."

"Chicks, Barry. Not corporate lawyers."

Who had authorized her to comment on his misery? He was too surprised to respond. All of his self-confidence flushed out of him just then. He walked to the window and leaned on the sill.

"I can't do this anymore."

"Sure you can," she said. He turned around. She was standing with her hands in her pockets, looking cold.

After she'd left, he turned on the radio, sat on the couch, and touched Justine's knitting.

"Yeah, okay, this is Ira in Queens," he heard, and he began to sweat. "Don't you dare give my tax dollars to those FAG HAGS on the school board. Spend it on prisons, yank those scumbags off the street. But what I really want to talk about is George Bush, that CIA DEGENERATE, and his minions—"

He twisted off the radio with shaking fingers. Holy shit.

He got into bed with a box of Cheerios. He turned on the TV.

"The 13's are the sufferers of life," said Resvan, the Public Access Numerologist. "They always do things they don't want to do. The fours are headstrong. Caller? I feel you vibrating on the number 11. Do you have a trip planned?" Resvan told three different people they would get jobs in September.

He decided against a shower. He wanted to sit and stew. Like in college. There was strength in it. It made sense. When he turned on the radio, a glass crashed to the floor.

Pippa had told him the trick in the kitchen was to slow down everything you did by ten percent. He slowly fiddled with the dial.

He stopped on a station because the singing voice was familiar and reassuring, if a little patronizing. He began to sweep up the shards. He should be careful—this morning he'd dropped the big knife on his foot. He was ripe for calamity, accident, cult conversion.

He realized he was listening to Barry Manilow. OH MY GOD.

Chapter 17

Details will be used against you

Justine was up until 4, knitting and turning things over and over in her mind. At this point, all of the fears she'd had about partnership were irrelevant. She didn't have children to take care of. She didn't have a husband or even a date to worry about. She'd turned down the London office more than once; but why not take a foreign assignment for a year?

Nana was drooling and shaking, staring into space through milky eyes. It was hard to watch. Justine left her room after a few minutes. Then she felt bad and turned back around. But Nana was being changed. She left again, feeling shaky and inadequate.

Back at the office, she called her mother. "I just saw Nana."

There was a pause. Neither of them said anything.

"So don't go anymore," her mother said. "I don't think she even knows we're there. If it upsets you, don't go."

"I want to be helpful."

"There's not much we can do," Carol said quietly.

"Barry and I aren't seeing each other anymore," she said, to hear how it sounded.

"Oh, I am SO relieved!" Carol shouted. "I think that was wise. I mean, a very nice guy, but a loser."

"Barry is not a loser."

"All right, then. Not a serious person. There's something wrong with him. Why should you have to deal with that?"

She pictured her mother doing a dance in her carpeted dressing room. Carol did this dance every time Justine stopped seeing someone. When Justine had cancelled her one-week engagement to Rob Principe, Carol danced so excitedly she was almost speechless with relief.

"I'll tell Rhoda to give that guy your number. You'll meet someone, don't worry. Come for dinner tonight."

That night, Justine had dinner plans with Harriet and Jenny Kravcek, who'd called out of the blue. Justine had agreed with a feeling of resignation—Jenny was a good party source, period. Carol loved Jenny. She'd do another little dance if she knew Justine was reactivating her. "Thanks, but I'll be here late."

"I can't wait for you to leave that job."

"Who said I was leaving," Justine said. She turned to a batch of annual reports from Driggs's new client, Precision, a Pittsburgh medical and cosmetic instruments company going into Chapter 11. As well they should: their tweezers were lousy, she'd tried them.

Justine walked to Harriet's through softening tar and exhaust fumes, yearning for lightness. The air was like syrup. She met Jenny in the lobby. Since they'd last seen each other, Jenny had dropped out of an MSW program to start her own business taking photo portraits of people with their pets; it was a raging success in Westchester.

"Uch, I had a date," Jenny began, and launched into the blow-by-blow description. It might have been a year ago.

"And you?"

Justine was supposed to spill her guts too. That's the way it worked. There was no way she was telling Jenny about Barry. "I *was* seeing somebody," she said, feeling the nausea deepen.

"You dumped him, he dumped you?"

Harriet opened the door nursing the child and looked Justine over. "Just checking for damage—she just broke up with her boyfriend," she explained to Jenny, who nodded; clearly they'd discussed this beforehand. They all walked into the baby's room and Harriet sat in a rocking chair.

"Well, it's going to be hard," Harriet said, while the baby fussed, "but you'll be so much better off in the long run."

"How do you know?" What right did they have to discuss this.

"He's been driving you crazy!" Harriet exclaimed. "He hid her bag in the onions, so she couldn't leave the house," she told Jenny incredulously. "And, he's got a family history of bankruptcy, gambling, anorexia, and temper tantrums. You're so much better off, it's not funny."

"I don't know about that. Wait. Who gambles?"

Jenny said, "Well, if you don't love him—"

Justine couldn't say she didn't love him. But what was love? If she loved him, she'd stand by while he wasted his life and called her a bitch? These people made no sense. "And you don't mind being alone, you never did," Harriet said, while the baby cried. "You're independent."

What the hell did that mean? Had Harriet been married so very long?

"You could do so much better, Justine," Jenny said wide-eyed, with smugness.

"He's a schmuck," Harriet concluded.

Just like her mother—either he was perfect, or he was a schmuck. If it didn't lead to a big wedding, there was something wrong with him. When was the last time Harriet gave her good advice on anything? Harriet was on another planet. She remembered a time, a year ago, when she went out with Harriet, Jenny, and a group of their friends. They went around the table, at Harriet's suggestion, and each woman detailed why she was miserable in her life, and the other women immediately offered suggestions. When it was Justine's turn, she said, "I'm not miserable. Sorry to disappoint you."

"So: where shall we order in from?" Harriet asked, tossing out take-out menus.

Justine didn't want advice. She didn't want to listen to her life turned into another Bad Man story. "Actually, I can't stay. My grandmother has taken a turn for the worse, and I have to go back to the hospital."

Jenny was miffed. Well, too bad. How much bonding could you do over being single and female in New York? She left, knowing they were dishing her dirt.

The following morning, while she was fixing herself a second breakfast in the pantry, Farlowe had her paged. She went into his office feeling fat and harassed.

"I'd like you to do some client development work," he announced, his head down in his papers. "A 50-state survey of indemnification provisions and takeover statutes."

She felt as if she'd been slapped. "Excuse me? I don't think my deal skills would be very well used on that."

"I really would be so grateful," he said tonelessly.

She had spent seven years of her life trying to please him. "Any parking tickets you want me to fix while I'm at it? Some dry cleaning I can pick up for you?"

He looked her in the eye and smiled slightly. "No thanks."

Well, he wasn't the only partner there. Justine grabbed two Danishes from the pantry and marched into Roberta's office, surprising her mid-Merit. She stubbed it out, embarrassed, took the Danish, and listened to the story.

"That bastard," Roberta said darkly. She dialed Ilana, brushing crumbs off her lapel. "Get over here. Now."

Ilana came in, her flaxen shellacked hair ablaze with new highlights. "What? What?" Justine told the story again.

"Let me take care of this," Ilana purred, her shiny coral lipstick making a mouth above her existing one.

"Wait." Justine was confused and ashamed. "I don't want it to seem like I ran to you right away. Even though I did."

She felt like a child. She had spent her childhood obsessed with injustice.

"No, of course not," Ilana said, and smoothed down her grosgrain lapel. "I'll skin his ass first thing tomorrow. By the by, Justine, First National of Sweden is selling their American venture capital group. I'm meeting them on Friday, you want in?"

"Sure," she said reluctantly.

"Get your hair done," Ilana added, giving Justine the name of her stylist. "I have an appointment on Friday morning. Use it."

That afternoon, Justine passed Farlowe's survey on to Roxy, who rolled her eyes. So now Justine would be in the doghouse with Sy, the head of Tax.

Roberta passed her in the hall. "Dinner?" she asked.

"Sure."

They took a cab down Second Avenue in the throbbing heat and Roberta chattered about a recruiting event she wanted Justine to run in the fall. Justine wondered what Roberta's place would be like. She'd been to Ilana's apartment once, which was the nightmarish explosion of pink chintz, striped silk, and tea roses she'd expected.

Over martinis in her blinding white kitchen, Ilana had said, swirling her olive, "Roberta isn't like us. A brilliant lawyer," she purred, "don't get me wrong. But can you imagine her kitchen? I shudder to think!" she added, in a savage stage whisper.

Roberta's apartment was in a brownstone on a lovely block. Inside, the place was clean, light, airy, with good reading light, big blue velvet art deco sofas, and no clutter.

"Nice pad, Roberta."

"You sound surprised," Roberta said, dropping her jacket and brief-case on a bench. A teenage boy, very tall and thin, wearing a tie-dyed T-shirt and pants with the crotch hanging low, came down the stairs.

"Hey," he said.

"Hey," Roberta said. She nodded at Justine. "Ben, this is Justine Schiff."

"Hey, Justine," he said, shaking her hand. "I've heard a lot about you." The boy had a nose ring.

She turned to Roberta in confusion.

"I guess it wasn't mutual," he said bashfully.

"Justine, this is Ben Jacobs. My son."

Justine stared at the nose ring. He also had three earrings and a dirty string bracelet. She was speechless. "Your son?"

The kid was smiling at her in a very superior way. How dare Roberta put her in this position, put her son in this position.

Her SON?

Roberta was doubled over in laughter. "The look on your face!"

"I'm shocked. I don't know what I am. How did you hide some-body this big?"

"He wasn't always this big," she said, and Ben flung himself on the couch and picked up a book. All these years, Roberta had been asking Justine up to her apartment, and she had misunderstood. She might have met this kid a long time ago.

"How did you swing this? You're always working."

Ben scoffed from the couch, reading *Nausea* with a pen in hand.

"I'm out of the office a lot," Roberta explained, taking off her blouse without embarrassment. "No one notices or cares. Why?" She put on a T-shirt. "Because I have bent my life, I have sacrificed, yea, my womanhood! For that firm. So what could I, the Old Maid, possibly be doing?"

All of her friends discussed their children endlessly and showed them off. Justine's own childhood was one of being trotted around—literally, at horse shows—on display everywhere.

"How could you not talk about him?"

Ben looked up from *Nausea* coyly.

"You know what happens when they find out you're in a family way. I needed the job. I needed the partnership. Now, I suppose, I could come out of the closet, but by now they'd react like you, like I cheated them out of something. Cheated them out of cheating me."

"I used to hate Packer Breebis Nishman Grabt," Ben said contemptuously, and sat up to light a cigarette. He looked just like Roberta!

"You don't still?"

He shrugged, exhaling. "I like the freedom."

"You look just like your mom," she told him. "Minus the nose ring, of course."

"Let's not discuss that." Roberta burst into a round of raspy cackles. "Oh, that was a very bad day . . . !"

They ordered in for barbecue, and Justine talked to Ben about school, Web sites, Martin Scorsese. This entirely new person sat gnawing on a corncob like a 6-foot miracle talking plant that had just popped up out of nowhere, with pimples, a nose ring, and a chess ranking. Roberta had a son old enough to smoke. Justine felt overwhelmed: she could have watched him grow up.

"If anyone asks," Roberta said, folding up a carton, "I say I'm divorced. Which is true."

"You are?" Justine was completely lost.

"Yes, I was married. It lasted a good six months, back in 1974. So

Ben has my maiden name and I have my married name. Ha!"

Roberta was married. "You didn't change back?"

"Eh, I was too lazy to go through the paperwork again, and then no one at the firm knew that I was married, so why tell them I was divorced? I pay all my taxes. I pay for independent health care. It's not like I'm doing anything illegal here."

"You've taken extraordinary chances," Justine said, and almost cried. Ben looked at her quizzically.

"Stop flagellating yourself," Roberta said, and squeezed her hand. "You've done the right thing every step of the way. Don't let them beat you down. Don't give up what you want. Don't be married to the firm. It'll ruin your life. I can say that—I'm not one of your mother's bridge ladies. It's not worth it, let me tell you."

"Why do you stay there? I really need to know."

"Are you kidding? Do you know what college tuition is?"

Justine lowered her voice, although Ben was right in front of her. "Does the father help?"

"Yes, but. Ben's not his primary concern," she said, gnawing on a sparerib bone. "He's got kids of his own, and two homes and two mortgages, and college tuition."

"He wouldn't leave . . . the wife?" She sounded like her mother.

"Who wanted him to?" Roberta shot back. "Hell no, I had no time and patience to set up housekeeping with that slob. What a slob! Forget about it, I didn't want him. But the baby, that was something else."

Justine looked at Ben, who had heard all this. He was wearing the same dour expression as when he'd told her about his chess tournaments. What did he think when his mother trashed his father like that?

When she told Roberta about the end of Barry, Ben wandered out of the room discreetly, his pants slung low on his hips.

"What a shame," Roberta said, her bare feet up on a chair. "I really thought he was going to be it."

A door slammed, and loud, percussive music spilled out of the back of the house.

"So this is your source on rap."

"Why, you think a 52-year-old Jewish corporate lawyer wouldn't know about 2DawgzKool on her own?"

"He's very cute," she offered.

"I know," Roberta exulted.

Justine went back to the office at 9:30, and spent two hours papering a conversion from a mutual thrift to a shareholder entity. She went into the library for a reference; Nicky was sitting in a chair, his freakishly long legs up on the table, surrounded by a year's worth of *Moody's*. He straightened up when he saw her. "Hi."

She sat down across from him. "Hi."

"I thought you'd gone for the day," he whispered.

"I just can't stay away," she whispered back wearily.

She told him about Farlowe's 50 state survey, and his eyebrows fused. "I passed it on to Roxy," she said, "but he's going to ask—"

"So what," Nicky said, angry for some reason. "He was out of line. Why are you obsessing about what he thinks? I should have thought you were old enough that you'd gone through all your parental issues by now."

Was he insulting her? Was she obsessing about Farlowe? Nicky was opaque. She put her cheek down on the table. "Normally, I'd ask you, What's that supposed to mean, but at the moment, I'm too tired to care."

He sat down next to her, very close. She looked at him from the table, his sharpness, his narrowness, his youngness. He was ageless. There was strange electrical tension. She was willing to bet that he'd kiss her, if it weren't Nicky, and it weren't the Library.

He put his hand on her head, and another hand on her arm. It was warm and interactive. At the *Moody's* table!

At the *Moody's* table in the library with your junior associate, who is 26 if he's a day, *now this is tacky*. No doubt Driggs would walk in and her career would be over.

She had a brief flash: the couch in the ladies' lounge.

She pulled him up and they walked, separate and dignified, into his office, which was the closer. He pressed her up against the door, but he was too tall. She pulled him down on the floor and kissed him.

He was salty and milky at once. Her tongue instantly gravitated to the scar and focused on it. It was very exciting. Nicky: who would have thought. He was so lean, so narrow—was he all there?

"Come home with me," he said after a while.

"You know, this really isn't right."

"I don't care."

With a single motion she pulled him up, pulled down her skirt, and slipped on her shoes. "Let's go."

"I live five blocks away," he said as they walked out into the humid night air.

"How convenient."

"Let's take a cab," he said, hailing one.

He lived as if in a hotel room, with a striped living room suite five feet from his bed and a TV mounted to the ceiling. It was a corporate apartment. Nicky Lukasch was such a cipher, so familiar, so strange. She hadn't even thought she was attracted to him, and now here she was, pelvis to the sky while he peeled off her panty hose.

They fell on the bed, and she didn't care about Barry, she didn't care about Nicky, and she didn't care about herself. She was focused. Her mouth found the scar again in the dark. His hipbones nearly impaled her. In short order, he was unwrapping a condom and within two minutes, not even, he was lying on top of her, shivering and spent.

"I'm so sorry," he said, in a normal voice. He might have been talking about missing a typo.

"Oh, don't worry about it."

"What do you mean?" he said suspiciously.

"Well, as long as we can have a rematch in a little while, that's fine."

He lifted his head up to look at her. "I don't think you understand. I mean, I think we have trouble here, I think you ought to look at this—"

The condom had torn, vertically.

She was up in a shot. "Get out! *Get out!* I can't believe this! Why didn't you tell me?"

"I've been telling you."

She leaned back against the upholstered headboard, which matched the living room suite. "When did this happen?"

"Okay, let's be calm."

"I can't believe this. I don't have time for this—I have a board meeting in Pittsburgh tomorrow. Today! I have to wake up in four hours to go to a board meeting in Pittsburgh!"

"I can go for you, if you want."

"You can't go, you know that. OH!"

"The timing was bad."

"Yes, and I'm ovulating, it just so happens."

"Ovulating. Is that a good thing?"

"In this context? No." She closed her eyes, and leaned her head back.

"Can't we do something? Can't you do that thing?"

"That thing? Are you talking about a process, or an application?"

"I don't know what I'm talking about . . . it's just a thing that women do."

"That thing?" she said derisively. "That vinegar and mustard thing?"

He put on his shorts. "Yes?"

"Grow up!"

"A doctor?" He pulled on his shirt. "Can we call a doctor?"

"I am not calling my gynecologist at 2 in the morning."

"I can take you to the hospital."

"Yeah, right."

He paced around his anonymous studio apartment. "Well, okay, you're not responding to any of my suggestions."

She sighed. How had this happened?

Nicky Lukasch stood in front of her primly. "I suppose now would be a good time to determine how each of us feels on the subject of Choice."

She exploded in laughter. "What's the matter, Nicky, don't you want to have kids?"

He didn't know she was joking. "Yes, children," he said solemnly. "But not at this juncture."

"Me neither," she said, thinking about Ben Jacobs.

He was silent in relief. She looked around the unfamiliar, generic apartment. Who was this man?

She rose and went to the bathroom. What was she even doing here? And yet, she did want children, and she supposed this was as good a juncture as any. But you couldn't just do that.

Or could you? Time was flying by. Children were sprouting up out of nowhere. Her dentist had brought over two kids from Vietnam. Roberta had had a child without the structure at 36. And Rob Principe, her former fiancé, had adopted the two-year-old daughter of a terminally ill colleague. People were doing things with a freedom she never believed existed. The idea was so foreign. Almost as foreign as hooking yourself up to a man for the rest of your life.

"You can't ever touch me in the office," she said, squeezing a swollen leg into panty hose.

"Never?" he said coyly, swinging his shoulders side to side.

Another playful little boy. "No one can know about this, for your sake as well as mine. Please."

"Of course," he said, and kissed her nervously.

She wouldn't panic. Panic was counterproductive. She had a board meeting in Pittsburgh at 11.

Happy birthday

Previously in life, Barry had felt like he was moving upward and forward. Now he was just going around. This hit him on the StairMaster: I am a hamster. Every year he said he was going to volunteer his time, get politically active, go to more concerts. And every year he didn't get around to it. Nothing changed. Life was endless. Life was full of shame. The closet where Justine's suits used to hang was so empty he felt winded.

His birthday was coming up. If he didn't find a job, he would die. He would explode. Commit suicide?

Ha. He sat on a bench in Strawberry Fields and read the *New York Post*. He was now addicted to it. Never the editorials, and never the news. But you couldn't beat it for local violence and celebrity gossip.

The flocks of Japanese tourists pointing at the Dakota made him mad. Bloodcurdling tragedies became just snapshot opportunities on the tour bus. You could rise, but then you had to take a fall. That was America. The mighty fall: they get shot, they commit murder, adultery, mail fraud, and child abuse. The beauty of it all was that you could watch it all on TV, and read about it in the *Post*.

No, Barry hadn't risen so high.

What was he waiting for? Justine wasn't going to call him. Lady Luxe wasn't going to call him. He'd lived his life like a slash-and-burn operation, and now he needed favors. It was late August. Everyone was out of town. It wasn't so easy to just fall in with a yogi anymore.

He sucked on a Popsicle in the sweltering park. Justine would have had a Wash'n Dri. He'd tease her, and she'd insist he use it, which he wanted to anyway. Nothing good could come of calling her. He'd spoil any chance of her missing him if he called too soon. He had to get it together, really.

Maybe she would call him on his birthday. He listened to the history of messages on his answering machine. That was back when people wanted to talk to him. Justine's messages were concise, courteous, and occasionally sly. His heart was overflowing. He'd been trying to get her attention, and in the meantime, she had a deadline, she had a conference, she had a dying grandmother, and three active cases. And there he was, biting her. He could understand her saying, Who needs this?

When his 35th birthday finally came, nothing happened. It was just another day. When the phone rang, it was his mother. Justine didn't call, and in the end, he didn't expect her to. He wanted to be maudlin about his life slipping away, his prime gone. But you could always make a case for the new day, the new month, the new year.

He had a new attitude: guilt and self-loathing were clearly getting him nowhere. So he would move on! Be proactive, organize his life! He was going to live every moment of every day towards attaining his goals.

This was very tiring. He got into bed with a box of Lucky Charms and watched the news. And the sports, and the talk shows. The Divorcée was probably thinking, TV, all day long: loser.

He went to the dentist. The dentist enthused about his fabulous vacation in Anguilla. "Some day, Barry, with a significant other," he added, smugly.

He couldn't get his teeth checked without being reminded of it? Was he wearing it as a sign on his forehead?

He looked in the mirror, and forgave himself for everything. And everyone around him. For everything. He was just living his life. The Divorcée was just living her life. The dentist probably meant well. He walked outside in bliss, and thanked West End Avenue for just being there. He had love in his heart, but soon he began to sweat. He took a misstep and landed in a pile of feces in his sandals.

God was a research psychologist, and he, Barry, was clearly in the control group.

Chapter 18

Not a good idea

Justine sat in the 16th floor conference room with the CEO of Precision Instruments, Vincent Barry (God was a comedian), his litigators, his bankers, and a staff attorney. The tweezer king had inherited a healthy business but was hit hard by the decline of steel, spent too much on acquisitions in surgical supply, and then was too strapped to modernize. At Tuesday's board meeting in Pittsburgh, a Philadelphia broker had convinced him to sell off the business piecemeal. Today's discussion in the Packer Breebis conference room concerned total liquidation.

Justine didn't know the first thing about Nicky Lukasch. He came from Boston, he swam at the Y, he didn't eat fish. She assumed he was Catholic, but he never talked about it, or anything else, for that matter, if she didn't initiate it. In some ways, she felt she knew even Mitch better than Nicky—odd, considering they had recently copulated (even if it was only for a minute and a half) and she might be carrying his child.

Oy! What had she been thinking?

Vincent Barry was a bald man with a fleshy white forehead and a habit of adding random s's to his words. "My brokers saids the first thing to sell is the Pittsburghs plants," he said, agitated. Barry would never look this bad if completely bald—he had a good head.

"Excuse me, but this yard sale makes no sense," Justine had to interject. "Your machinery is outdated, the plants are a mess, and you'll never recoup your investment. But, if you keep two plants and continue production, you'll be back in business in two years."

"Well, of course, that's an option," said one of the bankers, "but we thought it would be better to sell quickly, to end the anxiety for the company."

"If you do it this way, you can save those jobs," she added.

"I can't pays for those jobs," Vincent Barry said testily.

"The state of Pennsylvania will give you funding," she assured him. "The banks will finance the rest. There is very little that you personally have to be responsible for."

He stood up. "What the fuck do you thinks you're doings?"

Another gracious client. "Excuse me?"

"Excuse ME, but I'm askings you, what the fuck do you thinks you're doings?" He was tubby as well as ugly. "There's a reasons why we're letting peoples go. We are GOINGS INTO BANKRUPTCY."

She ignored the tone. "But it won't cost you anything, and it saves 219 jobs. Why wouldn't you do it?"

"Joes?" he called his ashen staff attorney.

"WE are the client, Miss Schiff," Joe said quietly.

"You think we're doings volunteers works here?"

Everyone looked at her. "But you've got nothing to lose," she began, but the client cut her off.

"Calls the partner," he said. "I've had its with you."

She asked Mitch to call Driggs, and walked carefully down the carpeted hallway to her office. She had been entirely reasonable.

But to the people who mattered, this was self-destruction.

She picked up her phone to call Roberta. No: she always did that. She should stop.

Nicky was right. She'd given them everything she had, routinely, religiously, without stopping to think. And now everything she'd worked for was in the toilet because of the selfish tantrum of a bald, inept, profligate tweezer king with a bizarre speech impediment.

Driggs barged in without knocking. "I don't know how you could have said that, Justine," he shouted, sweating and enraged. "I think you've totally fucked up our relationship with that client, Justine. What is WRONG with you?"

He was a tiny, tiny man with a high, squeaky voice. He had routinely chastised her and put her in awkward positions.

"I did what I thought was right," she said, on an even keel.

"Oh, shut up, Schiff," he said contemptuously. "It's a little late for you to sprout principles now."

"You're right. I'm not going to fight with you. The client can deal with you and Mitch from now on. I don't care."

"YOU DON'T CARE?" he shouted, practically strangling on his rage, and kicked her chair, which sent her papers flying.

"No, I don't," she laughed involuntarily, and picked the papers off the floor, replacing them in the file folder.

He snatched the folder, and slammed his fist into her door while stalking out.

Why was she always staring in amazement and trying to reason with a belligerent, irrational man?

She packed her stuff back in her shoulder bag and walked out. She bought an iced coffee, and wandered home in the sweltering heat. It was only 4 P.M.

At her desk at home, she made six phone calls: two headhunters, three clients, and Whitman Sklar. She was open for business. Anyone who wanted her could hire her. She spoke to machines and busy people who said they'd get back to her.

At 5:30, Mitch called her with questions.

"I suggests you looks in the files," she joked.

"Driggs is on the warpath," he whispered nervously. "His hand is turning colors. I've never seen him this mad."

"Do a good job, and you'll be his best friend," she advised. This was how she'd wound up as Farlowe's good girl, filling in for someone who'd just snapped one afternoon after years of faithful service.

Now she was wandering around her house with nothing to do.

What was the point of her life? To make partner, as quickly as possible, at this firm. Why? She couldn't even remember. It was as absurd as joining the circus. There at least you could make a case for the applause. She didn't want to spend her days and nights scrabbling for dominance among social misfits.

She wanted to talk to Barry. She couldn't call him not knowing whether she was pregnant. It was too soon for a test to be accurate. She'd have to wait it out. She took a shower, shaved her legs, bleached her mustache, and tweezed her eyebrows with a competitor's instrument.

At 9 she couldn't take it anymore. She put on a loose linen dress and walked the 21 blocks to Nicky's apartment. He had his tie on in the house. She couldn't help teasing him a little, and had a fleeting thought of Barry's baroque bathrobe.

No more Barry—she turned her attention to Nicky, who drew her in with pointy fingers and kissed her deeply, slowly, with his eyes closed. He had depth, but he was a foreign language. Would he ever be readable, knowable? Barry was constantly telling her something— what he thought, what he meant, asking her what she thought, what she meant. Could she deal with someone who didn't emit, emote, speak unless spoken to?

As if reading her thoughts, he spoke up now, clearing his throat first:

"I just got home."

"Hmm," she said, pulling off his tie.

"I heard about what happened," he said, touching her cheek.

"Most people have this crisis earlier."

"Why didn't you?"

"I have no idea," she said, settling into his sofa, kicking off her shoes. "I was very focused. I wanted to be the best."

"You are the best," he said, looming over her. Barry was tall, but somehow it was never an issue.

"You're very sweet."

"I think I'm having the crisis now," he said, but she didn't want to talk about it.

She pulled him to her and reached up to unbutton his shirt. The talking stopped. His stomach was concave. You could count his ribs. She missed Barry. She drew his face to hers and kissed his scar; it wasn't enough. She was just using him, wasn't she? She liked him. There was no question that it would lead nowhere, even if she was pregnant.

She couldn't possibly be pregnant. He unzipped her dress and started touching her.

She'd probably have fertility problems if she ever even tried to get pregnant.

She tried not to mind it, but he was kissing her wrong and rubbing her arms and legs as if he were sanding her. Everything was a problem.

"Nicky," she said, winded from struggling with him.

"Yes," he said, as if she'd called him on the phone.

"I don't feel right about this."

He sat up on the couch and stared at her in the dark.

"I'm sorry," she said. She wanted to leave. "I don't know what to say."

. . .

She walked home frustrated and depressed. She had thrown away her partnership. She might be pregnant. She smote her forehead with the heel of her hand. Life was ridiculous. Absolutely ridiculous.

She got in late the next morning. Bob had a thick wad of messages and she started returning calls. Noah Clurman had the perfect job for her: in-house Junior Counsel. It would pay less, she would do less, she'd have to commute to Hartford, and she'd be reporting to the man she'd dressed down six months ago for having no qualms about things like affiliate transactions. She said she'd think about it.

Headhunter #1 had the perfect job for her: a nonequity partnership at Shainwald Dickstein Schmertz, a third-tier firm on Wall Street in economic distress. She said no thank you.

Headhunter #2 had the perfect job for her: Of Counsel at Feinman, Dingle, O'Shaughnessey. They had seen her across the table many times and respected her work. After a year, nonequity partnership; after three, with good behavior, full partnership. She said she'd think about it.

She looked at her view of the building across the way. Wasn't that just moving to a different cell in the same prison?

She went into Nicky's office. "Do you have that agreement?"

He didn't look up. "No."

Justine had three nonactive and two active cases with Nicky. They had to work out a way around the awkwardness.

Mitch walked in.

"When will you have it?" she asked, embarrassed.

Nicky still didn't look up. "I don't know," he said bitterly.

All it took was one false move, one awkward silence, and everyone would know. "What's your best estimate?" she tried softly.

"I'll have it when I have it, all right, Justine?" he shouted.

"Woof!" said Mitch, and stood there gawking.

She had to leave now, before something else happened.

"Okay then." She walked out.

On second thought, leaving them together was not a good idea. She went back in. "Mitch, I need you."

"For what," he said cagily.

"We have to talk about Noah."

"We just talked about Noah." He was smiling in anticipation of good gossip. Uch! This was getting childish. Nicky would tell Mitch. Mitch would tell Ilana. And then it would hit the Quotron.

Why were people so fascinated by other people having sex? If you could call that sex. At that very moment, Ilana appeared, dressed like a knife.

"Jus-TINE," she called, and Justine followed her down the hall with the feeling that she was about to be taken to task.

"You didn't go to Remi," Ilana accused. "I could have used that appointment," she said, although her hair, as usual, was smoothly hovering two inches away from her scalp.

"Oh, I'm so sorry—I completely forgot." Now she'd pissed off Ilana.

"All right, you've had a tough week. I told Driggs he couldn't talk to an associate that way. He can talk to his partners that way, but I don't know how he expects to keep good help if he treats them like excrement."

"Thanks," Justine said. Ilana looked tootsed up and old, and Justine felt a wave of revulsion.

"And I told Farlowe that he was being sadistic and childish, as well as working against his own interests. Picking on you, in your seventh year!"

Justine heard it as "seventh month," and started to sweat.

"Look. I heard about Nicky." Ilana crossed her legs gracefully. "Now, I understand you're on the rebound, and you don't meet too many men. But. It just doesn't look right."

Justine almost gagged.

"Now, a partner, that's something else. That I could understand. A client. Noah Clurman—now there's a catch."

That Noah was married didn't make him any less appropriate, apparently.

"Anything else?" Justine asked.

Ilana raised a styled brow. "How was it?"

Justine left without responding. She went to her desk to read.

A good half-hour passed, and she hadn't absorbed a single sentence. She was losing her edge.

She went to get a Tab. Roberta cornered her outside the Xerox room, pulled her into her office, and shut the door. "I hear you've been seeing Nicky!"

Justine closed her eyes in disgust. Roberta had recently confided in her, and now she wanted payback.

"So?" She lit a Merit excitedly, and blew into a smoke-eating machine. "How could you not tell me! This is just too fabulous!"

Her life was turning into a bad movie.

"Roberta," she said slowly, pushing the air in front of her away until her arms were completely extended, "just mind your own business."

Roberta's face went blank and she sat down heavily. "Well, excuse me."

Justine walked out. She didn't mean that. Now she had alienated Roberta. Would she make it through the day with a single reference intact?

She sat at her desk. The phone rang.

It was her mother. "I understand you've got a new beau," she said, with chilly distance. Of course Carol had heard the news, and was unimpressed. A mere associate, 26 years old: come on.

Wait a minute! Justine wanted to shout. *It was nothing!* Nothing is going to come of it. And what if it did?

. . .

Ten days later, Justine went home at lunch. She got urine all over her hands and dropped the pregnancy detector wand into the toilet in her nerves. She fished it out, cursing. She'd bought two, just in case. At the drugstore, she'd thought: you should get a whole bunch of these. And then thought: why? You'll never have sex again, what's the point? She completed the steps of the second test without incident. She waited.

There was no line. She was negative, she wasn't pregnant. She walked back down Third Avenue in the heat, eating a pint of coffee ice cream in gratitude. And if she bumped into anyone, she didn't care. When she got back to the office, she realized she was menstruating.

Nicky stopped by her office to drop off an agreement that afternoon. He sat in her guest chair and she closed her door. Normally, they spent a fair amount of time with each other, with the door opened, with the door closed. But everything now was awkward.

"Well, you'll be glad to hear," she said, "that we aren't going to be parents. The home detector test was negative."

He nodded. "I want to see you."

"I don't think it's such a good idea. I'm sorry."

He walked out, looking like a little boy fighting for attention. She felt bad for him.

She'd never been involved with anyone from the firm, ever. There was a reason.

Justine and Nicky avoided each other carefully, but two weeks after the pregnancy test, they had to go to Boston together for the day. On the shuttle, Justine worked nonstop. Nicky read the *Economist* for a while and then pulled out *Lolita*, which was annoying. In Boston, they met with the principals of a radio station that was the target of a hostile bid from a very powerful media company with a chain of stations across the country. There were bankers, board members, the CEO, and the General Counsel, and in the middle of drafting the consent revocation statement, Justine spilled tea all over the keyboard of her laptop.

Everyone gasped. The machine paused, and the screen sputtered into end-of-the-world graphics and then snapped off into blackness while everyone held their breath. She almost cried.

In front of a client who was paying by the hour, whose every hour counted, who needed her complete attention and assistance in order to survive the onslaught of a media giant. Her face felt like fuchsia neon blinking at the boardroom: idiot! idiot! idiot!

Computer nightmares were traded across the mahogany table while she tried in vain to reboot. Without the computer, she might as well have been there to chat. She'd also managed to hit her skirt, her blouse, her jacket, a board member's pants, and the latest printout of the poison pill provision. The client was being a saint, and even the bankers were telling her to relax. Kissy kissy to her face, of course, but the minute she left the room, they'd be ripping apart her reputation and sucking on the bones. Investment bankers were worse than fashion models.

"Give me your computer," she said, and Nicky slid his laptop over. She found the file in the network—it had everything except the changes she'd just made. She redid the changes quickly and printed out a draft. They were back in business. She whispered to Nicky to call Floyd to get another laptop sent over.

"Sent here? Won't we be gone by the time—"

"Just do it, just in case."

She caught a flicker of something—a Don't Give Me Orders kind of a face. Well, too bad about him.

They were done in three hours. It was 1:18 and they jumped into a cab to catch the 2 o'clock shuttle. Her suit was ruined. The computer was ruined. What if they lost the proxy fight? What if they couldn't block the bid?

It was 1:38 and the entire city of Boston was under construction; the traffic was maddening, *maddening!* They might not make the flight. She didn't want another half hour of unstructured time with Nicky. She wondered if she could use his computer on the flight, and if he would make a big deal of it. They got to Logan at 1:44 and raced through the terminal.

She passed through the metal detector and met both laptops on the other side of the conveyer belt. Nicky let a whole adult family march right in front of him. Idiot. He was stalling to annoy her. She unzipped the cases, turned on Nicky's machine, and began explaining why hers was not working. The security guard wasn't buying her story. She was a suicide bomber, taking plastic explosives in a non-working laptop on the shuttle to LaGuardia?

Meanwhile, it was 1:56, and every single member of this family walked through the metal detector with a key ring the size of a baseball, setting off the alarms, and each one of them had to be electronically frisked separately by security. Nicky wasn't being nearly pushy enough. Who did he think he was, reading *Lolita* in front of her on a business trip. It was inappropriate. She slung both cases over her shoulders, and when he finally passed through the detector, she turned to take off for the gate.

She felt it happening, she saw it falling, she reached out to catch it but it grazed over her knuckle—the laptop, Nicky's laptop, slipped out of the case and skittered across the ground. She stood there, with fear in her mouth.

Nicky looked at her in disbelief. "What are you DOING?"

"Oh, my God. Oh, my God."

They knelt over the little machine in the middle of the concourse, while people tripped over them and cursed. She opened it up. The glass had cracked and the machine wouldn't start.

"I cannot . . . BELIEVE you!" he shouted, near tears.

"They'll give you another one right away. It's my fault."

"This was mine, not the firm's."

"I'll buy you another one. I am so sorry."

"It had all sorts of irreplaceable stuff on it."

"Well, you have everything backed up on disc, don't you?"

"Not necessarily." She had destroyed two laptops in the space of four hours. What were the odds of this happening?

"Well, you have hard copies of everything," she pleaded.

"Not necessarily! I have the entire genealogy of the Magyar clergy in there. From 1782 until present. Much of it is backed up, yes, but I haven't printed out in a while."

"Nicky, I am so sorry, I don't know what to say."

"Just to catch a shuttle, and there's one every half hour!" he shouted bitterly. "Just because you don't want to talk to me."

The genealogy of the Magyar clergy?

Back at the office, she went directly to Management Information Systems. "I have two nonworking laptops," she told Floyd, because Floyd's superior was on medical leave. "I need two new ones in the meantime, and I want these fixed immediately."

Floyd was unmoved. "What about the one I had sent to Boston?" He was thin and gawky and slightly touched in the head. "Do you know what I had to go through to do that? Do you even care?"

"I'm sorry, you can have that one brought back."

"Every last laptop is out right now. I'll put you on the list, but I have to say, I'm not impressed with the way you're treating this department or our equipment."

In the hall, she passed Farlowe and felt a pure, uncomplicated hatred for him and his whole dominion. He'd been waiting for her to come to him for help. He tilted his arrogant woolly head at her. She tilted hers right back. No help, no thank you.

No one would vote for her now.

. . .

At 8:30, she went into Dennis Delaney's office. He was a nice guy. Maybe he would have some idea of what she should do next.

"Holy cow, Justine," he gushed. "I heard about everything."

"Have you eaten," she asked.

"I'm starving, let's go."

They had Thai food within walking distance, and discussed laptops, Faustian bargains, and capital contributions.

"I don't think I have the stomach for this anymore," she concluded, surprised at herself. "Why did it take me so long to wake up?"

"You were billing too many hours," he said, and sipped his Scotch thoughtfully. "You didn't have time for doubts."

"Even so, most people wake up sooner," she said. He was sitting very near her on the banquette, his sleeves rolled up to show beefy forearms covered with soft drifts of red hair. Which was sweet, all of a sudden.

"Some people never wake up," Dennis offered. "Look at Driggs."

"Uch, please! Don't make me sick."

He laughed, and leaned into her, and kissed her on the mouth, a slow, soft, friendly kiss that tasted of cold Scotch and peanut sauce. Dennis Delaney. Married man. There they were, having noodles and kissing, in a completely natural way.

This was so easy! Why? Was she in heat or something?

He and his wife were trying to have a child and not getting one. She liked Ginny, sort of. She had to stop this. But why? He was kissing her so sweetly. It was a rainy night, in an empty restaurant where no one she knew ever came. She had known him since law school, had worked with him many long hours, and had always found him attractive. It was decadent, and unexpected, and completely outside her experience. He asked for the check.

She didn't want somebody else's husband. But what difference did it make? Nothing would come of it. He paid the check with his arm around her waist, something she needed, something she could never count on happening when she wanted it to. It was so rare that anything happened. Although plenty had been happening lately. Although nothing appropriate.

Oh, fuck appropriate! Why did she always have to be the appropriate one? She had busted her ass for seven years, denied herself basic, unremarkable things that most other people took for granted. When was it her turn? By the time the cab stopped in front of her building, she was completely ready to stop thinking. She paid in a hurry and they went upstairs.

The dog could wait. Any minute he might have second thoughts and run out of there. They kissed on the sofa. He was heating up very quickly. She wondered if he did this often. She didn't really care. Soon they were tangled on the bed. She started unbuckling his belt and suddenly he stopped, sat on the edge of the bed, and got sad.

She wrapped herself around him. He held her hands and apologized, breathing heavily with a slight wheeze.

She might have been getting into bed with anyone she saw, but she certainly wasn't getting very much out of it. They went into the living room. He asked for decaffeinated tea and she made it for him quickly while he sat on the sofa half-dressed and clumsily petted the dog. She missed Barry. One thing about Barry, sex was never a problem.

"I'm not used to this kind of generosity," he said, taking the cup in a trembling hand, about to cry.

"It's just tea, Dennis, relax."

No crying! She wanted him to get dressed and go.

Then he started talking. He spilled his marriage all over the table. She didn't want to hear about it. He was a nice guy, but this was ridiculous. Didn't he have to get home? She interrupted him to tell him she had to walk Stella. He put on his shirt reluctantly; he would've gone on and on. What had she been thinking? It was amazing that this had only happened half an hour ago. What the hell was she doing?

. . .

The next day, Justine and Mitch were due at Noah Clurman's office in Hartford at one o'clock. Driggs had Mitch on the run with the Precision bankruptcy, which was fine: she wanted to see Noah alone to discuss his offer. She wasn't so sure that the job didn't interest her. At 10 she marched into Mitch's office.

"I'm going without you," she said. "Give me your laptop."

"No way," Mitch laughed. "I've heard about you."

"I promise, promise, promise I will be so careful."

Driggs arrived. "Who do you think you are? You think you can order him around?"

"Yes, I do," she said, doing her best Roberta impression. It worked; he didn't challenge her, the twerp.

"I'll copy the draft and give you the disc," Mitch offered.

"Irrelevant. Floyd won't give me a laptop. I need yours."

"Stop wasting our time, Schiff," the little partner growled.

"Take it easy, Driggs," Mitch said, unbothered. "Can't you handle Floyd? You of all people, and *Floyd* of all people?"

"He says he doesn't have any, and I'm already late—"

"All right, but my screenplay's on it, and if anything happens to it, I will kill you, personally."

"You're using our laptop for personal business?" Driggs began braying. "I'm reporting you. You have no right."

"So copy it now," she said impatiently. "Come on, come on, I'm late."

Mitch had time to write a screenplay? He copied the file, and she took the computer, zipped it up securely in its carrying case, and ran out to the elevator. She was already too late to speak to Noah before the meeting. She'd have to pull him aside afterwards, and hope he could spare the time. Downstairs, on Park Avenue, she saw a brown traffic police car sidling up to what was probably her sedan. It might take her driver half an hour to circle the block—she darted out to catch him.

A car: she was hit in the knees, she fell backwards onto the pavement on her rear end. The machine flew out of her hands and landed a good 10 feet behind her.

She'd been hit by a car. She was late for a meeting that she had to attend. She'd been hit in the knees. She needed to get to Connecticut. The man who had hit her was squatting in front of her, sweating and pale. A crowd had gathered to watch as she dry heaved in the gutter. The laptop was now blocking traffic. She had to go to this meeting and make a good impression. She had to get herself together. She stood up and everyone screamed. She began to cry, and the car that had hit her was hit from behind by a gypsy cab.

A passing van swerved to watch, and ran over the laptop.

The crowd got more numerous. The man who had hit her was yelling at the Senegalese gypsy cab driver and hitting the hood of the gypsy cab; the woman in the gypsy cab was yelling at the traffic cop; the traffic cop was inspecting the damage; everyone was touching Justine, yelling that the police were coming; her coccyx bone was ringing, her hands and arm were scraped—raw skin and gravel and dirt. The noise was too much.

She had been hit by a car. She wouldn't make the meeting. She would lose her job. No one would give her a reference. She was sobbing in front of Packer Breebis Nishman Grabt. She was getting into bed with anyone who happened to be in the room. She had destroyed three laptops in two days.

Love the one you're with

Barry had to be light, he had to be hungry, he had to have energy. Energy: this was the problem. He was having an energy crisis. He needed vitamins. He needed protein powder, he needed power bars. He needed someone he could call on the phone who wouldn't answer with an intake of breath, and then, "Barry!" Pause. "How goes it?"

He needed to get laid.

He called his sister for advice.

"You must break your magic circles, Barry, because your magic circles are killing you."

What the hell did that mean? And was Karen a genius? He didn't want to think about it. He hung up the phone just as it rang again.

He was single and unemployed—he had to talk to everyone, whether he wanted to or not.

"Barry," Emily said smugly. "Thanks for picking up."

Was it possible? He was shaking. "What can I do for you?"

"Do you have next year's forecasts for Apricots? John thought you might have taken them home mistakenly."

"I don't have them."

"Okay, well, if you come across them in your travels," she said, trying to sound loose and sophisticated, "let me know."

Barry hung up, and screamed.

The doorbell rang, scaring him. Had the Divorcée heard him?

"Hi. Sorry to bother you," a short bearded man with a nice, dry handshake said breathlessly. "Colin Christie, Pippa's dad."

"You're Irish!" he exclaimed, and the man smiled, displaying awful teeth. "I had no idea! I mean, I knew she was a leprechaun, but I had no idea she came by it honestly! Come in, come in!"

The man stood just inside the door, unassuming, in a short-sleeved blue plaid shirt, shorts, and sneakers. "Pippa's running behind—she said she left a bag in the pantry."

Barry found a bag with the strap held on by safety pins. Sweet, sloppy Pippa. When she departed for Paris, he'd have no one left to talk to.

"Don't go," he pleaded. "Please sit down. Have some of your daughter's beautiful cookies and talk to me. Pippa is extraordinary. You've done a marvelous job with her."

"Oh, leprechauns are just born that way." Colin Christie sat down at the table and smiled sadly.

Barry wanted to drink pints with the guy. "I need your advice," he said, pouring iced coffee for two. In no time at all, he'd told about the Incident, the Unemployment, his mother's business, the plane crash, the classifieds, the dentist, the Divorcée, and Justine. He was beyond shame.

"Well," Colin said, chewing macaroons slowly with an abstract look. "Are you happy, are you comfortable unemployed?"

"Pshh!"

"So take a job in generics," he said.

"What if I hate it?"

"Get another."

"I have contacts in advertising," Barry chanced, "but I haven't activated them yet."

"And why not?" Colin leaned forward, freckly pink forearms resting lightly on the table.

"I want my own company," he said, but even as he said it, he knew he wasn't going to schlep across America blowing down steel doors. All the steak sandwiches in the world couldn't make him an entrepreneur if he didn't have the drive. "I was thinking about marketing Pippa's sesame mustard dressing."

"Isn't that beautiful? We have it on our beets. Lovely."

"But it isn't just stopping in a couple little stores and then boom, my children'll be set for life," he said. Colin nodded—he was pretty realistic, for a hippie. "Maybe I'm not an entrepreneur. Maybe I just don't like working for anyone."

Pippa's dad ran fingers through his red-brown beard and thought a while. "It seems to me," he said finally, "if you don't want your mum's business, and you don't have anything to sell, your best bet's advertising. You're far enough away from the product to live your life. You give advice, and if they don't take it, so what? It's not your problem."

"But I don't want 'so what.' I want it to be my problem."

"So call your mum." He stared at Barry with calm eyes. "Or start up a salad dressing."

"I can't do that."

"So send out résumés and wait for the phone to ring."

They looked at each other.

"Maybe this isn't the life choice," Barry sighed, finally. "Maybe this is the choice before the life choice."

"There you go," Colin Christie brightened, delighted.

"Hey, I didn't think hippies were into advertising."

"Well, I'm not," he said, folding his napkin slowly. "But it sounds like the right thing for you to do."

"So you disapprove of me. You find me base and vile."

"Absolutely not!" he said, smiling.

This was interesting. "I get it. You're a loyal oppositionist. You need people creating things you can despise."

"It has nothing to do with me," he said impatiently, and Barry felt immature. Colin Christie was, what, 45? Barry should have had kids by now, a family life.

"You're not sure. This would put you back on track till you are. Anyhow," he said, annoyed, "whatcha care what I think? I teach recorder to 10-year-olds in Vermont."

Barry wanted to play ball with him. "Recorder is important."

"Oh, come on now," he said, smiling knowingly.

"So you're a cynic then."

"No, just doing what I have to do," he said, smoothing down his mustache. "Something between what I love and what I hate."

So simple. "I think you just helped me out here. Thank you."

"Not at all, not at all."

"Okay! Now what about Justine?"

Colin let out a booming laugh. "You're on your own, there!"

.   .   .

When Colin had gone, Barry called Len Lefkowitz before he chickened out. "Do you remember me?"

"Barry Cantor, you're a household word. How are you?"

"Fine," he said, pacing in front of his windows.

"Glad to hear it."

"Not fine. Unemployed. Miserable. I'm calling for advice."

"We just signed on your old friends Courteous Crackers and Susie Strudel."

Just the names out loud made Barry fearful. The other day at Sloan's he'd broken out in hives, and he wasn't anywhere *near* the condiments.

"I'd say why don't we have lunch in a dark place next week," Len said seriously. "But the truth is I'm busy."

"Oh."

"You should call Bernie Steipell," Len said offhandedly. "He's knee-deep in new media. He could care less about a certain food conglomerate that pays my mortgage. Good luck to you."

Barry hung up and called Bernie. "What took you so long?" Bernie asked. "I heard about your, ah, fond farewell."

"I heard you lost some crackers."

"Crackers, croutons, and jam," Bernie said, stymied.

"Holy cow. So," Barry said, fast. "I want an interview."

"Okay," Bernie said optimistically. "Come in Wednesday at noon. I'll take you to lunch."

Barry hung up the phone carefully. He stood up. He felt cautiously triumphant. Why had everything seemed so difficult?

Andrew Carnegie didn't get married until he was 51. Ringo was doing children's television. People moved on.

That afternoon, Barry bumped into Debbie Wexler, a perky girl he'd dated briefly at Dartmouth. He remembered her chattering incessantly about classes, professors, requirements, the registrar's office.

He'd stopped calling her because she was so boring. It was odd to see her on a Broadway median.

"So, what are you," he asked, after they pecked hello. "Who are you doing?"

"Barry!" she said, embarrassed. And then, as if he'd fast-forwarded her, she started on her daughter's ballet classes, her son's teachers, the school requirements, the supervision. Her husband was a lawyer, they lived around the corner. She would have gone on endlessly if he hadn't pretended he had plans.

He walked away thinking: responsible, studious, perky, clean. But not smart. Justine was in a different layer of humanity.

Chapter 19

Where's the fella?

While she was being bandaged at New York Hospital, Justine's cell phone began ringing. She was sure it was going to be Roberta, asking her to go back to Boston—a vote of confidence she didn't deserve, after the laptop meltdown. She held the phone to her ear with her shoulder as the nurse cleaned her palms.

But it was Gene. Calling from Bedford.

Miriam had died at 10:30.

He would identify the body, Carol was arranging for the funeral. Could she come to the house?

Justine thanked him.

She asked the nurse to hang up for her and then dial Roberta's number.

"Justine!" Roberta shouted. News of her dry heaving in broad daylight on Park Avenue had apparently rocketed through the offices. "Where are you—are you okay?"

"I'm at the hospital," she said, wanting to cry, "and my life is just . . . disintegrating. Ow!" She flinched as the nurse blotted her wounds with acid.

Roberta told her to take as much time as she needed and call whenever she wanted to talk. Justine thanked her and asked the nurse to hang up.

Nana's body was somewhere in this building.

She took a taxi home—her legs were blue with bruises and her hands were wet with ointment under the bandages. Stella pounced on her, scratching her knees and licking her bandages. Justine tried to pack without using her hands. She called for a car and arrived in Bedford with the dog at close to 4 o'clock, her knees swollen and bruised, her oily palms stinging with every move she made.

Gene and Tom Zazlowe, Meredith's husband, were looking large on the couches in the living room. Carol came down the stairs in a blue sweat suit and her gold mule slippers. The dog raced to her and licked her hands enthusiastically. Her mother's face was swollen from crying. This was what grief looked like. This was what would happen to her when Carol died.

"She only weighed 88 pounds when she died," her mother said, wiping her eyes with her hand and sobbing openly, unashamed. She gave her mother a Kleenex and sat with her on the stairs.

Carol pulled herself together after a while. "What happened to you?" she demanded, noticing the bandages.

"Never mind."

"Donnie's coming tomorrow," her mother said. "He finally called today, to return my call. Of five days ago! I don't understand a person like that, who can't come to see his own mother. He wants to talk to her on the phone. She can't talk on the phone! That's the point!"

Meredith Zazlowe was suddenly there, reaching for her hands. Justine held up her bandages and shrank back protectively. So Meredith raised Justine up by the elbows to give her a hug. Meredith Zazlowe was so close, her stomach was touching Justine's.

"Your grandma loved you," she said, kissing her lips. Was Meredith going to stick her tongue in her mouth? "I want you to know that."

Justine disengaged herself, excused herself, and hobbled into the kitchen. Through the swinging door, she heard Meredith ask, "And where's the fella?"

"Don't ask," her mother said. And burst into more tears.

Gene, Meredith, and Justine split the list of people to call, and went to the various phones. Justine had never done this. There was no nice way of putting it.

Justine called Miriam's sister, Pearl, first. Pearl had to know the reason for the call. But she said, "Justine, darling, how are you? How's mother?" As if it were perfectly natural for a grandniece she hadn't seen in seventeen years to be calling on a Tuesday afternoon in September.

Her mother had too many friends. Justine spent the rest of the day calling them. A sister, or a brother, would be here now to help deal with this. A very old resentment from her childhood bubbled over. Her mother was on the phone, making arrangements, smoking, looking shaken, waxy, small, and alone. Gene was doing his bit. She shouldn't knock Gene. Thank God for him; if not for Gene, Carol would be living with her.

Justine gave up at 9:30. She couldn't climb the stairs to her old room, so she got into the rough, brand-new sheets of the twin bed in the downstairs guest room. It was unfair. She wished she had a sister or a brother. She wished she were at Barry's or at least at home. Nana was a dead person now. It was weird—at one point she was there, and then she wasn't. Death was better than the hospital. It should have happened sooner.

But it was sad. A whole life. Nana had gotten married at 19, had Carol at 20, and Donnie at 28, after the war. She'd never been to college. She'd never learned to drive. She'd had a standing appointment twice a week at the hairdresser's, and once a week at the nail salon. Until her husband died, she'd never paid a bill. She'd never opened a bill. All her friends had moved away and/or died. She'd stopped speaking to Pearl over an event in 1981, when she'd moved to Boca Raton. She hadn't had eggs in twenty-five years. Justine kept coming back to Herman—what an extraordinary thing.

Nana was a dead body. These brand-new sheets were killing her. Who would help her when her mother died? Who would she talk to when her mother died? If Justine didn't have kids, who would come to her funeral?

The next morning, she woke in deep pain. Her legs felt like they'd been whacked by I beams. She could barely stand. The undertaker at Brod's was not as grotesque as Justine had expected. The viewing was in a gray-green room with a box of Kleenex on every side table. The coffin was closed and covered with red roses.

"Nice flowers," Justine said, sitting down heavily.

"The undertaker did this pitch," Carol whispered to her. " 'For X you can have the coffin with two urns of flowers. For X plus 500 you can have two big urns. Don't you think she would've liked the bigger urns? And roses on top are extra, but isn't she worth it?' Isn't that disgusting?"

"You didn't tell me that," Justine said, shocked.

"The whole thing—" Carol said, and began to cry.

A flow of people trooped through the room in cocktail-party

clothes. Her mother sat on a couch and received. Gene stood by the door and smoked a cigar.

Marsha Salonika, one of Carol's college friends, put her hands on Justine's shoulders. "So. I know this is a terrible time. But are you seeing anybody?"

"Something just ended."

"Well, you let me know," she wagged her finger. "I have a guy for you. A real winner. Smart, for my Teenie." She took a cigarette from her bag and said, under her breath, "I hear the brother isn't coming?"

"Donnie's coming."

"And the wife, is she coming?"

"The wife is coming," she said, exhausted. Did these people listen to themselves?

More of her mother's friends were waiting back at the house. Rhoda Weisenblatt took her wrist in the dining room. "You loved your grandma, didn't you. Your mother is upset now, isn't she. It's very hard, I know. My mother died eight years ago, it was horrible." She paused, teary-eyed. She took a brownie from the buffet. "So how's work?"

"I just closed on a $10.7 billion stock swap. Maybe you read about it in the newspaper—"

"*Very* exciting! You're so impressive! So you weren't engaged, that time, you were just seeing someone, right?"

Justine stared at her. There was a pause.

Rhoda cocked her head, waiting. "Someone your mother wasn't wild about, hmm?"

Justine was not responding to this catty invasion.

"So are you seeing someone now?"

"I am not making further statements on this topic at this time."

Rhoda's eyes narrowed. That was the end of the chat. She put her hand on Justine's cheek. "Love your hair. Love it."

"Is there nothing else to talk about?" she demanded of Gene in the kitchen. "Your friends are mighty limited." He nodded, fatigued. He was hiding, too. "I mean, at a condolence call?"

People were in the downstairs guest room. Justine dragged herself up the stairs to lie down in her old room. She was in extreme discomfort. She had to be here, she couldn't go home. She wished she had bills or something to do. If Barry were here, she'd be introducing him, which wouldn't be much better.

The door opened.

"See, she redid this whole room, here—the carpet, the valances, the bedspreads—oh, hello, Justine. How ya doing, honey?" It was Connie Tischler and Pat Champion. "Sorry to bother you. Look at the valances," Connie whispered. Pat looked. They ducked out, leaving the door ajar.

Around 11, when everyone had gone, Justine and her mother sat in the kitchen, surrounded by fruit, flowers, and bakery boxes. "I have never seen so much food in my entire life," Carol said, lighting a Parliament.

"It's obscene," Justine agreed.

There was a pause. Her mother smoked.

"So, it must be nice to be back in your place," Carol said, with smugness. "With all your stuff."

"What do you mean."

"You have all your space. And peace and quiet."

"Enough." It wasn't her business to talk about.

"I know it's hard, what with all of this." Her mother squeezed her arm. Justine had to force herself not to pull away. "But it would be hard anyway, and you know you'd just have to get rid of him eventually."

"Don't do a dance, Carol," she warned, and leaned forward to get a cookie. As she said the following, she realized it was true: "I'm not a hundred percent on it."

"Am I stopping you?" Carol said, loud and defensive.

Justine ate the cookie fast. There was no one, no one in the world, as smug, as self-righteous, as critical, as negative as her mother. But after all, with the hospital, the nurses, the arrangements, Donnie—Carol wasn't herself.

No, that was just it: she was completely herself.

"The job problem really has to outweigh . . . the other things," Carol continued, with significant eye contact, and then looked down at the table, because she was talking about sex.

Her mother thought she was unable to make a decision because she was blinded by a man having sex with her. When Justine broke off her engagement to Rob Principe, Carol had said, primly, "It must have been very hard for you to make that decision." Because she thought that Justine thought it was sex with Rob or no sex ever. Carol actually believed that the only men Justine had been intimate with were the ones she'd introduced her to. If Carol actually knew how many men Justine had slept with, she might stop giving her advice.

Still: Nicky or Dennis or nobody at all was the shape of things to come. So Carol had a point, in a way. It really was Barry or nobody. For a very long time, anyway.

Carol changed the subject abruptly. "His Majesty, the managing partner, is coming in on the red-eye," she said, furious. " 'The funeral parlor is in Westchester,' " she imitated Donnie's disgusted, patronizing tone. " 'Yes,' I say. 'The cemetery is in Queens,' he says. A genius, my brother."

Justine watched her mother pacing in her gold mules.

"So we should've had it in Ozone Park? Like Miriam was a, a, a *Mafia don?*" She paced, furious. "He says, 'You should've done it in Manhattan.' As if you didn't have to drive from Manhattan."

"Well, he's too late," Justine said. "The arrangements are set. She's at the home." She thought about the 88-pound body in the coffin at Brod's, decomposing, and had to turn her head. "What are you wearing tomorrow?"

Business lunch

On Wednesday at high noon, Barry marched into lunch with Bernie Steipell without an agenda. He was just himself, Barry Cantor, looking for a job. Was this arrogant? Bernie had seen him work. He sat down at the table, the five empty months heavy on him. The night before, his father, Ira Cantor, had offered him a loan. There was nowhere to go but up.

But here he was, back in a suit, having a business lunch. Life was moving forward. Bernie was telling him that he'd always enjoyed working with him, that he was a pisser, a breath of fresh air, a brilliant strategist, and a natural ad man. But Barry had to understand that money was tight, that the agency was small, that he'd have to shift his whole outlook to the service side and learn to grovel.

"And I mean GROVEL," he added, laughing.

Barry felt a calmness take over him. He'd hit the bottom of the pool. He could push off now with complete control, and come up for air. "You'd hire me?"

"So you made a mistake," Bernie said grandly. "Whatever. I have a good feeling about you," he said, knocking back seltzer. "Don't make me regret it. You have to work on your temper."

"Agreed," Barry said, thinking incidentally about Rose. "Look, I need to know. Are you hiring me out of spite?"

Bernie took his red glasses off and thought about this. "Well, if I hadn't lost their business, I couldn't have hired you," he said. "I'd have wanted to—does that work for you?"

"Yeah, that works," Barry smiled. He was back in business. "You think I'll ever work on food again?"

"They can't enforce the ban, and they know it. But I can't afford a lawsuit, and they know it." Bernie chewed on a straw. "We'll keep you busy with cars and dish liquid until the dust clears. Then I might give you frozen fish sticks," he smiled, "but nothing fun." Bernie had a set of strong, sharp, very white teeth; Barry found them oddly reassuring.

He'd get the details on the health plan next week. Barry walked home in the sweltering heat with a promotion, a salary cut, a group of new products, and a boss who thought he was a naughty genius. The world was clean and beautiful!

On the other hand, what made him so sure that he'd hit bottom? What if there was no bottom. Anything could happen. People close to him could die. A job was nice, but it didn't mean everything was perfect from now on.

Why was he so neurotic? Just shut up and get the fucking suits to the cleaner's. He called everyone: Rose, Karen, Pippa, Hearne at home. No one picked up—he left messages on machines. He had a job, a good job, and he wanted to tell someone. He wanted to tell Justine. He made a pile for the dry cleaner. He called his cleaning lady to reinstate her; she cried, and he almost joined in with her.

The phone rang. It was Justine.

"Oh, you," he leaned back on the leather couch and let the jolt of excitement ebb into a feeling of well-being. "I'm glad you called. We have to talk about these rawhide chewy toys I have drifting through the house like tumbleweeds."

"Nana died."

"Died? Dead?" He wasn't shifting gears fast enough. He'd been about to make a wisecrack. "Where are you?"

"Bedford. I'm leaving in ten minutes."

"Can I see you?"

"I'll be there in about an hour."

He vacuumed frantically, took a shower, threw out the old pizzas and newspapers, stacked the baseball cards, and changed the sheets. He hadn't seen her in eight weeks and six days.

She rang the bell. She looked a total mess, scared and tired with dirty bandages unraveling on her hands. He gave her a big hug. The smell was back: hyacinths, tangerines, pencil shavings—strange, familiar, exciting.

"It's all a big mess," she sobbed, as the dog did laps around the living room. "But it's only going to get worse. The funeral's tomorrow. Every yenta in Westchester, Putnam, and Fairfield counties will be there."

They sat for a while not talking, her head on his chest, his arms wrapped around her back. It was good to have her there.

She looked up at him frankly. "Tell me something good."

"I got a job," he said. He loved the way it sounded.

She sat up, astounded.

"I start on Monday."

"What kind of job," she said, relaxing. She put her head in his lap and stretched her legs out on the couch.

He ran fingers through her hair. "You remember Bernie Steipell's agency?"

She lay in his lap, arms around him, asleep. The dog sat nearby, batting her eyelashes at him and waving her tail. He had no idea what to do. He felt nauseated. He had to be careful. He wasn't prepared to be this happy, all at once.

Later, they had a quiet dinner at the seafood place on Broadway. He fed her pieces of salmon. She smiled at him in spite of herself while she chewed. He looked at her bandages and her straight black bangs and his heart turned over. The whole thing with Justine was like a childhood crush—natural and unplanned. He didn't have to look for things about her he liked. He just wanted to be next to her.

"I missed you," she said, and spilled her coffee and looked up at him, ashamed, and he knew he had to ask her to marry him. She might say no, but he had to ask. Now, before he chickened out.

"Let's get married."

"Okay," she said, looking straight at him.

"I mean *married*," he said. "For good."

"Is there any other kind," she asked, looking around the room, fighting a smile.

"Did you say yes?"

She looked at him directly and laughed. He moved to sit next to her.

"You would have to propose in a restaurant," she said, her mouth open on his.

He felt like he'd just broken out of prison.

Funeral

All semblance of normalcy had blown out the window. Justine leaned back in the passenger seat. They were sailing down the Cross County. She was on her way to her grandmother's funeral in her fiancé's car. She had no idea what to think. Barry was driving so nicely. She loved the way he drove. He was such a good driver, she could put her head back and go to sleep and not worry about careening into the center lane divider of the Hutch. Her knees felt like wrecking balls. They were going to get married. They were driving to a funeral.

She burst into tears. He held his hand out.

"I'm so happy—it's terrible," she cried.

She needed time to absorb everything. Carol would say she was making a decision out of stress. She wasn't, though. She'd thought it through, and her objections had been dealt with.

"We can't spring this on her now," Justine decided, finally. "She's in no shape. Also. It would debase both things. Moreover, she needs time to absorb you again."

"I'll try to be absorbent," he said, and handed her a tissue.

But it was a funeral. Nana was dead. She couldn't be happy with Nana dead. She couldn't be sad with Barry there. He'd found a good job, something he really wanted to do. It was too much to process. She wouldn't have a single appropriate reaction today.

At Brod's they were whisked into a small family room off the chapel. Carol didn't seem at all surprised to see Barry.

"Oh, Barry. It's so good that you're here," she said, and burst into fresh tears. She gave Justine a kiss. Justine automatically took out a handkerchief, but her mother wasn't wearing lipstick.

Donnie was sitting upright in a chair, looking exactly like Carol, five foot five, drained, bloated, and grief-stricken. Justine hadn't seen him since he took her out to lunch eight years ago when she was hired by Packer Breebis, and told her if she worked her ass off, they just might not notice she was a girl. At the time, she hadn't realized how annoying that was.

Justine asked after the kids. Donnie's wife, Joyce, told her that they weren't coming—they'd just come back from camp and were tired. Carol shot her a meaningful glance.

The undertaker called Donnie to the phone, and conversation scattered.

Watching her uncle speaking deliberately on the phone triggered a series of childhood memories. She'd been impressed by the urgent calls Donnie constantly received from important people who needed his sober judgment during dinner. She'd been fascinated by the serious other place where he'd spent all his time. He was the only self-controlled adult in her family, and although she'd never liked him, Donnie was the reason she'd become a lawyer.

Barry put his arm around her and looked at her so sweetly she almost cried. She had forgotten that she was happy, and she had forgotten why. She had a splitting headache. She wanted a kiss.

"So," Donnie came back. "I hear you were key attorney on the Florida utilities swap. Terrific, Justine."

"That was so easy, it practically signed itself. And then I had this stupid little nothing case that was a nightmare. Nightmare, with two class action suits."

"That's how it goes," Donnie nodded. "Alex Schiff told me about you," he added, to include Barry.

"You're in touch with him?" Justine asked, surprised.

"I see him now and then at the club—he's friends with one of our members," he explained with a chilly superiority that reminded her of Driggs. "He asked me to come in on a real estate deal. Very shaky. I told him so, but he didn't want to hear it."

"Oh," she said.

"He's a very unstable person," Donnie said with distaste.

"Okay, enough," she said, surprised at her impatience.

"I'm just saying," Donnie said, and she held a hand up.

"We all know who my father is," she said. "Leave it alone."

Aunt Pearl came into the family room slowly, on a Lucite cane. She looked exactly like Miriam. It was eerie.

The coffin was very small. It was white. Justine thought white was vulgar for a coffin, although she didn't know why. It sat with the roses on top of it. The rabbi spoke in a vibrating baritone he was clearly impressed with. The ceremony was short, with hardly any Hebrew. Outside, it must have been 98 degrees.

At the grave in Queens, with planes screaming overhead, Carol turned to Justine while the coffin was being lowered into the hole, and said, "This is creepy." Justine took her mother's arm and tried not to sweat in the heat.

"I'm glad Barry came," her mother told her as they walked back to the cars, Barry and Gene behind them. Every time she took a step, her knees screamed in protest.

Justine said quietly, "He got a job."

"Thank God!" her mother whispered, and they tiptoed over other people's parents.

A whole spread, bigger even than the spread from the day before, was laid out in the dining room. Food and flowers were overflowing in the kitchen.

"Holy cow, look at all of this stuff," Barry said of a huge basket of beautiful tiny fruits.

"You think that's something? Look at this one—it's the same style, twice the size." Meredith Zazlowe stood at the foot of the table in a tennis outfit, holding her husband's glasses to her face to read the card. "Pat Champion sent the little one."

People came in talking. Mindy Frazier had snubbed Connie Tischler by not coming to the Children's Art Committee benefit, even though Connie had taken a whole table at the Friends of Zion fund-raiser. Her mother was responding to this talk; Justine was sitting with Barry by the fireplace, trying to calm her rushing head.

Rhoda Weisenblatt arrived and stood in front of them.

"Aren't you going to introduce me?" she said impatiently.

"Rhoda Weisenblatt, Barry Cantor," Justine said.

"We've missed you these last few days," Rhoda said, inspecting him.

"Well, I missed you, Rhoda."

Justine hooked her arm through Barry's and smirked. He knew exactly whom he was dealing with.

Connie Tischler veered towards the circle. "So here he is," she said matter-of-factly. "I knew there was someone."

"And what do you do," Rhoda continued the twice-over.

"I'm in advertising."

Rhoda raised her eyebrows at Justine. As if to say, I don't see any problem with that—what's wrong with your mother, anyway?

"Did you see it?" Rhoda Weisenblatt whispered viciously, referring to Meredith Zazlowe's tennis dress. "She should know better."

Arnold Tischler addressed Barry. "So: do you play golf?"

"Not really."

"No need to apologize," he said stoutly.

"I didn't think I had," Barry said.

Pearl was trying to walk and carry a plate of food simultaneously. Justine helped her to a small table, got herself a plate of chicken salad, and joined her. It was nice she didn't have to worry about Barry taking care of himself.

"So how's Cousin Linda?" Justine asked.

"Linda! I haven't heard from her in ten, fifteen years. You know, Neil never got over it when she left him."

"Wait: *she* left *him?*"

"Sure. For that guy in the real estate course."

"Wait. I thought the husband stole gloves at Macy's."

Pearl was adamant and shocked. "Oh, no. Neil was no genius, I grant you. But an honest man, Neil. No, they just let him go after Christmas. I remember Frieda and Joe coming over to our apartment, absolutely shocked. Neil had lost his job, but he couldn't go out for an interview—she was out all day and night selling real estate, and there was no one to stay with the kids. In *those days* this was unheard of. Unheard of. Nobody knew how to advise them. It didn't take him long to figure it out."

Justine felt a sadness take over. Pearl sounded just like Nana. "And Stacy?"

"Stacy is like a lost soul, Justine," Pearl said, shaking her head. "She was never very bright. A looker—oh, sure. She had those enormous blue eyes. Gorgeous. Gorgeous figure. But a moron? Absolute moron! Oh, those kids. The son, the drug addict? Was at MacLean's for a year. Then he was, oh, you know, selling vitamins over the phone. And the daughter married a Chinaman. A holistic practitioner."

Would she be like this when she got old? She spotted Connie Tischler wagging a finger at Barry. Was she like this now?

Wait a minute: wasn't Neil a doctor? Nana would have known.

. . .

In the late afternoon, Carol closed the door after her brother and his wife.

"He comes in for two minutes," she said spitefully, eyes like slits, "and he thinks he's God."

She walked into the kitchen and Justine followed. Barry was squatting down by the sink, up to his elbows in the garbage can.

He flushed. "I'm not looking through your garbage," he assured Carol, "I'm just throwing out your silverware."

Carol passed by as if he hadn't spoken. Barry rooted around until he fished out a silver knife, and held it up triumphantly.

"I'm so glad you found that," Carol said dryly.

Well, she'd been friendly to him earlier. Things weren't going to run smoothly. Why had Justine supposed they would?

"Would you like to take some air?" Barry suggested, and they slipped out the side door.

"I can't believe how callous they all are," Justine said as they passed by the parked cars. "The woman isn't even dead for five minutes, and it's whose basket is bigger, who's helping out more. Connie Tischler was giving tours of the house the other night. She strolled into my room while I was in bed and barely apologized."

The air was thick; they heard crickets, and the sound of the tree surgeon.

"Nobody knows what to do," Barry said. "If we lived in a little Sicilian fishing village, and someone died once a week, we'd know what to do."

She hooked her arm through his and steered him down the lane where the horse farm was.

"Nobody dies here, and nobody's sick," he continued. "They just hole up in their apartments and you never see them. And then they're dead, and nobody knows what to do."

There was a touch of fall in the humidity. As she passed the honeysuckle fence, the church bells rang for 6 o'clock, and Justine realized she'd been aroused all day. How perverse. She turned to him and pressed her face into his chest. "I know I'm not supposed to be happy, but I can't help it."

He gathered her in and they kissed with ardor under Meredith Zazlowe's enormous elm. There was crunching of gravel nearby.

"Vehicle, oh nine hundred," Barry chanted. Out of the corner of her eye, she saw the Weisenblatt Mercedes slowing down.

Go ahead, Rhoda, take a good look. She was engaged to be married to her husband. The very last one to get married, *the very last one.*

"Darling," Rhoda shouted out the window, "I just wanted to ask you—Mother had talked to me about something, you remember?"

She must have been referring to a blind date. "No."

"So I can forget about that thing, then," Rhoda said coyly.

Carol had asked her to beat the bushes for an available man. "What thing?" If Rhoda Weisenblatt was crass enough to bring up the no-confidence vote in front of Barry, then let her speak plainly.

"That thing," Barry turned to her. "You know, the tall Jewish one from the nice family and you'll know him by the full-time job he has, and the country house—that thing?"

Justine enjoyed the irritation this brought to Rhoda's face.

"Ttt. What a character you found," Rhoda said, and drove off. Justine looked at her future husband. She felt like she'd leveled out. She wondered if this was temporary, or what.

Journey Without Maps

It was sad and exciting, but Pippa kissed her father good-bye and boarded the plane with a thermos of tea. She was going to Paris. She had the window; the aisle was a man in his mid-30's, with a dark, brooding face like the man in *The Man Who Loved Women*. He had a sweater thrown around his neck, and was typing emphatically on a small computer with very clean-looking fingers. The seat between them was free. He gave a complicated sigh, and put his bag on the seat.

If he could do it, she could do it. After takeoff, she stood up to go to the bathroom, and dropped *Journey Without Maps* on the free seat next to his bag. He took off his glasses, paused, considered her, and rose gracefully as she climbed to get out.

The book was about Graham Greene being carried by bearers across Liberia in the 30's. There was a whole section on rats—rats in a famous Paris hotel, dead rats jumping with fleas in the English countryside, rats cascading down the walls of the huts in the Liberian interior.

Pippa was glad to be leaving New York for a while. The heat was making everyone crazy. Children were being shot for no reason. Yesterday, in a single day about town with her father, they saw: a man spewing white vomit in front of the Guggenheim SoHo, a woman defecating in the bus lane in front of Bergdorf Goodman, and a man urinating against a carpeted wall at the Walter Reade Theatre, not five feet from the men's room.

They'd seen *Pauline at the Beach*, and she'd thought about Vince. She hadn't spoken to him in months, and she hadn't missed him. If it had been nothing, then why had she spent so much time worrying about it? In French movies, everyone was always somewhere between seduction and betrayal, and they called it human nature. She wanted someone new.

She'd left her father at his bed and breakfast and walked west feeling wistful. On the No. 1 train uptown, a very nice-looking guy stood near her. The train had paused in a tunnel, in the heat. Then it started again. A woman with matted hair hanging down her back like a brisket came through singing for money. A man lying down on a bank of seats moaned. A pack of menacing teenagers ran through the car shouting. The lights went off. When they came on again, the guy smiled at her as if to say, What could possibly happen next?

She smiled back. They both looked away. He seemed very nice. He got off at the next stop. When she looked back after him, he was standing on the platform, holding a hand up to her. She was too stunned to respond. The doors were still open—he might come back; you had to be careful on the subway. She didn't wave. The doors closed. She saw him taking the steps slowly, dejected.

She should have waved! What had she turned into? When she got home, she called Vince to say good-bye. He said he was seeing Kiki again. He wished her luck. She hung up. That was that.

When she came back from the bathroom, her row mate was standing in the aisle in neat black loafers, holding two glasses of red wine. When she was seated, he gave her a glass, picked up her book distastefully, looked at her directly, and said, "You must tell me what it is you find so fascinating about the British writers. When there are so many far superior French ones."

"I read French ones," she said, but she hadn't read many. "But he's fabulous."

"London is a dead city," he said, bitterly. "No joy, no life. Nothing on the street. The food is disgusting. THERE IS NO FOOD! Always raining. How can you read such people?"

"Well this is about Africa—"

"By an English. They send their power-crazy homosexuals to rape the poor, lovely savages of Africa. They are gray, little people, the English. Constipated, small-minded, and spiteful."

"How can you say that?"

He raised his heavy brows in self-righteous astonishment. "They burned Jeanne d'Arc!"

Was he serious? She smiled, baffled. Life was getting interesting again.

Chapter 20

Is that it?

Suddenly, after six years of feeling behind in the count no matter what he did, Barry Cantor was having a fantastic season, breaking his own records, a legitimate stolen-base guy. He had joined the world, and it was as effortless as floating downstream. He strolled up Central Park West with *Magical Mystery Tour* on the Walkman; he was meeting Justine at the movies.

He had a whole new attitude at work. All the energy that used to go into resisting Maplewood Acres was now rechanneled into celebrating Steipell Associates. He was juggling ten accounts and overseeing three separate groups of people and he was thriving. Thriving! He was in constant contact with clients, and he was groveling. Groveling! Strangely, there was no ethical dilemma. Groveling came easily to him, and he was amused, indignant, and delighted to be good at it.

He crossed Central Park West and headed to Columbus. "Penny

Lane" was a Paul song, familiar and neighborly. The blue suburban skies were a relief after the acid meltdown of "Strawberry Fields." And how could Paul be angry, a gazillionaire, sitting on half of Scotland, adored and revered the world wide. Anger would be churlish, and Paul was nothing if not a statesman.

Two rollerbladers flew out of the park and swung left into the four-way intersection without looking. They missed colliding with him by an inch, and he felt a flash of fear in his stomach: everything was going too well for him. Something terrible was going to happen. What if someone died?

As usual, Justine was going out of her way to pretend that everything was normal. The engagement was announced three months after it had actually happened, because there was some sort of rule about mourning, or she decided that there ought to be one. So by the time everyone finally knew about it, the excitement had ebbed, and she was just going about her business calmly.

She had taken a position as in-house counsel at Fosdale Cleat, an investment bank she'd represented many times. For Barry, being new in his job at Steipell was like trying to have a personality in a foreign language. For Justine, being new at Fosdale Cleat was like moving to Larchmont and taking a part-time position in a yarn store. She was home most nights before 7. He wasn't sure how long she'd last there; her obsessive habits were curiously absent of late.

One night, she brought home a bread machine, an engagement present from Noah Clurman, the former client and tennis star. Justine Schiff, Barry Cantor's future wife, who hadn't turned her oven on in a good five years, mixed up the batter and set the egg timer. They ate leftovers from Szechuan Galaxy, and afterwards, he read about radial tires, and she read about Delaware case law.

The timer went off.

"This is good, that we can work together," Justine said, as she went into the kitchen. She let out a disappointed cry. The bread had emerged as a dry, gray, overcooked cube. When she cut into it, dust scattered. He found it so touching, he didn't know where to squeeze her or how hard. Justine had come out of nowhere—out of the sky!

They began discussing appliances, and almost immediately there began an argument about the minimum wage. She was against it.

"How can you be against the minimum wage!" he demanded. "You spend more on panty hose than those people make in a year."

"You have a real problem with the fact that I earn money," she said.

Of course, she was earning a lot less than she used to since she'd left Packer Breebis, but still significantly more than he did, and even significantly more than he used to.

"No, I have a problem with the fact that they don't make any money, and they never will."

"So what does that have to do with my panty hose. Which, incidentally, are a work-related expense, and anyway, I'm keeping the nylon makers of America in business."

"Growing up is accepting that you're part of the problem."

"What problem," she said contemptuously. "You watch too much TV. There is no ONE problem. You grow up, already."

Where did these arguments come from? She was so familiar, so attractive, so annoying, and such a kick in the pants. He was marrying the right woman. He could get on a smelly bus going to Passaic with her and have a good time.

Justine saw Barry coming towards her on Broadway and smiled. She kept telling herself that most marriages end in divorce, that familiarity breeds contempt, that stemware breaks. But she loved the great romping hulk of him, and she wanted to be hopeful.

Since the engagement, she'd been treated like Miss America everywhere she went. She wanted it to be like her regular life, only happy. But it wasn't like her regular life—it was a circus.

Part of it was starting the new job. All sorts of people she didn't know dropped in and broke the ice by discussing her publicly known attachment. Engagement: she could say it. She was finally legit.

But it was embarrassing: strangers were now camping out in her office and discussing their china patterns and their sex lives. The group of secretaries and young associates all getting engaged and married went around in a circle, telling about their dresses, their rings, their friends' rings, their photographers, their flowers, and their birth control. Who asked them?

She shooed them out—credibility was at stake.

Jenny Kravcek called to howl, and actually demanded details of how the engagement had been consummated. Her mother's friends were sending crystal and calling to squeal and ask about her trousseau. They got giggles saying the word trousseau. Justine was being congratulated, encouraged, respected, and admired. Where was all this interest and approval when she actually needed it, when she was alone and depressed? Carol wanted to carpet the Pierre in rose petals. Justine was dreading the wedding.

She met Barry at the Sony 84th Street and they kissed with propriety and got on the ticket buyers' line.

"Hey! What about a prenuptial," Barry said boisterously.

"Neh," Justine said.

"Sure? You could write it. You're my lawyer, you know."

The woman in front of them turned around and stared.

"Okay. You, Barry Cantor, will not bring, or in any way facilitate the bringing of, a rodent, reptile, or ferret into our current domicile, or any other dwelling in which we, as a partnership, shall reside."

"Hah!"

She liked it when she made him laugh.

"And you, Justine Schiff, will never look at another man as long as we both shall live!"

"The hell I won't."

"Well, I won't look at another woman!"

The woman turned around again. Who was this bitch to give them a look? So her fiancé was a little loud—was it against the law? Justine put her arm through his and kissed his cheek. "Of course you will."

"You're such a cynic."

"You can look all you like, but you, Barry Cantor, will never touch another woman, on any part of her body, as long as we both shall live."

"Yeah, okay," he said, bored with this by now.

The movie was sold out. It didn't really matter. They stopped at the video place on the way home. She went to Musicals and held up *The King and I*.

"No," he called from War/Action. He was looking so appealing in his glen plaid.

"A bald man is king," she tried.

"Funny," he said, holding up *Sudden Impact*.

She crossed the aisle to meet him in Comedy. "Certainly not." She was very pleased to be leaning on his arm, haggling lightheartedly on a Friday night. This was very much like how she imagined married life would be. This was the closest she'd ever come to that.

They went for Thai in the neighborhood.

"I have something to tell you," he said, as she spooned some fish sauce on her spring roll. "I wasn't going to Phoenix."

"What do you mean?"

"I mean, a year ago, when we met? I wasn't supposed to be on that plane. I was supposed to be going to Miami. With my mother, to visit her sister Sylvia."

She felt a hole opening up beneath her.

"In Miami," he repeated. "For Christmas?" he added, louder, as if trying to wake her up.

"So what are you saying," she asked, her face hot. "That you got on the wrong plane? That if you hadn't been so concussed, I'd never have met you?"

He smiled at her sadly. "I got on your plane because I overheard you say that that was where you were going," he said, lapping up rice from a serving spoon. "And so I switched my ticket." As she stared at him, his features began to congeal into a rubbery mask of beige and black. She was ill. "And here I am."

He followed a stranger on to a plane, throwing away his ticket and forgetting about his family plans? This was not a stable person. Was this the sort of man you married? This was the most frightening thing she'd ever heard.

She didn't know how to respond.

Just because it led to marriage, didn't necessarily mean that it was good. Roberta's sister's husband turned violent immediately after the wedding, and they had to get a restraining order. Doug had chased Harriet actively for two years, and two months after the wedding, he was basically a missing person who surfaced when he needed some sort of errand done for him. And then, of course, look at her father. Perfectly fine for ten years, and then he imploded.

On the other hand, could an alliance with an unpredictable, unstable man be much worse than spending her rare free evenings alone? Or with other depressed single women in inconvenient night spots, pretending it was fun to be pelted with ridiculous music while teenagers from New Jersey slowly filtered in?

Why had he waited until now to tell her this?

Every time she was relaxing into it, Barry came up with some bomb like this to throw her completely off-kilter. The previous week, on the one-year anniversary of the plane crash, Barry had taken her ice skating and told her that he knew they'd been married before, in a previous life.

"I could tell it at LaGuardia, from the way you looked at me," he said, his face glowing with love.

"Stop."

"I am utterly serious, and you know I'm not a spiritual person. And I feel such an affinity for the dog, too," he said, blowing on his hot chocolate. "I know that she and I—"

"Stop."

He was some kind of a nutcase. At the time, she'd looked at him closely and wondered what land mines could possibly be left.

And yet, when he was tired, when he was sick, when he was working, with his head bent down over spreadsheets on the coffee table, he looked so solid, so decent, that she thought she had him completely figured, and she had no panic.

"Well?" Barry was smiling at her now like a wolf, like he was pleased with himself in an ultimate way. "Say something?"

The spring rolls were getting cold. Justine didn't want to think about the ramifications of this new information. "Who knows about this?" she asked.

"Um, nobody," he said, turning from scary feral Barry into awkward teenage Barry.

"Let's keep it between us," she said, giving his arm a squeeze to end this disturbing conversation.

At home, they settled in on the couch to watch the compromise video, From Russia With Love. He kneaded her feet while she knitted.

"This is the most inane, sexist bullshit," Justine said, after giving it a chance to be merely dated. She went to the kitchen.

"Hey," Barry called after her. " 'A 111-year-old man in Chinatown was knocked down and robbed,'" he read from the *Post*. "'He refused treatment, was sent home, and died.'"

"Wow," she said, opening the freezer.

"He's been old for fifty years."

"More than that," she called, spooning ice cream into a bowl. "Fifty years ago, people got older earlier."

"Should you be eating that?" he asked as she walked in.

He'd better not start with her. "Yes," she said, and sat down. He grunted and held his hands out. She passed the bowl to him. He took a spoonful and gave it back.

"Uch, I don't want to live that long," he said, hand on her calf.

She looked up at him, alarmed.

"You do?" he asked. "Tell me you want to live that long."

"No, but. Don't talk about it," she said, disturbed.

The phone rang. It was Lily, a fourth-year associate at Feinman, Dingle, O'Shaughnessey, representing Fosdale Cleat in a recapitalization transaction. It was nice to be the one they were calling at home. Apropos of nothing, because she'd heard about Justine's engagement through the grapevine and felt perfectly authorized, Lily asked after Justine's stemware and told her that Justine *had* to go where her husband, a stunning Time Warner executive with an architecture degree, had picked out theirs.

Justine smiled inwardly and thought, Yes, but did he follow you on to an airplane just to meet you?

They watched the evil lady Russian intelligence chief talking on a red phone in a cave. Justine lay down with her head in his lap. They were both falling asleep.

"Are you watching?" she asked.

"Not really."

"Could we turn it off then?"

He glanced down at her and away with a half-lidded smile. "I want to see the rats in the sewer scene."

"You just want to annoy me."

When she woke up, he was singing the James Bond theme and sucking on her toes. Something suddenly occurred to her. Barry was Seventeen going on Eighteen, in a way. He was a pain in the ass, but he'd take care of her.